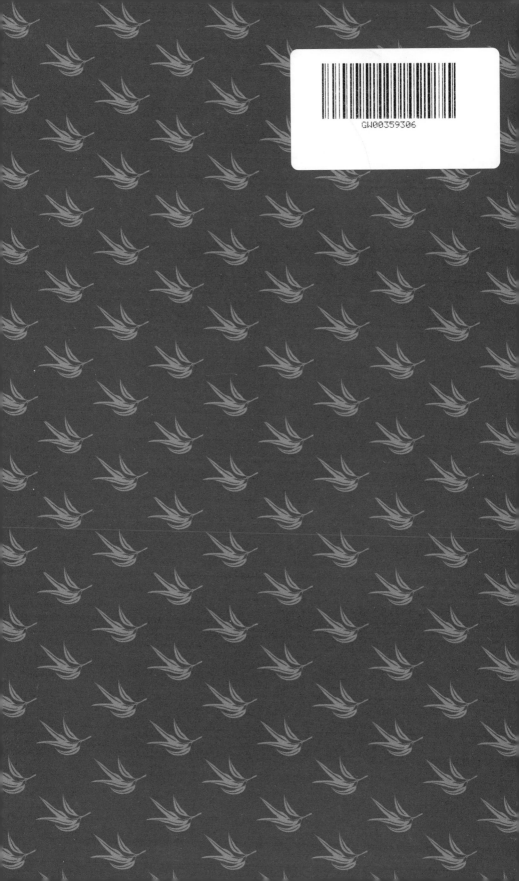

HENRY LAWSON

Greatest

SHORT STORIES

The Five Mile Press

The Five Mile Press

The Five Mile Press Pty Ltd
950 Stud Road, Rowville
Victoria 3178
Australia

Email: publishing@fivemile.com.au
Website: www.fivemile.com.au

This edition first published 2006

Series editor: A.K. Macdougall
Printed in China

National Library of Australia
Cataloguing-in-Publication data
Lawson, Henry, 1867–1922
Henry Lawson: greatest short stories

ISBN 1 74124 588 5.

1. Frontier and pioneer life – Australia – Fiction. I. Title
(Series: Australian classic edition).

A823.2

FRONT COVER IMAGE
Tom Roberts
Arrived Australia 1869
The Artists' Camp c. 1886 (detail)
Oil on canvas, 46.0 x 60.9 cm
Felton Bequest, 1943
National Gallery of Victoria

Contents

To Susan & Jim,
One of my nation's
great bush bards.
Warmest regards,
Lucas

2012

OVER THE SLIPRAILS

JOE WILSON

JOE WILSON'S MATES

THE ROMANCE OF THE SWAG

Introduction

'THE WORLD WAS encircled by the Mudgee hills,' wrote Henry Lawson in his *Fragment of Autobiography*, 'with Pipeclay as a centre. Mudgee, five miles away, was inside the world. Sydney was somewhere on the edge of the world, or just behind.'

To reach Pipeclay, which is now called Eurunderee, where Lawson spent much of his childhood, you take a side road out of Mudgee, and are soon disappointed. The Lawson house, built by his carpenter father, has gone. Only the brick chimney is left – surrounded, like the socket of a huge tooth, by a low wall of crazy paving. The place looks like a picnic shelter.

There's no sense of the spirit of Australia's greatest and most popular writer here. No sense that this was where the small boy used to listen to the quarrelling of his mother and father only a thin wall away, sometimes creeping out in despair to nurse the family dog. Nor that this was where the young Lawson could be suddenly turned out of his warm bed at dawn by his mother, telling him to get up quick because the cows were getting away, and he'd have to run barefoot across the frosty flats.

The shell of the house looks across rolling country to the blue ranges beyond. The prospect is pleasant, almost idyllic. Whatever grimness Lawson saw in the landscape is long gone: he doesn't seem to belong here. Lawson in fact was a city man, but you won't find his spirit in whatever pubs are left between the *Bulletin* office and Circular Quay, where he drank his penny-a-line magazine payments. Nor does he haunt the old Darlinghurst Gaol, where he often did time between 1908 and 1910 for failing to keep up his maintenance payments to his estranged family.

Lawson country is not a place but a land of the imagination. For him, the western plains of New South Wales are a vast theatre, lit by a blinding sun, under which those foolish enough to lead their lives there struggle unceasingly, and usually lose.

At the top of the Lawson food chain are the squatters – men with tight fists, large properties, and no sympathy for those battling it out below them. Though they don't appear often, the squatters are always there, hovering like unforgiving gods – though sometimes, in a crisis, they can soften. In 'The Bush-fire', Wall is a hard man who despises Ross, his selector neighbour, and is horrified when he learns that his daughter Mary intends to marry Ross's son.

But when a bushfire threatens the selector's hard-won wheat, he relents, and sends his men to save the crop.

Ross belongs to the class of small farmers who break their backs and their spirits trying to wring a living from their land. They're everywhere in Lawson's stories, locked in constant conflict with the elements. Tom Hopkins, in 'Settling the Land', is typical. Everything goes against him. The tree-stumps seem to be set in the earth like concrete, his crops fail, his sheep are impounded for grazing on the squatter's land, and his horses refuse to pull the plough. The cheekiness of the boy he hires to help him is the last straw – so Tom 'cursed the boy along with the horses, the plough, the selection, the squatters, and Australia. Yes, he cursed Australia.'

If these men fail, they sink to the group below them. These are the ones Lawson knows best – the gnarled and whiskered wanderers who carry their swags from property to property, usually on foot, looking for work. We get some memorable portraits – con men such as 'The Man Who Forgot', who does an award-winning impression of amnesia, is ordered off the property by the boss because he won't work, but remembers to go through everybody's swag before he leaves. We get bush characters, like the inveterate yarn-spinner Mitchell, who has an opinion on everything, or Poisonous Jimmy, or Gentleman Once. And crazies – 'hatters' as they were then called – off their rockers because of hardship and loneliness, as in '"Rats"', where an old swagman gets into an argument with his swag, challenges it to a fight, and they go a few rounds together, urged on by an appreciative audience.

These wanderers, pilgrims to nowhere strung out across the vast western plains, share a bush religion: campfire yarns, humour as dry as the land around them, and mateship. It makes hardship endurable – a burden shared, and thereby lightened. It's a bond so powerful it can even reach upwards to bosses ('Our hands came together and gripped,' says Jack Ellis in 'The Babies in the Bush' after he's learned the boss's tragic secret, 'the ghostly Australian daybreak was over the Bathurst plains') and downwards to dogs ('That There Dog of Mine').

It's a man's world. There weren't many women out in the west in the 1890s, and there aren't many in Lawson's stories. The title of one – 'No Place for a Woman' – sums up his view of the matter. But when they do appear they can be unforgettable. 'The Drover's Wife' is the best known and most anthologised, but Lawson's finest creation is Mrs Spicer in '"Water Them Geraniums".' Abandoned by her husband, weighed down by kids and poverty, she struggles on in her bark humpy, selling eggs and butter in town and watering her geraniums, until she just can't go on any more, turns her face to the wall and dies.

'"Water Them Geraniums"' is one of the Joe Wilson series – eight interlocking stories, Lawson's most ambitious and best fiction, which form the centrepiece of this collection. Joe Wilson and his wife Mary start their new life on an isolated selection at Lahey's Creek in a depressing landscape: 'Mary drove with me the rest of the way to the creek, along the lonely branch track across native apple-tree flats. It was a dreary, hopeless track. There was no horizon, nothing but the rough ashen trunks of the gnarled and stunted trees in all directions.'

These stories offer more than typically Lawsonian renditions of bush tribulation. Vivid as they are, these accounts are transcended by a searching exploration of character. There's a sustained attempt to examine what happens when a marriage is put under stress by deprivation and loneliness. With most of Lawson's fiction, the narrative is what we remember most. In the Joe Wilson series we remember character. The silences of the bush reflect the silences that develop in the couple's relationship and mark its deterioration. The country's sheer unyieldingness dehumanises them.

The Joe Wilson stories select themselves, but picking the others – he wrote more than 150 – wasn't so easy. The thirty-nine finally chosen are intended to show Lawson's skill across a range of genres.

There are vivid sketches, such as 'Hungerford', a portrait of the outback town he visited in January 1893 and never forgot: 'There is no distant prospect of Hungerford – you don't see the town till you are quite close to it, and then two or three white-washed galvanised-iron roofs start out of the mulga.'

There are bush tales like 'A Droving Yarn', where apparent artlessness conceals considerable cunning and craft. And more rounded and developed stories, where Lawson takes greater pains with his plot – as in 'When the Sun Went Down', where two brothers settle their differences as one of them is dying. It teeters on the edge of melodrama, and perhaps overbalances, but manages to be moving nevertheless. And there are also virtual essays – 'Bush Cats' ('Cats will kill rabbits and drag them home. We knew a fossicker whose cat used to bring him a bunny nearly every night') and 'The Romance of the Swag', a delightful series of variations on what a bushman carries with him, including 'three boots of different sizes, all belonging to the right foot, and a left slipper.'

Lawson was a master of all these modes, and he salts them with wry humour and a keen eye for human frailty – something he suffered very much from himself, as he declined into alcoholism and depression over the last years of his life, until his death in 1922. But it takes more than literary skills to make an author Australia's necessary writer. Though Lawson often seems to hate the bush he so unforgettably describes, underneath the gritty cynicism there's a profound feeling for his characters that sometimes comes close to love.

Which is why 'Shall We Gather at the River?' rounds off the collection so well. It's the story of a bush preacher called Peter McLaughlan, who 'had a beard like you see in some Bible pictures of Christ.' He preaches in a time of drought and despair for the weary farmers gathered around him. Nothing is wasted, he tells them, nothing is without reason. There is beauty even in this place, a moral beauty, where people help one another when in trouble. And so simple and direct is McLaughlan's speech, says the narrator, who sounds suspiciously like Lawson himself, that men move uncomfortably in their seats and women break down and weep. The preacher ends with a song – the title of the story – and men who have hated each other for years 'shake hands silently'.

'Shall We Gather at the River?' is as much a sermon as a story, and it is undeniably sentimental, but powerfully and movingly so. It is Lawson gathering his characters in an emotional embrace. After all their trials, he offers them catharsis. It wasn't the last story he wrote, but it reads as if it were, and makes a deeply satisfying finale.

BARRY OAKLEY
Wentworth Falls, 2006

WHILE THE BILLY BOILS

FIRST SERIES

An Old Mate of Your Father's

YOU REMEMBER when we hurried home from the old bush school how we were sometimes startled by a bearded apparition, who smiled kindly down on us, and whom our mother introduced, as we raked off our hats, as 'An old mate of your father's on the diggings, Johnny.' And he would pat our heads and say we were fine boys, or girls – as the case may have been – and that we had our father's nose but our mother's eyes, or the other way about; and say that the baby was the dead spit of its mother, and then added, for father's benefit: 'But yet he's like you, Tom.' It did seem strange to the children to hear him address the old man by his Christian name – considering that the mother always referred to him as 'Father.' She called the old mate Mr So-and-so, and father called him Bill, or something to that effect.

Occasionally the old mate would come dressed in the latest city fashion, and at other times in a new suit of reach-me-downs, and yet again he would turn up in clean white moleskins, washed tweed coat, Crimean shirt, blucher boots, soft felt hat, with a fresh-looking speckled handkerchief round his neck. But his face was mostly round and brown and jolly, his hands were always horny, and his beard grey. Sometimes he might have seemed strange and uncouth to us at first, but the old man never appeared the least surprised at anything he said or did – they understood each other so well – and we would soon take to this relic of our father's past, who would have fruit or lollies for us – strange that he always remembered them – and would surreptitiously slip 'shilluns' into our dirty little hands, and tell us stories about the old days, 'when me an' yer father was on the diggin's, an' you wasn't thought of, my boy.'

Sometimes the old mate would stay over Sunday, and in the forenoon or after dinner he and father would take a walk amongst the deserted shafts of Sapling Gully or along Quartz Ridge, and criticise old ground, and talk of past diggers' mistakes, and second bottoms, and feelers, and dips, and leads – also outcrops – and absently pick up pieces of quartz and slate, rub them on their sleeves, look at them in an abstracted manner, and drop them again; and they would talk of some old lead they had worked on: 'Hogan's party was here on one side of us, Macintosh was here on the other, Mac was getting good gold and so was Hogan, and now, why the blanky blank weren't we on gold?' And the mate would always agree that there was 'gold in them ridges and gullies yet, if a man only had the money behind him to git at it.' And then perhaps the guv'nor would show him a spot where he intended to put down a shaft some day – the old man was always thinking of putting down a shaft.

And these two old fifty-niners would mooch round and sit on their heels on the sunny mullock heaps and break clay lumps between their hands, and lay plans for the putting down of shafts, and smoke, till an urchin was sent to 'look for your father and Mr So-and-so, and tell 'em to come to their dinner.'

And again – mostly in the fresh of the morning – they would hang about the fences on the selection and review the live stock: five dusty skeletons of cows, a hollow-sided calf or two, and one shocking piece of equine scenery – which, by the way, the old mate always praised. But the selector's heart was not in farming nor on selections – it was far away with the last new rush in Western Australia or Queensland, or perhaps buried in the worked-out ground of Tambaroora, Married Man's Creek, or Araluen; and by and by the memory of some half-forgotten reef or lead or Last Chance, Nil Desperandum, or Brown Snake claim would take their thoughts far back and away from the dusty patch of sods and struggling sprouts called the crop, or the few discouraged, half-dead slips which comprised the orchard. Then their conversation would be pointed with many Golden Points, Bakery Hills, Deep Creeks, Maitland Bars, Specimen Flats, and Chinamen's Gullies. And so they'd yarn till the youngster came to tell them that 'Mother sez the breakfus is gettin' cold,' and then the old mate would rouse himself and stretch and say, 'Well, we mustn't keep the missus waitin', Tom!'

And, after tea, they would sit on a log of the wood-heap, or the edge of the veranda – that is, in warm weather – and yarn about Ballarat and Bendigo – of the days when we spoke of being 'on' a place oftener than at it: on Gulgong, on Lambing Flat, on Creswick – and they would use the definite article before the names, as: 'on The Turon; The Lachlan; The Home Rule; The Canadian Lead.' Then again they'd yarn of the old mates, such as Tom Brook, Jack Henright, and poor Martin Ratcliffe – who was killed in his golden hole – and of other men whom they didn't seem to have known much about, and who went by the names of 'Adelaide Adolphus', 'Corney George', and other names which might have been more or less applicable.

And sometimes they'd get talking, low and mysterious like, about 'Th' Eureka Stockade'; and if we didn't understand and asked questions, 'what was the Eureka Stockade?' or 'what did they do it for?' father'd say: 'Now, run away, sonny, and don't bother; me and Mr So-and-so want to talk.' Father had the mark of a hole on his leg, which he said he got through a gun accident when a boy, and a scar on his side, that we saw when he was in swimming with us; he said he got that in an accident in a quartz-crushing machine. Mr So-and-so had a big scar on the side of his forehead that was caused by a pick accidentally slipping out of a loop in the rope, and falling down a shaft where he was working. But how was it they talked low, and their eyes brightened up, and they didn't look at each other, but away over sunset, and had to get up and walk about, and take a stroll in the cool of the evening when they talked about Eureka?

And, again they'd talk lower and more mysterious like, and perhaps mother would be passing the wood-heap and catch a word, and ask:

'Who was she, Tom?'

And Tom – father – would say:

'Oh, you didn't know her, Mary; she belonged to a family Bill knew at home.'

And Bill would look solemn till mother had gone, and then they would smile a quiet smile, and stretch and say, 'Ah, well!' and start something else.

They had yarns for the fireside, too, some of those old mates of our father's, and one of them would often tell how a girl – a queen of the diggings – was married, and had her wedding-ring made out of the gold of that field; and how the diggers weighed their gold with the new wedding-ring – for luck – by hanging the ring on the hook of the scales and attaching their chamois-leather gold bags to it (whereupon she boasted that four hundred ounces of the precious metal passed through her wedding-ring); and how they lowered the young bride, blindfolded, down a golden hole in a big bucket, and got her to point out the drive from which the gold came that her ring was made out of. The point of this story seems to have been lost – or else we forget it – but it was characteristic. Had the girl been lowered down a duffer, and asked to point out the way to the gold, and had she done so successfully, there would have been some sense in it.

And they would talk of King, and Maggie Oliver, and G. V. Brooke, and others, and remember how the diggers went five miles out to meet the coach that brought the girl actress, and took the horses out and brought her in in triumph, and worshipped her, and sent her off in glory, and threw nuggets into her lap. And how she stood upon the box-seat and tore her sailor hat to pieces, and threw the fragments amongst the crowd; and how the diggers fought for the bits and thrust them inside their shirt bosoms; and how she broke down and cried, and could in her turn have worshipped those men – loved them, every one. They were boys all, and gentlemen all. There were college men, artists, poets, musicians, journalists – Bohemians all. Men from all the lands and one. They understood art – and poverty was dead.

And perhaps the old mate would say slyly, but with a sad, quiet smile:

'Have you got that bit of straw yet, Tom?'

Those old mates had each three pasts behind them. The two they told each other when they became mates, and the one they had shared.

And when the visitor had gone by the coach we noticed that the old man would smoke a lot, and think as much, and take great interest in the fire, and be a trifle irritable perhaps.

Those old mates of our father's are getting few and far between, and only happen along once in a way to keep the old man's memory fresh, as it were. We met one to-day, and had a yarn with him, and afterwards we got thinking, and somehow began to wonder whether those ancient friends of ours were, or were not, better and kinder to their mates than we of the rising generation are to our fathers; and the doubt is painfully on the wrong side.

SETTLING ON THE LAND

THE WORST BORE in Australia just now is the man who raves about getting the people on the land, and button-holes you in the street with a little scheme of his own. He generally does not know what he is talking about.

There is in Sydney a man named Tom Hopkins who settled on the land once, and sometimes you can get him to talk about it. He did very well at his trade in the city, years ago, until he began to think that he could do better up-country. Then he arranged with his sweetheart to be true to him and wait whilst he went west and made a home. She drops out of the story at this point.

He selected on a run at Dry Hole Creek, and for months awaited the arrival of the government surveyors to fix his boundaries; but they didn't come, and, as he had no reason to believe they would turn up within the next ten years, he grubbed and fenced at a venture, and started farming operations.

Does the reader know what grubbing means? Tom does. He found the biggest, ugliest, and most useless trees on his particular piece of ground; also the greatest number of adamantine stumps. He started without experience, or with very little, but with plenty of advice from men who knew less about farming than he did. He found a soft place between two roots on one side of the first tree, made a narrow, irregular hole, and burrowed down till he reached a level where the tap-root was somewhat less than four feet in diameter, and not quite as hard as flint: then he found that he hadn't room to swing the axe, so he heaved out another ton or two of earth – and rested. Next day he sank a shaft on the other side of the gum; and after tea, over a pipe, it struck him that it would be a good idea to burn the tree out, and so use up the logs and lighter rubbish lying round. So he widened the excavation, rolled in some logs, and set fire to them – with no better result than to scorch the roots.

Tom persevered. He put the trace harness on his horse, drew in all the logs within half a mile, and piled them on the windward side of that gum; and during the night the fire found a soft place, and the tree burnt off about six feet above the surface, falling on a squatter's boundary fence, and leaving the ugliest kind of stump to occupy the selector's attention; which it did, for a week. He waited till the hole cooled, and then he went to work with pick, shovel, and axe: and even now he gets interested in drawings of machinery, such as are published in the agricultural weeklies, for getting out stumps without graft. He thought he would be able to get some posts and rails out of that tree, but found reason to think that a cast-iron column would split sooner – and straighter. He traced some of the surface roots to the other side of the selection, and broke most of his trace-chains trying to get them out by horse-power – for they had other roots going down from underneath. He cleared a patch in the course of time and for several seasons he broke more ploughshares than he could pay for.

Meanwhile the squatter was not idle. Tom's tent was robbed several times, and his hut burnt down twice. Then he was charged with killing some sheep and a steer on the run, and converting them to his own use, but got off mainly because there was a difference of opinion between the squatter and the other local J.P. concerning politics and religion.

Tom ploughed and sowed wheat, but nothing came up to speak of – the ground was too poor; so he carted stable manure six miles from the nearest town, manured the land, sowed another crop, and prayed for rain. It came. It raised a flood which washed the crop clean off the selection, together with several acres of manure, and a considerable portion of the original surface soil; and the water brought down enough sand to make a beach, and spread it over the field to a depth of six inches. The flood also took half a mile of fencing from along the creek-bank, and landed it in a bend, three miles down, on a dummy selection, where it was confiscated. Tom didn't give up – he was energetic. He cleared another piece of ground on the siding, and sowed more wheat; it had the rust in it, or the smut – and averaged three shillings per bushel. Then he sowed lucerne and oats, and bought a few cows: he had an idea of starting a dairy. First, the cows' eyes got bad, and he sought the advice of a German cocky, and acted upon it; he blew powdered alum through paper tubes into the bad eyes, and got some of it snorted and butted back into his own. He cured the cows' eyes and got the sandy blight in his own, and for a week or so he couldn't tell one end of a cow from the other, but sat in a dark corner of the hut and groaned, and soaked his glued eyelashes in warm water. Germany stuck to him and nursed him, and saw him through.

Then the milkers got bad udders, and Tom took his life in his hands whenever he milked them. He got them all right presently – and butter fell to fourpence a pound. He and the aforesaid cocky made arrangements to send their butter to a better market; and then the cows contracted a disease which was known in those parts as 'plooro permoanyer,' but generally referred to as 'th' ploorer.'

Again Tom sought advice, acting upon which he slit the cows' ears, cut their tails half off to bleed them, and poured pints of 'pain killer' into them through their nostrils; but they wouldn't make an effort, except, perhaps, to rise and poke the selector when he tried to tempt their appetites with slices of immature pumpkin. They died peacefully and persistently, until all were gone save a certain dangerous, barren, slab-sided luny bovine with white eyes and much agility in jumping fences, who was known locally as Queen Elizabeth.

Tom shot Queen Elizabeth, and turned his attention to agriculture again. Then his plough horses took bad with something the Teuton called 'der shtranguls.' He submitted them to a course of treatment in accordance with Jacob's advice – and they died.

Even then Tom didn't give in – there was grit in that man. He borrowed a broken-down dray-horse in return for its keep, coupled it with his own old riding hack, and started to finish ploughing. The team wasn't a success. Whenever the draught horse's knees gave way and he stumbled forward, he jerked the lighter horse back into the plough, and something would break. Then Tom would blaspheme till he was refreshed, mend up things with wire and bits of clothes-line, fill his pockets with stones to throw at the team, and start again. Finally he hired a dummy's child to drive the horses. That brat did his best: he tugged at the head of the team, prodded it behind, heaved rocks at it, cut a sapling, got up his enthusiasm, and wildly whacked the light horse whenever the other showed signs of moving – but he never succeeded in starting both horses at one and the same time. Moreover the youth was cheeky, and the selector's temper had been soured: he cursed the boy along with the horses, the plough, the selection, the squatter, and Australia. Yes, he cursed Australia. The boy cursed back, was chastised, and immediately went home and brought his father.

Then the dummy's dog tackled the selector's dog and this precipitated things. The dummy would have gone under had his wife not arrived on the scene with the eldest son and the rest of the family. They all fell foul of Tom. The woman was the worst. The selector's dog chawed the other and came to his master's rescue just in time – or Tom Hopkins would never have lived to become the inmate of a lunatic asylum.

Next year there happened to be good grass on Tom's selection and nowhere else, and he thought it wouldn't be a bad idea to get a few poor sheep, and fatten them up for market: sheep were selling for about seven-and-sixpence a dozen at that time. Tom got a hundred or two, but the squatter had a man stationed at one side of the selection with dogs to set on the sheep directly they put their noses through the fence (Tom's was not a sheep fence). The dogs chased the sheep across the selection and into the run again on the other side, where another man waited ready to pound them.

Tom's dog did his best; but he fell sick while chawing up the fourth capitalistic canine, and subsequently died. The dummies had rubbed that cur with poison before starting it across – that was the only way they could get at Tom's dog.

Tom thought that two might play at the game, and he tried; but his nephew, who happened to be up from the city on a visit, was arrested at the instigation of the squatter for alleged sheep-stealing, and sentenced to two years' hard; during which time the selector himself got six months for assaulting the squatter with intent to do him grievous bodily harm – which, indeed, he more than attempted, if a broken nose, a fractured jaw, and the loss of most of the squatter's teeth amounted to anything. The squatter by this time had made peace with the other local Justice, and had become his father-in-law.

When Tom came out there was little left for him to live for; but he took a job of fencing, got a few pounds together, and prepared to settle on the land some more. He got a 'missus' and a few cows during the next year; the missus robbed him and ran away with the dummy, and the cows died in the drought, or were impounded by the squatter while on their way to water. Then Tom rented an orchard up the creek, and a hailstorm destroyed all the fruit. Germany happened to be represented at the time, Jacob having sought shelter at Tom's hut on his way home from town. Tom stood leaning against the door post with the hail beating on him through it all. His eyes were very bright and very dry, and every breath was a choking sob. Jacob let him stand there, and sat inside with a dreamy expression on his hard face, thinking of childhood and fatherland, perhaps. When it was over he led Tom to a stool and said, 'You waits there, Tom. I must go home to somedings. You sits there still and waits twenty minutes;' then he got on his horse and rode off muttering to himself; 'Dot man moost gry, dot man moost gry.' He was back inside of twenty minutes with a bottle of wine and a cornet under his overcoat. He poured the wine into two pint-pots, made Tom drink, drank himself, and then took his cornet, stood up at the door, and played a German march into the rain after the retreating storm. The hail had passed over his vineyard and he was a ruined man too. Tom did 'gry' and was all right. He was a bit disheartened, but he did another job of fencing, and was just beginning to think about 'puttin' in a few vines an' fruit-trees' when the government surveyors – whom he'd forgotten all about – had a resurrection and came and surveyed, and found that the real selection was located amongst some barren ridges across the creek. Tom reckoned it was lucky he didn't plant the orchard, and he set about shifting his home and fences to the new site. But the squatter interfered at this point, entered into possession of the farm and all on it, and took action against the selector for trespass – laying the damages at £2500.

Tom was admitted to the lunatic asylum at Parramatta next year, and the squatter was sent there the following summer, having been ruined by the drought, the rabbits, the banks, and a wool-ring. The two became very friendly, and had many a sociable argument about the feasibility – or otherwise – of blowing open the flood-gates of Heaven in a dry season with dynamite.

Tom was discharged a few years since. He knocks about certain suburbs a good deal. He is seen in daylight seldom, and at night mostly in connection with a dray and a lantern. He says his one great regret is that he wasn't found to be of unsound mind before he went up-country.

Enter Mitchell

THE WESTERN TRAIN had just arrived at Redfern railway station with a lot of ordinary passengers and one swagman.

He was short, and stout, and bow-legged, and freckled, and sandy. He had red hair and small, twinkling, grey eyes, and – what often goes with such things – the expression of a born comedian. He was dressed in a ragged, well-washed print shirt, an old black waistcoat with a calico back, a pair of cloudy moleskins patched at the knees and held up by a plaited greenhide belt buckled loosely round his hips, a pair of well-worn, fuzzy blucher boots, and a soft felt hat, green with age, and with no brim worth mentioning, and no crown to speak of. He swung a swag on to the platform, shouldered it, pulled out a billy and water-bag, and then went to a dog-box in the brake van.

Five minutes later he appeared on the edge of the cab-platform, with an anxious-looking cattle-dog crouching against his legs, and one end of the chain in his hand. He eased down the swag against a post, turned his face to the city, tilted his hat forward, and scratched the well-developed back of his head with a little finger. He seemed undecided what track to take.

'Cab, sir!'

The swagman turned slowly and regarded cabby with a quiet grin.

'Now, do I look as if I want a cab?'

'Well, why not? No harm, anyway – I thought you might want a cab.'

Swaggy scratched his head, reflectively.

'Well,' he said, ' you're the first man that has thought so these ten years. What do I want with a cab?'

'To go where you're going, of course.'

'Do I look knocked up?'

'I didn't say you did.'

'And I didn't say you said I did … Now, I've been on the track this five years. I've tramped two thousan' miles since last Chris'mas, and I don't see why I can't tramp the last mile. Do you think my old dog wants a cab?'

The dog shivered and whimpered; he seemed to want to get away from the crowd.

'But then, you see, you ain't going to carry that swag through the streets, are you?' asked the cabman.

'Why not? Who'll stop me? There ain't no law agin it, I b'lieve?'

'But then, you see, it don't look well, you know.'

'Ah! I thought we'd get to it at last.'

The traveller up-ended his bluey against his knee, gave it an affectionate pat, and then straightened himself up and looked fixedly at the cabman.

'Now, look here!' he said, sternly and impressively, 'can you see anything wrong with that old swag o' mine?'

It was a stout, dumpy swag, with a red blanket outside, patched with blue, and the edge of a blue blanket showing in the inner rings at the end. The swag might have been newer; it might have been cleaner; it might have been hooped with decent straps, instead of bits of clothes-line and greenhide – but otherwise there was nothing the matter with it, as swags go.

'I've humped that old swag for years,' continued the bushman; 'I've carried that old swag thousands of miles – as that old dog knows – an' no one ever bothered about the look of it, or of me, or of my old dog, neither; and do you think I'm going to be ashamed of that old swag, for a cabby or anyone else? Do you think I'm going to study anybody's feelings? No one ever studied mine! I'm in two minds to summon you for using insulting language towards me!'

He lifted the swag by the twisted towel which served for a shoulder-strap, swung it into the cab, got in himself and hauled the dog after him.

'You can drive me somewhere where I can leave my swag and dog while I get some decent clothes to see a tailor in,' he said to the cabman. 'My old dog ain't used to cabs, you see.'

Then he added, reflectively: 'I drove a cab myself, once, for five years in Sydney.'

WHEN THE SUN WENT DOWN

JACK DREW sat on the edge of the shaft, with his foot in the loop and one hand on the rope, ready to descend. His elder brother, Tom, stood at one end of the windlass and the third mate at the other. Jack paused before swinging off, looked up at his brother, and impulsively held out his hand:

'You ain't going to let the sun go down, are you, Tom?'

But Tom kept both hands on the windlass-handle and said nothing.

'Lower away!'

They lowered him to the bottom, and Tom shouldered his pick in silence and walked off to the tent. He found the tin plate, pint-pot, and things set ready for him on the rough slab table under the bush shed. The tea was made, the cabbage and potatoes strained and placed in a billy near the fire. He found the fried bacon and steak between two plates in the camp-oven. He sat down to the table but he could not eat. He felt mean. The inexperience and hasty temper of his brother had caused the quarrel between them that morning; but then Jack admitted that, and apologised when he first tried to make it up.

Tom moved round uneasily and tried to smoke: he could not get Jack's last appeal out of his ears – 'You ain't going to let the sun go down, Tom?'

Tom found himself glancing at the sun. It was less than two hours from sunset. He thought of the words of the old Hebrew – or Chinese – poet; he wasn't religious, and the authorship didn't matter. The old poet's words began to haunt him: 'Let not the sun go down upon your wrath – Let not the sun go down upon your wrath.'

The line contains good, sound advice; for quick-tempered men are often the most sensitive, and when they let the sun go down on the aforesaid wrath that quality is likely to get them down and worry them during the night.

Tom started to go to the claim, but checked himself, and sat down and tried to draw comfort from his pipe. He understood his brother thoroughly, but his brother never understood him – that was where the trouble was. Presently he got thinking how Jack would worry about the quarrel and have no heart for his work. Perhaps he was fretting over it now, all alone by himself, down at the end of the damp, dark drive. Tom had a lot of the old woman about him, in spite of his unsociable ways and brooding temper.

He had almost made up his mind to go below again, on some excuse, when his mate shouted from the top of the shaft:

'Tom! Tom! For Christ's sake come here!'

Tom's heart gave a great thump, and he ran like a kangaroo to the shaft. All the diggers within hearing were soon on the spot. They saw at a glance what had happened. It was madness to sink without timber in such treacherous ground. The sides of the shaft were closing in. Tom sprang forward and shouted through the crevice:

'To the "face," Jack! To the "face," for your life!'

'The old workings!' he cried, turning to the diggers. 'Bring a fan and tools. We'll dig him out.'

A few minutes later a fan was rigged over a deserted shaft close by, where fortunately the windlass had been left for bailing purposes, and men were down in the old drive. Tom knew that he and his mates had driven very close to the old workings.

He knelt in the damp clay before the 'face' and worked like a madman; he refused to take turn about, and only dropped the pick to seize a shovel in his strong hands, and snatch back the loose clay from under his feet; he reckoned that he had six or, perhaps, eight feet to drive, and he knew that the air could not last long in the new drive – even if that had not already fallen in and crushed his brother. Great drops of perspiration stood out on Tom's forehead, and his breath began to come in choking sobs, but he still struck strong, savage blows into the clay before him, and the drive lengthened quickly. Once he paused a moment to listen, and then distinctly heard a sound as of a tool or stone being struck against the end of the new drive. Jack was safe!

Tom dug on until the clay suddenly fell away from his pick and left a hole, about the size of a plate, in the 'face' before him. 'Thank God!' said a hoarse, strained voice at the other side.

'All right, Jack?'

'Yes, old man; you are just in time; I've hardly got room to stand in, and I'm nearly smothered.' He was crouching against the 'face' of the new drive.

Tom dropped his pick and fell back against the man behind him.

'Oh, God! my back!' he cried.

Suddenly he struggled to his knees, and then fell forward on his hand and dragged himself close to the hole in the end of the drive.

'Jack!' he gasped, 'Jack!'

'Right, old man; what's the matter?'

'I've hurt my heart, Jack! – Put your hand – quick! ... The sun's going down.'

Jack's hand came out through the hole. Tom gripped it, and then fell with his face in the damp clay.

They half carried, half dragged him from the drive, for the roof was low and they were obliged to stoop. They took him to the shaft and sent him up, lashed to the rope.

A few blows of the pick, and Jack scrambled from his prison and went to the surface, and knelt on the grass by the body of his brother. The diggers gathered round and took off their hats. And the sun went down.

THE MAN WHO FORGOT

'WELL, I DUNNO,' said Tom Marshall – known as 'The Oracle' –
'I've heerd o' sich cases before: they ain't commin, but – I've heerd o' sich cases
before,' and he screwed up the left side of his face whilst he reflectively scraped
his capacious right ear with the large blade of a pocket-knife.

They were sitting at the western end of the rouseabouts' hut, enjoying
the breeze that came up when the sun went down, and smoking and yarning.
The 'case' in question was a wretchedly forlorn-looking specimen of the
swag-carrying clan whom a boundary-rider had found wandering about the
adjacent plain, and had brought into the station. He was a small, scraggy man,
painfully fair, with a big, baby-like head, vacant watery eyes, long thin hairy
hands, that felt like pieces of damp seaweed, and an apologetic cringe-and-look-
up-at-you manner. He professed to have forgotten who he was and all about
himself.

The Oracle was deeply interested in this case, as indeed he was in anything else
that 'looked curious.' He was a big, simple-minded shearer, with more heart than
brains, more experience than sense, and more curiosity than either. It was a
wonder that he had not profited, even indirectly, by the last characteristic. His
heart was filled with a kind of reverential pity for anyone who was fortunate or
unfortunate enough to possess an 'affliction'; and amongst his mates had been
counted a deaf man, a blind man, a poet, and a man who 'had rats.' Tom had
dropped across them individually, when they were down in the world, and had
befriended them, and studied them with great interest – especially the poet; and
they thought kindly of him, and were grateful – except the individual with the
rats, who reckoned Tom had an axe to grind – that he, in fact, wanted to cut his
(Rat's) liver out as a bait for Darling cod – and so renounced the mateship.

It was natural, then, for the Oracle to take the present case under his wing. He
used his influence with the boss to get the Mystery on 'picking up,' and studied
him in spare time, and did his best to assist the poor hushed memory, which
nothing the men could say or do seemed able to push further back than the day
on which the stranger 'kind o' woke up' on the plain, and found a swag beside
him. The swag had been prospected and fossicked for a clue, but yielded none.
The chaps were sceptical at first, and inclined to make fun of the Mystery; but
Tom interfered, and intimated that if they were skunks enough to chyack or try
on any of their 'funny business' with a 'pore afflicted chap,' he (Tom) would be
obliged to 'perform.' Most of the men there had witnessed Tom's performance,
and no one seemed ambitious to take a leading part in it. They preferred to be
in the audience.

'Yes,' reflected the Oracle, 'it's a curious case, and I dare say some of them big doctors, like Morell Mackenzie, would be glad to give a thousand or two to get holt on a case like this.'

'Done,' cried Mitchell, the goat of the shed. 'I'll go halves! – or stay, let's form a syndicate and work the Mystery.'

Some of the rouseabouts laughed, but the joke fell as flat with Tom as any other joke.

'The worst of it is,' said the Mystery himself, in the whine that was natural to him, and with a timid side look up at Tom – 'the worst of it is I might be a lord or duke, and don't know anything about it. I might be a rich man, with a lot of houses and money. I might be a lord.'

The chaps guffawed.

'Wot'yer laughing at?' asked Mitchell. 'I don't see anything unreasonable about it; he might be a lord as far as looks go. I've seen two.'

'Yes,' reflected Tom, ignoring Mitchell, 'there's something in that; but then again, you see, you might be Jack the Ripper. Better let it slide, mate; let the dead past bury its dead. Start fresh with a clean sheet.'

'But I don't even know my name, or whether I'm married or not,' whined the outcast. 'I might have a good wife and little ones.'

'Better keep on forgetting, mate,' Mitchell said, 'and as for a name, that's nothing. I don't know mine, and I've had eight. There's plenty good names knocking round. I knew a man named Jim Smith that died. Take his name, it just suits you, and he ain't likely to call round for it; if he does, you can say you was born with it.'

So they called him Smith, and soon began to regard him as a harmless lunatic and to take no notice of his eccentricities.

Great interest was taken in the case for a time, and even Mitchell put in his oar and tried all sorts of ways to assist the Mystery in his weak, helpless, and almost pitiful endeavours to recollect who he was. A similar case happened to appear in the papers at this time, and the thing caught on to such an extent that the Oracle was moved to impart some advice from his store of wisdom.

'I wouldn't think too much over it if I was you,' said he to Mitchell, 'hundreds of sensible men went mad over that there Tichborne case who didn't have anything to do with it, but just through thinking on it; and you're ratty enough already, Jack. Let it alone and trust me to find out who's Smith just as soon as ever we cut out.'

Meanwhile Smith ate, worked, and slept, and borrowed tobacco and forgot to return it – which was made a note of. He talked freely about his case when asked, but if he addressed anyone, it was with the air of the timid but good young man, who is fully aware of the extent and power of this world's wickedness, and stands somewhat in awe of it, but yet would beg you to favour a humble worker in the vineyard by kindly accepting a tract, and passing it on to friends after perusal.

One Saturday morning, about a fortnight before cut out, the Oracle came late to his stand, and apparently with something on his mind. Smith hadn't turned up, and the next rouseabout was doing his work, to the mutual dissatisfaction of all parties immediately concerned.

'Did you see anything of Smith?' asked Mitchell of the Oracle. 'Seems to have forgot to get up this morning.'

Tom looked disheartened and disappointed.

'He's forgot again,' said he, slowly and impressively.

'Forgot what? We know he's blessed well forgot to come to graft.'

'He's forgot again,' repeated Tom. 'He woke up this morning and wanted to know who he was and where he was.' Comments.

'Better give him best, Oracle,' said Mitchell presently. 'If he can't find out who he is and where he is, the boss'll soon find it out for him.'

'No,' said Tom, 'when I take a thing in hand I see it through.'

This was also characteristic of the boss-over-the-board, though in another direction. He went down to the hut and inquired for Smith.

'Why ain't you at work?'

'Who am I, sir? Where am I?' whined Smith. 'Can you please tell me who I am and where I am?'

The boss drew a long breath and stared blankly at the Mystery; then he erupted.

'Now, look here!' he howled, 'I don't know who the gory sheol you are, except that you're a gory lunatic, and what's more, I don't care a damn. But I'll soon show you where you are! You can call up at the store and get your cheque, and soon as you blessed well like; and then take a walk, and don't forget to take your lovely swag with you.'

The matter was discussed at the dinner-table. The Oracle swore that it was a cruel, mean way to treat a 'pore afflicted chap,' and cursed the boss. Tom's admirers cursed in sympathy, and trouble seemed threatening, when the voice of Mitchell was heard to rise in slow, deliberate tones over the clatter of cutlery and tin plates.

'I wonder,' said the voice, 'I wonder whether Smith forgot his cheque?'

It was ascertained that Smith hadn't.

There was some eating and thinking done.

Soon Mitchell's voice was heard again, directed at the Oracle. It said:

'Do you keep any vallabels about your bunk, Oracle?'

Tom looked hard at Mitchell. 'Why?'

'Oh, nothin': only I think it wouldn't be a bad idea for you to look at your bunk and see whether Smith forgot.'

The chaps grew awfully interested. They fixed their eyes on Tom, and he looked with feeling from one face to another; then he pushed his plate back, and slowly extracted his long legs from between the stool and the table. He climbed to his bunk, and carefully reviewed the ingredients of his swag. Smith hadn't forgot.

When the Oracle's face came round again there was in it a strange expression which a close study would have revealed to be more of anger than of sorrow, but that was not all. It was an expression such as a man might wear who is undergoing a terrible operation, without chloroform, but is determined not to let a whimper escape him. Tom didn't swear, and by that token they guessed how mad he was. 'Twas a rough shed, with a free and lurid vocabulary, but had they all sworn in chorus, with One-eyed Bogan as lead, it would not have done justice to Tom's feelings – and they realised this.

The Oracle took down his bridle from its peg, and started for the door amid a respectful and sympathetic silence, which was only partly broken once by the voice of Mitchell, which asked in an awed whisper:

'Going ter ketch yer horse, Tom?'

The Oracle nodded, and passed on; he spake no word – he was too full for words.

Five minutes passed, and then the voice of Mitchell was heard again, uninterrupted by the clatter of tinware. It said in impressive tones:

'It would not be a bad idea for some of you chaps that camp in the bunks along there, to have a look at your things. Scotty's bunk is next to Tom's.'

Scotty shot out of his place as if a snake had hold of his leg, starting a plank in the table and upsetting three soup plates. He reached for his bunk like a drowning man clutching at a plant, and tore out the bedding. Again, Smith hadn't forgot.

Then followed a general overhaul, and it was found in most cases that Smith had remembered. The pent-up reservoir of blasphemy burst forth.

The Oracle came up with Smith that night at the nearest shanty, and found that he had forgotten again, and in several instances, and was forgetting some more under the influence of rum and of the flattering interest taken in his case by a drunken Bachelor of Arts who happened to be at the pub. Tom came in quietly from the rear, and crooked his finger at the shanty-keeper. They went apart from the rest, and talked together a while very earnestly. Then they secretly examined Smith's swag, the core of which was composed of Tom's and his mate's valuables.

Then the Oracle stirred up Smith's recollections and departed.

Smith was about again in a couple of weeks. He was damaged somewhat physically, but his memory was no longer impaired.

HUNGERFORD

ONE OF THE HUNGRIEST cleared roads in New South Wales runs to within a couple of miles of Hungerford, and stops there; then you strike through the scrub to the town. There is no distant prospect of Hungerford – you don't see the town till you are quite close to it, and then two or three white-washed galvanised-iron roofs start out of the mulga.

They say that a past Ministry commenced to clear the road from Bourke, under the impression that Hungerford was an important place, and went on, with the blindness peculiar to governments, till they got to within two miles of the town. Then they ran short of rum and rations, and sent a man on to get them, and make inquiries. The member never came back, and two more were sent to find him – or Hungerford. Three days later the two returned in an exhausted condition, and submitted a motion of want-of-confidence, which was lost. Then the whole House went on and was lost also. Strange to relate, that Government was never missed.

However, we found Hungerford and camped there for a day. The town is right on the Queensland border, and an interprovincial rabbit-proof fence – with rabbits on both sides of it – runs across the main street.

This fence is a standing joke with Australian rabbits – about the only joke they have out there, except the memory of Pasteur and poison and inoculation. It is amusing to go a little way out of town, about sunset, and watch them crack Noah's Ark rabbit jokes about that fence, and burrow under and play leap-frog over it till they get tired. One old buck rabbit sat up and nearly laughed his ears off at a joke of his own about that fence. He laughed so much that he couldn't get away when I reached for him. I could hardly eat him for laughing. I never saw a rabbit laugh before; but I've seen a possum do it.

Hungerford consists of two houses and a humpy in New South Wales and five houses in Queensland. Characteristically enough, both the pubs are in Queensland. We got a glass of sour yeast at one and paid sixpence for it – we had asked for English ale.

The post office is in New South Wales, and the police-barracks in Bananaland. The police cannot do anything if there's a row going on across the street in New South Wales, except to send to Brisbane and have an extradition warrant applied for; and they don't do much if there's a row in Queensland. Most of the rows are across the border, where the pubs are.

At least, I believe that's how it is, though the man who told me might have been a liar. Another man said he was a liar, but then he might have been a liar himself – a third person said he was one. I heard that there was a fight over it, but the man who told me about the fight might not have been telling the truth.

One part of the town swears at Brisbane when things go wrong, and the other part curses Sydney.

The country looks as though a great ash-heap had been spread out there, and mulga scrub and firewood planted – and neglected. The country looks just as bad for a hundred miles round Hungerford, and beyond that it gets worse – a blasted, barren wilderness that doesn't even howl. If it howled it would be a relief.

I believe that Burke and Wills found Hungerford, and it's a pity they did; but if I ever stand by the graves of the men who first travelled through this country, when there were neither roads nor stations, nor tanks, nor bores, nor pubs, I'll – I'll take my hat off. There were brave men in the land in those days.

It is said that the explorers gave the district its name chiefly because of the hunger they found there, which has remained there ever since. I don't know where the ford comes in – there's nothing to ford, except in flood-time. Hungerthirst would have been better. The town is supposed to be situated on the banks of a river called the Paroo, but we saw no water there, except what passed for it in a tank. The goats and sheep and dogs and the rest of the population drink there. It is dangerous to take too much of that water in a raw state.

Except in flood-time you couldn't find the bed of the river without the aid of a spirit-level and a long straight-edge. There is a Custom-house against the fence on the northern side. A pound of tea often costs six shillings on that side, and you can get a common lead pencil for fourpence at the rival store across the street in the mother province. Also, a small loaf of sour bread sells for a shilling at the humpy aforementioned. Only about sixty per cent of the sugar will melt.

We saw one of the storekeepers give a dead-beat swagman five shillings' worth of rations to take him on into Queensland. The storekeepers often do this, and put it down on the loss side of their books. I hope the recording angel listens, and puts it down on the right side of his book.

We camped on the Queensland side of the fence, and after tea had a yarn with an old man who was minding a mixed flock of goats and sheep; and we asked him whether he thought Queensland was better than New South Wales, or the other way about.

He scratched the back of his head, and thought a while, and hesitated like a stranger who is going to do you a favour at some personal inconvenience.

At last, with the bored air of a man who has gone through the same performance too often before, he stepped deliberately up to the fence and spat over it into New South Wales. After which he got leisurely through and spat back on Queensland.

'That's what I think of the blanky colonies!' he said.

He gave us time to become sufficiently impressed; then he said:

'And if I was at the Victorian and South Australian border I'd do the same thing.'

He let that soak into our minds, and added: 'And the same with West Australia – and – and Tasmania.' Then he went away.

The last would have been a long spit – and he forgot Maoriland.

We heard afterwards that his name was Clancy and he had that day been offered a job droving at 'twenty-five shillings a week and find your own horse.' Also find your own horse-feed and tobacco and soap and other luxuries, at station prices. Moreover, if you lost your own horse you would have to find another, and if that died or went astray you would have to find a third – or forfeit your pay and return on foot. The boss drover agreed to provide flour and mutton – when such things were procurable.

Consequently, Clancy's unfavourable opinion of the colonies.

My mate and I sat down on our swags against the fence to talk things over. One of us was very deaf. Presently a black tracker went past and looked at us, and returned to the pub. Then a trooper in Queensland uniform came along and asked us what the trouble was about, and where we came from and were going, and where we camped. We said we were discussing private business, and he explained that he thought it was a row, and came over to see. Then he left us, and later on we saw him sitting with the rest of the population on a bench under the hotel veranda. Next morning we rolled up our swags and left Hungerford to the north-west.

A CAMP-FIRE YARN

'THIS GIRL,' said Mitchell, continuing a yarn to his mate, 'was about the ugliest girl I ever saw, except one, and I'll tell you about her directly. The old man had a carpenter's shop fixed up in a shed at the back of his house, and he used to work there pretty often, and sometimes I'd come over and yarn with him. One day I was sitting on the end of the bench, and the old man was working away, and Mary was standing there too, all three of us yarning – she mostly came poking round where I was if I happened to be on the premises – or at least I thought so – and we got yarning about getting married, and the old cove said he'd get married again if the old woman died.

'"You get married again!" said Mary. "Why, father, you wouldn't get anyone to marry you – who'd have you?"

'"Well," he said, "I bet I'll get someone sooner than you, anyway. You don't seem to be able to get anyone, and it's pretty near time you thought of settlin' down and gettin' married. I wish someone would have you."

'He hit her pretty hard there, but it served her right. She got as good as she gave. She looked at me and went all colours, and then she went back to her washtub.

'She was mighty quiet at tea-time – she seemed hurt a lot, and I began to feel sorry I'd laughed at the old man's joke, for she was really a good, hard-working girl, and you couldn't help liking her.

'So after tea I went out to her in the kitchen, where she was washing up, to try and cheer her up a bit. She'd scarcely speak at first, except to say Yes or No, and kept her face turned away from me; and I could see that she'd been crying. I began to feel sorry for her and mad at the old man, and I started to comfort her. But I didn't go the right way to work about it. I told her that she mustn't take any notice of the old cove, as he didn't mean half he said. But she seemed to take it harder than ever, and at last I got so sorry for her that I told her that I'd have her if she'd have me.'

'And what did she say?' asked Mitchell's mate, after a pause.

'She said she wouldn't have me at any price!'

The mate laughed, and Mitchell grinned his quiet grin.

'Well, this set me thinking,' he continued. 'I always knew I was a dashed ugly cove, and I began to wonder whether any girl would really have me; and I kept on it till at last I made up my mind to find out and settle the matter for good – or bad.

'There was another farmer's daughter living close by, and I met her pretty often coming home from work, and sometimes I had a yarn with her. She was plain, and no mistake: Mary was a Venus alongside of her. She had feet like a Lascar, and hands about ten sizes too large for her, and a face like that camel – only red; she walked like a camel, too. She looked like a ladder with a dress on, and she didn't know a great A from a corner cupboard.

'Well, one evening I met here at the sliprails, and presently I asked her, for a joke, if she'd marry me. Mind you, I never wanted to marry her; I was only curious to know whether any girl would have me.

'She turned away her face and seemed to hesitate, and I was just turning away and beginning to think I was a dashed hopeless case, when all of a sudden she fell up against me and said she'd be my wife ... And it wasn't her fault that she wasn't.'

'What did she do?'

'Do! What didn't she do? Next day she went down to our place when I was at work, and hugged and kissed mother and the girls all round, and cried, and told mother that she'd try and be a dutiful daughter to her. Good Lord! You should have seen the old woman and the girls when I came home.

'Then she let every one know that Bridget Page was engaged to Jack Mitchell, and told her friends that she went down on her knees every night and thanked the Lord for getting the love of a good man. Didn't the fellows chyack me, though! My sisters were raving mad about it, for their chums kept asking them how they liked their new sister, and when it was going to come off, and who'd be bridesmaids and best man, and whether they weren't surprised at their brother Jack's choice; and then I'd gammon at home that it was all true.

'At last the place got too hot for me. I got sick of dodging that girl. I sent a mate of mine to tell her that it was all a joke, and that I was already married in secret; but she didn't see it, then I cleared, and got a job in Newcastle, but had to leave there when my mates sent me the office that she was coming. I wouldn't wonder but what she is humping her swag after me now. In fact, I thought you was her in disguise when I set eyes on you first ... You needn't get mad about it: I don't mean to say that you're quite as ugly as she was, because I never saw a man that was – or a woman either. Anyway, I'll never ask a woman to marry me again unless I'm ready to marry her.'

Then Mitchell's mate told a yarn.

'I knew a case once something like the one you were telling me about; the landlady of a hash-house where I was stopping in Albany told me. There was a young carpenter staying there, who'd run away from Sydney from an old maid who wanted to marry him. He'd cleared from the church door, I believe. He was scarcely more'n a boy – about nineteen – and a soft kind of a fellow, something like you, only good-looking – that is, he was passable. Well, as soon as the woman found out where he'd gone, she came after him. She turned up at the boarding-house one Saturday morning when Bobbie was at work; and the first thing she did was to rent a double room from the landlady and buy some cups and saucers to start housekeeping with. When Bobbie came home he just gave her one look and gave up the game.

'"Get your dinner, Bobbie," she said, after she'd slobbered over him a bit, "and then get dressed and come with me and get married!"

'She was about three times his age, and had a face like that picture of a lady over Sappho Smith's letters in the Sydney Bulletin.

'Well, Bobbie went with her like a – like a lamb; never gave a kick or tried to clear.'

'Hold on,' said Mitchell, 'did you ever shear lambs?'

'Never mind. Let me finish the yarn. Bobbie was married; but she wouldn't let him out of her sight all that afternoon, and he had to put up with her before them all. About bedtime he sneaked out and started along the passage to his room that he shared with two or three mates. But she'd her eye on him.

'"Bobbie, Bobbie!" she says, "Where are you going?"

'"I'm going to bed," said Bobbie. "Good night!"

'"Bobbie, Bobbie," she says, sharply. "That isn't our room; this is our room, Bobbie. Come back at once! What do you mean, Bobbie? Do you hear me, Bobbie?"

'So Bobbie came back, and went in with the scarecrow. Next morning she was first at the breakfast table, in a dressing-gown and curl papers. And when they were all sitting down Bobbie sneaked in, looking awfully sheepish, and sidled for his chair at the other end of the table. But she'd her eyes on him.

'"Bobbie, Bobbie!" she said, "Come and kiss me, Bobbie!"

'And he had to do it in front of them all.

'But I believe she made him a good wife.'

THAT THERE DOG OF MINE

MACQUARIE THE SHEARER had met with an accident. To tell the truth, he had been in a drunken row at a wayside shanty, from which he had escaped with three fractured ribs, a cracked head, and various minor abrasions. His dog, Tally, had been a sober but savage participator in the drunken row, and had escaped with a broken leg. Macquarie afterwards shouldered his swag and staggered and struggled along the track ten miles to the Union Town hospital. Lord knows how he did it. He didn't exactly know himself. Tally limped behind all the way, on three legs.

The doctors examined the man's injuries and were surprised at his endurance. Even doctors are surprised sometimes – though they don't always show it. Of course they would take him in, but they objected to Tally. Dogs were not allowed on the premises.

'You will have to turn that dog out,' they said to the shearer, as he sat on the edge of a bed.

Macquarie said nothing.

'We cannot allow dogs about the place, my man,' said the doctor in a louder tone, thinking the man was deaf.

'Tie him up in the yard then.'

'No. He must go out. Dogs are not permitted on the grounds.'

Macquarie rose slowly to his feet, shut his agony behind his set teeth, painfully buttoned his shirt over his hairy chest, took up his waistcoat, and staggered to the corner where the swag lay.

'What are you going to do?' they asked.

'You ain't going to let my dog stop?'

'No. It's against the rules. There are no dogs allowed on the premises.'

He stooped and lifted his swag, but the pain was too great, and he leaned back against the wall.

'Come, come now! man alive!' exclaimed the doctor, impatiently. 'You must be mad. You know you are not in a fit state to go out. Let the wardsman help you to undress.'

'No!' said Macquarie. 'No. If you won't take my dog in you don't take me. He's got a broken leg and wants fixing up just – just as much as – as I do. If I'm good enough to come in, he's good enough – and – and better.'

He paused a while, breathing painfully, and then went on.

'That – that there old dog of mine has follered me faithful and true, these twelve long hard and hungry years. He's about – about the only thing that ever cared whether I lived or fell and rotted on the cursed track.'

He rested again; then he continued: 'That – that there dog was pupped on the track,' he said, with a sad sort of a smile. 'I carried him for months in a billy, and afterwards on my swag when he knocked up ... And the old slut – his mother – she'd foller along quite contented – and sniff the billy now and again – just to see if he was all right ... She follered me for God knows how many years. She follered me till she was blind – and for a year after. She follered me till she could crawl along through the dust no longer, and – and then I killed her, because I couldn't leave her behind alive!'

He rested again.

'And this here old dog,' he continued, touching Tally's upturned nose with his knotted fingers, 'this here old dog has follered me for – for ten years; through floods and droughts, through fair times and – and hard – mostly hard; and kept me from going mad when I had no mate nor money on the lonely track; and watched over me for weeks when I was drunk – drugged and poisoned at the cursed shanties; and saved my life more'n once, and got kicks and curses very often for thanks; and forgave me for it all; and – and fought for me. He was the only living thing that stood up for me against that crawling push of curs when they set onter me at the shanty back yonder – and he left his mark on some of 'em too; and – and so did I.'

He took another spell.

Then he drew in his breath, shut his teeth hard, shouldered his swag, stepped into the doorway, and faced round again.

The dog limped out of the corner and looked up anxiously.

'That there dog,' said Macquarie to the hospital staff in general, 'is a better dog that I'm a man – or you too, it seems – and a better Christian. He's been a better mate than I ever was to any man – or any man to me. He's watched over me; kep' me from getting robbed many a time; fought for me; saved my life and took drunken kicks and curses for thanks – and forgave me. He's been a true, straight, honest, and faithful mate to me – and I ain't going to desert him now. I ain't going to kick him out in the road with a broken leg. I – Oh, my God! my back!'

He groaned and lurched forward, but they caught him, slipped off the swag, and laid him on a bed.

Half an hour later the shearer was comfortably fixed up. 'Where's my dog?' he asked, when he came to himself.

'Oh, the dog's all right,' said the nurse, rather impatiently. 'Don't bother. The doctor's setting his leg out in the yard.'

GOING BLIND

I MET HIM in the Full-and-Plenty Dining-rooms. It was a cheap place in the city, with good beds upstairs let at one shilling per night – 'Board and residence for respectable single men, fifteen shillings per week.' I was a respectable single man then. I boarded and resided there. I boarded at a greasy little table in the greasy little corner under the fluffy little staircase in the hot and greasy little dining-room or restaurant downstairs. They called it dining-rooms, but it was only one room, and there wasn't half enough room in it to work your elbows when the seven little tables and forty-nine chairs were occupied. There was not room for an ordinary-sized steward to pass up and down between the tables; but our waiter was not an ordinary-sized man – he was a living skeleton in miniature. We handed the soup, and the 'roast beef one,' and 'roast lamb one,' 'corn beef and cabbage one,' 'veal and stuffing one,' and the 'veal and pickled pork,' one – or two, or three, as the case might be – and the tea and coffee, and the various kinds of puddings – we handed them over each other, and dodged the drops as well as we could. The very hot and very greasy little kitchen was adjacent, and it contained the bathroom and other conveniences, behind screens of white-washed boards.

I resided upstairs in a room where there were five beds and one wash-stand; one candle-stick, with a very short bit of soft yellow candle in it; the back of a hair-brush, with about a dozen bristles in it; and half a comb – the big-tooth end – with nine and a half teeth at irregular distances apart.

He was a typical bushman, not one of those tall, straight, wiry, brown men of the West, but from the old Selection Districts, where many drovers came from, and of the old bush school; one of those slight active little fellows whom we used to see in cabbage-tree hats, Crimean shirts, strapped trousers, and elastic-side boots – 'larstins,' they called them. They could dance well; sing indifferently, and mostly through their noses, the old bush songs; play the concertina horribly; and ride like – like – well, they could ride.

He seemed as if he had forgotten to grow old and die out with this old colonial school to which he belonged. They had careless and forgetful ways about them. His name was Jack Gunther, he said, and he'd come to Sydney to try to get something done to his eyes. He had a portmanteau, a carpet bag, some things in a three-bushel bag, and a tin box. I sat beside him on his bed, and struck up an acquaintance, and he told me all about it. First he asked me would I mind shifting round to the other side, as he was rather deaf in that ear. He'd been kicked by a horse, he said, and had been a little dull o' hearing on that side ever since.

He was as good as blind. 'I can see the people near me,' he said, 'but I can't make out their faces. I can just make out the pavement and the houses close at hand, and all the rest is a sort of white blur.' He looked up: 'That ceiling is a kind of white, ain't it? And this,' tapping the wall and putting his nose close to it, 'is a sort of green, ain't it?' The ceiling might have been whiter. The prevalent tints of the wall-paper had originally been blue and red, but it was mostly green enough now – a damp, rotten green; but I was ready to swear that the ceiling was snow and that the walls were as green as grass if it would have made him feel more comfortable. His sight began to get bad about six years before, he said; he didn't take much notice of it at first, and then he saw a quack, who made his eyes worse. He had already the manner of the blind – the touch of every finger, and even the gentleness in his speech. He had a boy down with him – a 'sorter cousin of his,' and the boy saw him round. 'I'll have to be sending that youngster back,' he said, 'I think I'll send him home next week. He'll be picking up and learning too much down here.'

I happened to know the district he came from, and we would sit by the hour and talk about the country, and chaps by the name of this and chaps by the name of that – drovers mostly, whom we had met or had heard of. He asked me if I'd ever heard of a chap by the name of Joe Scott – a big sandy-complexioned chap, who might be droving; he was his brother, or, at least, his half-brother, but he hadn't heard of him for years; he'd last heard of him at Blackall, in Queensland; he might have gone overland to Western Australia with Tyson's cattle to the new country.

We talked about grubbing and fencing and digging and droving and shearing – all about the bush – and it all came back to me as we talked. 'I can see it all now,' he said once, in an abstracted tone, seeming to fix his helpless eyes on the wall opposite. But he didn't see the dirty blind wall, nor the dingy window, nor the skimpy little bed, nor the greasy wash-stand: he saw the dark blue ridges in the sunlight, the grassy sidlings and flats, the creek with clumps of she-oak here and there, the course of the willow-fringed river below, the distant peaks and ranges fading away into a lighter azure, the granite ridge in the middle distance, and the rocky rises, the stringy-bark and the apple-tree flats, the scrubs, and the sunlit plains – and all. I could see it, too – plainer than ever I did.

He had done a bit of fencing in his time, and we got talking about timber. He didn't believe in having fencing-posts with big butts; he reckoned it was a mis- take. 'You see,' he said, 'the top of the butt catches the rain water and makes the post rot quicker. I'd back posts without any butt at all to last as long or longer than posts with 'em – that's if the fence is well put up and well rammed.' He had supplied fencing stuff, and fenced by contract, and – well, you can get more posts without butts out of a tree than posts with them. He also objected to charring the butts. He said it only made more work – and wasted time – the butts lasted longer without being charred.

I asked him if he'd ever got stringy-bark palings or shingles out of mountain ash, and he smiled a smile that did my heart good to see, and said he had. He had also got them out of various other kinds of trees.

We talked about soil and grass, and gold-digging, and many other things which came back to one like a revelation as we yarned.

He had been to the hospital several times. 'The doctors don' say they can cure me,' he said, 'they say they might be able to improve my sight and hearing, but it would take a long time – anyway, the treatment would improve my general health. They know what's the matter with my eyes,' and he explained it as well as he could. 'I wish I'd seen a good doctor when my eyes first began to get weak; but young chaps are always careless over things. It's harder to get cured of anything when you're done growing.'

He was always hopeful and cheerful. 'If the worst comes to the worst,' he said, 'there's things I can do where I come from. I might do a bit o' wool-sorting, for instance. I'm a pretty fair expert. Or else when they're weeding out I could help. I'd just have to sit down and they'd bring the sheep to me, and I'd feel the wool and tell them what it was – being blind improves the feeling, you know.'

He had a packet of portraits, but he couldn't make them out very well now. They were sort of blurred to him, but I described them and he told me who they were. 'That's a girl o' mine,' he said, with reference to one – a jolly, good-looking bush girl. 'I got a letter from her yesterday. I managed to scribble something, but I'll get you, if you don't mind, to write something more I want to put in on another piece of paper, and address an envelope for me.'

Darkness fell quickly upon him now – or, rather, the 'sort of white blur' increased and closed in. But his hearing was better, he said, and he was glad of that and still cheerful. I thought it natural that his hearing should improve as he went blind.

One day he said that he did not think he would bother going to the hospital any more. He reckoned he'd get back to where he was known. He'd stayed down too long already, and the 'stuff' wouldn't stand it. He was expecting a letter that didn't come. I was away for a couple of days, and when I came back he had been shifted out of the room and had a bed in an angle of the landing on top of the staircase, with the people brushing against him and stumbling over his things all day on their way up and down. I felt indignant, thinking that – the house being full – the boss had taken advantage of the bushman's helplessness and good nature to put him there. But he said that he was quite comfortable. 'I can get a whiff of air here,' he said.

Going in next day I thought for a moment that I had dropped suddenly back into the past and into a bush dance, for there was a concertina going upstairs. He was sitting on the bed, with his legs crossed, and a new cheap concertina on his knee, and his eyes turned to the patch of ceiling as if it were a piece of music and he could read it. 'I'm trying to knock a few tunes into my head,' he said, with a brave smile, 'in case the worst comes to the worst.' He tried to be cheerful, but seemed worried and anxious. The letter hadn't come. I thought of the many blind musicians in Sydney, and I thought of the bushman's chance, standing at a corner swanking a cheap concertina, and I felt sorry for him.

I went out with a vague idea of seeing someone about the matter, and getting something done for the bushman – of bringing a little influence to his assistance; but I suddenly remembered that my clothes were worn out, my hat in a shocking state, my boots burst, and that I owed for a week's board and lodging, and was likely to be thrown out at any moment myself; and so I was not in a position to go where there was influence.

When I went back to the restaurant there was a long, gaunt, sandy-complexioned bushman sitting by Jack's side. Jack introduced him as his brother, who had returned unexpectedly to his native district, and had followed him to Sydney. The brother was rather short with me at first, and seemed to regard the restaurant people, all of us, in fact – in the light of spielers who wouldn't hesitate to take advantage of Jack's blindness if he left him a moment; and he looked ready to knock down the first man who stumbled against Jack, or over his luggage – but that soon wore off. Jack was going to stay with Joe at the Coffee Palace for a few weeks, and then go back up-country, he told me. He was excited and happy. His brother's manner towards him was as if Jack had just lost his wife, or boy, or someone very dear to him. He would not allow him to do anything for himself, nor try to – not even lace up his boots. He seemed to think that he was thoroughly helpless, and when I saw him pack up Jack's things, and help him at the table, and fix his tie and collar with his great brown hands, which trembled all the time with grief and gentleness, and make Jack sit down on the bed whilst he got a cab and carried the traps down to it, and take him downstairs as if he were made of thin glass, and settle with the landlord – then I knew that Jack was all right.

We had a drink together – Joe, Jack, the cabman, and I. Joe was very careful to hand Jack the glass, and Jack made a joke about it for Joe's benefit. He swore he could see a glass yet, and Joe laughed, but looked extra troubled the next moment.

I felt their grips on my hand for five minutes after we parted.

THE UNION BURIES ITS DEAD

WHILE out boating one Sunday afternoon on a billabong across the river, we saw a young man on horseback driving some horses along the bank. He said it was a fine day, and asked if the water was deep there. The joker of our party said it was deep enough to drown him, and he laughed and rode farther up. We didn't take much notice of him.

Next day a funeral gathered at a corner pub and asked each other in to have a drink while waiting for the hearse. They passed away some of the time dancing jigs to a piano in the bar parlour. They passed away the rest of the time skylarking and fighting.

The defunct was a young Union labourer, about twenty-five, who had been drowned the previous day while trying to swim some horses across a billabong of the Darling.

He was almost a stranger in town, and the fact of his having been a Union man accounted for the funeral. The police found some Union papers in his swag, and called at the General Labourers' Union Office for information about him. That's how we knew. The secretary had very little information to give. The departed was a 'Roman,' and the majority of the town were otherwise – but Unionism is stronger that creed. Liquor, however, is stronger than Unionism; and, when the hearse presently arrived, more than two-thirds of the funeral were unable to follow.

The procession numbered fifteen, fourteen souls following the broken shell of a soul. Perhaps not one of the fourteen possessed a soul any more than the corpse did – but that doesn't matter.

Four or five of the funeral, who were boarders at the pub, borrowed a trap which the landlord used to carry passengers to and from the railway station. They were strangers to us who were on foot, and we to them. We were all strangers to the corpse.

A horseman, who looked like a drover just returned from a big trip, dropped into our dusty wake and followed us a few hundred yards, dragging his packhorse behind him, but a friend made wild and demonstrative signals from an hotel veranda – hooking at the air in front with his right hand and jobbing his left thumb over his shoulder in the direction of the bar – so the drover hauled off and didn't catch up to us any more. He was a stranger to the entire show.

We walked in twos. There were three twos. It was very hot and dusty; the heat rushed in fierce dazzling rays across every iron roof and light-coloured wall that was turned to the sun. One or two pubs closed respectfully until we got past. They closed their bar doors and the patrons went in and out through some side

or back entrance for a few minutes. Bushmen seldom grumble at an inconvenience of this sort, when it is caused by a funeral. They have too much respect
for the dead.

On the way to the cemetery we passed three shearers sitting on the shady side
of a fence. One was drunk – very drunk. The other two covered their right ears
with their hats, out of respect for the departed – whoever he might have been –
and one of them kicked the drunk and muttered something to him.

He straightened himself up, stared, and reached helplessly for his hat, which
he shoved half off and then on again. Then he made a great effort to pull
himself together – and succeeded. He stood up, braced his back against the fence,
knocked off his hat, and remorsefully placed his foot on it – to keep it off his
head till the funeral passed.

A tall, sentimental drover, who walked by my side, cynically quoted Byronic
verses suitable to the occasion – to death – and asked with pathetic humour
whether we thought the dead man's ticket would be recognised 'over yonder.' It
was a G.L.U. ticket, and the general opinion was that it would be recognised.

Presently my friend said:

'You remember when we were in the boat yesterday, we saw a man driving some
horses along the bank?'

'Yes.'

He nodded at the hearse and said:

'Well, that's him.'

I thought a while.

'I didn't take any particular notice of him,' I said. 'He said something, didn't
he?'

'Yes; said it was a fine day. You'd have taken more notice if you'd known that
he was doomed to die in the hour, and that those were the last words he would
say to any man in this world.'

'To be sure,' said a full voice from the rear. 'If ye'd known that, ye'd have
prolonged the conversation.'

We plodded on across the railway line and along the hot, dusty road which ran
to the cemetery, some of us talking about the accident, and lying about the
narrow escapes we had had ourselves. Presently someone said:

'There's the Devil.'

I looked up and saw a priest standing in the shade of the tree by the
cemetery gate.

The hearse was drawn up and the tail-boards were opened. The funeral
extinguished its right ear with its hat as four men lifted the coffin out and laid
it over the grave. The priest – a pale, quiet young fellow – stood under the shade
of a sapling which grew at the head of the grave. He took off his hat, dropped

it carelessly on the ground, and proceeded to business. I noticed that one or two heathens winced slightly when the holy water was sprinkled on the coffin. The drops quickly evaporated, and the little round black spots they left were soon dusted over; but the spots showed, by contrast, the cheapness and shabbiness of the cloth with which the coffin was covered. It seemed black before; now it looked a dusky grey.

Just here man's ignorance and vanity made a farce of the funeral. A big, bull-necked publican, with heavy, blotchy features, and a supremely ignorant expression, picked up the priest's straw hat and held it about two inches over the head of his reverence during the whole of the service. The father, be it remembered, was standing in the shade. A few shoved their hats on and off uneasily, struggling between their disgust for the living and their respect for the dead. The hat had a conical crown and a brim sloping down all round like a sunshade, and the publican held it with his great red claw spread over the crown. To do the priest justice, perhaps he didn't notice the incident. A stage priest or parson in the same position might have said, 'Put the hat down, my friend; is not the memory of our departed brother worth more than my complexion?' A wattle-bark layman might have expressed himself in stronger language, none the less to the point. But my priest seemed unconscious of what was going on. Besides, the publican was a great and important pillar of the church. He couldn't, as an ignorant and conceited ass, lose such a good opportunity of asserting his faithfulness and importance to his church.

The grave looked very narrow under the coffin, and I drew a breath of relief when the box slid easily down. I saw a coffin get stuck once, at Rookwood, and it had to be yanked out with difficulty, and laid on the sods at the feet of the heart-broken relations, who howled dismally while the grave-diggers widened the hole. But they don't cut contracts so fine in the West. Our grave-digger was not altogether bowelless, and, out of respect for that human quality described as 'feelin's,' he scraped up some light and dusty soil and threw it down to deaden the fall of the clay lumps on the coffin. He also tried to steer the first few shovelfuls gently down against the end of the grave with the back of the shovel turned outwards, but the hard dry Darling River clods rebounded and knocked all the same. It didn't matter much – nothing does. The fall of lumps of clay on a stranger's coffin doesn't sound any different from the fall of the same things on an ordinary wooden box – at least I didn't notice anything awesome or unusual in the sound; but, perhaps, one of us – the most sensitive – might have been impressed by being reminded of a burial of long ago, when the thump of every sod jolted his heart.

I have left out the wattle – because it wasn't there. I have also neglected to mention the heart-broken old mate, with his grizzled head bowed and great pearly drops streaming down his rugged cheeks. He was absent – he was probably 'out back.' For similar reasons I have omitted reference to the suspicious moisture in the eyes of a bearded bush ruffian named Bill. Bill failed to turn up, and the only moisture was that which was induced by the heat. I have left out the 'sad Australian sunset,' because the sun was not going down at the time. The burial took place exactly at midday.

The dead bushman's name was Jim, apparently; but they found no portraits, nor locks of hair, nor any love letters, nor anything of that kind in his swag – not even a reference to his mother; only some papers relating to Union matters. Most of us didn't know the name till we saw it on the coffin; we knew him as 'that poor chap that got drowned yesterday.'

'So his name's James Tyson,' said my drover acquaintance, looking at the plate.

'Why! Didn't you know that before?' I asked.

'No; but I knew he was a Union man.'

It turned out, afterwards, that J.T. wasn't his real name – only 'the name he went by.'

Anyhow he was buried by it, and most of the 'Great Australian Dailies' have mentioned in their brevity columns that a young man named James John Tyson was drowned in a billabong of the Darling last Sunday.

We did hear, later on, what his real name was; but if we ever chance to read it in the 'Missing Friends Column,' we shall not be able to give any information to heart-broken mother or sister or wife, nor to anyone who could let him hear something to his advantage – for we have already forgotten the name.

STEELMAN

STEELMAN was a hard case. If you were married, and settled down, and were so unfortunate as to have known Steelman in other days, he would, if in your neighbourhood and deadbeat, be sure to look you up. He would find you anywhere, no matter what precautions you might take. If he came to your house, he would stay to tea without invitation, and if he stayed to tea, he would ask you to 'fix up a shake-down on the floor, old man,' and put him up for the night; and, if he stopped all night, he'd remain – well, until something better turned up.

There was no shaking off Steelman. He had a way about him which would often make it appear as if you had invited him to stay, and pressed him against his roving inclination, and were glad to have him round for company, while he remained only out of pure goodwill to you. He didn't like to offend an old friend by refusing his invitation.

Steelman knew his men.

The married victim generally had neither the courage nor the ability to turn him out. He was cheerfully blind and deaf to all hints, and if the exasperated missus said anything to him straight, he would look shocked, and reply, as likely as not:

'Why, my good woman, you must be mad! I'm your husband's guest!'

And if she wouldn't cook for him, he'd cook for himself.

There was no choking him off. Few people care to call the police in a case like this; and besides, as before remarked, Steelman knew his men. The only way to escape from him was to move – but then, as likely as not, he'd help pack up and come along with his portmanteau right on top of the last load of furniture, and drive you and your wife to the verge of madness by the calm style in which he proceeded to superintend the hanging of your pictures.

Once he quartered himself like this on an old schoolmate of his, named Brown, who had got married and steady and settled down. Brown tried all ways to get rid of Steelman, but he couldn't do it. One day Brown said to Steelman:

'Look here, Steely, old man, I'm very sorry, but I'm afraid we won't be able to accommodate you any longer – to make you comfortable, I mean. You see, a sister of the missus is coming down on a visit for a month or two, and we ain't got anywhere to put her, except in your room. I wish the missus's relations to blazes! I didn't marry the whole family; but it seems I've got to keep them.'

Pause – very awkward and painful for poor Brown. Discouraging silence from Steelman. Brown rested his elbows on his knees, and, with a pathetic and appealing movement of his hand across his forehead, he continued desperately:

'I'm very sorry, you see, old man – you know I'd like you to stay – I want you to stay ... It isn't my fault – it's the missus's doings. I've done my best with her, but I can't help it. I've been more like a master in my own house – more comfortable – and I've been better treated since I've had you to back me up ... I'll feel mighty lonely, anyway, when you're gone ... But ... you know ... as soon as her sister goes ... you know ...'

Here poor Brown broke down – very sorry he had spoken at all; but Steely came to the rescue with a ray of light.

'What's the matter with the little room at the back?' he asked.

'Oh, we couldn't think of putting you there,' said Brown, with a last effort; 'it's not fixed up; you wouldn't be comfortable, and, besides, it's damp, and you'd catch your death of cold. It was never meant for anything but a wash-house. I'm sorry I didn't get another room built on to the house.'

'Bosh!' interrupted Steelman cheerfully. 'Catch a cold! Here I've been knocking about the country for the last five years – sleeping out in all weathers – and do you think a little damp is going to hurt me? Pooh! What do you take me for? Don't you bother your head about it any more, old man; I'll fix up the lumber-room for myself, all right; and all you've got to do is to let me know when the sister-in-law business is coming on, and I'll shift out of my room in time for the missus to get it ready for her. Here, have you got a bob on you? I'll go out and get some beer. A drop'll do you good.'

'Well, if you can make yourself comfortable, I'll be only too glad for you to stay,' said Brown, wearily.

'You'd better invite some woman you know to come on a visit, and pass her off as your sister,' said Brown to his wife, while Steelman was gone for the beer. 'I've made a mess of it.'

Mrs Brown said, 'I knew you would.'

Steelman knew his man.

But at last Brown reckan was sitting beside Brown's bed with a saucer of vinegar, some brown paper, a raw beef-steak, and a bottle of soda.

'Well, what have you got to say for yourself now, Brown?' he said sternly. 'Ain't you jolly well ashamed of yourself to come home in the beastly state you did last night, and insult a guest in your house, to say nothing of an old friend – and perhaps the best friend you ever had, if you only knew it? Anybody else would have given you in charge and got you three months for the assault. You ought to have some consideration for your wife and children, and your own character – even if you haven't any for your old mate's feelings. Here, drink this, and let me fix you up a bit; the missus has got the breakfast waiting.'

SHOOTING THE MOON

WE LAY IN CAMP in the fringe of the mulga, and watched the big, red, smoky, rising moon out on the edge of the misty plain, and smoked and thought together sociably. Our nose-bags were nice and heavy, and we still had about a pound of nailrod between us.

The moon reminded my mate, Jack Mitchell, of something – anything reminded him of something, in fact.

'Did you ever notice,' said Jack, in a lazy tone, just as if he didn't want to tell a yarn – 'Did you ever notice that people always shoot the moon when there's no moon? Have you got the matches?'

He lit up; he was always lighting up when he was reminded of something.

'This reminds me – Have you got the knife? My pipe's stuffed up.'

He dug it out, loaded afresh, and lit up again.

'I remember once, at a pub I was staying at, I had to leave without saying goodbye to the landlord. I didn't know him very well at that time.

'My room was upstairs at the back with the window opening on to the backyard. I always carried a bit of clothes-line in my swag or portmanteau those times. I travelled along with a portmanteau those times. I carried the rope in case of accident, or in case of fire, to lower my things out of the window – hang myself, maybe, if things got too bad. No, now I come to think of it, I carried a revolver for that, and it was the only thing I never pawned.'

'To hang yourself with?' asked the mate.

'Yes – you're very smart,' snapped Mitchell; 'never mind – This reminds me that I got a chap at a pub to pawn my last suit, while I stopped inside and waited for an old mate to send me a pound; but I kept the shooter, and if he hadn't sent it I'd have been the late John Mitchell long ago.'

'And sometimes you lower'd out when there wasn't a fire.'

'Yes, that will pass; you're improving in the funny business. But about the yarn. There was two beds in my room at the pub, where I had to go away without shouting for the boss, and, as it happened, there was a strange chap sleeping in the other bed that night, and, just as I raised the window and was going to lower my bag out, he woke up.

'"Now, look here," I said, shaking my fist at him, like that, "if you say a word, I'll stoush yer!"

'"Well," he said, "well, you needn't be in such a sweat to jump down a man's throat. I've got my swag under the bed, and I was just going to ask you for the loan of the rope when you're done with it."

'Well, we chummed. His name was Tom – Tom – something, I forget the other name, but it doesn't matter. Have you got the matches?'

He wasted three matches, and continued:

'There was a lot of old galvanised iron lying about under the window, and I was frightened the swag would make a noise; anyway, I'd have to drop the rope, and that was sure to make a noise. So we agreed for one of us to go down and land the swag. If we were seen going down without the swags it didn't matter, for we could say we wanted to go out in the yard for something.'

'If you had the swag you might pretend you were walking in your sleep,' I suggested, for the want of something funnier to say.

'Bosh,' said Jack, 'and get woke up with a black eye. Bushies don't generally carry their swags out of pubs in their sleep, or walk neither; it's only city swells who do that. Where's the blessed matches?

'Well, Tom agreed to go, and presently I saw a shadow under the window, and lowered away.

'"All right?" I asked in a whisper.

'"All right!" whispered the shadow.

'I lowered the other swag.

'"All right?"

'"All right!" said the shadow, and just then the moon came out.

'"All right!" says the shadow.

'But it wasn't all right. It was the landlord himself!

'It seems he got up and went out to the back in the night, and just happened to be coming in when my mate Tom was sneaking out of the back door. He saw Tom, and Tom saw him, and smoked through a hole in the palings into the scrub. The boss looked up at the window, and dropped to it. I went down, funky enough, I can tell you, and faced him. He said:

'"Look here, mate, why didn't you some straight to me, and tell me how you was fixed, instead of sneaking round the trouble in that fashion? There's no occasion for it."

'I felt mean at once, but I said: "Well, you see, we didn't know you, boss."

'"So it seems. Well, I didn't think of that. Anyway, call up your mate and come and have a drink; we'll talk over it afterwards." So I called Tom. "Come on," I shouted. "It's all right."

'And the boss kept us a couple of days, and then gave us as much tucker as we could carry, and a drop of stuff and a few bob to go on the track again with.'

'Well, he was white, any road.'

'Yes. I knew him well after that, and only heard one man say a word against him.'

'And did you stoush him?'

'No; I was going to, but Tom wouldn't let me. He said he was frightened I might make a mess of it, and he did it himself.'

'Did what? Make a mess of it?'

'He made a mess of the other man that slandered that publican. I'd be funny if I was you. Where's the matches?'

'And could Tom fight?'

'Yes. Tom could fight.'

'Did you travel long with him after that?'

'Ten years.'

'And where is he now?'

'Dead – Give us the matches.'

WHILE THE BILLY BOILS
SECOND SERIES

THE DROVER'S WIFE

THE TWO-ROOMED house is built of round timber, slabs, and string-bark, and floored with split slabs. A big bark kitchen standing at one end is larger than the house itself, veranda included.

Bush all round – bush with no horizon, for the country is flat. No ranges in the distance. The bush consists of stunted, rotten native apple-trees. No undergrowth. Nothing to relieve the eye save the darker green of a few she-oaks which are sighing above the narrow, almost waterless creek. Nineteen miles to the nearest sign of civilisation – a shanty on the main road.

The drover, an ex-squatter, is away with sheep. His wife and children are left here alone.

Four ragged, dried-up-looking children are playing about the house. Suddenly one of them yells: 'Snake! Mother, here's a snake!'

The gaunt, sun-browned bushwoman dashes from the kitchen, snatches her baby from the ground, holds it on her left hip, and reaches for a stick.

'Where is it?'

'Here! gone into the wood-heap!' yells the eldest boy – a sharp-faced urchin of eleven. 'Stop there, mother! I'll have him. Stand back! I'll have the beggar!'

'Tommy, come here, or you'll be bit. Come here at once when I tell you, you little wretch!'

The youngster comes reluctantly, carrying a stick bigger than himself. Then he yells, triumphantly:

'There it goes – under the house!' and darts away with club uplifted. At the same time the big, black, yellow-eyed dog-of-all-breeds, who has shown the wildest interest in the proceedings, breaks his chain and rushes after that snake. He is a moment late, however, and his nose reaches the crack in the slabs just as the end of its tail disappears. Almost at the same moment the boy's club comes down and skins the aforesaid nose. Alligator takes small notice of this, and proceeds to undermine the building; but he is subdued after a struggle and chained up. They cannot afford to lose him.

The drover's wife makes the children stand together near the dog-house while she watches for the snake. She gets two small dishes of milk and sets them down near the wall to tempt it to come out; but an hour goes by and it does not show itself.

It is near sunset, and a thunderstorm is coming. The children must be brought inside. She will not take them into the house, for she knows the snake is there, and may at any moment come up through a crack in the rough slab floor; so she carries several armfuls of firewood into the kitchen and then takes the children there. The kitchen has no floor – or, rather, an earthen one – called a 'ground floor' in this part of the bush. There is a large, roughly-made table in the centre of the place. She brings the children in, and makes them get on this table. They are two boys and two girls – mere babies. She gives them some supper, and then, before it gets dark, she does into the house, and snatches up some pillows and bedclothes – expecting to see or lay her hand on the snake any minute. She makes a bed on the kitchen table for the children, and sits down beside it to watch all night.

She has an eye on the corner, and a green sapling club laid in readiness on the dresser by her side; also her sewing basket and a copy of the Young Ladies' Journal. She has brought the dog into the room.

Tommy turns in, under protest, but says he'll lie awake all night and smash that blinded snake.

His mother asks him how many times she has told him not to swear.

He has his club with him under the bedclothes, and Jacky protests:

'Mummy! Tommy's skinnin' me alive wif his club. Make him take it out.'

Tommy: 'Shet up, you little —! D'yer want to be bit with the snake?'

Jacky shuts up.

'If yer bit,' says Tommy, after a pause, 'you'll swell up, an' smell, an' turn red an' green an' blue all over till yer bust. Won't he, mother?'

'Now then, don't frighten the child. Go to sleep,' she says.

The two younger children go to sleep, and now and then Jacky complains of being 'skeezed.' More room is made for him. Presently Tommy says: 'Mother! Listen to them (adjective) little possums. I'd like to screw their blanky necks.'

And Jacky protests drowsily.

'But they don't hurt us, the little blanks!'

Mother: 'There, I told you you'd teach Jacky to swear.' But the remark makes her smile. Jacky goes to sleep.

Presently Tommy asks:

'Mother! Do you think they'll ever extricate the (adjective) kangaroo?'

'Lord! How am I to know, child? Go to sleep.'

'Will you wake me if the snake comes out?'

'Yes. Go to sleep.'

Near midnight. The children are all asleep and she sits there still, sewing and reading by turns. From time to time she glances round the floor and wall-plate, and, whenever she hears a noise, she reaches for the stick. The thunderstorm comes on, and the wind, rushing through the cracks in the slab wall, threatens to blow out her candle. She places it on a sheltered part of the dresser and fixes up a newspaper to protect it. At every flash of lightning, the cracks between the slabs gleam like polished silver. The thunder rolls, and the rain comes down in torrents.

Alligator lies at full length on the floor, with his eyes turned towards the partition. She knows by this that the snake is there. There are large cracks in that wall opening under the floor of the dwelling-house.

She is not a coward, but recent events have shaken her nerves. A little son of her brother-in-law was lately bitten by a snake, and died. Besides, she has not heard from her husband for six months, and is anxious about him.

He was a drover, and started squatting here when they were married. The drought of 18— ruined him. He had to sacrifice the remnant of his flock and go droving again. He intends to move his family into the nearest town when he comes back, and, in the meantime, his brother, who keeps a shanty on the main road, comes over about once a month with provisions. The wife has still a couple of cows, one horse, and a few sheep. The brother-in-law kills one of the latter occasionally, gives her what she needs of it, and takes the rest in return for other provisions.

She is used to being left alone. She once lived like this for eighteen months. As a girl she built the usual castles in the air; but all her girlish hopes and aspirations have long been dead. She finds all the excitement and recreation she needs in the Young Ladies' Journal, and Heaven help her! takes a pleasure in the fashion-plates.

Her husband is an Australian, and so is she. He is careless, but a good enough husband. If he had the means he would take her to the city and keep her there like a princess. They are used to being apart, or at least she is. 'No use fretting,' she says. He may forget sometimes that he is married; but if he has a good cheque when he comes back he will give most of it to her. When he had money he took her to the city several times – hired a railway sleeping compartment, and put up at the best hotels. He also bought her a buggy, but they had to sacrifice that along with the rest.

The last two children were born in the bush – one while her husband was bringing a drunken doctor, by force, to attend to her. She was alone on this occasion, and very weak. She had been ill with a fever. She prayed to God to send her assistance. God sent Black Mary – the 'whitest' gin in all the land. Or, at least, God sent King Jimmy first, and he sent Black Mary. He put his black face round the door-post, took in the situation at a glance, and said cheerfully: 'All right, missus – I bring my old woman, she down alonga creek.'

One of the children died while she was here alone. She rode nineteen miles for assistance, carrying the dead child.

It must be near one or two o'clock. The fire is burning low. Alligator lies with his hand resting on his paws, and watches the wall. He is not a very beautiful dog, and the light shows numerous old wounds where the hair will not grow. He is afraid of nothing on the face of the earth or under it. He will tackle a bullock as readily as he will tackle a flea. He hates all other dogs – except kangaroo-dogs – and has a marked dislike to friends or relations of the family. They seldom call, however. He sometimes makes friends with strangers. He hates snakes and has killed many, but he will be bitten some day and die; most snake-dogs end that way.

Now and then the bushwoman lays down her work and watches, and listens, and thinks. She thinks of things in her own life, for there is little else to think about.

The rain will make the grass grow, and this reminds her how she fought a bush-fire once while her husband was away. The grass was long, and very dry, and the fire threatened to burn her out. She put on an old pair of her husband's trousers and beat out the flames with a green bough, till great drops of sooty perspiration stood out on her forehead and ran in streaks down her blackened arms. The sight of his mother in trousers greatly amused Tommy, who worked like a little hero by her side, but the terrified baby howled lustily for his 'mummy.' The fire would have mastered her but for four excited bushmen who arrived in the nick of time. It was a mixed-up affair all round; when she went to take up the baby he screamed and struggled convulsively, thinking it was a 'blackman;' and Alligator, trusting more to the child's sense than his own instinct, charged furiously, and (being old and slightly deaf) did not in his excitement at first recognise his mistress's voice, but continued to hang on to the moleskins until choked off by Tommy with a saddle-strap. The dog's sorrow for his blunder, and his anxiety to let it be known that it was all a mistake, was as evident as his ragged tail and a twelve-inch grin could make it. It was a glorious time for the boys; a day to look back to, and talk about, and laugh over for many years.

She thinks how she fought a flood during her husband's absence. She stood for hours in the drenching downpour, and dug an overflow gutter to save the dam across the creek. But she could not save it. There are things that a bushwoman cannot do. Next morning the dam was broken and her heart was nearly broken too, for she thought how her husband would feel when he came home and saw the result of years of labour swept away. She cried then.

She also fought the pleuro-pneumonia – dosed and bled the few remaining cattle, and wept again when her two best cows died.

Again, she fought a mad bullock that besieged the house for a day. She made bullets and fired at him through cracks in the slabs with an old shot-gun. He was dead in the morning. She skinned him and got seventeen-and-sixpence for the hide.

She also fights the crows and eagles that have designs on her chickens. Her plan of campaign is very original. The children cry 'Crows, mother!' and she rushes out and aims a broomstick at the birds as though it were a gun, and says, 'Bung!' The crows leave in a hurry; they are cunning, but a woman's cunning is greater.

Occasionally a bushman in the horrors, or a villainous-looking sundowner, comes and nearly scares the life out of her. She generally tells the suspicious-looking stranger that her husband and two sons are at work below the dam, or over at the yard, for he always cunningly inquires for the boss.

Only last week a gallows-faced swagman – having satisfied himself that there were no men on the place – threw his swag down on the veranda, and demanded tucker. She gave him something to eat; then he expressed his intention of staying the night. It was sundown then. She got a batten from the sofa, loosened the dog, and confronted the stranger, holding the batten in one hand and the dog's collar with the other. 'Now you go!' she said. He looked at her and at the dog, said 'All right mum,' in a cringing tone, and left. She was a determined-looking woman, and Alligator's yellow eyes glared unpleasantly – besides, the dog's chawing-up apparatus greatly resembled that of the reptile he was named after.

She has few pleasures to think of as she sits here alone by the fire, on guard against a snake. All days are much the same to her; but on Sunday afternoon she dresses herself, tidies the children, smartens up baby, and goes for a lonely walk along the bush-track, pushing an old perambulator in front of her. She does this every Sunday. She takes as much care to make herself and the children look smart as she would if she were going to do the block in the city. There is nothing to see, however, and not a soul to meet. You might walk for twenty miles along this track without being able to fix a point in you mind, unless you are a bushman. This is because of the everlasting, maddening sameness of the stunted trees – that monotony which makes a man long to break away and travel as far as trains can go, and sail as far as ships can sail – and further.

But this bushwoman is used to the loneliness of it. As a girl-wife she hated it, but now she would feel strange away from it.

She is glad when her husband returns, but she does not gush or make a fuss about it. She gets him something good to eat, and tidies up the children.

She seems contented with her lot. She loves her children, but has no time to show it. She seems harsh to them. Her surroundings are not favourable to the development of the 'womanly' or sentimental side of nature.

It must be near morning now; but the clock is in the dwelling-house. Her candle is nearly done; she forgot that she was out of candles. Some more wood must be got to keep the fire up, and so she shuts the dog inside and hurries round to the wood-heap. The rain has cleared off. She seizes a stick, pulls it out, and – crash! the whole pile collapses.

Yesterday she bargained with a stray blackfellow to bring her some wood, and while he was at work she went in search of a missing cow. She was absent an hour or so, and the native black made good use of his time. On her return she was so astonished to see a good heap of wood by the chimney, that she gave him an extra fig of tobacco, and praised him for not being lazy. He thanked her, and left with head erect and chest well out. He was the last of his tribe and a King; but he had built that wood-heap hollow.

She is hurt now, and tears spring to her eyes as she sits down again by the table. She takes up a handkerchief to wipe the tears away, but pokes her eyes with her bare fingers instead. The handkerchief is full of holes, and she finds that she has put her thumb through one, and her forefinger through another.

This makes her laugh, to the surprise of the dog. She has a keen, very keen, sense of the ridiculous; and some time or other she will amuse bushmen with the story.

She had been amused before like that. One day she sat down 'to have a good cry,' as she said – and the old cat rubbed against her dress and 'cried too.' Then she had to laugh.

It must be near daylight now. The room is very close and hot because of the fire. Alligator still watches the wall from time to time. Suddenly he becomes greatly interested; he draws himself a few inches nearer the partition, and a thrill runs through his body. The hair on the back of his neck begins to bristle, and the battle-light is in his yellow eyes. She knows what this means, and lays her hand on the stick. The lower end of one of the partition slabs has a large crack on both sides. An evil pair of small, bright bead-like eyes glisten at one of these holes. The snake – a black one – comes slowly out, about a foot, and moves its head up and down. The dog lies still, and the woman sits as one fascinated. The snake comes out a foot further. She lifts her stick, and the reptile, as though suddenly aware of danger, sticks his head in through the crack on the other side of the slab, and hurries to get his tail round after him. Alligator springs, and his jaws come together with a snap. He misses, for his nose is large, and the snake's body close down in the angle formed by the slabs and the floor. He snaps again as the tail comes round. He has the snake now, and tugs it out eighteen inches. Thud, thud, comes the woman's club on the ground. Alligator pulls again. Thud, thud. Alligator gives another pull and he has the snake out – a black brute, five feet long. The head rises to dart about, but the dog has the enemy close to the neck. He is a big, heavy dog, but quick as a terrier. He shakes the snake as though he felt the original curse in common with mankind. The eldest boy wakes up, seizes his stick, and tries to get out of bed, but his mother forces him back with a grip of iron. Thud, thud – the snake's back is broken in several places. Thud, thud – its head is crushed, and Alligator's nose skinned again.

She lifts the mangled reptile on the point of her stick, carries it to the fire, and throws it in; then piles on the wood and watches the snake burn. The boy and dog watch too. She lays her hand on the dog's head, and all the fierce, angry light dies out of his yellow eyes. The younger children are quieted, and presently go to sleep. The dirty-legged boy stands for a moment in his shirt, watching the fire. Presently he looks up at her, sees the tears in her eyes, and, throwing his arms round her neck exclaims:

'Mother, I won't never go drovin'; blarst me if I do!'

And she hugs him to her worn-out breast and kisses him; and they sit thus together while the sickly daylight breaks over the bush.

'RATS'

'WHY, THERE'S TWO of them, and they're having a fight! Come on.'

It seemed a strange place for a fight – that hot, lonely, cotton-bush plain. And yet not more than half a mile ahead there were apparently two men struggling together on the track.

The three travellers postponed their smoke-ho and hurried on. They were shearers – a little man and a big man, known respectively as 'Sunlight' and 'Macquarie,' and a tall, thin, young jackeroo whom they called 'Milky.'

'I wonder where the other man sprang from? I didn't see him before,' said Sunlight.

'He muster bin layin' down in the bushes,' said Macquarie. 'They're goin' at it proper, too. Come on! Hurry up and see the fun!'

They hurried on.

'It's a funny-lookin' feller, the other feller,' panted Milky. 'He don't seem to have no head. Look! he's down – they're both down! They must ha' clinched on the ground. No! they're up an' at it again ... Why, good Lord! I think the other's a woman!'

'My oath! so it is!' yelled Sunlight. 'Look, the brute's got her down again! He's kickin' her. Come on, chaps; come on, or he'll do for her!'

They dropped swags, water-bags and all, and raced forward; but presently Sunlight, who had the best eyes, slackened his pace and dropped behind. His mates glanced back at his face, saw a peculiar expression there, looked again, and then dropped into a walk.

They reached the scene of the trouble, and there stood a little withered old man by the track, with his arms folded close up under his chin; he was dressed mostly in calico patches; and half a dozen corks, suspended on bits of string from the brim of his hat, dangled before his bleared optics to scare away the flies. He was scowling malignantly at a stout, dumpy swag which lay in the middle of the track.

'Well, old Rats, what's the trouble?' asked Sunlight.

'Oh, nothing, nothing,' answered the old man, without looking round. 'I fell out with my swag, that's all. He knocked me down, but I've settled him.'

'But look here,' said Sunlight, winking at his mate, 'we saw you jump on him when he was down. That ain't fair, you know.'

'But you didn't see it all,' cried Rats, getting excited. 'He hit me first! And look here, I'll fight him again for nothing, and you can see fair play.'

They talked a while; then Sunlight proposed to second the swag, while his mate supported the old man, and after some persuasion, Milky agreed, for the sake of the lark, to act as time-keeper on referee.

Rats entered into the spirit of the thing; he stripped to the waist, and while he was getting ready the travellers pretended to bet on the result.

Macquarie took his place behind the old man, and Sunlight upended the swag. Rats shaped and danced around; then he rushed, feinted, ducked, retreated, darted in once more, and suddenly went down like a shot on the broad of his back. No actor could have done it better; he went down from that imaginary blow as if a cannon-ball had struck him in the forehead.

Milky called time, and the old man came up, looking shaky. However, he got in a tremendous blow which knocked the swag into the bushes.

Several rounds followed with varying success.

The men pretended to get more and more excited, and betted freely; and Rats did his best. At last they got tired of the fun, Sunlight let the swag lie after Milky called time, and the jackeroo awarded the fight to Rats. They pretended to hand over the stakes, and then went back for their swags, while the old man put on his shirt.

Then he calmed down, carried his swag to the side of the track, sat down on it and talked rationally about bush matters for a while; but presently he grew silent and began to feel his muscles and smile idiotically.

'Can you len' us a bit o' meat?' said he suddenly.

They spared him half a pound; but he said he didn't want it all, and cut off about an ounce, which he laid on the end of his swag. Then he took the lid off his billy and produced a fishing-line. He baited the hook, threw the line across the track, and waited for a bite. Soon he got deeply interested in the line, jerked it once or twice, and drew it in rapidly. The bait had been rubbed off in the grass. The old man regarded the hook disgustedly.

'Look at that!' he cried. 'I had him, only I was in such a hurry. I should ha' played him a little more.'

Next time he was more careful. He drew the line in warily, grabbed an imaginary fish and laid it down on the grass. Sunlight and Co. were greatly interested by this time.

'Wot yer think o' that?' asked Rats. 'It weighs thirty pound if it weighs an ounce! Wot yer think o' that for a cod? The hook's half-way down his blessed gullet!'

He caught several cod and a bream while they were there, and invited them to camp and have tea with him. But they wished to reach a certain shed next day, so – after the ancient had borrowed about a pound of meat for bait – they went on, and left him fishing contentedly.

But first Sunlight went down into his pocket and came up with half a crown, which he gave to the old man, along with some tucker. 'You'd best push on to the water before dark, old chap,' he said, kindly.

When they turned their heads again, Rats was still fishing: but when they looked back for the last time before entering the timber, he was having another row with his swag; and Sunlight reckoned that the trouble arose out of some lies which the swag had been telling about the bigger fish it caught.

ON THE TRACK

ANDY PAGE'S RIVAL

Tall and freckled and sandy,
  Face of a country lout;
That was the picture of Andy –
  Middleton's rouseabout.
On Middleton's wide dominions
  Plied the stock-whip and shears;
Hadn't any opinions —

AND HE HADN'T any 'ideers' – at least, he said so himself – except as regarded anything that looked to him like what he called 'funny business,' under which heading he catalogued tyranny, treachery, interference with the liberty of the subject by the subject, 'blanky' lies, or swindles – all things, in short, that seemed to his slow understanding dishonest, mean or paltry; most especially, and above all, treachery to a mate. That he could never forget. Andy was uncomfortably 'straight.' His mind worked slowly and his decisions were, as a rule, right and just; and when he once came to a conclusion concerning any man or matter, or decided upon a course of action, nothing short of an earthquake or a Nevertire cyclone could move him back an inch – unless a conviction were severely shaken, and then he would require as much time to 'back' to his starting point as he did to come to the decision.

Andy had come to a conclusion with regard to a selector's daughter – name, Lizzie Porter – who lived (and slaved) on her father's selection, near the township corner of the run on which Andy was a general 'hand.' He had been in the habit for several years of calling casually at the selector's house, as he rode to and fro between the station and the town, to get a drink of water and exchange the time of day with old Porter and his 'missus.' The conversation concerned the drought, and the likelihood or otherwise of their ever going to get a little rain; or about Porter's cattle, with an occasional inquiry concerning, or reference to, a stray cow belonging to the selection, but preferring the run; a little, plump, saucy, white cow, by the way, practically pure white, but referred to by Andy – who had eyes like a blackfellow – as 'old Speckledy.' No one else could detect a spot or speckle on her at a casual glance. Then after a long bovine silence, which would have been painfully embarrassing in any other society, and a tilting of his cabbage-tree hat forward, which came of tickling and scratching the sun-blotched nape of his neck with his little finger, Andy would slowly say: 'Ah well. I must be gettin'. So-long, Mr Porter. So-long, Mrs Porter.' And if she were in evidence – as she generally was on such occasions – 'So-long, Lizzie.' And they'd shout:

'So-long, Andy,' as he galloped off from the jump. Strange that those shy, quiet, gentle-voiced bushmen seem the hardest and most reckless riders.

But of late his horse had been seen hanging up outside Porter's for an hour or so after sunset. He smoked, talked over the results of the last drought (if it happened to rain), and the possibilities of the next one, and played cards with old Porter; who took to winking, automatically, at his 'old woman,' and nudging, and jerking his thumb in the direction of Lizzie when her back was turned, and Andy was scratching the nape of his neck and staring at the cards.

Lizzie told a lady friend of mine, years afterwards, how Andy popped the question; told it in her quiet way – you know Lizzie's quiet way (something of the old, privileged house-cat about her); never a sign in expression or tone to show whether she herself saw or appreciated the humour of anything she was telling, no matter how comical it might be. She had witnessed two tragedies, and had found a dead man in the bush, and related the incidents as though they were commonplace.

It happened one day – after Andy had been coming two or three times a week for about a year – that she found herself sitting with him on a log of the wood-heap, in the cool of the evening, enjoying the sunset breeze. Andy's arm had got round her – just as it might have gone round a post he happened to be leaning against. They hadn't been talking about anything in particular. Andy said he wouldn't be surprised if they had a thunderstorm before mornin' – it had been so smotherin' hot all day.

Lizzie said, 'Very likely.'

Andy smoked a good while, then he said: 'Ah, well! It's a weary world.'

Lizzie didn't say anything.

By and by Andy said: 'Ah, well, it's a lonely world, Lizzie.'

'Do you feel lonely, Andy?' asked Lizzie, after a while.

'Yes, Lizzie; I do.'

Lizzie let herself settle, a little, against him, without either seeming to notice it, and after another while she said, softly: 'So do I, Andy.'

Andy knocked the ashes from his pipe very slowly and deliberately, and put it away; then he seemed to brighten suddenly, and said briskly: 'Well, Lizzie! Are you satisfied?'

'Yes, Andy; I'm satisfied.'

'Quite sure, now?'

'Yes; I'm quite sure, Andy. I'm perfectly satisfied.'

'Well, then, Lizzie – it's settled!'

But to-day – a couple of months after the proposal described above – Andy had trouble on his mind, and the trouble was connected with Lizzie Porter. He was putting up a two-rail fence along the old log paddock on the frontage, and working like a man in trouble, trying to work it off his mind; and evidently not succeeding – for the last two panels were out of line. He was ramming a post – Andy rammed honestly, from the bottom of the hole, not the last few shovelfuls below the surface, as some do. He was ramming the last layer of clay when a cloud of white dust came along the road, paused, and drifted or poured off into the scrub, leaving long Dave Bentley, the horse-breaker, on his last victim.

"'Ello, Andy! Graftin'?'

'I want to speak to you, Dave,' said Andy, in a strange voice.

'All – all right!' said Dave, rather puzzled. He got down, wondering what was up, and hung his horse to the last post but one.

Dave was Andy's opposite in one respect: he jumped to conclusions, as women do; but, unlike women, he was mostly wrong. He was an old chum and mate of Andy's who had always liked, admired, and trusted him. But now, to his helpless surprise, Andy went on scraping the earth from the surface with his long-handled shovel, and heaping it conscientiously round the butt of the post, his face like a block of wood, and his lips set grimly. Dave broke out first (with bush oaths):

'What's the matter with you? Spit it out! What have I been doin' to you? What's yer got yer rag out about, anyway?'

Andy faced him suddenly, with hatred for 'funny business' flashing in his eyes.

'What did you say to my sister Mary about Lizzie Porter?'

Dave started; then he whistled long and low. 'Spit it all out, Andy!' he advised.

'You said she was travellin' with a feller!'

'Well, what's the harm in that? Everybody knows that ——'

'If any crawler says a word about Lizzie Porter – look here, me and you's got to fight, Dave Bentley!' Then, with still greater vehemence, as though he had a share in the garment: 'Take off that coat!'

'Not if I know it!' said Dave, with the sudden quietness that comes to brave but headstrong and impulsive men at a critical moment: 'Me and you ain't goin' to fight, Andy; and' (with sudden energy) 'if you try it on I'll knock you into jim-rags!'

Then, stepping close to Andy and taking him by the arm: 'Andy, this thing will have to be fixed up. Come here; I want to talk to you.' And he led him some paces aside, inside the boundary line, which seemed a ludicrously unnecessary precaution, seeing that there was no one within sight or hearing save Dave's horse.

'Now, look here, Andy; let's have it over. What's the matter with you and Lizzie Porter?'

'I'm travellin' with her, that's all; and we're going to get married in two years!'

Dave gave vent to another long, low whistle. He seemed to think and make up his mind.

'Now, look here, Andy: we're old mates, ain't we?'

'Yes; I know that.'

'And do you think I'd tell you a blanky lie, or crawl behind your back? Do you? Spit it out!'

'N – no, I don't!'

'I've always stuck up for you, Andy, and – why, I've fought for you behind your back!'

'I know that, Dave.'

'There's my hand on it!'

Andy took his friend's hand mechanically, but gripped it hard.

'Now, Andy, I'll tell you straight: It's Gorstruth about Lizzie Porter!'

They stood as they were for a full minute, hands clasped; Andy with his jaw dropped and staring in a dazed sort of way at Dave. He raised his disengaged hand helplessly to his thatch, gulped suspiciously, and asked in a broken voice:

'How – how do you know it, Dave?'

'Know it? Andy, I seen 'em meself!'

'You did, Dave?' in a tone that suggested sorrow more than anger at Dave's part in the seeing of them.

'Gorstruth, Andy!'

'Tell me, Dave, who was the feller? That's all I want to know.'

'I can't tell you that. I only seen them when I was canterin' past in the dusk.'

'Then how'd you know it was a man at all?'

'It wore trousers, anyway, and was as big as you; so it couldn't have been a girl. I'm pretty safe to swear it was Mick Kelly. I saw his horse hangin' up at Porter's once or twice. But I'll tell you what I'll do: I'll find out for you, Andy. And, what's more, I'll job him for you if I catch him!'

Andy said nothing; his hands clenched and his chest heaved. Dave laid a friendly hand on his shoulder.

'It's red-hot, Andy, I know. Anybody else but you and I wouldn't have cared. But don't be a fool; there's any Gorsquantity of girls knockin' round. You just give it to her straight and chuck her, and have done with it. You must be bad off to bother about her. Gorstruth! she ain't much to look at anyway! I've got to ride like blazes to catch the coach. Don't knock off till I come back; I won't be above an hour. I'm goin' to give you some points in case you've got to fight Mick; and I'll have to be there to back you!' And, thus taking the right moment instinctively, he jumped on his horse and galloped on towards the town.

His dust-cloud had scarcely disappeared round a corner of the paddocks when Andy was aware of another one coming towards him. He had a dazed idea that it was Dave coming back, but went on digging another post-hole, mechanically, until a spring-cart rattled up, and stopped opposite him. Then he lifted his head. It was Lizzie herself, driving home from town. She turned towards him with her usual faint smile. Her small features were 'washed out' and rather haggard.

"Ello, Andy!'

But, at the sight of her, all his hatred of 'funny business' – intensified, perhaps, by a sense of personal injury – came to a head, and he exploded:

'Look here, Lizzie Porter! I know all about you. You needn't think you're goin' to cotton on with me any more after this! I wouldn't be seen in a paddock with yer! I'm satisfied about you! Get on out of this!'

The girl stared at him for a moment thunderstruck; then she lammed into the old horse with a stick she carried in place of a whip.

She cried, and wondered what she'd done, and trembled so that she could scarcely unharness the horse, and wondered if Andy had got a touch of the sun, and went in and sat down and cried again; and pride came to her aid and she hated Andy; thought of her big brother, away droving, and made a cup of tea. She shed tears over the tea, and went through it all again.

Meanwhile Andy was suffering a reaction. He started to fill the hole before he put the post in; then to ram the post before the rails were in position. Dubbing off the ends of the rails, he was in danger of amputating a toe or a foot with every stroke of the adze. And, at last, trying to squint along the little lumps of clay which he had placed in the centre of the top of each post for several panels back – to assist him to take a line – he found that they swam and doubled, and ran off in watery angles, for his eyes were too moist to see straight and single.

Then he threw down the tools hopelessly, and was standing helplessly undecided whether to go home or go down to the creek and drown himself, when Dave turned up again.

'Seen her?' asked Dave.

'Yes,' said Andy.

'Did you chuck her?'

'Look here, Dave; are you sure the feller was Mick Kelly?'

'I never said I was. How was I to know? It was dark. You don't expect I'd "fox" a feller I see doing a bit of a bear-up to a girl, do you? It might have been you, for all I knowed. I suppose she's been talking you round?'

'No, she ain't,' said Andy. 'But, look here, Dave; I was properly gone on that girl, I was, and – and I want to be sure I'm right.'

The business was getting altogether too psychological for Dave Bentley. 'You might as well,' he rapped out, 'call me a liar at once!'

"Taint that at all, Dave. I want to get at who the feller is; that's what I want to get at now. Where did you see them, and when?'

'I seen them Anniversary night, along the road, near Ross's farm; and I seen 'em Sunday night afore that – in the trees near the old culvert – near Porter's sliprails; and I seen 'em one night outside Porter's, on a log near the wood-heap. They was thick that time, and bearin' up proper, and no mistake. So I can swear to her. Now, are you satisfied about her?'

But Andy was wildly pitchforking his thatch under his hat with all ten fingers and staring at Dave, who began to regard him uneasily; then there came to Andy's eyes an awful glare, which caused Dave to step back hastily.

'Good God, Andy! Are yer goin' ratty?'

'No!' cried Andy, wildly.

'Then what the blazes is the matter with you? You'll have rats if you don't look out!'

'Jimminy froth! – it was me all the time!'

'What?'

'It was me that was with her all them nights. It was me that you seen. Why, I popped on the wood-heap!'

Dave was taken too suddenly to whistle this time.

'And you went for her just now?'

'Yes!' yelled Andy.

'Well – you've done it!'

'Yes,' said Andy, hopelessly; 'I've done it!'

Dave whistled now – a very long, low whistle. 'Well, you're a bloomin' goat, Andy, after this. But this thing'll have to be fixed up!' and he cantered away. Poor Andy was too badly knocked to notice the abruptness of Dave's departure, or to see that he turned through the sliprails on to the track that led to Porter's.

Half an hour later Andy appeared at Porter's back door, with an expression on his face as though the funeral was to start in ten minutes. In a tone befitting such an occasion, he wanted to see Lizzie.

Dave had been there with the laudable determination of fixing the business up, and had, of course, succeeded in making it much worse than it was before. But Andy made it all right.

THE IRON-BARK CHIP

DAVE REGAN and party – bush-fencers, tank-sinkers, and rough carpenters – were finishing the third and last culvert of their contract on the last section of the new railway line, and had already sent in their vouchers for the completed contract, so that there might be no excuse for extra delay in connection with the cheque.

Now it had been expressly stipulated in the plans and specifications that the timber for certain beams and girders was to be ironbark and no other, and government inspectors were authorised to order the removal from the ground of any timber or material they might deem inferior, or not in accordance with the stipulations. The railway contractor's foreman and inspector of sub-contractors was a practical man and a bushman, but he had been a timber-getter himself; his sympathies were bushy, and he was on winking terms with Dave Regan. Besides, extended time was expiring, and the contractors were in a hurry to complete the line. But the government inspector was a reserved man who poked round on his independent own and appeared in lonely spots at unexpected times – with apparently no definite object in life – like a grey kangaroo bothered by a new wire fence, but unsuspicious of the presence of humans. He wore a grey suit, rode, or mostly led, an ashen-grey horse; the grass was long and grey, so he was seldom spotted until he was well within the horizon and bearing leisurely down on a party of sub-contractors, leading his horse.

Now iron-bark was scarce and distant on those ridges, and another timber, similar in appearance, but much inferior in grain and 'standing' quality, was plentiful and close at hand. Dave and party were 'about full of' the job and place, and wanted to get their cheque and be gone to another 'spec' they had in view. So they came to reckon they'd get the last girder from a handy tree, and have it squared, in place, and carefully and conscientiously tarred before the inspector happened along, if he did. But they didn't. They got it squared, and ready to be lifted into its place; the kindly darkness of tar was ready to cover a fraud that took four strong men with crowbars and levers to shift; and now (such is the regular cussedness of things) as the fraudulent piece of timber lay its last hour on the ground, looking and smelling, to their guilty imaginations like anything but iron-bark, they were aware of the government inspector drifting down upon them obliquely, with something of the atmosphere of a casual Bill or Jim who had dropped out of his easygoing track to see how they were getting on, and borrow a match. They had more than half hoped that, as he had visited them pretty frequently during the progress of the work, and knew how near it was to completion, he wouldn't bother coming any more. But it's the way with the

Government. You might move heaven and earth in vain endeavour to get the 'guvermunt' to flutter an eyelash over something of the most momentous importance to yourself and mates and the district – even to the country; but just when you are leaving authority severely alone, and have strong reasons for not wanting to worry or interrupt it, and not desiring it to worry about you, it will take a fancy into its head to come along and bother.

'It's always the way!' muttered Dave to his mates. 'I knew the beggar would turn up! ... And the only cronk log we've had, too!' he added, in an injured tone. 'If this had 'a' been the only blessed iron-bark in the whole contract, it would have been all right ... Good day, sir!' (to the inspector). 'It's hot?'

The inspector nodded. He was not of an impulsive nature. He got down from his horse and looked at the girder in an abstracted way; and presently there came into his eyes a dreamy, far-away, sad sort of expression, as if there had been a very sad and painful occurrence in his family, way back in the past, and that piece of timber in some way reminded him of it and brought the old sorrow home to him. He blinked three times, and asked, in a subdued tone:

'Is that iron-bark?'

Jack Bentley, the fluent liar of the party, caught his breath with a jerk and coughed, to cover the gasp and gain time. 'I–iron-bark? Of course it is! I thought you would know iron-bark, mister.' (Mister was silent.) 'What else d'yer think it is?'

The dreamy, abstracted expression was back. The inspector, by the way, didn't know much about timber, but he had a great deal of instinct, and went by it when in doubt.

'L–look here, mister!' put in Dave Regan, in a tone of innocent puzzlement and with a blank bucolic face. 'B–but don't the plans and specifications say iron-bark? Ours does, anyway. I–I'll git the papers from the tent and show yer, if yer like.'

It was not necessary. The inspector admitted the fact slowly. He stooped, and with an absent air picked up a chip. He looked at it abstractedly for a moment, blinked his threefold blink; then, seeming to recollect an appointment, he woke up suddenly and asked briskly:

'Did this chip come off that girder?'

Blank silence. The inspector blinked six times, divided in threes, rapidly, mounted his horse, said 'Day,' and rode off.

Regan and party stared at each other.

'Wha–what did he do that for?' asked Andy Page, the third in the party.

'Do what for, you fool?' inquired Dave.

'Ta–take that chip for?'

'He's taking it to the office!' snarled Jack Bentley.

'What—what for? What does he want to do that for?'

'To get it blanky well analysed! You ass! Now are yer satisfied?' And Jack sat down hard on the timber, jerked out his pipe, and said to Dave, in a sharp, toothache tone:

'Gimmiamatch!'

'We—well! What are we to do now?' inquired Andy, who was the hardest grafter, but altogether helpless, hopeless, and useless in a crisis like this.

'Grain and varnish the bloomin' culvert!' snapped Bentley.

But Dave's eyes, that had been ruefully following the inspector, suddenly dilated. The inspector had ridden a short distance along the line, dismounted, thrown the bridle over a post, laid the chip (which was too big to go in his pocket) on top of it, got through the fence, and was now walking back at an angle across the line in the direction of the fencing party, who had worked up on the other side, a little more than opposite the culvert.

Dave took in the lay of the country at a glance and thought rapidly.

'Gimme an iron-bark chip!' he said suddenly.

Bentley, who was quick-witted when the track was shown him, as is a kangaroo-dog (Jack ran by sight, not scent), glanced in the line of Dave's eyes, jumped up, and got a chip about the same size as that which the inspector had taken.

Now the 'lay of the country' sloped generally to the line from both sides, and the angle between the inspector's horse, the fencing party, and the culvert was well within a clear concave space; but a couple of hundred yards back from the line and parallel to it (on the side on which Dave's party worked their timber) a fringe of scrub ran to within a few yards of a point which would be about in line with a single tree on the cleared slope, the horse, and the fencing party.

Dave took the iron-bark chip, ran along the bed of the water-course into the scrub, raced up the sidling behind the bushes, got safely through without breathing, across the exposed space, and brought the tree into line between him and the inspector who was talking to the fencers. Then he began to work quickly down the slope towards the tree (which was a thin one), keeping it in line, his arms close to his sides, and working, as it were, down the trunk of the tree, as if the fencing party were kangaroos and Dave was trying to get a shot at them. The inspector, by the by, had a habit of glancing now and then in the direction of his horse, as though under the impression that it was flighty and restless and inclined to bolt on opportunity. It was an anxious moment for all parties concerned – except the inspector. They didn't want him to be perturbed. And, just as Dave reached the foot of the tree, the inspector finished what he had to say to the fencers, turned, and started to walk briskly back to his horse. There was a thunderstorm coming. Now was the critical moment – there were certain prearranged signals between Dave's party and the fencers which might have interested the inspector, but none to meet a case like this.

Jack Bentley gasped, and started forward with an idea of intercepting the inspector and holding him for a few minutes in bogus conversation. Inspirations come to one at a critical moment, and it flashed on Jack's mind to send Andy instead. Andy looked as innocent and guileless as he was, but was uncomfortable in the vicinity of 'funny business,' and must have an honest excuse. 'Not that that mattered,' commented Jack afterwards; 'it would have taken the inspector ten minutes to get at what Andy was driving at, whatever it was.'

'Run, Andy! Tell him there's a heavy thunderstorm coming and he'd better stay in our humpy till it's over. Run! Don't stand staring like a blanky fool. He'll be gone!'

Andy stared. But just then, as luck would have it, one of the fencers started after the inspector, hailing him as 'Hi, mister!' He wanted to be set right about the survey or something – or to pretend to want to be set right – from motives of policy which I haven't time to explain here.

That fencer explained afterwards to Dave's party that he 'seen what you coves was up to,' and that's why he called the inspector back. But he told them that after they had told their yarn – which was a mistake.

'Come back, Andy!' cried Jack Bentley.

Dave Regan slipped round the tree, down on his hands and knees, and made quick time through the grass which, luckily, grew pretty tall on the thirty or forty yards of slope between the tree and the horse. Close to the horse, a thought struck Dave that pulled him up, and sent a shiver along his spine and a hungry feeling under it. The horse would break away and bolt! But the case was desperate. Dave ventured an interrogatory 'Cope, cope, cope?' The horse turned his head wearily and regarded him with a mild eye, as if he'd expected him to come, and come on all fours, and wondered what had kept him so long; then he went on thinking. Dave reached the foot of the post; the horse obligingly leaning over on the other leg. Dave reared head and shoulders cautiously behind the post, like a snake; his hand went up twice, swiftly – the first time he grabbed the inspector's chip, and the second time he put the iron-bark one in its place. He drew down and back, and scuttled off for the tree like a gigantic tailless goanna.

A few minutes later he walked up to the culvert from along the creek, smoking hard to settle his nerves.

The sky seemed to darken suddenly; the first great drops of the thunderstorm came pelting down. The inspector hurried to his horse, and cantered off along the line in the direction of the fettlers' camp.

He had forgotten all about the chip, and left it on top of the post!

Dave Regan sat down on the beam in the rain and swore comprehensively.

MIDDLETON'S PETER

I

THE FIRST BORN

THE STRUGGLING squatter is to be found in Australia as well as the 'struggling farmer.' The Australian squatter is not always the mighty wool king that English and American authors and other uninformed people apparently imagine him to be. Squatting, at the best, is but a game of chance. It depends mainly on the weather, and that, in New South Wales at least, depends on nothing.

Joe Middleton was a struggling squatter, with a station some distance to the westward of the furthest line reached by the ordinary new chum. His run, at the time of our story, was only about six miles square, and his stock was limited in proportion. The hands on Joe's run consisted of his brother Dave, a middle-aged man known only as 'Middleton's Peter' (who had been in the service of the Middleton family ever since Joe Middleton could remember), and an old black shepherd, with his gin and two boys.

It was in the first year of Joe's marriage. He had married a very ordinary girl, as far as Australian girls go, but in his eyes she was an angel. He really worshipped her.

One sultry afternoon in midsummer all the station-hands, with the exception of Dave Middleton, were congregated about the homestead door, and it was evident from their solemn faces that something unusual was the matter. They appeared to be watching for something or someone across the flat, and the old black shepherd, who had been listening intently with bent head, suddenly straightened himself up and cried:

'I can hear the cart. I can see it!'

You must bear in mind that our blackfellows do not always talk the gibberish with which they are credited by story writers.

It was not until some time after Black Bill had spoken that the white – or, rather, the brown – portion of the party could see or even hear the approaching vehicle. At last, far out through the trunks of the native apple-trees, the cart was seen approaching; and as it came nearer it was evident that it was being driven at a breakneck pace, the horses cantering all the way, while the motion of the cart, as first one wheel and then the other sprang from a root or a rut, bore a striking resemblance to the Highland Fling. There were two persons in the cart. One was Mother Palmer, a stout, middle-aged party (who sometimes did the duties of a midwife), and the other was Dave Middleton, Joe's brother.

The cart was driven right up to the door with scarcely any abatement of speed, and was stopped so suddenly that Mrs Palmer was sent sprawling on to the horse's rump. She was quickly helped down, and, as soon as she had recovered sufficient breath, she followed Black Mary into the bedroom where young Mrs Middleton was lying, looked very pale and frightened. The horse which had been driven so cruelly had not done blowing before another cart appeared, also driven very fast. It contained old Mr and Mrs Middleton, who lived comfortably on a small farm not far from Palmer's place.

As soon as he had dumped Mrs Palmer, Dave Middleton left the cart and, mounting a fresh horse which stood ready saddled in the yard, galloped off through the scrub in a different direction.

Half an hour afterwards Joe Middleton came home on a horse that had been almost ridden to death. His mother came out at the sound of his arrival, and he anxiously asked her:

'How is she?'

'Did you find Doc. Wild?' asked the mother.

'No, confound him!' exclaimed Joe bitterly. 'He promised me faithfully to come over on Wednesday and stay until Maggie was right again. Now he has left Dean's and gone – Lord knows where. I suppose he is drinking again. How is Maggie?'

'It's all over now – the child is born. It's a boy; but she is very weak. Dave got Mrs Palmer here just in time. I had better tell you at once that Mrs Palmer says if we don't get a doctor here tonight poor Maggie won't live.'

'Good God! and what am I to do?' cried Joe desperately.

'Is there any other doctor within reach?'

'No; there is only the one at B—; that's forty miles away, and he is laid up with the broken leg he got in the buggy accident. Where's Dave?'

'Gone to Black's shanty. One of Mrs Palmer's sons thought he remembered someone saying that Doc. Wild was there last week. That's fifteen miles away.'

'But it is our only hope,' said Joe dejectedly. 'I wish to God that I had taken Maggie to some civilised place a month ago.'

Doc. Wild was a well-known character among the bushmen of New South Wales, and although the profession did not recognise him, and denounced him as an empiric, his skill was undoubted. Bushmen had great faith in him, and would often ride incredible distances in order to bring him to the bedside of a sick friend. He drank fearfully, but was seldom incapable of treating a patient; he would, however, sometimes be found in an obstinate mood and refuse to travel to the side of a sick person, and then the devil himself could not make the doctor budge. But for all this he was very generous – a fact that could, no doubt, be testified to by many a grateful sojourner in the lonely bush.

II

THE ONLY HOPE

Night came on, and still there was no change in the condition of the young wife, and no sign of the doctor. Several stockmen from the neighbouring stations, hearing that there was trouble at Joe Middleton's, had ridden over, and had galloped off on long, hopeless rides in search of a doctor. Being generally free from sickness themselves, these bushmen look upon it as a serious business even in its mildest form; what is more, their sympathy is always practical where it is possible for it to be so. One day, while out on the run after an 'outlaw,' Joe Middleton was badly thrown from his horse, and the breakneck riding that was done on that occasion from the time the horse came home with empty saddle until the rider was safe in bed and attended by a doctor was something extraordinary, even for the bush.

Before the time arrived when Dave Middleton might reasonably have been expected to return, the station people were anxiously watching for him, all except the old blackfellow and the two boys, who had gone to yard the sheep.

The party had been increased by Jimmy Nowlett, the bullocky, who had just arrived with a load of fencing wire and provisions for Middleton. Jimmy was standing in the moonlight, whip in hand, looking as anxious as the husband himself, and endeavouring to calculate by mental arithmetic the exact time it ought to take Dave to complete his double journey, taking into consideration the distance, the obstacles in the way, and the chances of horse-flesh.

But the time which Jimmy fixed for the arrival came without Dave.

Old Peter (as he was generally called, though he was not really old) stood aside in his usual sullen manner, his hat drawn down over his brow and eyes, and nothing visible but a thick and very horizontal black beard, from the depth of which emerged large clouds of very strong tobacco smoke, the product of a short, black, clay pipe.

They had almost given up all hope of seeing Dave return that night, when Peter slowly and deliberately removed his pipe and grunted:

'He's a-comin'.'

He then replaced the pipe, and smoked on as before.

All listened, but not one of them could hear a sound.

'Yer ears must be pretty sharp for yer age, Peter. We can't hear him,' remarked Jimmy Nowlett.

'His dog ken,' said Peter.

The pipe was again removed and its abbreviated stem pointed in the direction of Dave's cattle-dog, who had risen beside his kennel with pointed ears, and was looking eagerly in the direction from which his master was expected to come.

Presently the sound of horse's hoofs was distinctly heard.

'I can hear two horses,' cried Jimmy Nowlett excitedly.

'There's only one,' said old Peter quietly.

A few moments passed, and a single horseman appeared on the far side of the flat.

'It's Doc. Wild on Dave's horse,' cried Jimmy Nowlett. 'Dave don't ride like that.'

It's Dave,' said Peter, replacing his pipe and looking more unsociable than ever.

Dave rode up and, throwing himself wearily from the saddle, stood ominously silent by the side of his horse.

Joe Middleton said nothing, but stood aside with an expression of utter hopelessness on his face.

'Not there?' asked Jimmy Nowlett at last, addressing Dave.

'Yes, he's there,' answered Dave, impatiently.

This was not the answer they expected, but nobody seemed surprised.

'Drunk?' asked Jimmy.

'Yes.'

Here old Peter removed his pipe, and pronounced the one word 'How?'

'What the hell do you mean by that?' muttered Dave, whose patience had evidently been severely tried by the clever but intemperate bush doctor.

'How drunk?' explained Peter, with great equanimity.

'Stubborn drunk, blind drunk, beastly drunk, dead drunk, and damned well drunk, if that's what you want to know!'

'What did Doc. say?' asked Jimmy.

'Said he was sick – had lumbago – wouldn't come for the Queen of England; said he wanted a course of treatment himself. Curse him! I have no patience to talk about him.'

'I'd give him a course of treatment,' muttered Jimmy viciously, trailing the long lash of his bullock-whip through the grass and spitting spitefully at the ground.

Dave turned away and joined Joe, who was talking earnestly to his mother by the kitchen door. He told them that he had spent an hour trying to persuade Doc. Wild to come, and, that before he had left the shanty, Black had promised him faithfully to bring the doctor over as soon as his obstinate mood wore off.

Just then a low moan was heard from the sick room, followed by the sound of Mother Palmer's voice calling old Mrs Middleton, who went inside immediately.

No one had noticed the disappearance of Peter, and when he presently returned from the stockyard, leading the only fresh horse that remained, Jimmy Nowlett began to regard him with some interest. Peter transferred the saddle from Dave's horse to the other, and then went into a small room off the kitchen, which served him as a bedroom; from it he soon returned with a formidable-looking revolver, the chambers of which he examined in the moonlight in full view of all the company. They thought for a moment the man had gone mad. Old Middleton leaped quickly behind Nowlett, and Black Mary, who had come out to the cask at the corner for a dipper of water, dropped the dipper and was inside like a shot. One of the black boys came softly up at that moment; as soon as his sharp eye 'spotted' the weapon, he disappeared as though the earth had swallowed him.

'What the mischief are yer goin' ter do, Peter?' asked Jimmy.

'Goin' to fetch him,' said Peter, and, after carefully emptying his pipe and replacing it in a leather pouch at his belt, he mounted and rode off at any easy canter.

Jimmy watched the horse until it disappeared at the edge of the flat, and then after coiling up the long lash of his bullock-whip in the dust until it looked like a sleeping snake, he prodded the small end of the long pine handle into the middle of the coil, as though driving home a point, and said in a tone of intense conviction:

'He'll fetch him.'

III

DOC. WILD

Peter gradually increased his horse's speed along the rough bush track until he was riding at a good pace. It was ten miles to the main road, and five from there to the shanty kept by Black.

For some time before Peter started the atmosphere had been very close and oppressive. The great black edge of a storm-cloud had risen in the east, and everything indicated the approach of a thunderstorm. It was not long coming. Before Peter had completed six miles of his journey, the clouds rolled over, obscuring the moon, and an Australian thunderstorm came on with its mighty downpour, its blinding lightning, and its earth-shaking thunder. Peter rode steadily on, only pausing now and then until a flash revealed the track in front of him.

Black's shanty – or, rather, as the sign had it, 'Post Office and General Store' – was, as we have said, five miles along the main road from the point where Middleton's track joined it. The building was of the usual style of bush architecture. About two hundred yards nearer the creek, which crossed the road further on, stood a large bark-and-slab stable, large enough to have met the requirements of a legitimate bush 'public.'

The reader may doubt that a sly-grog shop could openly carry on business on a main government road along which mounted troopers were continually passing. But then, you see, mounted troopers get thirsty like other men; moreover, they could always get their thirst quenched gratis at these places; so the reader will be prepared to hear that on this very night two troopers' horses were stowed snugly away in the stable, and two troopers were stowed snugly away in the back room of the shanty, sleeping off the effects of their cheap but strong potations.

There were two rooms, of a sort, attached to the stables – one at each end. One was occupied by a man who was 'generally useful,' and the other was the surgery, office, and bedroom pro tem. of Doc. Wild.

Doc. Wild was a tall man, of spare proportions. He had a cadaverous face, black hair, bushy black eyebrows, eagle nose, and eagle eyes. He never slept while he was drinking. On this occasion he sat in front of the fire on a low three-legged stool. His knees were drawn up, his toes hooked round the front legs of the stool, one hand resting on one knee, and one elbow (the hand supporting the chin) resting on the other. He was staring intently into the fire, on which an old black saucepan was boiling and sending forth a pungent odour of herbs. There seemed something uncanny about the doctor as the red light of the fire fell on his hawk-like face and gleaming eyes. He might have been Mephistopheles watching some infernal brew.

He had sat there some time without stirring a finger, when the door suddenly burst open and Middleton's Peter stood within, dripping wet. The doctor turned his black, piercing eyes upon the intruder (who regarded him silently) for a moment, and then asked quietly:

'What the hell do you want?'

'I want you,' said Peter.

'And what do you want me for?'

'I want you to come to Joe Middleton's wife. She's bad,' said Peter calmly.

'I won't come,' shouted the doctor. 'I've brought enough horse-stealers into the world already. If any more want to come they can go to blazes for me. Now, you get out of this!'

'Don't get yer rag out,' said Peter quietly. 'The hoss-stealer's come, an' nearly killed his mother ter begin with; an' if yer don't get yer physic-box an' come wi' me, by the great God I'll ——'

Here the revolver was produced and pointed at Doc. Wild's head. The sight of the weapon had a sobering effect upon the doctor. He rose, looked at Peter critically for a moment, knocked the weapon out of his hand, and said slowly and deliberately:

'Wall, ef the case es as serious as that, I (hic) reckon I'd better come.'

Peter was still of the same opinion, so Doc. Wild proceeded to get his medicine-chest ready. He explained afterwards, in one of his softer moments, that the shooter didn't frighten him so much as it touched his memory – 'sorter put him in mind of the old days in California, and made him think of the man he might have been,' he'd say – 'kinder touched his heart and slid the durned old panorama in front of him like a flash; made him think of the time when he slipped three leaden pills into 'Blue Shirt' for winking at a new chum behind his (the doc's) back when he was telling a truthful yarn, and charged the said 'Blue Shirt' a hundred dollars for extracting the said pills.'

Joe Middleton's wife is a grandmother now.

Peter passed after the manner of his sort; he was found dead in his bunk.

Poor Doc. Wild died in a shepherd's hut at the Dry Creeks. The shepherds (white men) found him, 'naked as he was born and with the hide half burned off him with the sun,' rounding up imaginary snakes on a dusty clearing, one blazing hot day. The hut-keeper had some 'quare' (queer) experiences with the doctor during the next three days and used, in after years, to tell of them, between the puffs of his pipe, calmly and solemnly as if the story was rather to the doctor's credit than otherwise. The shepherds sent for the police and a doctor, and sent word to Joe Middleton. Doc. Wild was sensible towards the end. His interview with the other doctor was characteristic. 'And, now you see how far I am,' he said in conclusion – 'have you brought the brandy?' The other doctor had. Joe Middleton came with his wagonette and in it the softest mattress and pillows the station afforded. He also, in his innocence, brought a dozen of soda-water. Doc. Wild took Joe's hand feebly, and a little later, he 'passed out' (as he would have said) murmuring 'something that sounded like poetry,' in an unknown tongue. Joe took the body to the home station. 'Who's the boss bringin'?' asked the shearers, seeing the wagonette coming very slowly and the boss walking by the horses' heads. 'Doc. Wild,' said a station-hand. 'Take yer hats off.'

They buried him with bush honours, and chiselled his name on a slab of blue-gum – a wood that lasts.

No Place For A Woman

HE HAD A selection on a long box-scrub sidling of the ridges, about half a mile back and up from the coach road. There were no neighbours that I ever heard of, and the nearest 'town' was thirty miles away. He grew wheat among the stumps of his clearing, sold the crop standing to a cocky who lived ten miles away, and had some surplus sons; or, some seasons, he reaped it by hand, had it thrashed by travelling 'steamer' (portable steam engine and machine), and carried the grain, a few bags at a time, into the mill on his rickety dray.

He had lived alone for upwards of fifteen years, and was known to those who knew him as 'Ratty Howlett.'

Trav'lers and strangers failed to see anything uncommonly ratty about him. It was known, or, at least, it was believed, without question, that while at work he kept his horse saddled and bridled, and hung up to the fence, or grazing about, with the saddle on – or, anyway, close handy for a moment's notice – and whenever he caught sight, over the scrub and through the quarter-mile break in it, of a traveller on the road, he would jump on his horse and make after him. If it was a horseman he usually pulled him up inside of a mile. Stories were told of unsuccessful chases, misunderstandings, and complications arising out of Howlett's mania for running down and bailing up travellers. Sometimes he caught one every day for a week, sometimes not one for weeks – it was a lonely track.

The explanation was simple, sufficient, and perfectly natural – from a bushman's point of view. Ratty only wanted to have a yarn. He and the traveller would camp in the shade for half an hour or so and yarn and smoke. The old man would find out where the traveller came from, and how long he'd been there, and where he was making for, and how long he reckoned he'd be away; and ask if there had been any rain along the traveller's back track, and how the country looked after the drought; and he'd get the traveller's ideas on abstract questions – if he had any. If it was a footman (swagman), and he was short of tobacco, old Howlett always had half a stick ready for him. Sometimes, but very rarely, he'd invite the swagman back to the hut for a pint of tea, or a bit of meat, flour, tea, or sugar, to carry him along the track.

And, after the yarn by the road, they said, the old man would ride back, refreshed, to his lonely selection, and work on into the night as long as he could see his solitary old plough-horse, or the scoop of his long-handled shovel.

And so it was that I came to make his acquaintance – or, rather, that he made mine. I was cantering easily along the track – I was making for the north-west with a packhorse – when about a mile beyond the track to the selection I heard,

'Hi, mister!' and saw a dust-cloud following me. I had heard of 'Old Ratty Howlett' casually, and so was prepared for him.

A tall, gaunt man on a little horse. He was clean-shaven, except for a frill beard round under his chin, and his long wavy, dark hair was turning grey; a square, strong-faced man, and reminded me of one full-faced portrait of Gladstone more than any other face I had seen. He had large reddish-brown eyes, deep set under heavy eyebrows, and with something of the blackfellow in them – the sort of eyes that will peer at something on the horizon that no one else can see. He had a way of talking to the horizon, too – more than to his companion; and he had a deep vertical wrinkle in his forehead that no smile could lessen.

I got down and got out my pipe, and we sat on a log and yarned a while on bush subjects; and then, after a pause, he shifted uneasily, it seemed to me, and asked rather abruptly, and in an altered tone, if I was married. A queer question to ask a traveller; more especially in my case, as I was little more than a boy then.

He talked on again of old things and places where we had both been, and asked after men he knew, or had known – drovers and others – and whether they were living yet. Most of his inquiries went back before my time; but some of the drovers, one or two overlanders with whom he had been mates in his time, had grown old into mine, and I knew them. I notice now, though I didn't then – and if I had it would not have seemed strange from a bush point of view – that he didn't ask for news, nor seem interested in it.

Then after another uneasy pause, during which he scratched crosses in the dirt with a stick, he asked me, in the same queer tone and without looking at me or looking up, if I happened to know anything about doctoring – if I'd ever studied it.

I asked him if any one was sick at his place. He hesitated and said 'No.' Then I wanted to know why he had asked me that question, and he was so long about answering that I began to think he was hard of hearing, when, at last, he muttered something about my face reminding him of a young fellow he knew of who'd gone to Sydney to 'study for a doctor.' That might have been, and looked natural enough; but why didn't he ask me straight out if I was the chap he 'knowed of?' Travellers do not like beating about the bush in conversation.

He sat in silence for a good while, with his arms folded, and looking absently away over the dead level of the great scrubs that spread from the foot of the ridge we were on to where a blue peak or two of a distant range showed above the bush on the horizon.

I stood up and put my pipe away and stretched. Then he seemed to wake up. 'Better come back to the hut and have a bit of dinner,' he said. 'The missus will about have it ready, and I'll spare you a handful of hay for the horses.'

The hay decided it. It was a dry season. I was surprised to hear of a wife, for I thought he was a hatter – I had always heard so; but perhaps I had been mistaken, and he had married lately; or had got a housekeeper. The farm was an irregularly-shaped clearing in the scrub, with a good many stumps in it, with a broken down two-rail fence along the frontage, and logs and 'dog-leg' the rest. It was about as lonely-looking a place as I had seen, and I had seen some out-of-the-way, God-forgotten holes where men lived alone. The hut was in the top corner, a two-roomed slab hut, with a shingle roof, which must have been uncommon round there in the days when that hut was built. I was used to bush carpentering, and saw that the place had been put up by a man who had plenty of life and hope in front of him, and for someone else beside himself. But there were two unfinished skilling-rooms built on to the back of the hut; the posts, sleepers, and wall-plates had been well put up and fitted, and the slab walls were up, but the roof had never been put on. There was nothing but burrs and nettles inside those walls, and an old wooden bullock-plough and a couple of yokes were dry-rotting across the back doorway. The remains of a straw-stack, some hay under a bark humpy, a small iron plough, and an old stiff coffin-headed grey draught-horse, were all that I saw about the place.

But there was a bit of a surprise for me inside, in the shape of a clean white table-cloth on the rough slab table which stood on stakes driven into the ground. The cloth was coarse, but it was a table-cloth – not a spare sheet put on in honour of unexpected visitors – and perfectly clean. The tin plates, pannikins, and jam tins that served as sugar-bowls and salt-cellars were polished brightly. The walls and fire-place were white-washed, the clay floor swept, and clean sheets of newspaper laid on the slab mantelshelf under the row of biscuit-tins that held the groceries. I thought that his wife, or housekeeper, or whatever she was, was a clean and tidy woman about the house. I saw no woman; but on the sofa – a light, wooden, batten one, with runged arms at the ends – lay a woman's dress on a lot of sheets of old stained and faded newspapers. He looked at it in a puzzled way, knitting his forehead, then took it up absently and folded it. I saw then that it was a riding-skirt and jacket. He bundled them into the newspapers and took them into the bedroom.

'The wife was going on a visit down the creek this afternoon,' he said rapidly and without looking at me, but stooping as if to have another look through the door at those distant peaks. 'I suppose she got tired o' waitin', and went and took the daughter with her. But, never mind, the grub is ready.' There was a camp-oven with a leg of mutton and potatoes sizzling in it on the hearth, and billies hanging over the fire. I noticed the billies had been scraped, and the lids polished.

There seemed to be something queer about the whole business, but then he and his wife might have had a 'breeze' during the morning. I thought so during the meal, when the subject of women came up, and he said one never knew how to take a woman; but there was nothing in what he said that need necessarily have referred to his wife or to any woman in particular. For the rest he talked of old bush things, droving, digging, and old bushranging – but never about live things and living men, unless any of the old mates he talked about happened to be alive by accident. He was very restless in the house, and never took his hat off.

There was a dress and a woman's old hat hanging on the wall near the door, but they looked as if they might have been hanging there for a lifetime. There seemed something queer about the whole place – something wanting; but then all out-of-the-way bush homes are haunted by that something wanting or, more likely, by the spirits of the things that should have been there, but never had been.

As I rode down the track to the road I looked back and saw old Howlett hard at work in a hole round a big stump with his long-handled shovel.

I'd noticed that he moved and walked with a slight list to port, and put his hand once or twice to the small of his back, and I set it down to lumbago, or something of that sort.

Up in the Never-Never I heard from a drover who had known Howlett that his wife had died in the first year, and so this mysterious woman, if she was his wife, was, of course, his second wife. The drover seemed surprised and rather amused at the thought of old Howlett going in for matrimony again.

I rode back that way five years later, from the Never-Never. It was early in the morning – I had ridden since midnight. I didn't think the old man would be up and about; and besides, I wanted to get on home, and have a look at the old folk, and the mates I'd left behind – and the girl. But I hadn't got far past the point where Howlett's track joined the road, when I happened to look back, and saw him on horseback, stumbling down the track. I waited till he came up.

He was riding the old grey draught-horse this time, and it looked very much broken down. I thought it would have come down every step, and fallen like an old rotten humpy in a gust of wind. And the old man was not much better off. I saw at once that he was a very sick man. His face was drawn, and he bent forward as if he was hurt. He got down stiffly and awkwardly, like a hurt man, and as soon as his feet touched the ground he grabbed my arm, or he would have gone down like a man who steps off a train in motion. He hung towards the bank of the road, feeling blindly, as it were, for the ground, with his free hand, as I eased him down. I got my blanket and calico from the pack-saddle to make him comfortable.

'Help me with my back agen the tree,' he said. 'I must sit up – it's no use lyin' me down.'

He sat with his hand gripping his side, and breathed painfully.

'Shall I run up to the hut and get the wife?' I asked.

'No,' He spoke painfully. 'No!' Then, as if the words were jerked out of him by a spasm: 'She ain't there.'

I took it that she had left him.

'How long have you been bad? How long has this been coming on?'

He took no notice of the question. I thought it was a touch of rheumatic fever, or something of that sort. 'It's gone into my back and sides now – the pain's worse in me back,' he said presently.

I had once been mates with a man who died suddenly of heart disease, while at work. He was washing a dish of dirt in the creek near a claim we were working; he let the dish slip into the water, fell back, crying, 'Oh, my back!' and was gone. And now I felt by instinct that it was poor old Howlett's heart that was wrong. A man's heart is in his back as well as in his arms and hands.

The old man had turned pale with the pallor of a man who turns faint in a heat wave, and his arms fell loosely, and his hands rocked helplessly with the knuckles in the dust. I felt myself turning white, too, and the sick, cold, empty feeling in my stomach, for I knew the signs. Bushmen stand in awe of sickness and death.

But after I'd fixed him comfortably and given him a drink from the water-bag the greyness left his face, and he pulled himself together a bit; he drew up his arms and folded them across his chest. He let his head rest back against the tree – his slouch hat had fallen off revealing a broad, white brow, much higher than I expected. He seemed to gaze on the azure fin of the range, showing above the dark blue-green bush on the horizon.

Then he commenced to speak – taking no notice of me when I asked him if he felt better now – to talk in that strange, absent, far-away tone that awes one. He told his story mechanically, monotonously – in set words, as I believe now, as he had often told it before; if not to others, then to the loneliness of the bush. And he used the names of people and places that I had never heard of – just as if I knew them as well as he did.

'I didn't want to bring her up the first year. It was no place for a woman. I wanted her to stay with her people and wait till I'd got the place a little more shipshape. The Phippses took a selection down the creek. I wanted her to wait and come up with them so's she'd have some company – a woman to talk to. They came afterwards, but they didn't stop. It was no place for a woman.

'But Mary would come. She wouldn't stop with her people down-country. She wanted to be with me, and look after me, and work and help me.'

He repeated himself a great deal – said the same thing over and over again sometimes. He was only mad on one track. He'd tail off and sit silent for a while; then he'd become aware of me in a hurried, half-scared way, and apologise for putting me to all that trouble, and thank me. 'I'll be all right d'reckly. Best take the horses up to the hut and have some breakfast; you'll find it by the fire. I'll foller you, d'reckly. The wife'll be waitin' an' ——' He would drop off, and be going again presently on the old track:

'Her mother was coming up to stay a while at the end of the year, but the old man hurt his leg. Then her married sister was coming, but one of the youngsters got sick and there was trouble at home. I saw the doctor in the town – thirty miles from here – and fixed it up with him. He was a boozer – I'd 'a shot him afterwards. I fixed up with a woman in the town to come and stay. I thought Mary was wrong in her time. She must have been a month or six weeks out. But I listened to her ... Don't argue with a woman. Don't listen to a woman. Do the right thing. We should have had a mother woman to talk to us. But it was no place for a woman!'

He rocked his head, as if from some old agony of mind, against the tree-trunk.

'She was took bad suddenly one night, but it passed off. False alarm. I was going to ride somewhere, but she said to wait till daylight. Someone was sure to pass. She was a brave and sensible girl, but she had a terror of being left alone. It was no place for a woman!

'There was a black shepherd three or four miles away. I rode over while Mary was asleep, and started the black boy into town. I'd 'a shot him afterwards if I'd 'a caught him. The old black gin was dead the week before, or Mary would 'a bin all right. She was tied up in a bunch with strips of blanket and greenhide, and put in a hole. So there wasn't even a gin near the place. It was no place for a woman!

'I was watchin' the road at daylight, and I was watchin' the road at dusk. I went down in the hollow and stooped down to get the gap agen the sky, so's I could see if any one was comin' over ... I'd get on the horse and gallop along towards the town for five miles, but something would drag me back, and then I'd race for fear she'd die before I got to the hut. I expected the doctor every five minutes.

'It came on about daylight next morning. I ran back'ards and for'ards between the hut and the road like a madman. And no one come. I was running amongst the logs and stumps, and fallin' over them, when I saw a cloud of dust agen sunrise. It was her mother and sister in the spring-cart, an' just catchin' up to them was the doctor in his buggy with the woman I'd arranged with in town. The mother and sister were staying at the town for the night, when they heard of the black boy. It took him a day to ride there. I'd 'a shot him if I'd 'a caught him ever after. The doctor'd been on the drunk. If I'd had the gun and known she was gone I'd have shot him in the buggy. They said she was dead. And the child was dead, too.

'They blamed me, but I didn't want her to come; it was no place for a woman. I never saw them again after the funeral. I didn't want to see them any more.'

He moved his head wearily against the tree, and presently drifted on again in a softer tone – his eyes and voice were growing more absent and dreamy and far away.

'About a month after – or a year, I lost count of the time long ago – she came back to me. At first she'd come in the night, then sometimes when I was at work – and she had the baby – it was a girl – in her arms. And by and by she came to stay altogether ... I didn't blame her for going away that time – it was no place for a woman ... She was a good wife to me. She was a jolly girl when I married her. The little girl grew up like her. I was going to send her down-country to be educated – it was no place for a girl.

'But a month, or a year ago, Mary left me, and took the daughter, and never came back till last night – this morning, I think it was. I thought at first it was the girl with her hair done up, and her mother's skirt on, to surprise her old dad. But it was Mary, my wife – as she was when I married her. She said she couldn't stay, but she'd wait for me on the road; on – the road.'

His arms fell, and his face went white. I got the water-bag. 'Another turn like that and you'll be gone,' I thought, as he came to again. Then I suddenly thought of a shanty that had been started, when I came that way last, ten or twelve miles along the road, towards the town. There was nothing for it but to leave him and ride on for help, and a cart of some kind.

'You wait here till I come back,' I said. 'I'm going for the doctor.'

He roused himself a little. 'Best come up to the hut and get some grub. The wife'll be waiting ...' He was off the track again.

'Will you wait while I take the horse down to the creek?'

'Yes – I'll wait by the road.'

'Look!' I said, 'I'll leave the water-bag handy. Don't move till I come back.'

'I won't move – I'll wait by the road,' he said.

I took the packhorse, which was the freshest and best, threw the pack-saddle and bags into a bush, left the other horse to take care of itself, and started for the shanty, leaving the old man with his back to the tree, his arms folded, and his eyes on the horizon.

One of the chaps at the shanty rode on for the doctor at once, while the other came back with me in a spring-cart. He told me that old Howlett's wife had died in child-birth the first year on the selection – 'she was a find girl he'd heerd!' He told me the story as the old man had told it, and in pretty well the same words, even to giving it as his opinion that it was no place for a woman. 'And he "hatted" and brooded over it till he went ratty.'

I knew the rest. He not only thought that his wife, or the ghost of his wife, had been with him all those years, but that the child had lived and grown up, and that the wife did the housework; which, of course, he must have done himself.

When we reached him his knotted hands had fallen for the last time, and they were at rest. I only took one quick look at his face, but could have sworn that he was gazing at the blue fin of the range on the horizon of the bush.

Up at the hut the table was set as on the first day I saw it, and breakfast in the camp-oven by the fire.

BUSH CATS

'DOMESTIC CATS' we mean – the descendants of cats who came from the northern world during the last hundred odd years. We do not know the name of the vessel in which the first Thomas and his Maria came out to Australia, but we suppose that it was one of the ships of the First Fleet. Most likely Maria had kittens on the voyage – two lots, perhaps – the majority of which were buried at sea; and no doubt the disembarkation caused her much maternal anxiety.

The feline race has not altered much in Australia, from a physical point of view – not yet. The rabbit has developed into something like a cross between a kangaroo and a possum, but the bush has not begun to develop the common cat. She is just as sedate and motherly as the mummy cats of Egypt were, but she takes longer strolls of nights, climbs gum-trees instead of roofs, and hunts stranger vermin than ever came under the observation of her northern ancestors. Her views have widened. She is mostly thinner than the English farm cat – which is, they say, on account of eating lizards.

English rats and English mice – we say 'English' because everything which isn't Australian in Australia, is English (or British) – English rats and English mice are either rare or non-existent in the bush; but the hut cat has a wider range for game. She is always dragging in things which are unknown in the halls of zoology; ugly, loathsome, crawling abortions which have not been classified yet – and perhaps could not be.

The Australian zoologist ought to rake up some more dead languages, and then go out back with a few bush cats.

The Australian bush cat has a nasty, unpleasant habit of dragging a long, wriggling, horrid, black snake – she seems to prefer black snakes – into a room where there are ladies, proudly laying it down in a conspicuous place (usually in front of the exit), and then looking up for approbation. She wonders, perhaps, why the visitors are in such a hurry to leave.

Pussy doesn't approve of live snakes round the place, especially if she has kittens; and if she finds a snake in the vicinity of her progeny – well, it is bad for that particular serpent.

This brings recollections of a neighbour's cat who went out in the scrub, one midsummer's day, and found a brown snake. Her name – the cat's name – was Mary Ann. She got hold of the snake all right, just within an inch of its head; but it got the rest of its length wound round her body and squeezed about eight lives out of her. She had the presence of mind to keep her hold; but it struck her that she was in a fix and that if she wanted to save her ninth life, it wouldn't be a bad idea to go home for help. So she started home, snake and all.

The family were at dinner when Mary Ann came in, and, although she stood on an open part of the floor, no one noticed her for a while. She couldn't ask for help, for her mouth was too full of snake. By and by one of the girls glanced round, and then went over the table, with a shriek, and out of the back door. The room was cleared very quickly. The eldest boy got a long-handled shovel, and in another second would have killed more cat than snake; but his father interfered. The father was a shearer, and Mary Ann was a favourite cat with him. He got a pair of shears from the shelf and deftly shore off the snake's head, and one side of Mary Ann's whiskers. She didn't think it safe to let go yet. She kept her teeth in the neck until the selector snipped the rest of the snake off her. The bits were carried out on a shovel to die at sundown. Mary Ann had a good drink of milk and then got her tongue out and licked herself back into the proper shape for a cat; after which she went out to look for the snake's mate. She found it, too, and dragged it home the same evening.

Cats will kill rabbits and drag them home. We knew a fossicker whose cat used to bring him a bunny nearly every night. The fossicker had rabbits for breakfast until he got sick of them, and then he used to swap them with a butcher for meat. The cat was named Ingersoll, which indicates his sex and gives an inkling to his master's religious and political opinions. Ingersoll used to prospect round in the gloaming until he found some rabbit holes which showed encouraging indications. He would shepherd one hole for an hour or so every evening until he found it was a duffer, or worked it out; then he would shift to another. One day he prospected a big hollow log with a lot of holes in it, and more going down underneath. The indications were very good, but Ingersoll had no luck. The game had too many ways of getting out and in. He found that he could not work that claim by himself, so he floated it into a company. He persuaded several cats from a neighbouring selection to take shares, and they watched the holes together, or in turns – they worked shifts. The dividends more than realised even their wildest expectations, for each cat took home at least one rabbit every night for a week.

A selector started a vegetable garden about the time when rabbits were beginning to get troublesome up-country. The hare had not shown itself yet. The farmer kept quite a regiment of cats to protect his garden – and they protected it. He would shut the cats up all day with nothing to eat, and let them out about sundown; then they would mooch off to the turnip patch like farm-labourers going to work. They would drag the rabbits home to the back door, and sit there and watch them until the farmer opened the door and served out the ration of milk. Then the cats would turn in. He nearly always found a semicircle of dead rabbits and watchful cats round the door in the morning. They sold the product of their labour direct to the farmer for milk. It didn't matter if one cat had been unlucky – had not got a rabbit – each had an equal share in the general result. They were true socialists, those cats.

One of those cats was a mighty big Tom, named Jack. He was death on rabbits; he would work hard all night, laying for them and dragging them home. Some weeks he would graft every night, and at other times every other night, but he was generally pretty regular. When he reckoned he had done an extra night's work, he would take his Maria and take her out for a stroll. Well, one evening Jack went into the garden and chose a place where there was good cover, and lay low. He was a bit earlier than usual, so he thought he would have a doze till rabbit time. By and by he heard a noise, and slowly, cautiously opening one eye, he saw two big ears sticking out of the leaves in front of him. He judged that it was an extra big bunny, so he put some extra style into his manoeuvres. In about five minutes he made his spring. He must have thought (if cats think) that it was a whopping, old-man rabbit, for it was a pioneer hare – not an ordinary English hare, but one of those great coarse lanky things which the bush is breeding. The selector was attracted by an unusual commotion and a cloud of dust among his cabbages, and came along with his gun in time to witness the fight. First Jack would drag the hare, and then the hare would drag Jack; sometimes they would be down together, and then Jack would use his hind claws with effect; finally he got his teeth in the right place, and triumphed. Then he started to drag the corpse home, but he had to give it best and ask his master to lend a hand. The selector took up the hare, and Jack followed home, much to the family's surprise. He did not go back to work that night; he took a spell. He had a drink of milk, licked the dust off himself, washed it down with another drink, and sat in front of the fire and thought for a goodish while. Then he got up, walked over to the corner where the hare was lying, had a good look at it, came back to the fire, sat down again, and thought hard. He was still thinking when the family retired.

HOW STEELMAN TOLD HIS STORY

IT WAS STEELMAN'S humour, in some of his moods, to take Smith into his confidence, as some old bushmen do their dogs.

'You're nearly as good as an intelligent sheep-dog to talk to, Smith – when a man gets tired of thinking to himself and wants a relief. You're a bit of a mug and a good deal of an idiot, and the chances are that you don't know what I'm driving at half the time – that's the main reason why I don't mind talking to you. You ought to consider yourself honoured; it ain't every man I take into my confidence, even that far.'

Smith rubbed his head.

'I'd sooner talk to you – or a stump – any day than to one of those silent, suspicious, self-contained, worldly-wise chaps that listen to everything you say – sense and rubbish alike – as if you were trying to get them to take shares in a mine. I drop the man who listens to me all the time and doesn't seem to get bored. He isn't safe. He isn't to be trusted. He mostly wants to grind his axe against yours, and there's too little profit for me where there are two axes to grind, and no stone – though I'd manage it once, anyhow.'

'How'd you do it?' asked Smith.

'There are several ways. Either you join forces, for instance, and find a grindstone – or make one of the other man's axe. But the last way is too slow, and, as I said, takes too much brain-work – besides, it doesn't pay. It might satisfy your vanity or pride, but I've got none. I had once, when I was younger, but it – well, it nearly killed me, so I dropped it.

'You can mostly trust the man who wants to talk more than you do; he'll make a safe mate – or a good grindstone.'

Smith scratched the nape of his neck and sat blinking at the fire, with the puzzled expression of a woman pondering over a life-question or the trimming of a hat. Steelman took his chin in his hand and watched Smith thoughtfully.

'I – I say, Steely,' exclaimed Smith, suddenly, sitting up and scratching his head and blinking harder than ever – 'wha – what am I?'

'How do you mean?'

'Am I the axe or the grindstone?'

'Oh, your brain seems in extra good working order to-night, Smith. Well, you turn the grindstone and I grind.' Smith settled. 'If you could grind better than I, I'd turn the stone and let you grind, I'd never go against the interests of the firm – that's fair enough, isn't it?'

'Ye-es,' admitted Smith; 'I suppose so.'

'So do I. Now, Smith, we've got along all right together for years, off and on, but you never know what might happen. I might stop breathing, for instance – and so might you.'

Smith began to look alarmed.

'Poetical justice might overtake one or both of us – such things have happened before, though not often. Or, say, misfortune or death might mistake us for honest, hard-working mugs with big families to keep, and cut us off in the bloom of all our wisdom. You might get into trouble, and, in that case, I'd be bound to leave you there, on principle; or I might get into trouble, and you wouldn't have the brains to get me out – though I know you'd be mug enough to try. I might make a rise and cut you, or you might be misled into showing some spirit, and clear out after I'd stoushed you for it. You might get tired of me calling you a mug and bossing you and making a tool or convenience of you, you know. You might go in for honest graft (you were always a bit weak-minded) and then I'd have to wash my hands of you (unless you agreed to keep me) for an irreclaimable mug. Or it might suit me to become a respected and worthy fellow townsman, and then, if you came within ten miles of me or hinted that you ever knew me, I'd have you up for vagrancy, or soliciting alms, or attempting to levy blackmail. I'd have to fix you – so I give you fair warning. Or we might get into some desperate fix (and it needn't be very desperate, either) when I'd be obliged to sacrifice you for my own personal safety, comfort, and convenience. Hundreds of things might happen.

'Well, as I said, we've been at large together for some years, and I've found you sober, trustworthy, and honest; so in case we do part – as we will sooner or later – and you survive, I'll give you some advice from my own experience.

'In the first place: If you ever happen to get born again – and it wouldn't do you much harm – get born with the strength of a bullock and the hide of one as well, and a swelled head, and no brains – at least no more brains that you've got now. I was born with a skin like tissue-paper, and brains; also a heart.

'Get born without relatives, if you can: if you can't help it, clear out on your own just as soon after you're born as you possibly can. I hung on.

'If you have relations, and feel inclined to help them any time when you're flush (and there's no telling what a weak-minded man like you might take it into his head to do) – don't do it. They'll get a down on you if you do. It only causes family troubles and bitterness. There's no dislike like that of a dependant. You'll get neither gratitude nor civility in the end, and be lucky if you escape with a character. (You've got no character, Smith; I'm only just supposing you have.) There's no hatred too bitter for, and nothing too bad to be said of, the mug who turns. The worst yarns about a man are generally started by his own tribe, and the world believes them at once on that very account. Well, the first thing to do in life is to escape from your friends.

'If you ever go to work – and miracles have happened before – no matter what your wages are, or how you are treated, you can take it for granted that you're sweated; act on that to the best of your ability, or you'll never rise in the world. If you go to see a show on the nod you'll be found a comfortable seat in a good place; but if you pay the chances are the ticket clerk will tell you a lie, and you'll have to hustle for standing room. The man that doesn't ante gets the best of this world; anything he'll stand is good enough for the man that pays. If you try to be too sharp you'll get into jail sooner or later; if you try to be too honest the chances are that the bailiff will get into your house – if you have one – and make a holy show of you before the neighbours. The honest softy is more often mistaken for a swindler, and accused of being one, than the out-and-out scamp; and the man that tells the truth too much is set down as an irreclaimable liar. But most of the time crow low and roost high, for it's a funny world, and you never know what might happen.

'And if you get married (and there's no accounting for a woman's taste) be as bad as you like, and then moderately good, and your wife will love you. If you're bad all the time she can't stand it for ever, and if you're good all the time she'll naturally treat you with contempt. Never explain what you're going to do, and don't explain afterwards, if you can help it. If you find yourself between two stools, strike hard for your own self, Smith – strike hard, and you'll be respected more than if you fought for all the world. Generosity isn't understood nowadays, and what the people don't understand is either "mad" or "cronk." Failure has no case, and you can't build one for it ... I started out in life very young – and very soft.'

'I thought you were going to tell me your story, Steely,' remarked Smith.

Steelman smiled sadly.

OVER THE SLIPRAILS

THE SHANTY-KEEPER'S WIFE

THERE WERE about a dozen of us jammed into the coach, on the box-seat and hanging on to the roof and tailboard as best we could. We were shearers, bagmen, agents, a squatter, a cockatoo, the usual joker – and one or two professional spielers, perhaps. We were tired and stiff and nearly frozen – too cold to talk and too irritable to risk the inevitable argument which an interchange of ideas would have led up to. We had been looking forward for hours, it seemed, to the pub where we were to change horses. For the last hour or two all that our united efforts had been able to get out of the driver was a grunt to the effect that it was ''bout a couple o' miles.' Then he said, or grunted, ''Tain't fur now,' a couple of times, and refused to commit himself any further; he seemed grumpy about having committed himself so far.

He was one of those men who take everything in dead earnest; who regard any expression of ideas outside their own sphere of life as trivial, or, indeed, if addressed directly to them, as offensive; who, in fact, are darkly suspicious of anything in the shape of a joke or laugh on the part of an outsider in their own particular dust-hole. He seemed to be always thinking, and thinking a lot; when his hands were not both engaged, he would tilt his hat forward and scratch the base of his skull with his little finger, and let his jaw hang. But his intellectual powers were mostly concentrated on a doubtful swingle-tree, a misfitting collar, or that there bay or piebald (on the off or near side) with the sore shoulder.

Casual letters or papers, to be delivered on the road, were matters which troubled him vaguely, but constantly – like the abstract ideas of his passengers.

The joker of our party was a humorist of the dry order, and had been slyly taking rises out of the driver for the last two or three stages. But the driver only brooded. He wasn't the one to tell you straight if you offended him, or if he fancied you offended him, and thus gain your respect, or prevent a misunderstanding which would result in life-long enmity. He might meet you in after years when you had forgotten all about your trespass – if indeed you had ever been conscious of it – and 'stoush' you unexpectedly on the ear.

Also you might regard him as your friend, on occasion, and yet he would stand by and hear a perfect stranger tell you the most outrageous lies, to your hurt, and know that the stranger was telling lies, and never put you up to it. It would never enter his head to do so. It wouldn't be any affair of his – only an abstract question.

It grew darker and colder. The rain came as if the frozen south were spitting at our face and neck and hands, and our feet grew as big as camels', and went dead, and we might as well have stamped the footboards with wooden legs for all the feeling we got into our own. But they were more comfortable that way, for the toes didn't curl up and pain so much, nor did our corns stick out so hard against the leather, and shoot.

We looked out eagerly for some clearing, or fence, or light – some sign of the shanty where we were to change horses – but there was nothing save blackness all round. The long, straight, cleared road was no longer relieved by the ghostly patch of light, far ahead, where the bordering tree-walls came together in perspective and framed the ether. We were down in the bed of the bush.

We pictured a haven of rest with a suspended lamp burning in the frosty air outside and a big log fire in a cosy parlour off the bar, and a long table set for supper. But this is a land of contradictions; wayside shanties turn up unexpectedly, and in the most unreasonable places, and are, as likely as not, prepared for a banquet when you are not hungry and can't wait, and as cold and dark as a bushman's grave when you are and can.

Suddenly the driver said: 'We're there now.' He said this as if he had driven us to the scaffold to be hanged, and was fiercely glad that he'd got us there safely at last. We looked but saw nothing; then a light appeared ahead and seemed to come towards us; and presently we saw that it was a lantern held up by a man in a slouch hat, with a dark bushy beard, and a three-bushel bag around his shoulders. He held up his other hand, and said something to the driver in a tone that might have been used by the leader of a search party who had just found the body. The driver stopped and then went on slowly.

'What's up?' we asked. 'What's the trouble?'

'Oh, it's all right,' said the driver.

'The publican's wife is sick,' somebody said, 'and he wants us to come quietly.'

The usual little slab-and-bark shanty was suggested in the gloom, with a big bark stable looming in the background. We climbed down like so many cripples. As soon as we began to feel our legs and be sure we had the right ones and the proper allowance of feet, we helped, as quietly as possible, to take the horses out and round to the stable.

'Is she very bad?' we asked the publican, showing as much concern as we could.

'Yes,' he said, in the subdued voice of a rough man who had spent several anxious, sleepless nights by the sick-bed of a dear one. 'But, God willing, I think we'll pull her through.'

Thus encouraged we said, sympathetically: 'We're very sorry to trouble you, but I suppose we could manage to get a drink and a bit to eat?'

'Well,' he said, 'there's nothing to eat in the house, and I've only got rum and milk. You can have that if you like.'

One of the pilgrims broke out here.

'Well, of all the pubs,' he began, 'that I've ever —'

'Hush-sh-sh!' said the publican.

The pilgrim scowled and retired to the rear. You can't express your feelings freely when there's a woman dying close handy.

'Well, who says rum and milk?' asked the joker in a low voice.

'Wait here,' said the publican, and disappeared into the little front passage.

Presently a light showed through a window with a scratched and fly-bitten B and A on two panes, and a mutilated R on the third, which was broken. A door opened, and we sneaked into the bar. It was like having drinks after hours where the police are strict and independent.

When we came out the driver was scratching his head and looking at the harness on the veranda floor.

'You fellows'll have ter put in the time for an hour or so. The horses is out back somewheres,' and he indicated the interior of Australia with a side jerk of his head, 'and the boy ain't back with 'em yet.'

'But dash it all,' said the pilgrim, 'me and my mate —'

'Hush!' said the publican.

'How long are the horses likely to be?' we asked the driver.

'Dunno,' he grunted. 'Might be three or four hours. It's all accordin'.'

'Now, look here,' said the pilgrim, 'me and my mate wanter catch the train.'

'Hush-sh-sh!' from the publican in a fierce whisper.

'Well, boss,' said the joker, 'can you let us have beds, then? I don't want to freeze here all night, anyway.'

'Yes,' said the landlord, 'I can do that, but some of you will have to sleep double and some of you'll have to take it out of the sofas, and one or two'll have to make a shake-down on the floor. There's plenty of bags in the stable, and you've got rugs and coats with you. Fix it up amongst yourselves.'

'But look here!' interrupted the pilgrim, desperately, 'we can't afford to wait! We're only "battlers," me and my mate, pickin' up crumbs by the wayside. We've got to catch the —'

'Hush!' said the publican savagely. 'You fool, didn't I tell you my missus was bad? I won't have any noise.'

'But look here,' protested the pilgrim, 'we must catch the train at Dead Camel —'

'You'll catch my boot presently,' said the publican, with a savage oath, 'and go further than Dead Camel. I won't have my missus disturbed for you or any other man! Just you shut up or get out, and take your blooming mate with you.'

We lost patience with the pilgrim and sternly took him aside.

'Now for God's sake, hold your jaw,' we said. 'Haven't you got any consideration at all? Can't you see the man's wife is ill – dying perhaps – and he nearly worried off his head?'

The pilgrim and his mate were scraggy little bipeds of the city push variety, so they were suppressed.

'Well,' yawned the joker, 'I'm not going to roost on a stump all night. I'm going to turn in.'

'It'll be eighteenpence each,' hinted the landlord. 'You can settle now if you like to save time.'

We took the hint, and had another drink. I don't know how we 'fixed it up amongst ourselves,' but we got settled down somehow. There was a lot of mysterious whispering and scuffling round by the light of a couple of dirty greasy bits of candle. Fortunately we dared not speak loud enough to have a row, though most of us were by this time in the humour to pick a quarrel with a long-lost brother.

The joker got the best bed, as good-humoured, good-natured chaps generally do, without seeming to try for it. The growler of the party got the floor and chaff-bags, as selfish men mostly do – without seeming to try for it either. I took it out of one of the 'sofas,' or rather that sofa took it out of me. It was short and narrow and down by the head, with a leaning to one corner on the outside, and had more nails and bits of gin-case than original sofa in it.

I had been asleep for three seconds, it seemed, when somebody shook me by the shoulder and said:

'Take yer seats.'

When I got out, the driver was on the box, and the others were getting rum and milk inside themselves (and in bottles) before taking their seats.

It was colder and darker than ever and the South Pole seemed nearer; and pretty soon, but for the rum, we should have been in a worse fix than before.

There was a spell of grumbling. Presently someone said:

'I don't believe them horses was lost at all. I was round behind the stable before I went to bed, and seen horses there; and if they wasn't them same horses there, I'll eat 'em raw!'

'Would yer?' said the driver, in a disinterested tone.

'I would,' said the passenger. Then, with a sudden ferocity, 'and you too!'

The driver said nothing. It was an abstract question which didn't interest him.

We saw that we were on delicate ground, and changed the subject for a while. Then someone else said:

'I wonder where his missus was? I didn't see any signs of her about, or any other woman about the place, and we was pretty well all over it.'

'Must have kept her in the stable,' suggested the joker.

'No, she wasn't, for Scotty and that chap on the roof was there after bags.'

'She might have been in the loft,' reflected the joker.

'There was no loft,' put in a voice from the top of the coach.

'I say, Mister – Mister man,' said the joker suddenly to the driver, 'Was his missus sick at all?'

'I dunno,' replied the driver. 'She might have been. He said so, anyway. I ain't got no call to call a man a liar.'

'See here,' said the cannibalistic individual to the driver, in the tone of a man who has made up his mind for a row, 'has that shanty-keeper got a wife at all?'

'I believe he has.'

'And is she living with him?'

'No, she ain't – if yer wanter know.'

'Then where is she?'

'I dunno. How am I to know? She left him three or four years ago. She was in Sydney last time I heard of her. It ain't no affair of mine, anyways.'

'And is there any woman about the place at all, driver?' inquired a professional wanderer reflectively.

'No – not that I knows of. There useter to be an old black gin come pottering round sometimes, but I ain't seen her lately.'

'And excuse me, driver, but is there any one round there at all?' inquired the professional wanderer, with the air of a conscientious writer, collecting material for an Australian novel from life, and with an eye to detail.

'Naw,' said the driver – and recollecting that he was expected to be civil and obliging to his employers' patrons, he added in surly apology, 'Only the boss and the stableman, that I knows of.' Then repenting of the apology, he asserted his manhood again, and asked, in a tone calculated to risk a breach of the peace, 'Any more questions, gentlemen – while the shop's open?'

There was a long pause.

'Driver,' asked the pilgrim appealingly, 'was them horses lost at all?'

'I dunno,' said the driver. 'He said they was. He's got the looking after them. It was nothing to do with me.'

'Twelve drinks at sixpence a drink' – said the joker, as if calculating to himself – 'that's six bob, and, say on an average, four shouts – that's one pound four. Twelve beds at eighteenpence a bed – that's eighteen shillings; and say ten bob in various drinks and the stuff we brought with us, that's two pound twelve. That publican didn't do so bad out of us in two hours.'

We wondered how much the driver got out of it, but thought it best not to ask him.

We didn't say much for the rest of the journey. There was the usual man who thought as much and knew all about it from the first, but he wasn't appreciated. We suppressed him. One or two wanted to go back and 'stoush' that landlord, and the driver stopped the coach cheerfully at their request; but they said they'd come across him again, and allowed themselves to be persuaded out of it. It made us feel bad to think how we had allowed ourselves to be delayed, and robbed, and had sneaked round on tiptoe, and how we had sat on the inoffensive pilgrim and his mate, and all on account of a sick wife who didn't exist.

The coach arrived at Dead Camel in an atmosphere of mutual suspicion and distrust, and we spread ourselves over the train and departed.

A Case For The Oracle

THE ORACLE and I were camped together. The Oracle was a brick-layer by trade, and had two or three small contracts on hand. I was 'doing a bit of house-painting.' There were a plasterer, a carpenter, and a plumber – we were all T'othersiders, and old mates, and we worked things together. It was in Westralia – the Land of T'othersiders – and, therefore, we were not surprised when Mitchell turned up early one morning, with his swag and an atmosphere of salt water about him.

He'd had a rough trip, he said, and would take a spell that day and take the lay of the land and have something cooked for us by the time we came home; and go to graft himself next morning. And next morning he went to work, 'labouring' for the Oracle.

The Oracle and his mates, being small contractors and not pressed for time, had dispensed with the services of a labourer, and had done their own mixing and hod-carrying in turns. They didn't want a labourer now, but the Oracle was a vague fatalist, and Mitchell a decided one. So it passed.

The Oracle had a 'Case' right under his nose – in his own employ, in fact; but was not aware of the fact until Mitchell drew his attention to it. The Case went by the name of Alfred O'Briar – which hinted a mixed parentage. He was a small, nervous working-man, of no particular colour, and no decided character, apparently. If he had a soul above bricks, he never betrayed it. He was not popular on the jobs. There was something sly about Alf, they said.

The Oracle had taken him on in the first place as a day-labourer, but afterwards shared the pay with him as with Mitchell. O'Briar shouted – judiciously, but on every possible occasion – for the Oracle; and, as he was an indifferent workman, the boys said he only did this so that the Oracle might keep him on. If O'Briar took things easy and did no more than the rest of us, at least one of us would be sure to get it into his head that he was loafing on us; and if he grafted harder than we did, we'd be sure to feel indignant about that too, and reckon that it was done out of nastiness or crawlsomeness, and feel a contempt for him accordingly. We found out accidentally that O'Briar was an excellent mimic and a bit of a ventriloquist, but he never entertained us with his peculiar gifts; and we set that down to churlishness.

O'Briar kept his own counsel, and his history, if he had one; and hid his hopes, joys, and sorrows, if he had any, behind a vacant grin, as Mitchell hid his behind a quizzical one. He never resented alleged satire – perhaps he couldn't see it – and therefore he got the name of being a cur. As a rule, he was careful with his money, and was called mean – not, however, by the Oracle, whose philosophy was simple, and whose sympathy could not realise a limit; nor yet by Mitchell. Mitchell waited.

O'Briar occupied a small tent by himself, and lived privately of evenings. When we began to hear two men talking at night in his tent, we were rather surprised, and wondered in a vague kind of way how any of the chaps could take sufficient interest in Alf to go in and yarn with him. In the days when he was supposed to be sociable, we had voted him a bore; even the Oracle was moved to admit that he was 'a bit slow.'

But late one night we distinctly heard a woman's voice in O'Briar's tent. The Oracle suddenly became hard of hearing, and, though we heard the voice on several occasions, he remained exasperatingly deaf, yet aggressively unconscious of the fact. 'I have got enough to do puzzling over me own whys and wherefores,' he said. Mitchell began to take some interest in O'Briar, and treated him with greater respect. But our camp had the name of being the best constructed, the cleanest, and the most respectable in the vicinity. The health officer and constable in charge had complimented us on the fact, and we were proud of it. And there were three young married couples in camp, also a Darby and Joan; therefore, when the voice of a woman began to be heard frequently and at disreputable hours of the night in O'Briar's tent, we got uneasy about it. And when the constable who was on night duty gave us a friendly hint, Mitchell and I agreed that something must be done.

'Av coorse, men will be men,' said the constable, as he turned his horse's head, 'but I thought I'd mention it. O'Briar is a dacent man, and he's one of yer mates. Av coorse. There's a bad lot in that camp in the scrub over yander, and – av coorse. Good day to ye, byes.'

Next night we heard the voice in O'Briar's tent again, and decided to speak to Alf in a friendly way about it in the morning. We listened outside in the dark, but could not distinguish the words, though I thought I recognised the voice.

'It's the hussy from the camp over there; she's got holt of that fool, and she'll clean him out before she's done,' I said. 'We're Alf's mates, any way it goes, and we ought to put a stop to it.'

'What hussy?' asked Mitchell; 'there's three or four there.'

'The one with her hair all over her head,' I answered.

'Where else should it be?' asked Mitchell. 'But I'll just have a peep and see who it is. There's no harm in that.'

He crept up to the tent and cautiously moved the flap. Alf's candle was alight; he lay on his back in his bunk, with his arms under his head, calmly smoking. We withdrew.

'They must have heard us,' said Mitchell; 'and she's slipped out under the tent at the back, and through the fence into the scrub.'

Mitchell's respect for Alf increased visibly.

But we began to hear ominous whispers from the young married couples and next Saturday night, which was pay-night, we decided to see it through. We did not care to speak to Alf until we were sure. He stayed in camp, as he often did, on Saturday evening, while the others went up town. Mitchell and I returned earlier than usual, and leaned on the fence at the back of Alf's tent.

We were scarcely there when we were startled by a 'rat-tat-tat' as of someone knocking at a door. Then an old woman's voice inside the tent asked: 'Who's there?'

'It's me,' said Alf's voice from the front, 'Mr O'Briar from Perth.'

'Mary, go and open the door!' said the old woman. (Mitchell nudged me to keep quiet.)

'Come in, Mr O'Breer,' said the old woman. 'Come in. How do you do? When did you get back?'

'Only last night,' said Alf.

'Look at that now! Bless us all! And how did you like the country at all?'

'I didn't care much for it,' said Alf. We lost the thread of it until the old woman spoke again.

'Have you had your tea, Mr O'Breer?'

'Yes thank you, Mrs O'Connor.'

'Are you quite sure, man?'

'Quite sure, thank you, Mrs O'Connor.' (Mitchell trod on my foot.)

'Will you have a drop of whisky or a glass of beer, Mr O'Breer?'

'I'll take a glass of beer, thank you, Mrs O'Connor.'

There seemed to be a long pause. Then the old woman said, 'Ah well, I must get my work done, and Mary will stop here and keep you company, Mr O'Breer.' The arrangement seemed satisfactory to all parties, for there was nothing more said for a while. (Mitchell nudged me again, with emphasis, and I kicked his shin.)

Presently Alf said: 'Mary!' And a girl's voice said, 'Yes, Alf.'

'You remember the night I went away, Mary?'

'Yes, Alf, I do.'

'I have travelled long ways since then, Mary; I worked hard and lived close. I didn't make my fortune, but I managed to rub a note or two together. It was a hard time and a lonesome time for me, Mary. The summer's awful over there, and livin's bad and dear. You couldn't have any idea of it, Mary.'

'No, Alf.'

'I didn't come back so well off as I expected.'

'But that doesn't matter, Alf.'

'I got heart-sick and tired of it, and couldn't stand it any longer, Mary.'

'But that's all over now, Alf; you mustn't think of it.'

'Your mother wrote to me.'

'I know she did' – (very low and gently).

'And do you know what she put in it, Mary?'

'Yes, Alf.'

'And did you ask her to put it in?'

'Don't ask me, Alf.'

'And it's all true, Mary?'

There was no answer, but the silence seemed satisfactory.

'And be sure you have yourself down here on Sunday, Alf, me son.' ('There's the old woman come back!' said Mitchell.)

'An' since the girl's willin' to have ye, and the ould woman's willin' – there's me hand on it, Alf, me boy. An' God bless ye both.' ('The old man's come now,' said Mitchell.)

'Come along,' said Mitchell, leading the way to the front of the tent.

'But I wouldn't like to intrude on them. It's hardly right, Mitchell, is it?'

'That's all right,' said Mitchell. He tapped the tent pole.

'Come in,' said Alf. Alf was lying on his bunk as before, with his arms under his head. His face wore a cheerful, not to say happy, expression. There was no one else in the tent. I was never more surprised in my life.

'Have you got the paper, Alf?' said Mitchell.

'Yes. You'll find it there at the foot of the bunk. There it is. Won't you sit down, Mitchell?'

'Not to-night,' said Mitchell. 'We brought you a bottle of ale. We're just going to turn in.'

And we said good night. 'Well,' I said to Mitchell when we got inside, 'what do you think of it?'

'I don't think of it at all,' said Mitchell. 'Do you mean to say you can't see it now?'

'No, I'm dashed if I can,' I said. 'Some of us must be drunk, I think, or getting rats. It's not to be wondered at, and the sooner we get out of this country the better.'

'Well, you must be a fool, Joe,' said Mitchell. 'Can't you see? Alf thinks aloud.'

'What?'

'Talks to himself. He was thinking about going back to his sweetheart. Don't you know he's a bit of a ventriloquist?'

Mitchell lay awake a long time, in the position that Alf usually lay in, and thought. Perhaps he thought on the same lines as Alf did that night. But Mitchell did his thinking in silence.

We thought it best to tell the Oracle quietly. He was deeply interested, but not surprised. 'I've heerd of such cases before,' he said. But the Oracle was a gentleman. 'There's things that a man wants to keep to himself that ain't his business,' he said. And we understood this remark to be intended for our benefit, and to indicate a course of action upon which the Oracle had decided, with respect to this case, and which we, in his opinion, should do well to follow. Alf got away a week or so later, and we all took a holiday and went down to Fremantle to see him off. Perhaps he wondered why Mitchell gripped his hand so hard and wished him luck so earnestly, and was surprised when he gave him three cheers.

'Ah, well!' remarked Mitchell, as we turned up the wharf.

'I've heerd of such cases before,' said the Oracle, meditatively. 'They ain't common, but I've heerd of such cases before.'

JOE WILSON

JOE WILSON'S COURTSHIP

THERE ARE MANY times in this world when a healthy boy is happy. When he is put into knickerbockers, for instance, and 'comes a man to-day,' as my little Jim used to say. When they're cooking something at home that he likes. When the 'sandy blight' or measles breaks out amongst the children, or the teacher or his wife falls dangerously ill – or dies, it doesn't matter which – 'and there ain't no school.' When a boy is naked and in his natural state for a warm climate like Australia, with three or four of his schoolmates, under the shade of the creek-oaks in the bend where there's a good clear pool with a sandy bottom. When his father buys him a gun, and he starts out after kangaroos or possums. When he gets a horse, saddle, and bridle of his own. When he has his arm in splints or a stitch in his head – he's proud then, the proudest boy in the district.

I wasn't a healthy-minded, average boy; I reckon I was born for a poet by mistake, and grew up to be a bushman, and didn't know what was the matter with me – or the world – but that's got nothing to do with it.

There are times when a man is happy. When he finds out that the girls loves him. When he's just married. When he's a lawful father for the first time, and everything's going on all right: some men make fools of themselves then – I know I did. I'm happy to-night because I'm out of debt and can see clear ahead, and because I haven't been easy for a long time.

But I think that the happiest time in a man's life is when he's courting a girl, and finds out for sure that she loves him, and hasn't a thought for any one else. Make the most of your courting days, you young chaps, and keep them clean, for they're about the only days when there's a chance of poetry and beauty coming into this life. Make the best of them, and you'll never regret it the longest day you live. They're the days that the wife will look back to, anyway, in the brightest of times as well as in the blackest, and there shouldn't be anything in those days that might hurt her when she looks back. Make the most of your courting days, you young chaps, for they will never come again.

A married man knows all about it – after a while; he sees the woman world through the eyes of his wife; he knows what an extra moment's pressure of the hand means, and, if he has had a hard life, and is inclined to be cynical, the knowledge does him no good. It leads him into awful messes sometimes, for a married man, if he's inclined that way, has three times the chance with a woman that a single man has – because the married man knows. He is privileged; he can guess pretty closely what a woman means when she says something else; he knows just how far he can go; he can go farther in five minutes towards coming to the point with a woman than an innocent young man dares go in three weeks.

Above all, the married man is more decided with women; he takes them and things for granted. In short he is – well, he is a married man. And, when he knows all this, how much better or happier is he for it? Mark Twain says that he lost all the beauty of the river when he saw it with a pilot's eye – and there you have it.

But it's all new to a young chap, provided he hasn't been a young blackguard. It's all wonderful, new, and strange to him. He's a different man. He finds that he never knew anything about women. He sees none of woman's little ways and tricks in his girl. He is in heaven one day and down near the other place the next; and that's the sort of thing that makes life interesting. He takes his new world for granted. And, when she says she'll be his wife —!

Make the most of your courting days, you young chaps, for they've got a lot of influence on your married life afterwards – a lot more than you'd think. Make the best of them, for they'll never come any more, unless we do our courting over again in another world. If we do, I'll make the most of mine.

But, looking back, I didn't do so badly after all. I never told you about the days I courted Mary. The more I look back the more I come to think that I made the most of them, and if I had no more to regret in married life than I have in my courting days, I wouldn't walk to and fro in the room, or up and down the yard in the dark sometimes, or lie awake some nights thinking … Ah, well!

I was between twenty-one and thirty then: birthdays had never been any use to me, and I'd left off counting them. You don't take much stock in birthdays in the bush. I'd knocked about the country for a few years, shearing and fencing and droving a little, and wasting my life without getting anything for it. I drank now and then, and made a fool of myself. I was reckoned 'wild'; but I only drank because I felt less sensitive, and the world seemed a lot saner and better and kinder when I had a few drinks: I loved my fellow-man then and felt nearer to him. It's better to be thought 'wild' than to be considered eccentric or ratty. Now, my old mate, Jack Barnes, drank – as far as I could see – first because he'd inherited the gambling habit from his father along with his father's luck; he'd the habit of being cheated and losing very bad, and when he lost he drank. Till drink got a hold on him. Jack was sentimental too, but in a different way. I was sentimental about other people – more fool I! – whereas Jack was sentimental about himself. Before he was married, and when he was recovering from a spree, he'd write rhymes about 'Only a boy, drunk by the roadside,' and that sort of thing; and he'd call 'em poetry, and talk about signing them and sending them to the Town and Country Journal. But he generally tore them up when he got better. The bush is breeding a race of poets, and I don't know what the country will come to in the end.

Well. It was after Jack and I had been out shearing at Beenaway Shed in the big scrubs. Jack was living in the little farming town of Solong, and I was hanging round. Black, the squatter, wanted some fencing done, and a new stable built, or buggy and harness-house, at his place at Haviland, a few miles out of Solong. Jack and I were good bush carpenters, so we took the job to keep us going till something else turned up. 'Better than doing nothing,' said Jack.

'There's a nice little girl in the service at Black's,' he said. 'She's more like an adopted daughter, in fact, than a servant. She's a real good little girl, and good-looking into the bargain. I hear that young Black is sweet on her, but they say she won't have anything to do with him. I know a lot of chaps that have tried for her, but they've never had any luck. She's a regular little dumpling, and I like dumplings. They call her Possum. You ought to try a bear up in that direction, Joe.'

I was always shy with women – except perhaps some that I should have fought shy of; but Jack wasn't – he was afraid of no woman, good, bad, or indifferent. I haven't time to explain why, but somehow, whenever a girl took any notice of me I took it for granted that she was only playing with me, and felt nasty about it. I made one or two mistakes, but – ah well!

'My wife knows little Possum,' said Jack. 'I'll get her to ask her out to our place, and let you know.'

I reckoned that he wouldn't get me there then, and made a note to be on the watch for tricks. I had a hopeless little love-story behind me, of course. I suppose most married men can look back to their lost love; few marry the first flame. Many a married man looks back and thinks it was damned lucky that he didn't get the girl he couldn't have. Jack had been my successful rival, only he didn't know it – I don't think his wife knew it either. I used to think her the prettiest and sweetest little girl in the district.

But Jack was mighty keen on fixing me up with the little girl at Haviland. He seemed to take it for granted that I was going to fall in love with her at first sight. He took too many things for granted as far as I was concerned, and got me into awful tangles sometimes.

'You let me alone, and I'll fix you up, Joe,' he said, as we rode up to the station. 'I'll make it all right with the girl. You're rather a good-looking chap. You've got the sort of eyes that take with girls, only you don't know it; you haven't got the go. If I had your eyes along with my other attractions, I'd be in trouble on account of a woman once a week.'

'For God's sake shut up, Jack,' I said.

Do you remember the first glimpse you got of your wife? Perhaps not in England, where so many couples grow up together from childhood; but it's different in Australia, where you may hail from two thousand miles away from where your wife was born, and yet she may be a countrywoman of yours, and a countrywoman in ideas and politics too. I remember the first glimpse I got of Mary.

It was a two-story brick house with wide balconies and verandas all round, and a double row of pines down to the front gate. Parallel at the back was an old slab-and-shingle place, one room deep, and about eight rooms long, with a row of skillions at the back: the place was used for kitchen, laundry and servants' rooms. This was the old homestead before the new house was built. There was a wide, old-fashioned brick-floored veranda in front, with an open end; there was ivy climbing up the veranda-post on one side and a baby-rose on the other, and a grape-vine near the chimney. We rode up to the end of the veranda, and Jack called to see if there was any one at home, and Mary came trotting out; so it was in the frame of vines that I first saw her.

More than once since then I've had a fancy to wonder whether the rose-bush killed the grape-vine or the ivy smothered 'em both in the end. I used to have a vague idea of riding that way some day to see. You do get strange fancies at odd times.

Jack asked her if the boss was in. He did all the talking. I saw a little girl, rather plump, with a complexion like a New England or Blue Mountain girl, or a girl from Tasmania, or from Gippsland in Victoria. Red and white girls were very scarce in the Solong district. She had the biggest and brightest eyes I'd seen round there, dark hazel eyes, as I found out afterwards, and bright as a possum's. No wonder they called her 'Possum.' I forgot at once that Mrs Jack Barnes was the prettiest girl in the district. I felt a sort of comfortable satisfaction in the fact that I was on horseback; most bushmen look better on horseback. It was a black filly, a fresh young thing, and she seemed as shy of girls as I was myself. I noticed Mary glanced in my direction once or twice to see if she knew me; but, when she looked, the filly took all my attention. Mary trotted in to tell old Black he was wanted, and after Jack had seen him and arranged to start work next day, we started back to Solong.

I expected Jack to ask me what I thought of Mary – but he didn't. He squint-ed at me sideways once or twice, and didn't say anything for a long time, and then he started talking of other things. I began to feel wild at him. He seemed so damnably satisfied with the way things were going. He seemed to reckon that I was a gone case now; but as he didn't say so, I had no way of getting at him. I felt sure he'd go home and tell his wife that Joe Wilson was properly gone on lit-tle Possum at Haviland. That was all Jack's way.

Next morning we started to work. We were to build the buggy-house at the back near the end of the old house, but first we had to take down a rotten old place that might have been the original hut in the bush before the old house was built. There was a window in it, opposite the laundry window in the old place, and the first thing I did was to take out the sash. I'd noticed Jack yarning with Possum before he started work. While I was at work at the window he called me around to the other end of the hut to help him lift a grindstone out of the way; and when we'd done it, he took the top of my ear between his fingers and thumb and stretched it and whispered into it:

'Don't hurry with that window, Joe; the strips are hardwood and hard to get off – you'll have to take the sash out very carefully so as not to break the glass.' Then he stretched my ear a little more and put his mouth closer:

'Make a looking-glass of that window, Joe,' he said.

I was used to Jack, and when I went back to the window I started to puzzle out what he meant, and presently I saw it by chance.

That window reflected the laundry window: the room was dark inside, and there was a good clear reflection; and presently I saw Mary come to the laundry window and stand with her hands behind her back, thoughtfully watching me. The laundry window had an old-fashioned hinged sash, and I like that sort of window – there's more romance about it, I think. There was a thick dark-green ivy all round the window, and Mary looked prettier than a picture. I squared up my shoulders and put my heels together, and put as much style as I could into my work. I couldn't have turned round to save my life.

Presently Jack came round, and Mary disappeared.

'Well?' he whispered.

'You're a fool, Jack,' I said. 'She's only interested in the old house being pulled down.'

'That's all right,' he said. 'I've been keeping an eye on the business round the corner, and she ain't interested when I'm round this end.'

'You seem mighty interested in the business,' I said.

'Yes,' said Jack. 'This sort of thing just suits a man of my rank in times of peace.'

'What made you think of the window?' I asked.

'Oh, that's as simple as striking matches. I'm up to all those dodges. Why, where there wasn't a window, I've fixed up a piece of looking-glass to see if a girl was taking any notice of me when she thought I wasn't looking.'

He went away and presently Mary was at the window again, and this time she had a tray with cups of tea and a plate of cake and bread-and-butter. I was prising off the strips that held the sash, very carefully, and my heart suddenly commenced to gallop, without any reference to me. I'd never felt like that before, except once or twice. It was just as if I'd swallowed some clock-work arrangement, unconsciously, and it had started to go, without warning. I reckon it was all on account of that blarsted Jack working me up. He had a quiet way of working you up to a thing, that made you want to hit him sometimes – after you'd made an ass of yourself.

I didn't hear Mary at first. I hoped Jack would come round and help me out of the fix, but he didn't.

'Mr – Mr Wilson!' said Mary. She had a sweet voice.

I turned round.

'I thought you and Mr Barnes might like a cup of tea.'

'Oh, thank you!' I said, and I made a dive for the window, as if hurry would help it. I trod on an old cask-hoop; it sprang up and dinted my shin and I stumbled – and that didn't help matters much.

'Oh! did you hurt yourself, Mr Wilson?' cried Mary.

'Hurt myself! Oh no, not at all, thank you,' I blurted out. 'It takes more than that to hurt me.'

I was about the reddest shy lanky fool of a bushman that ever was taken at a disadvantage on foot, and when I took the tray my hands shook so that a lot of the tea was spilt into the saucers. I embarrassed her too, like the damned fool I was, till she must have been as red as I was, and it's a wonder we didn't spill the whole lot between us. I got away from the window in as much of a hurry as if Jack had cut his leg with a chisel and fainted, and I was running with whisky for him. I blundered round to where he was, feeling like a man feels when he has just made an ass of himself in public. The memory of that sort of thing hurts you worse and makes you jerk your head more impatiently than the thought of a past crime would, I think.

I pulled myself together when I got to where Jack was.

'Here, Jack!' I said. 'I've struck something all right; here's some tea and brownie – we'll hang out here all right.'

Jack took a cup of tea and a piece of cake and sat down to enjoy it, just as if he'd paid for it and ordered it to be sent out about that time.

He was silent for a while, with the sort of silence that always made me wild at him. Presently he said, as if he'd just thought of it:

'That's a very pretty little girl, Possum, isn't she, Joe? Do you notice how she dresses? – always fresh and trim. But she's got on her best bib-and-tucker to-day, and a pinafore with frills to it. And it's ironing-day, too. It can't be on your account. If it was Saturday or Sunday afternoon, or some holiday, I could understand it. But perhaps one of her admirers is going to take her to the church bazaar in Solong to-night. That's what it is.'

He gave me time to think over that.

'But yet she seems interested in you, Joe,' he said. 'Why didn't you offer to take her to the bazaar instead of letting another chap get in ahead of you? You miss all your chances, Joe.'

Then a thought struck me. I ought to have known Jack well enough to have thought of it before.

'Look here, Jack,' I said. 'What have you been saying to that girl about me?'

'Oh, not much,' said Jack. 'There isn't much to say about you.'

'What did you tell her?'

'Oh, nothing in particular. She'd heard all about you before.'

'She hadn't heard much good, I suppose,' I said.

'Well, that's true, as far as I could make out. But you've only got yourself to blame. I didn't have the breeding and rearing of you. I smoothed over matters with her as much as I could.'

'What did you tell her? I said. 'That's what I want to know.'

'Well, to tell the truth, I didn't tell her anything much. I only answered questions.'

'And what questions did she ask?'

'Well, in the first place, she asked if your name wasn't Joe Wilson; and I said it was, as far as I knew. Then she said she heard that you wrote poetry, and I had to admit that that was true.'

'Look here, Jack.' I said, 'I've two minds to punch your head.'

'And she asked me if it was true that you were wild,' said Jack, 'and I said you was, a bit. She said it seemed a pity. She asked me if it was true that you drank, and I drew a long face and said that I was sorry to say it was true. She asked me if you had any friends, and I said none that I knew of, except me. I said that you'd lost all your friends; they stuck to you as long as they could, but they had to give you best, one after the other.'

'What next?'

'She asked me if you were delicate, and I said no, you were as tough as fencing-wire. She said you looked rather pale and thin, and asked me if you'd had an illness lately. And I said no – it was all on account of the wild dissipated life you'd led. She said it was a pity you hadn't a mother or a sister to look after you – it was a pity that something couldn't be done for you, and I said it was, but I was afraid that nothing could be done. I told her that I was doing all I could to keep you straight.'

I knew enough of Jack to know that most of this was true. And so she only pitied me after all. I felt as if I'd been courting her for six months and she'd thrown me over – but I didn't know anything about women yet.

'Did you tell her I was in jail?' I growled.

'No, by gum! I forgot that. But never mind, I'll fix that up all right. I'll tell her that you got two years' hard for horse-stealing. That ought to make her interested in you, if she isn't already.'

We smoked a while.

'And was that all she said?' I asked.

'Who? – oh! Possum,' said Jack, rousing himself. 'Well, no; let me think – we got chatting of other things – you know a married man's privileged, and can say a lot more to a girl than a single man can. I got talking nonsense about sweethearts, and one thing led to another till at last she said, 'I suppose Mr Wilson's got a sweetheart, Mr Barnes?'

'And what did you say?' I growled.

'Oh, I told her that you were a holy terror amongst the girls,' said Jack. 'You'd better take back that tray, Joe, and let us get to work.'

I wouldn't take back the tray – but that didn't mend matters, for Jack took it back himself.

I didn't see Mary's reflection in the window again, so I took the window out. I reckoned that she was just a big-hearted, impulsive little thing, as many Australian girls are, and I reckoned that I was a fool for thinking for a moment that she might give me a second thought, except by way of kindness. Why! young Black and half a dozen better men than me were sweet on her, and young Black was to get his father's station and the money – or rather his mother's money, for she held the stuff (she kept it close, too, by all accounts). Young Black was away at the time, and his mother was dead against him about Mary, but that didn't make any difference, as far as I could see. I reckoned that it was only just going to be a hopeless, heart-breaking, stand-off-and-worship affair, as far as I was concerned – like my first love affair, that I haven't told you about yet. I was tired of being pitied by good girls. You see, I didn't know women then. If I had known, I think I might have made more than one mess of my life.

Jack rode home to Solong every night. I was staying at a pub some distance out of town, between Solong and Haviland. There were three or four wet days, and we didn't get on with the work. I fought shy of Mary till one day she was hanging out clothes and the line broke. It was the old-style sixpenny clothes-line. The clothes were all down, but it was clean grass, so it didn't matter much. I looked at Jack.

'Go and help her, you capital idiot!' he said, and I made the plunge.

'Oh, thank you, Mr Wilson!' said Mary, when I came to help. She had the broken end of the line, and was trying to hold some of the clothes off the ground, as if she could pull it an inch with the heavy wet sheets and table-cloths and things on it, or as if it would do any good if she did. But that's the way with women – especially little women – some of 'em would try to pull a store bullock if they got the end of the rope on the right side of the fence. I took the line from Mary and accidentally touched her soft, plump little hand as I did so: it sent a thrill right through me. She seemed a lot cooler than I was.

Now, in cases like this, especially if you lose your head a bit, you get hold of the loose end of the rope that's hanging from the post with one hand, and the end of the line with the clothes on with the other, and try to pull 'em far enough together to make a knot. And that's about all you do for the present, except look like a fool. Then I took off the post end, spliced the line, took it over the fork, and pulled, while Mary helped me with the prop. I thought Jack might have come and taken the prop from her, but he didn't; he just went on with his work as if nothing was happening inside the horizon.

She'd got the line about two-thirds full of clothes, it was a bit short now, so she had to jump and catch it with one hand and hold it down while she pegged a sheet she'd thrown over. I'd made the plunge now, so I volunteered to help her. I held down the line while she threw the things over and pegged out. As we got near the post and higher I straightened out some ends and pegged myself. Bushmen are handy at most things. We laughed, and now and again Mary would say, 'No, that's not the way, Mr Wilson; that's not right; the sheet isn't far enough over; wait till I fix it.' I'd a reckless idea once of holding her up while she pegged, and I was glad afterwards that I hadn't made such a fool of myself.

'There's only a few more things in the basket, Miss Brand,' I said. 'You can't reach – I'll fix 'em up.'

She seemed to give a little gasp.

'Oh, those things are not ready yet,' she said, 'they're not rinsed,' and she grabbed the basket and held it away from me. The things looked the same to me as the rest on the line; they looked rinsed enough and blued too. I reckoned that she didn't want me to take the trouble, or thought that I mightn't like to be seen hanging out clothes, and was only doing it out of kindness.

'Oh, it's no trouble,' I said, 'let me hang 'em out. I like it. I've hung out clothes at home on a windy day,' and I made a reach into the basket. But she flushed red, with temper, I thought, and snatched the basket away.

'Excuse me, Mr Wilson,' she said, 'but those things are not ready yet!' and she marched into the wash-house.

'Ah, well! You've got a little temper of your own,' I thought to myself.

When I told Jack, he said that I'd made another fool of myself. He said I'd both disappointed and offended her. He said that my line was to stand off a bit and be serious and melancholy in the background.

That evening when we'd started home, we stopped some time yarning with a chap we met at the gate; and I happened to look back and saw Mary hanging out the rest of the things – she thought that we were out of sight. Then I understood why those things weren't ready while we were round.

For the next day or two Mary didn't take the slightest notice of me, and I kept out of her way. Jack said I'd disillusioned her – and hurt her dignity – which was a thousand times worse. He said I'd spoilt the thing altogether. He said that she'd got an idea that I was shy and poetic, and I'd only shown myself the usual sort of bushwhacker.

I noticed her talking and chatting with other fellows once or twice, and it made me miserable. I got drunk two evenings running, and then, as it appeared afterwards, Mary consulted Jack, and at last she said to him, when we were together:

'Do you play draughts, Mr Barnes?'

'No,' said Jack.

'Do you, Mr Wilson?' she asked, suddenly turning her big bright eyes on me, and speaking to me for the first time since last washing-day.

'Yes,' I said, 'I do a little.' Then there was a silence, and I had to say something else.

'Do you play draughts, Miss Brand?' I asked.

'Yes,' she said, 'but I can't get any one to play with me here of an evening, the men are generally playing cards or reading.' Then she said, 'It's very dull these long winter evenings when you've got nothing to do. Young Mr Black used to play draughts, but he's away.'

I saw Jack winking at me urgently.

'I'll play a game with you, if you like,' I said, 'but I ain't much of a player.'

'Oh, thank you, Mr Wilson! When shall you have an evening to spare?'

We fixed it for that same evening. We got chummy over the draughts. I had a suspicion even then that it was a put-up job to keep me away from the pub.

Perhaps she found a way of giving a hint to old Black without committing herself. Women have ways – or perhaps Jack did it. Anyway, next day the boss came round and said to me:

'Look here, Joe, you've got no occasion to stay at the pub. Bring along your blankets and camp in one of the spare rooms of the old house. You can have your tucker here.'

He was a good sort, was Black the squatter: a squatter of the old school, who'd shared the early hardships with his men, and couldn't see why he should not shake hands and have a smoke and a yarn over old times with any of his old station-hands that happened to come along. But he'd married an Englishwoman after the hardships were over, and she'd never got any Australian notions.

Next day I found one of the skillion rooms scrubbed out and a bed fixed up for me. I'm not sure to this day who did it, but I suppose that good-natured old Black had given one of the women a hint. After tea I had a yarn with Mary, sitting on a log of the wood-heap. I don't remember exactly how we came to be there, or who sat down first. There was about two feet between us. We got very chummy and confidential. She told me about her childhood and her father.

He'd been an old mate of Black's, a younger son of a well-to-do English family (with blue blood in it, I believe), and sent out to Australia with a thousand pounds to make his way, as many younger sons are, with more or less. They think they're hard done by; they blue their thousand pounds in Melbourne or Sydney, and they don't make any more nowadays, for the Roarin' Days have been dead these thirty years. I wish I'd had a thousand pounds to start on!

Mary's mother was the daughter of a German immigrant, who selected up there in the old days. She had a will of her own as far as I could understand, and bossed the home till the day of her death. Mary's father made money, and lost it, and drank – and died. Mary remembered him sitting on the veranda one evening with his hand on her head, and singing a German song (the 'Lorelei,' I think it was) softly, as if to himself. Next day he stayed in bed, and the children were kept out of the room; and, when he died, the children were adopted round (there was a little money coming from England).

Mary told me all about her girlhood. She went first to live with a sort of cousin in town, in a house where they took cards in on a tray, and then she came to live with Mrs Black, who took a fancy to her at first. I'd had no boyhood to speak of, so I gave her some of my ideas on what the world ought to be, and she seemed interested.

Next day there were sheets on my bed, and I felt pretty cocky until I remembered that I'd told her I had no one to care for me; then I suspected pity again.

But the next evening we remembered that both our fathers and mothers were dead, and discovered that we had no friends except Jack and old Black, and things went on very satisfactorily.

And next day there was a little table in my room with a crocheted cover and a looking-glass.

I noticed the other girls began to act mysterious and giggle when I was round, but Mary didn't seem aware of it.

We got very chummy. Mary wasn't comfortable at Haviland. Old Black was very fond of her and always took her part, but she wanted to be independent. She had a great idea of going to Sydney and getting into the hospital as a nurse. She had friends in Sydney, but she had no money. There was a little money coming to her when she was twenty-one – a few pounds – and she was going to try and get it before that time.

'Look here, Miss Brand,' I said, after we'd watched the moon rise. 'I'll lend you the money. I've got plenty – more than I know what to do with.'

But I saw I'd hurt her. She sat up very straight for a while, looking before her; then she said it was time to go in, and said, 'Good night, Mr Wilson.'

I reckoned I'd done it that time; but Mary told me afterwards that she was only hurt because it struck her that what she said about money might have been taken for a hint. She didn't understand me yet, and I didn't know human nature. I didn't say anything to Jack – in fact about this time I left off telling him about things. He didn't seem hurt; he worked hard and seemed happy.

I really meant what I said to Mary about the money. It was pure good nature. I'd be a happier man now, I think, and a richer man perhaps, if I'd never grown more selfish than I was that night on the wood-heap with Mary. I felt a great sympathy for her – but I got to love her. I went through all the ups and downs of it. One day I was having tea in the kitchen, and Mary and another girl, named Sarah, reached me a clean plate at the same time: I took Sarah's because she was first, and Mary seemed very nasty about it, and that gave me great hopes. But all next evening she played draughts with a drover that she'd chummed up with. I pretended to be interested in Sarah's talk, but it didn't seem to work.

A few days later a Sydney jackeroo visited the station. He had a good pea-rifle, and one afternoon he started to teach Mary to shoot at a target. They seemed to get very chummy. I had a nice time for three or four days, I can tell you. I was worse than a wall-eyed bullock with the pleuro. The other chaps had a shot out of the rifle. Mary called 'Mr Wilson' to have a shot, and I made a worse fool of myself by sulking. If it hadn't been a blooming jackeroo I wouldn't have minded so much.

Next evening the jackeroo and one or two other chaps and the girls went out possum shooting. Mary went. I could have gone, but I didn't. I mooched round all the evening like an orphan bandicoot on a burnt ridge, and then I went up to the pub and filled myself up with beer, and damned the world, and came home and went to bed. I think that evening was the only time I ever wrote poetry down on a piece of paper. I got so miserable that I enjoyed it.

I felt better next morning, and reckoned I was cured. I ran against Mary accidentally, and had to say something.

'How did you enjoy yourself yesterday evening, Miss Brand?' I asked.

'Oh, very well, thank you, Mr Wilson,' she said. Then she asked, 'How did you enjoy yourself, Mr Wilson?'

I puzzled over that afterwards, but couldn't make anything out of it. Perhaps she only said it for the sake of saying something. But about this time my handkerchiefs and collars disappeared from the room and turned up washed and ironed, and laid tidily on my table. I used to keep an eye out, but could never catch anybody near my room. I straightened up, and kept my room a bit tidy, and when my handkerchief got too dirty, and I was ashamed of letting it go to the wash, I'd slip down to the river after dark and wash it out, and dry it next day, and rub it up to look as if it hadn't been washed, and leave it on my table. I felt so full of hope and joy that I worked twice as hard as Jack, till one morning he remarked casually:

'I see you've made a new mash, Joe. I saw the half-caste cook tidying up your room this morning and taking your collars and things to the wash-house.'

I felt very much off colour all the rest of the day, and I had such a bad night of it that I made up my mind next morning to look the hopelessness square in the face and live the thing down.

It was the evening before Anniversary Day. Jack and I had put in a good day's work to get the job finished, and Jack was having a smoke and a yarn with the chaps before he started home. We sat on an old log along by the fence at the back of the house. There was Jimmy Nowlett the bullock-driver, and long Dave Regan the drover, and Jim Bullock the fencer, and one or two others. Mary and the station girls and one or two visitors were sitting under the old veranda. The jackeroo was there too, so I felt happy. It was the girls who used to bring the chaps hanging round. They were getting up a dance party for Anniversary night. Along in the evening another chap came riding up to the station: he was a big shearer, a dark, handsome fellow, who looked like a gipsy; it was reckoned that there was foreign blood in him. He went by the name of Romany. He was supposed to be shook after Mary too. He had the nastiest temper and the best violin in the district, and the chaps put up with him a lot because they wanted him to play at bush dances. The moon had risen over Pine Ridge, but it was dusky where we were. We saw Romany loom up, riding in from the gate; he rode round the end of the coach-house and across towards where we were – I suppose he was going to tie up his horse at the fence; but about half-way across the grass he disappeared. It struck me that there was something peculiar about the way he got down, and I heard a sound like a horse stumbling.

'What the hell's Romany trying to do?' said Jimmy Nowlett. 'He couldn't have fell off his horse – or else he's drunk.'

A couple of chaps got up and went to see. Then there was the waiting, mysterious silence that comes when something happens in the dark, and nobody knows what it is. I went over, and the thing dawned on me. I'd stretched a wire clothes-line across there during the day and had forgotten all about it for the moment. Romany had no idea of the line and, as he rode up, it caught him on a level with his elbows, and scraped him off his horse. He was sitting on the grass, swearing in a surprised voice, and the horse looked surprised too. Romany wasn't hurt, but the sudden shock had spoilt his temper. He wanted to know who'd put up that bloody line. He came over and sat on the log. The chaps smoked for a while.

'What did you git down so sudden for, Romany?' asked Jim Bullock, presently. 'Did you hurt yerself on the pommel?'

'Why didn't you ask the horse to go round?' asked Dave Regan.

'I'd only like to know who put up that bleeding wire!' growled Romany.

'Well,' said Jimmy Nowlett, 'if we'd put up a sign to beware of the line you couldn't have seen it in the dark.'

'Unless it was a transparency with a candle behind it,' said Dave Regan. 'But why didn't you get down on one end, Romany, instead of all along? It wouldn't have jolted yer so much.'

All this with the bush drawl, and between the puffs of their pipes. But I didn't take any interest in it. I was brooding over Mary and the jackeroo.

'I've heard of men getting down over their horse's head,' said Dave presently, in a reflective sort of way – 'In fact, I've done it myself – but I never saw a man get off backwards over his horse's rump.'

But they saw that Romany was getting nasty, and they wanted him to play the fiddle next night, so they dropped it.

Mary was singing an old song. I always thought she had a sweet voice, and I'd have enjoyed it if that damned jackeroo hadn't been listening too. We listened in silence until she'd finished.

'That gal's got a nice voice,' said Jimmy Nowlett.

'Nice voice!' snarled Romany, who'd been waiting for a chance to be nasty. 'Why, I've heard a tom-cat sing better.'

I moved and Jack, he was sitting next me, nudged me to keep quiet. The chaps didn't like Romany's talk about Possum at all. They were all fond of her: she wasn't a pet or tomboy, for she wasn't built that way, but they were fond of her in such a way that they didn't like to hear anything said about her. They said nothing for a while, but it meant a lot. Perhaps the single men didn't care to speak for fear that it would be said that they were gone on Mary. But presently Jimmy Nowlett gave a big puff at his pipe and spoke:

'I suppose you got bit, too, in that quarter, Romany?'

'Oh, she tried it on, but it didn't go,' said Romany. 'I've met her sort before. She's setting her cap at that jackeroo now. Some girls will run after anything with trousers on,' and he stood up.

Jack Barnes must have felt what was coming, for he grabbed my arm, and whispered, 'Sit still, Joe, damn you! He's too good for you!' But I was on my feet and facing Romany as if a giant hand had reached down and wrenched me off the log and set me there.

'You're a damned crawler, Romany!' I said.

Little Jimmy Nowlett was between us, and the other fellows round us before a blow got home. 'Hold on, you damned fools!' they said. 'Keep quiet till we get away from the house!' There was a little clear flat down by the river, and plenty of light there, so we decided to go down there and have it out.

Now I never was a fighting man; I'd never learnt to use my hands. I scarcely knew how to put them up. Jack often wanted to teach me, but I wouldn't bother about it. He'd say, 'You'll get into a fight some day, Joe, or out of one, and shame me'; but I hadn't the patience to learn. He'd wanted me to take lessons at the station after work, but he used to get excited, and I didn't want Mary to see him knocking me about. Before he was married, Jack was always getting into fights – he generally tackled a better man and got a hiding; but he didn't seem to care so long as he made a good show – though he used to explain the thing away from a scientific point of view for weeks after. To tell the truth, I had a horror of fighting; I had a horror of being marked about the face; I think I'd sooner stand off and fight a man with revolvers than fight him with fists; and then I think I would say, last thing, 'Don't shoot me in the face!' Then again I hated the idea of hitting a man. It seemed brutal to me. I was too sensitive and sentimental, and that was what the matter was. Jack seemed very serious on it as we walked down to the river, and he couldn't help hanging out blue lights.

'Why didn't you let me teach you to use your hands?' he said. 'The only chance now is that Romany can't fight after all. If you'd waited a minute I'd have been at him.' We were a bit behind the rest, and Jack started giving me points about lefts and rights, and 'half-arms,' and that sort of thing. 'He's left-handed, and that's the worst of it,' said Jack. 'You must only make as good a show as you can, and one of us will take him on afterwards.'

But I just heard him and that was all. It was to be my first fight since I was a boy, but somehow I felt cool about it – sort of dulled. If the chaps had known all they would have set me down as a cur. I thought of that, but it didn't make any difference with me then; I knew it was a thing they couldn't understand. I knew I was reckoned pretty soft. But I knew one thing that they didn't know. I knew that it was going to be a fight to a finish, one way or the other. I had more brains and imagination than the rest put together, and I suppose that that was the real cause of most of my trouble. I kept saying to myself, 'You'll have to go through with it now, Joe, old man! It's the turning point of your life.' If I won the fight, I'd set to work and win Mary; if I lost, I'd leave the district for ever. A man thinks a lot in a flash sometimes; I used to get excited over little things, because of the very paltriness of them, but I was mostly cool in a crisis – Jack was the reverse. I looked ahead: I wouldn't be able to marry a girl who could look back and remember when her husband was beaten by another man – no matter what sort of brute the other man was.

I never in my life felt so cool about a thing. Jack kept whispering instructions, and showing with his hands, up to the last moment, but it was all lost on me.

Looking back, I think there was a bit of romance about it: Mary singing under the vines to amuse a jackeroo dude, and a coward going down to the river in the moonlight to fight for her.

It was very quiet in the little moonlit flat by the river. We took off our coats and were ready. There was no swearing or barracking. It seemed an understood thing with the men that if I went out first round Jack would fight Romany; and if Jack knocked him out somebody else would fight Jack to square matters. Jim Bullock wouldn't mind obliging for one; he was a mate of Jack's, but he didn't mind who he fought so long as it was for the sake of fair play – or 'peace and quietness,' as he said. Jim was very good-natured. He backed Romany, and of course Jack backed me.

As far as I could see, all Romany knew about fighting was to jerk one arm up in front of his face and duck his head by way of a feint, and then rush and lunge out. But he had the weight and strength and length of reach, and my first lesson was a very short one. I went down early in the round. But it did me good; the blow and the look I'd seen in Romany's eyes knocked all the sentiment out of me. Jack said nothing – he seemed to regard it as a hopeless job from the first. Next round I tried to remember some things Jack had told me, and made a better show, but I went down in the end.

I felt Jack breathing quick and trembling as he lifted me up.

'How are you, Joe?' he whispered.

'I'm all right,' I said.

'It's all right,' whispered Jack in a voice as if I was going to be hanged, but it would soon be all over. 'He can't use his hands much more than you can – take your time, Joe – try to remember something I told you, for God's sake!'

When two men fight who don't know how to use their hands, they stand a show of knocking each other about a lot. I got some awful thumps, but mostly on the body. Jimmy Nowlett began to get excited and jump around – he was an excitable little fellow.

'Fight! You —!' he yelled. 'Why don't you fight? That ain't fightin'. Fight, and don't try to murder each other. Use your crimson hands, or, by God, I'll chip you! Fight, or I'll blanky well bullock-whip the pair of you'; then his language got awful. They said we went like windmills, and that nearly every one of the blows we made was enough to kill a bullock if it had got home. Jimmy stopped us once, but they held him back.

Presently I went down pretty flat, but the blow was well up on the head, and didn't matter much – I had a good thick skull. And I had one good eye yet.

'For God's sake, hit him!' whispered Jack – he was trembling like a leaf. 'Don't mind what I told you. I wish I was fighting him myself! Get a blow home, for God's sake. Make a good show this round and I'll stop the fight.'

That showed how little even Jack, my old mate, understood me.

I had the bushman up in me now, and wasn't going to be beaten while I could think. I was wonderfully cool, and learning to fight. There's nothing like a fight to teach a man. I was thinking fast, and learning more in three seconds than Jack's sparring could have taught me in three weeks. People think that blows hurt in a fight, but they don't – not till afterwards. I fancy that a fighting man, if he isn't altogether an animal, suffers more mentally than he does physically.

While I was getting my wind I could hear through the moonlight and still air the sound of Mary's voice singing up at the house. I thought hard into the future, even as I fought. The fight only seemed something that was passing.

I was on my feet again and at it, and presently I lunged out and felt such a jar on my arm that I thought it was telescoped. I thought I'd put out my wrist and elbow. And Romany was lying on the broad of his back.

I heard Jack draw three breaths of relief in one. He said nothing as he straightened me up, but I could feel his heart beating. He said afterwards that he didn't speak because he thought a word might spoil it.

I went down again, but Jack told me afterwards that he felt I was all right when he lifted me.

Then Romany went down, then we fell together and the chaps separated us. I got another knock-down blow in, and was beginning to enjoy the novelty of it, when Romany staggered and limped.

'I've done,' he said. 'I've twisted my ankle.' He'd caught his heel against a tuft of grass.

'Shake hands,' yelled Jimmy Nowlett.

I stepped forward, but Romany took his coat, and limped to his horse.

'If yer don't shake hands with Wilson, I'll lam yer', howled Jimmy; but Jack told him to let the man alone, and Romany got on his horse somehow and rode off.

I saw Jim Bullock stoop and pick up something from the grass, and heard him swear in surprise. There was some whispering, and presently Jim said:

'If I thought that, I'd kill him.'

'What is it?' asked Jack.

Jim held up a butcher's knife. It was common for a man to carry a butcher's knife in a sheath fastened to his belt.

'Why did you let your man fight with a butcher's knife in his belt?' asked Jimmy Nowlett.

But the knife could easily have fallen out when Romany fell, and we decided it that way.

'Any way,' said Jimmy Nowlett, 'if he'd stuck Joe in hot blood before us all it wouldn't be so bad as if he sneaked up and stuck him in the back in the dark.

But you'd best keep an eye over yer shoulder for a year or two, Joe. That chap's got Eye-talian blood in him somewhere. And now the best thing you chaps can do is to keep your mouth shut and keep all this dark from the gals.'

Jack hurried me on ahead. He seemed to act queer, and when I glanced at him I could have sworn that there was water in his eyes. I said that Jack had no sentiment except for himself, but I forgot, and I'm sorry I said it.

'What's up, Jack?' I asked.

'Nothing,' said Jack.

'What's up, you old fool?' I said.

'Nothing,' said Jack, 'except that I'm damned proud of you, Joe, you old ass!' and he put his arm round my shoulders and gave me a shake. 'I didn't know it was in you, Joe – I wouldn't have said it before, or listened to any other man say it, but I didn't think you had the pluck – God's truth, I didn't. Come along and get your face fixed up.'

We got into my room quietly, and Jack got a dish of water, and told one of the chaps to sneak a piece of fresh beef from somewhere.

Jack was as proud as a dog with a tin tail as he fussed around me. He fixed up my face in the best style he knew, and he knew a good many – he'd been mended himself so often.

While he was at work we heard a sudden hush and a scraping of feet amongst the chaps that Jack had kicked out of the room, and a girl's voice whispered. 'Is he hurt? Tell me. I want to know – I might be able to help.'

It made my heart jump, I can tell you. Jack went out at once, and there was some whispering. When he came back he seemed wild.

'What is it, Jack?' I said.

'Oh, nothing,' he said, 'only that damned slut of a half-caste cook overheard some of those blanky fools arguing as to how Romany's knife got out of the sheath, and she's put a nice yarn round amongst the girls. There's a regular bobbery, but it's all right now, Jimmy Nowlett's telling 'em lies at a great rate.'

Presently there was another hush outside, and a saucer with vinegar and brown paper was handed in.

One of the chaps brought some beer and whisky from the pub, and we had a quiet little time in my room. Jack wanted to stay all night, but I reminded him that his little wife was waiting for him in Solong, so he said he'd be round early in the morning, and went home.

I felt the reaction pretty bad. I didn't feel proud of the affair at all. I thought it was a low brutal business all round. Romany was a quiet chap after all, and the chaps had no right to chyack him. Perhaps he'd had a hard life, and carried a big swag of trouble that we didn't know anything about. He seemed a lonely man. I'd gone through enough myself to reach me not to judge men. I made up my mind to tell him how I felt about the matter next time we met. Perhaps I made my usual mistake of bothering about 'feelings' in another party that hadn't any feelings at all – perhaps I didn't; but it's generally best to chance it on the kind side in a case like this. Altogether I felt as if I'd made another fool of myself, and been a weak coward. I drank the rest of the beer and went to sleep.

About daylight I woke and heard Jack's horse on the gravel. He came round the back of the buggy-shed and up to my door, and then, suddenly, a girl screamed out. I pulled on my trousers and 'lastic-side boots and hurried out. It was Mary herself, dressed, and sitting on an old stone step at the back of the kitchen with her face in her hands, and Jack was off his horse and stooping by her side with his hand on her shoulder. She kept saying, 'I thought you were —!' I didn't catch the name. An old single-barrel muzzle-loader shot-gun was lying in the grass at her feet. It was the gun they used to keep loaded and hanging in straps in a room off the kitchen ready for a shot at a cunning old hawk that they called "Tarnal Death,' and that used to be always after the chickens.

When Mary lifted her face it was as white as notepaper and her eyes seemed to grow wilder when she caught sight of me.

'Oh, you did frighten me, Mr Barnes,' she gasped. Then she gave a little ghost of a laugh and stood up, and some colour came back.

'Oh, I'm a little fool!' she said quickly. 'I thought I heard old 'Tarnal Death at the chickens, and I thought it would be a great thing if I got the gun and brought him down; so I got up and dressed quietly so as not to wake Sarah. And then you came round the corner and frightened me. I don't know what you must think of me, Mr Barnes.'

'Never mind,' said Jack. 'You go and have a sleep, or you won't be able to dance tonight. Never mind the gun – I'll put that away.' And he steered her round to the door of her room off the brick veranda where she slept with one of the other girls.

'Well, that's a rum start!' I said.

'Yes, it is,' said Jack; 'it's very funny. Well, how's your face this morning, Joe?' He seemed a lot more serious than usual.

We were hard at work all the morning cleaning out the big wool-shed and getting it ready for the dance, hanging hoops for the candles, and making seats. I kept out of sight of the girls as much as I could. One side of my face was a sight, and the other wasn't too classical. I felt as if I had been stung by a swarm of bees.

'You're a fresh, sweet-scented beauty now, and no mistake, Joe,' said Jimmy Nowlett – he was going to play the accordion that night.

'You ought to fetch the girls now, Joe. But never mind, your face'll go down in about three weeks. My lower jaw is crooked yet; but that fight straightened my nose, that had been knocked crooked when I was a boy – so I didn't lose much beauty by it.'

When we'd done in the shed, Jack took me aside and said:

'Look here, Joe; if you won't come to the dance tonight – and I can't say you'd ornament it – I tell you what you'll do. You get little Mary away on the quiet and take her out for a stroll – and act like a man. The job's finished now, and you won't get another chance like this.'

'But how am I to get her out?' I said.

'Never you mind. You be mooching round down by the big peppermint-tree near the river-gate, say about half-past ten.'

'What good'll that do?'

'Never you mind. You just do as you're told, that's all you've got to do,' said Jack, and he went home to get dressed and bring his wife.

After the dancing started that night I had a peep in once or twice. The first time I saw Mary dancing with Jack, and looking serious; and the second time she was dancing with the blarsted jackeroo dude, and looking excited and happy. I noticed that some of the girls, that I could see sitting on a stool along the opposite wall, whispered, and gave Mary black looks as the jackeroo swung her past. It struck me pretty forcibly that I should have taken fighting lessons from him instead of from poor Romany. I went away and walked about four miles down the river road, getting out of the way into the bush whenever I saw any chap riding along. I thought of poor Romany and wondered where he was, and thought that there wasn't much to choose between us as far as happiness was concerned. Perhaps he was walking by himself in the bush, and feeling like I did. I wished I could shake hands with him.

But somehow, about half-past ten, I drifted back to the river sliprails, and leant over them in the shadow of the peppermint-tree, looking at the rows of river-willows in the moonlight. I didn't expect anything, in spite of what Jack said.

I didn't like the idea of hanging myself: I'd been with a party who found a man hanging in the bush, and it was no place for a woman round where he was. And I'd helped drag two bodies out of the Cudgegong River in a flood, and they weren't sleeping beauties. I thought it was a pity that a chap couldn't lie down on a grassy bank in a graceful position in the moonlight, and die just by thinking of it – and die with his eyes and mouth shut. But then I remembered that I wouldn't make a beautiful corpse anyway it went, with the face I had on me.

I was just getting comfortably miserable when I heard a step behind me, and my heart gave a jump. And I gave a start, too.

'Oh, is that you, Mr Wilson?' said a timid little voice.

'Yes,' I said. 'Is that you, Mary?'

And she said yes. It was the first time I called her Mary, but she did not seem to notice it.

'Did I frighten you?' I asked.

'No – yes – just a little,' she said. 'I didn't know there was any one —' then she stopped.

'Why aren't you dancing?' I asked her.'

'Oh, I'm tired,' she said. 'It was too hot in the wool-shed. I thought I'd like to come out, and get my head cool, and be quiet a little while.'

'Yes,' I said. 'It must be hot in the wool-shed.'

She stood looking out over the willows. Presently she said: 'It must be very dull for you, Mr Wilson – you must feel lonely. Mr Barnes said —' Then she gave a little gasp and stopped – as if she was just going to put her foot in it.

'How beautiful the moonlight looks on the willows!' she said.

'Yes,' I said, 'doesn't it? Supposing we have a stroll by the river.'

'Oh, thank you, Mr Wilson. I'd like it very much.'

I didn't notice it then, but, now I come to think of it, it was a beautiful scene: there was a horse-shoe of high blue hills round behind the house, with the river running round under the slopes, and in front was a rounded hill covered with pines, and pine ridges, and a soft blue peak away over the ridges, ever so far in the distance.

I had a handkerchief over the worst of my face, and kept the best side turned to her. We walked down by the river, and didn't say anything for a good while. I was thinking hard. We came to a white smooth log in a quiet place out of sight of the house.

'Suppose we sit down for a while, Mary,' I said.

'If you like, Mr Wilson,' she said.

There was about a foot of log between us.

'What a beautiful night!' she said.

'Yes,' I said, 'isn't it?'

Presently she said, 'I suppose you know I'm going away next month, Mr Wilson?'

I felt suddenly empty. 'No,' I said, 'I didn't know that.'

'Yes,' she said, 'I thought you knew. I'm going to try to get into the hospital to be trained for a nurse, and if that doesn't come off I'll get a place as assistant public-school teacher.'

We didn't say anything for a good while.

'I suppose you won't be sorry to go, Miss Brand?' I said.

'I – I don't know,' she said. 'Everybody's been so kind to me here.'

She sat looking straight before her, and I fancied her eyes glistened. I put my arm round her shoulders, but she didn't seem to notice it. In fact, I scarcely noticed it myself at the time.

'So you think you'll be sorry to go away?' I said.

'Yes, Mr Wilson. I suppose I'll fret for a while. It's been my home, you know.'

I pressed my hand on her shoulder, just a little, so she couldn't pretend not to know it was there. But she didn't seem to notice.

'Ah, well,' I said, 'I suppose I'll be on the wallaby again next week.'

'Will you, Mr Wilson?' she said. Her voice seemed very soft.

I slipped my arm round her waist, under her arm. My heart was going like clockwork now.

Presently she said:

'Don't you think it's time to go back now, Mr Wilson?'

'Oh, there's plenty of time!' I said. I shifted up, and put my arm further round, and held her closer. She sat straight up, looking right in front of her, but she began to breathe hard.

'Mary,' I said.

'Yes,' she said.

'Call me Joe,' I said.

'I – I don't like to,' she said. 'I don't think it would be right.'

So I just turned her face round and kissed her. She clung to me and cried.

'What is it, Mary?' I said.

She only held me tighter and cried.

'What is it, Mary?' I said. 'Ain't you well? Ain't you happy?'

'Yes, Joe,' she said, 'I'm very happy.' Then she said, 'Oh, your poor face! Can't I do anything for it?'

'No,' I said. 'That's all right. My face doesn't hurt me a bit now.'

But she didn't seem right.

'What is it, Mary?' I said. 'Are you tired? You didn't sleep last night —' Then I got an inspiration.

'Mary,' I said, 'what were you doing out with the gun this morning?'

And after some coaxing it all came out a bit hysterical.

'I couldn't sleep – I was frightened. Oh! I had such a terrible dream about you, Joe! I thought Romany came back and got into your room and stabbed you with his knife. I got up and dressed, and about daybreak I heard a horse at the gate; then I got the gun down from the wall – and – and Mr Barnes came round the corner and frightened me. He's something like Romany, you know.'

Then I got as much of her as I could into my arms.

And, oh, but wasn't I happy walking home with Mary that night! She was too little for me to put my arm round her waist, so I put it round her shoulder, and that felt just as good. I remember I asked her who'd cleaned up my room and washed my things, but she wouldn't tell.

She wouldn't go back to the dance yet; she said she'd go into her room and rest a while. There was no one near the old veranda; and when she stood on the end of the floor she was just on a level with my shoulder.

'Mary,' I whispered, 'put your arms round my neck and kiss me.'

She put her arms round my neck, but she didn't kiss me; she only hid her face.

'Kiss me, Mary!' I said.

'I – I don't like to,' she whispered.

'Why not, Mary?'

Then I felt her crying or laughing, or half-crying and half-laughing. I'm not sure to this day which it was.

'Why won't you kiss me, Mary? Don't you love me?'

'Because,' she said, 'because – because I – I don't – I don't think it's right for – for a girl to – to kiss a man unless she's going to be his wife.'

Then it dawned on me! I'd forgot all about proposing.

'Mary,' I said, 'would you marry a chap like me?'

And that was all right.

Next morning Mary cleared out my room and sorted out my things, and didn't take the slightest notice of the other girls' astonishment.

But she made me promise to speak to old Black, and I did the same evening. I found him sitting on the log by the fence, having a yarn on the quiet with an old bushman; and when the old bushman got up and went away, I sat down.

'Well, Joe,' said Black, 'I see somebody's been spoiling your face for the dance.' And after a bit he said, 'Well, Joe, what is it? Do you want another job? If you do, you'll have to ask Mrs Black, or Bob' (Bob was his eldest son); 'they're managing the station for me now, you know.' He could be bitter sometimes in his quiet way.

'No,' I said; 'it's not that, boss.'

'Well, what is it, Joe?'

'I – well, the fact is, I want little Mary.'

He puffed at his pipe for a long time, then I thought he spoke.

'What did you say, boss?' I said.

'Nothing, Joe,' he said. 'I was going to say a lot, but it wouldn't be any use. My father used to say a lot to me before I was married.'

I waited a good while for him to speak.

'Well, boss,' I said, 'what about Mary?'

'Oh! I suppose that's all right, Joe,' he said. 'I – I beg your pardon. I got thinking of the days when I was courting Mrs Black.'

BRIGHTEN'S SISTER-IN-LAW

JIM WAS BORN on Gulgong, New South Wales. We used to say 'on' Gulgong – and old diggers still talked of being 'on th' Gulgong' – though the goldfield there had been worked out for years, and the place was only a dusty little pastoral town in the scrubs. Gulgong was about the last of the great alluvial 'rushes' of the 'roaring days' – and dreary and dismal enough it looked when I was there. The expression 'on' came from being on the 'diggings' or goldfield – the workings or the goldfield was all underneath, of course, so we lived (or starved) on them – not in nor at 'em.

Mary and I had been married about two years when Jim came. His name wasn't 'Jim,' by the way, it was 'John Henry,' after an uncle godfather; but we called him Jim from the first – (and before it) – because Jim was a popular bush name, and most of my old mates were Jims. The bush is full of good-hearted scamps called Jim.

We lived in an old weather-board shanty that had been a sly-grog shop, and the Lord knows what else! in the palmy days of Gulgong; and I did a bit of digging ('fossicking,' rather), a bit of shearing, a bit of fencing, a bit of bush-carpentering, tank-sinking – anything, just to keep the billy boiling.

We had a lot of trouble with Jim with his teeth. He was bad with every one of them, and we had most of them lanced – couldn't pull him through without. I remember we got one lanced and the gum healed over before the tooth came through, and we had to get it cut again. He was a plucky little chap, and after the first time he never whimpered when the doctor was lancing his gum: he used to say 'tar' afterwards, and want to bring the lance home with him.

The first turn we got with Jim was the worst. I had had the wife and Jim camping with me in a tent at a dam I was making at Cattle Creek; I had two men working for me, and a boy to drive one of the tip-drays, and I took Mary out to cook for us. And it was lucky for us that the contract was finished and we got back to Gulgong, and within reach of a doctor, the day we did. We were just camping in the house, with our goods and chattels anyhow, for the night; and we were hardly back home an hour when Jim took convulsions for the first time.

Did you ever see a child in convulsions? You wouldn't want to see it again: it plays the devil with a man's nerves. I'd got the beds fixed up on the floor and the billies on the fire – I was going to make some tea, and put a piece of corned beef on to boil overnight – when Jim (he'd been queer all day, and his mother was trying to hush him to sleep) – Jim, he screamed out twice. He'd been crying a good deal, and I was dog-tired and worried (over some money a man owed me) or I'd have noticed at once that there was something unusual in the way the child cried out: as it was I didn't turn round till Mary screamed 'Joe! Joe!' You know how a woman cries out when her child is in danger or dying – short, and sharp, and terrible. 'Joe! Look! look! Oh my God, our child! Get the bath, quick! Quick! it's convulsions!'

Jim was bent back like a bow, stiff as a bullock-yoke, in his mother's arms, and his eyeballs were turned up and fixed – a thing I saw twice afterwards and don't want ever to see again.

I was falling over things getting the tub and the hot water, when the woman who lived next door rushed in. She called to her husband to run for the doctor, and before the doctor came she and Mary had got Jim into a hot bath and pulled him through.

The neighbour woman made me up a shake-down in another room, and stayed with Mary that night; but it was a long while before I got Jim and Mary's screams out of my head and fell asleep.

You may depend I kept the fire in, and a bucket of water hot over it for a good many nights after that; but (it always happens like this) there came a night, when the fright had worn off, when I was too tired to bother about the fire, and that night Jim took us by surprise. Our wood-heap was done, and I broke up a new chair to get a fire, and had to run a quarter of a mile for water; but this turn wasn't so bad as the first, and we pulled him through.

You never saw a child in convulsions? Well, you don't want to. It must be only a matter of seconds, but it seems long minutes; and half an hour afterwards the child might be laughing and playing with you, or stretched out dead. It shook me up a lot. I was always pretty high-strung and sensitive. After Jim took the first fit, every time he cried, or turned over, or stretched out in the night, I'd jump: I was always feeling his forehead in the dark to see if he was feverish, or feeling his limbs to see if he was 'limp' yet. Mary and I often laughed about it – afterwards. I tried sleeping in another room, but for nights after Jim's first attack I'd just be dozing off into a sound sleep, when I'd hear him scream, as plain as could be, and I'd hear Mary cry, 'Joe! – Joe!' – short, sharp, and terrible – and I'd be up and into their room like a shot, only to find them sleeping peacefully. Then I'd feel Jim's head and his breathing for signs of convulsions, see to the fire and water, and go back to bed and try to sleep. For the first few nights I was like that all night, and I'd feel relieved when daylight came. I'd be in first thing to see if they were all right; then I'd sleep till dinner-time if it was Sunday or I had no work. But then I was run down about that time: I was worried about some money for a wool-shed I put up and never got paid for; and besides, I'd been pretty wild before I met Mary.

I was fighting hard then – struggling for something better. Both Mary and I were born to better things, and that's what made the life so hard for us.

Jim got on all right for a while: we used to watch him well, and have his teeth lanced in time.

It used to hurt and worry me to see how – just as he was getting fat and rosy and like a natural happy child, and I'd feel proud to take him out – a tooth would come along, and he'd get thin and white and pale and bigger-eyed and old-fashioned. We'd say, 'He'll be safe when he gets his eye-teeth;' but he didn't get them till he was two; then, 'He'll be safe when he gets his two-year-old teeth;' they didn't come till he was going on for three.

He was a wonderful little chap – Yes, I know all about parents thinking that their child is the best in the world. If your boy is small for his age, friends will say that small children make big men; that he's a very bright, intelligent child, and that it's better to have a bright, intelligent child than a big, sleepy lump of fat. And if your boy is dull and sleepy, they say that the dullest boys make the cleverest men – and all the rest of it. I never took any notice of that sort of chatter – took it for what it was worth; but, all the same, I don't think I ever saw such a child as Jim was when he turned two. He was everybody's favourite. They spoilt him rather. I had my own ideas about bringing up a child. I reckoned Mary was too soft with Jim. She'd say, 'Put that' (whatever it was) 'out of Jim's reach, will you, Joe?' and I'd say, 'No! leave it there, and make him understand he's not to have it. Make him have his meals without any nonsense and go to bed at a regular hour,' I'd say. Mary and I had many a breeze over Jim. She'd say that I forgot he was only a baby: but I held that a baby could be trained from the first week; and I believe I was right.

But, after all, what are you to do? You'll see a boy that was brought up strict turn out a scamp; and another that was dragged up anyhow (by the hair of the head, as the saying is) turn out well. Then, again, when a child is delicate – and you might lose him any day – you don't like to spank him, though he might be turning out a little fiend, as delicate children often do. Suppose you gave a child a hammering, and the same night he took convulsions, or something, and died – how'd you feel about it? You never know what a child is going to take, any more than you can tell what some women are going to say or do.

I was very fond of Jim, and we were great chums. Sometimes I'd sit and wonder what the deuce he was thinking about, and often, the way he talked, he'd make me uneasy. When he was two he wanted a pipe above all things, and I'd get him a clean new clay and he'd sit by my side, on the edge of the veranda, or on a log of the wood-heap, in the cool of the evening, and suck away at his pipe, and try to spit when he saw me do it. He seemed to understand that a cold empty pipe wasn't quite the thing, yet to have the sense to know that he couldn't smoke tobacco yet: he made the best he could of things. And if he broke a clay pipe he wouldn't have a new one, and there'd be a row; the old one had to be mended up, somehow, with string or wire. If I got my hair cut, he'd want his cut too; and it always troubled him to see me shave – as if he thought there must be something wrong somewhere, else he ought to have to be shaved too. I lathered him one day, and pretended to shave him: he sat through it as solemn as an owl, but didn't seem to appreciate it – perhaps he had sense enough to know that it couldn't possibly be the real thing. He felt his face, looked very hard at the lather I scraped off, and whimpered, 'No blood, daddy!'

I used to cut myself a good deal: I was always impatient over shaving.

Then he went in to interview his mother about it. She understood his lingo better than I did.

But I wasn't always at ease with him. Sometimes he'd sit looking into the fire, with his head on one side, and I'd watch him and wonder what he was thinking about (I might as well have wondered what a Chinaman was thinking about) till he seemed at least twenty years older than me: sometimes, when I moved or spoke, he'd glance round just as if to see what that old fool of a dadda of his was doing now.

I used to have a fancy that there was something Eastern, or Asiatic – something older than our civilisation or religion – about old-fashioned children. Once I started to explain my idea to a woman I thought would understand – and as it happened she had an old-fashioned child, with very slant eyes – a little tartar he was too. I suppose it was the sight of him that unconsciously reminded me of my infernal theory, and set me off on it, without warning me. Anyhow it got me mixed up in an awful row with the woman and her husband – and all their tribe. It wasn't an easy thing to explain myself out of it, and the row hasn't been fixed up yet. There were some Chinamen in the district.

I took a good-sized fencing contract, the frontage of a ten-mile paddock, near Gulgong, and did well out of it. The railway had got as far as the Cudgegong River – some twenty miles from Gulgong and two hundred from the coast – and 'carrying' was good then. I had a couple of draught-horses, that I worked in the tip-drays when I was tank-sinking, and one or two others running in the bush. I bought a broken-down wagon cheap, tinkered it up myself – christened it 'The Same Old Thing' – and started carrying from the railway terminus through Gulgong and along the bush roads and tracks that branch out fanlike through the scrubs to the one-pub towns and sheep and cattle stations out there in the howling wilderness. It wasn't much of a team. There were the two heavy horses for 'shafters;' a stunted colt, that I'd bought out of the pound for thirty shillings; a light, spring-cart horse; an old grey mare, with points like a big red-and-white Australian store bullock, and with the grit of an old washerwoman to work; and a horse that had spanked along in Cobb & Co's mail-coach in his time. I had a couple there that didn't belong to me: I worked them for the feeding of them in the dry weather. And I had all sorts of harness, that I mended and fixed up myself. It was a mixed team, but I took light stuff, got through pretty quick, and freight rates were high. So I got along.

Before this, whenever I made a few pounds I'd sink a shaft somewhere, prospecting for gold; but Mary never let me rest till she had talked me out of that.

I made up my mind to take on a small selection farm – that an old mate of mine had fenced in and cleared, and afterwards chucked up – about thirty miles out west of Gulgong, at a placed called Lahey's Creek. (The places were all called Lahey's Creek, or Spicer's Flat, or Murphy's Flat, or Ryan's Crossing, or some such name – round there.) I reckoned I'd have a run for the horses and be able to grow a bit of feed. I always had a dread of taking Mary and the children too far away from a doctor – or a good woman neighbour; but there were some people came to live on Lahey's Creek, and besides, there was a young brother of Mary's – a young scamp (his name was Jim, too, and we called him 'Jimmy' at first to make room for our Jim – he hated the name 'Jimmy' or James). He came to live with us – without asking – and I thought he'd find enough work at Lahey's Creek to keep him out of mischief. He wasn't to be depended on much – he thought nothing of riding off, five hundred miles or so, 'to have a look at the country' – but he was fond of Mary, and he'd stay by her till I got someone else to keep her company while I was on the road. He would be a protection against 'sundowners' or any shearers who happened to wander that way in the 'd.t's' after a spree. Mary had a married sister come to live at Gulgong just before we left, and nothing would suit her and her husband but we must leave little Jim with them for a month or so – till we got settled down at Lahey's Creek. They were newly married.

Mary was to have driven into Gulgong, in the spring-cart, at the end of the month, and taken Jim home; but when the time came she wasn't too well – and besides, the tyres of the cart were loose, and I hadn't time to get them cut, so we let Jim's time run on a week or so longer, till I happened to come out through Gulgong from the river with a small load of flour for Lahey's Creek way. The roads were good, the weather grand – no chance of it raining, and I had a spare tarpaulin if it did – I would only camp out one night; so I decided to take Jim home with me.

Jim was turning three then, and he was a cure. He was so old-fashioned that he used to frighten me sometimes – I'd almost think that there was something supernatural about him; though of course, I never took any notice of that rot about some children being too old-fashioned to live. There's always the ghoulish old hag (and some not so old nor haggish either) who'll come round and shake up young parents with such croaks as, 'You'll never rear that child –

he's toobright for his age.' To the devil with them!
I say.

But I really thought that Jim was too intelligent for his age, and I often told
Mary that he ought to be kept back, and not let talk too much to old diggers and
long lanky jokers of bushmen who rode in and hung their horses outside my
place on Sunday afternoons.

I don't believe in parents talking about their own children everlastingly – you
get sick of hearing them; and their kids are generally little devils, and turn out
larrikins as likely as not.

But, for all that, I really think that Jim, when he was three years old, was the
most wonderful little chap, in every way, that I ever saw.

For the first hour or so, along the road, he was telling me all about his
adventures at his auntie's.

'But they spoilt me too much, dad,' he said, as solemn as a native bear. 'An'
besides, a boy ought to stick to his parrans!'

I was taking out a cattle-pup for a drover I knew, and the pup took up a good
deal of Jim's time.

Sometimes he'd jolt me the way he talked; and other times I'd have to turn
away my head and cough, or shout at the horses, to keep from laughing outright.
And once, when I was taken that way, he said:

'What are you jerking your shoulders and coughing, and grunting, and going
on that way for, dad? Why don't you tell me something?'

'Tell you what, Jim?'

'Tell me some talk.'

So I told him all the talk I could think of. And I had to brighten up, I can tell
you, and not draw too much on my imagination – for Jim was a terror at
cross-examination when the fit took him; and he didn't think twice about telling
you when he thought you were talking nonsense. Once he said:

'I'm glad you took me home with you, dad. You'll get to know Jim.'

'What!' I said.

'You'll get to know Jim.'

'But don't I know you already?'

'No, you don't. You never has time to know Jim at home.'

And, looking back, I saw that it was cruel true. I had known in my heart all
along that this was the truth; but it came to me like a blow from Jim. You see, it
had been a hard struggle for the last year or so; and when I was home for a day
or two I was generally too busy, or too tired and worried, or full of schemes for
the future to take much notice of Jim. Mary used to speak to me about it,
sometimes. 'You never take notice of the child,' she'd say. 'You could surely find
a few minutes of an evening. What's the use of always worrying and brooding?

Your brain will go with a snap some day, and, if you get over it, it will teach you a lesson. You'll be an old man, and Jim a young one, before you realise that you had a child once. Then it will be too late.'

This sort of talk from Mary always bored me and made me impatient with her, because I knew it all too well. I never worried for myself – only for Mary and the children. And often, as the days went by, I said to myself, 'I'll take more notice of Jim and give Mary more of my time, just as soon as I can see things clear ahead a bit.' And the hard days went on, and the weeks, and the months, and the years. Ah, well!

Mary used to say, when things would get worse, 'Why don't you talk to me, Joe? Why don't you tell me your thoughts, instead of shutting yourself up in yourself and brooding – eating your heart out? It's hard for me: I get to think you're tired of me, and selfish. I might be cross and speak sharp to you when you are in trouble. How am I to know, if you don't tell me?'

But I didn't think she'd understand.

And so, getting acquainted, and chumming and dozing, with the gums closing over our heads here and there, and the ragged patches of sunlight and shade passing up, over the horses, over us, on the front of the load, over the load, and down on to the white, dusty road again – Jim and I got along the lonely bush road and over the ridges some fifteen miles before sunset, and camped at Ryan's Crossing on Sandy Creek for the night. I got the horses out and took the harness off. Jim wanted badly to help me, but I made him stay on the load; for one of the horses – a vicious, red-eyed chestnut – was a kicker: he'd broken a man's leg. I got the feed-bags stretched across the shafts, and the chaff and corn into them; and there stood the horses all round with their rumps north, south, and west, and their heads between the shafts, munching and switching their tails. We use double shafts, you know, for horse-teams – two pairs side by side – and prop them up, and stretch bags between them, letting the bags sag to serve as feed boxes. I threw the spare tarpaulin over the wheels on one side, letting about half of it lie on the ground in case of damp, and so making a floor and a breakwind. I threw down bags and the blankets and possum rug against the wheel to make a camp for Jim and the cattle-pup, and got a gin-case we used for a tucker-box, the frying-pan and billy down, and made a good fire at a log close handy, and soon everything was comfortable. Ryan's Crossing was a grand camp. I stood with my pipe in my mouth, my hands behind my back, and my back to the fire, and took the country in.

Reedy Creek came down along a western spur of the range: the banks here were deep and green, and the water ran clear over the granite bars, boulders, and gravel. Behind us was a dreary flat covered with those gnarled, grey-barked, dry-rotted 'native apple-trees' (about as much like apple-trees as the native bear is like any other), and a nasty bit of sandy-dusty road that I was always glad to get over in wet weather. To the left on our side of the creek were reedy marshes, with frogs croaking, and across the creek the dark box-scrub-covered ridges ended in steep 'sidings' coming down to the creek-bank, and to the main road that skirted them, running on west up over a 'saddle' in the ridges and on towards Dubbo. The road by Lahey's Creek to a place called Cobborah branched off, through dreary apple-tree and stringy-bark flats to the left, just beyond the crossing: all these fanlike branch tracks from the Cudgegong were inside a big horse-shoe in the Great Western Line, and so they gave small carriers a chance, now that Cobb & Co's coaches and the big teams and vans had shifted out of the main western terminus. There were tall she-oaks all along the creek and a clump of big ones over a deep waterhole just above the crossing. The creek oaks have rough barked trunks, like English elms, but are much taller and higher to the branches – and the leaves are reedy; Kendall, the Australian poet, calls them the 'she-oak harps Aeolian.' Those trees are always sigh-sigh-sighing – more of a sigh than a sough or the 'whoosh' of gum-trees in the wind. You always hear them sighing, even when you can't feel any wind. It's the same with telegraph wires: put your head against a telegraph-post on a dead, still day, and you'll hear and feel the far-away roar of the wires. But then the oaks are not connected with the distance, where there might be wind; and they don't roar in a gale, only sigh louder and softer according to the wind, and never seem to go above or below a certain pitch – like a big harp with all the strings the same. I used to have a theory that those creek oaks got the wind's voice telephoned to them, so to speak, through the ground.

I happened to look round and there was Jim (I thought he was on the tarpaulin playing with the pup): he was standing close beside me with his legs wide apart, his hands behind his back, and his back to the fire.

He held his head a little on one side, and there was such an old, old, wise expression in his big brown eyes – just as if he'd been a child for a hundred years or so, or as though he were listening to those oaks, and understanding them in a fatherly sort of way.

'Dad!' he said presently – 'Dad! Do you think I'll ever grow up to be a man?'

'Wh – why, Jim?' I gasped.

'Because I don't want to.'

I couldn't think of anything against this. It made me uneasy. But I remember I used to have a childish dread of growing up to be a man.

'Jim,' I said, to break the silence, 'do you hear what the she-oaks say?'

'No, I don't. Is they talking?'

'Yes,' I said, without thinking.

'What is they saying?' he asked.

I took the bucket and went down to the creek for some water for tea. I thought Jim would follow with a little tin billy he had, but he didn't: when I got back to the fire he was again on the possum rug, comforting the pup. I fried some bacon and eggs that I'd brought out with me. Jim sang out from the wagon:

'Don't cook too much, dad – I mightn't be hungry.'

I got the tin plates, and pint-pots and things out on a clean new flour-bag, in honour of Jim, and dished up. He was leaning back on the rug looking at the pup in a listless sort of way. I reckoned he was tired out, and pulled the gin-case up close to him for a table and put his plate on it. But he only tried a mouthful or two, and then he said:

'I ain't hungry, dad! You'll have to eat it all.'

It made me uneasy – I never liked to see a child of mine turn from his food. They had given him some tinned salmon in Gulgong, and I was afraid that that was upsetting him. I was always against tinned muck.

'Sick, Jim?' I asked.

'No, dad, I ain't sick; I don't know what's the matter with me.'

'Have some tea, sonny?'

'Yes, dad.'

I gave him some tea, with some milk in it that I'd brought in a bottle from his aunt's for him. He took a sip or two and then put the pint-pot on the gin-case.

'Jim's tired, dad,' he said.

I made him lie down while I fixed up a camp for the night. It had turned a bit chilly, so I let the big tarpaulin down all round – it was made to cover a high load, the flour in the wagon didn't come above the rail, so the tarpaulin came down well on to the ground. I fixed Jim up a comfortable bed under the tail-end of the wagon: when I went to lift him in he was lying back, looking up at the stars in a half-dreamy, half-fascinated way that I didn't like. Whenever Jim was extra old-fashioned, or affectionate, there was danger.

'How do you feel now, sonny?'

It seemed a minute before he heard me and turned from the stars.

'Jim's better, dad.' Then he said something like, 'The stars are looking at me.' I thought he was half asleep. I took off his jacket and boots and carried him in under the wagon and made him comfortable for the night.

'Kiss me 'night-night, daddy,' he said.

I'd rather he hadn't asked me – it was a bad sign. As I was going to the fire he called me back.

'What is it, Jim?'

'Get me my things and the cattle-pup, please, daddy.'

I was scared now. His things were some toys and rubbish he'd brought from Gulgong, and I remembered, the last time he had convulsions, he took all his toys and a kitten to bed with him. And "night-night' and 'daddy' were two-year-old language to Jim. I'd thought he'd forgotten those words – he seemed to be going back.

'Are you quite warm enough, Jim?'

'Yes, dad.'

I started to walk up and down – I always did this when I was extra worried.

I was frightened now about Jim, though I tried to hide the fact from myself. Presently he called again. 'What is it, Jim?'

'Take the blankets off me, fahver – Jim's sick!' (They'd been teaching him to say father.)

I was scared now. I remembered a neighbour of ours had a little girl die (she swallowed a pin), and when she was going she said:

'Take the blankets off me, muvver – I'm dying.'

And I couldn't get that out of my head.

I threw back a fold of the possum rug, and felt Jim's head – he seemed cool enough.

'Where do you feel bad, sonny?'

No answer for a while; then he said suddenly, but in a voice as if he were talking in his sleep:

'Put my boots on, please, daddy. I want to go home to muvver!'

I held his hand, and comforted him for a while; then he slept – in a restless, feverish sort of way.

I got the bucket I used for water for the horses and stood it over the fire; I ran to the creek with the big kerosene-tin bucket and got it full of cold water and stood it handy. I got the spade (we always carried one to dig wheels out of bogs in wet weather) and turned a corner of the tarpaulin back, dug a hole, and trod the tarpaulin down into the hole to serve for a bath, in case of the worst. I had a tin of mustard, and meant to fight a good round for Jim, if death came along.

I stooped in under the tail-board of the wagon and felt Jim. His head was burning hot, and his skin parched and dry as a bone.

Then I lost nerve and started blundering backward and forward between the wagon and the fire, and repeating what I'd heard Mary say the last time we fought for Jim: 'God! don't take my child! God! don't take my boy!' I'd never had much faith in doctors, but, my God! I wanted one then. The nearest was fifteen miles away.

I threw back my head and stared up at the branches in desperation; and – well, I don't ask you to take much stock in this, though most old bushmen will believe anything of the bush by night; and – now, it might have been that I was unstrung, or it might have been a patch of the sky outlined in the gently moving branches, or the blue smoke rising up. But I saw the figure of a woman, all white, come down, down, nearly to the limbs of the trees, point on up the main road, and then float up and up and vanish, still pointing. I thought Mary was dead! Then it flashed on me.

Four or five miles up the road, over the 'saddle,' was an old shanty that had been a half-way inn before the Great Western Line got round as far as Dubbo, and took the coach traffic off those old bush roads. A man named Brighten lived there. He was a selector; did a little farming, and as much sly-grog selling as he could. He was married – but it wasn't that: I'd thought of them, but she was a childish, worn-out, spiritless woman, and both were pretty 'ratty' from hardship and loneliness – they weren't likely to be of any use to me. But it was this: I'd heard talk, among some women in Gulgong, of a sister of Brighten's wife who'd gone out to live with them lately: she'd been a hospital matron in the city, they said; and there were yarns about her. Some said she got the sack for exposing the doctors – carrying on with them – I didn't remember which. The fact of a city woman going out to live in such a place, with such people, was enough to make talk among women in a town twenty miles away, but then there must have been something extra about her, else bushmen wouldn't have talked and carried her name so far; and I wanted a woman out of the ordinary now. I even reasoned this way, thinking like lightning, as I knelt over Jim between the big back wheels of the wagon.

I had an old racing mare that I used as a riding hack, following the team. In a minute I had her saddled and bridled; I tied the end of a half-full chaff-bag, shook the chaff into each end and dumped it on to the pommel as a cushion or buffer for Jim; I wrapped him in a blanket, and scrambled into the saddle with him.

The next minute we were stumbling down the steep bank, clattering and splashing over the crossing, and struggling up the opposite bank to the level. The mare, as I told you, was an old racer, but broken-winded – she must have run without wind after the first half-mile. She had the old racing instinct in her strong, and whenever I rode in company I'd have to pull her hard else she'd race the other horse or burst. She ran low fore and aft, and was the easiest horse I ever rode. She ran like wheels on rails, with a bit of a tremble now and then – like a railway carriage – when she settled down to it.

The chaff-bag had slipped off, in the creek I suppose, and I let the bridle-rein go and held Jim up to me like a baby the whole way. Let the strongest man, who isn't used to it, hold a baby in one position for five minutes – and Jim was fairly heavy. But I never felt the ache in my arms that night – it must have gone before I was in a fit state of mind to feel it. And at home I'd often growled about being asked to hold the baby for a few minutes. I could never brood comfortably and nurse a baby at the same time. It was a ghostly moonlight night. There's no timber in the world so ghostly as the Australian bush in moonlight – or just about daybreak. The all-shaped patches of moonlight falling between ragged, twisted boughs; the ghostly blue-white bark of the 'white-box' trees; a dead, naked white ring-barked tree, or dead white stump starting out here and there, and the ragged patches of shade and light on the road that made anything, from the shape of a spotted bullock to a naked corpse laid out stark. Roads and tracks through the bush made by moonlight – every one seeming straighter and clearer than the real one; you have to trust to your horse then. Sometimes the naked white trunk of a red stringy-bark tree, where a sheet of bark had been taken off, would start out like a ghost from the dark bush. And dew or frost glistening on these things according to the season. Now and again a great grey kangaroo, that had been feeding on a green patch down by the road, would start with a 'thump-thump,' and away up the siding.

The bush seemed full of ghosts that night – all going my way – and being left behind by the mare. Once I stopped to look at Jim: I just sat back and the mare 'propped' – she'd been a stock-horse, and was used to 'cutting-out.' I felt Jim's hands and forehead; he was in a burning fever. I bent forward, and the old mare settled down to it again. I kept saying out loud – and Mary and me often laughed about it (afterwards): 'He's limp yet! – Jim's limp yet!' (the words seemed jerked out of me by sheer fright) – 'He's limp yet!' till the mare's feet took it up. Then, just when I thought she was doing her best and racing her hardest, she suddenly started forward, like a cable tram gliding along on its own and the grip put on suddenly. It was just what she'd do when I'd be riding alone and a strange horse drew up from behind – the old racing instinct. I felt the thing too! I felt as if a strange horse was there! And then – the words just jerked out of me by sheet funk – I started saying, 'Death is riding tonight! ... Death is racing tonight! ... Death is riding tonight!' till the hoof-beats took that up. And I believe the old mare felt the black horse at her side and was going to beat him or break her heart.

I was mad with anxiety and fright: I remember I kept saying, 'I'll be kinder to Mary after this! I'll take more notice of Jim!' and the rest of it.

I don't know how the old mare got up the last 'pinch.' She must have slackened pace, but I never noticed it: I just held Jim up to me and gripped the saddle with my knees – I remember the saddle jerked from the desperate jumps of her till I thought the girth would go. We topped the gap and were going down into the gully they called Dead Man's Hollow, and there, at the back of a ghostly clearing that opened from the road where there were some black-soil springs, was a long, low, oblong weather-board-and-shingle building, with blind, broken windows in the gable-ends, and a wide steep veranda roof slanting down almost to the level of the window-sills – there was something sinister about it. I thought – like the hat of a jail-bird slouched over his eyes. The place looked both deserted and haunted. I saw no light, but that was because of the moonlight outside. The mare turned in at the corner of the clearing to take a short cut to the shanty, and, as she struggled across some marshy ground, my heart kept jerking out the words, 'It's deserted! They've gone away! It's deserted!' The mare went round to the back and pulled up between the back door and a big bark-and-slab kitchen. Someone shouted from inside:

'Who's there?'

'It's me. Joe Wilson. I want your sister-in-law – I've got the boy – he's sick and dying!'

Brighten came out, pulling up his moleskins. 'What boy?' he asked.

'Here, take him,' I shouted, 'and let me get down.'

'What's the matter with him?' asked Brighten, and he seemed to hang back. And just as I made to get my leg over the saddle, Jim's head went back over my arm, he stiffened, and I saw his eyeballs turned up and glistening in the moonlight.

I felt cold all over then and sick in the stomach – but clear-headed in a way: strange, wasn't it? I don't know why I didn't get down and rush into the kitchen to get a bath ready. I only felt as if the worst had come, and I wished it were over and gone. I even thought of Mary and the funeral.

Then a woman ran out of the house – a big, hard-looking woman. She had on a wrapper of some sort, and her feet were bare. She laid her hand on Jim, looked at his face, and then snatched him from me and ran into the kitchen – and me down and after her. As great good luck would have it they had some dirty clothes on to boil in a kerosene-tin – dish-cloths or something.

Brighten's sister-in-law dragged a tub out from under the table, wrenched the bucket off the hook, and dumped in the water, dish-cloths and all, snatched a can of cold water from a corner, dashed that in, and felt the water with her hand – holding Jim up to her hip all the time – and I won't say how he looked. She stood him in the tub and started dashing water over him, tearing off his clothes between the splashes.

'Here, that tin of mustard – there on the shelf!' she shouted to me.

She knocked the lid off the tin on the edge of the tub, and went on splashing and spanking Jim.

It seemed an eternity. And I? Why, I never thought clearer in my life. I felt cold-blooded – I felt as if I'd like an excuse to go outside till it was all over. I thought of Mary and the funeral – and wished that that was past. All this in a flash, as it were. I felt that it would be a great relief, and only wished the funeral was months past. I felt – well, altogether selfish. I only thought of myself.

Brighten's sister-in-law splashed and spanked him hard – hard enough to break his back I thought, and – after about half an hour it seemed – the end came: Jim's limbs relaxed, he slipped down into the tub, and the pupils of his eyes came down. They seemed dull and expressionless, like the eyes of a new baby, but he was back for the world again.

I dropped on the stool by the table.

'It's all right,' she said. 'It's all over now. I wasn't going to let him die.' I was only thinking, 'Well, it's over now, but it will come on again. I wish it was over for good. I'm tired of it.'

She called to her sister, Mrs Brighten, a washed-out, helpless little fool of a woman, who'd been running in and out and whimpering all the time:

'Here, Jessie! Bring the new white blanket off my bed. And you, Brighten, take some of that wood off the fire, and stuff something in that hole there to stop the draught.'

Brighten – he was a nuggety little hairy man with no expression to be seen for whiskers – had been running in with sticks and back logs from the wood-heap. He took the wood out, stuffed up the crack, and went inside and brought out a black bottle – got a cup from the shelf, and put both down near my elbow.

Mrs Brighten started to get some supper or breakfast, or whatever it was, ready. She had a clean cloth, and set the table tidily. I noticed that all the tins were polished bright (old coffee and mustard-tins and the like, that they used instead of sugar-basins and tea-caddies and salt-cellars), and the kitchen was kept as clean as possible. She was all right at little things. I knew a haggard, worked-out bushwoman who put her whole soul – or all she'd got left – into polishing old tins till they dazzled your eyes.

I didn't feel inclined for corned beef and damper, and post-and-rail tea. So I sat and squinted, when I thought she wasn't looking, at Brighten's sister-in-law. She was a big woman, her hands and feet were big, but well-shaped and all in proportion – they fitted her. She was a handsome woman – about forty I should think. She had a square chin, and a straight thin-lipped mouth – straight save for a hint of a turn down at the corners, which I fancied (and I have strange fancies) had been a sign of weakness in the days before she grew hard. There was no sign of weakness now. She had hard grey eyes and blue-black hair. She hadn't spoken yet. She didn't ask me how the boy took ill or how I got there, or who or what I was – at least not until the next evening at tea-time.

She sat upright with Jim wrapped in the blanket and laid across her knees, with one hand under his neck and the other laid lightly on him, and she just rocked him gently.

She sat looking hard and straight before her, just as I've seen a tired needlewoman sit with her work in her lap, and look away back into the past. And Jim might have been the work in her lap, for all she seemed to think of him. Now and then she knitted her forehead and blinked.

Suddenly she glanced round and said – in a tone as if I was her husband and she didn't think much of me:

'Why don't you eat something?'

'Beg pardon?'

'Eat something!'

I drank some tea, and sneaked another look at her. I was beginning to feel more natural, and wanted Jim again, now that the colour was coming back into his face, and he didn't look like an unnaturally stiff and staring corpse. I felt a lump rising, and wanted to thank her. I sneaked another look at her.

She was staring straight before her – I never saw a woman's face change so suddenly – I never saw a woman's eyes so haggard and hopeless. Then her great chest heaved twice, I heard her draw a long shuddering breath, like a knocked-out horse, and two great tears dropped from her wide open eyes down her cheeks like rain-drops on a face of stone. And in the firelight they seemed tinged with blood.

I looked away quick, feeling full up myself. And presently (I hadn't seen her look round) she said:

'Go to bed.'

'Beg pardon?' (Her face was the same as before the tears.)

'Go to bed. There's a bed made for you inside on the sofa.'

'But – the – team – I must'

'What?'

'The team. I left it at the camp. I must look at it.'

'Oh! Well, Brighten will ride down and bring it up in the morning – or send the half-caste. Now you go to bed, and get a good rest. The boy will be all right. I'll see to that.'

I went out – it was a relief to get out – and looked to the mare. Brighten had got her some corn and chaff in a candle-box, but she couldn't eat yet. She just stood or hung resting one hind leg and then the other, with her nose over the box – and she sobbed. I put my arms round her neck and my face down on her ragged mane, and cried for the second time since I was a boy.

As I started to go in I heard Brighten's sister-in-law say, suddenly and sharply:

'Take that away, Jessie.'

And presently I saw Mrs Brighten go into the house with the black bottle.

The moon had gone behind the range. I stood for a minute between the house and the kitchen and peeped in through the kitchen window.

She had moved away from the fire and sat near the table. She bent over Jim and held him up close to her and rocked herself to and fro.

I went to bed and slept till the next afternoon. I woke just in time to hear the tail-end of a conversation between Jim and Brighten's sister-in-law. He was asking her out to our place, and she promising to come.

'And now,' says Jim, 'I want to go home to "muffer" in "The Same Ol' Fling."'

'What?'

Jim repeated.

'Oh! "The Same Old Thing," – the wagon.'

The rest of the afternoon I poked round the gullies with old Brighten, looking at some 'indications' (of the existence of gold) he had found. It was no use trying to 'pump' him concerning his sister-in-law; Brighten was an 'old hand,' and had learned in the old bushranging and cattle-stealing days to know nothing about other people's business. And, by the way, I noticed then that the more you talk and listen to a bad character, the more you lose your dislike for him.

I never saw such a change in a woman as in Brighten's sister-in-law that evening. She was bright and jolly, and seemed at least ten years younger. She bustled round and helped her sister to get tea ready. She rooted out some old china that Mrs Brighten had stowed away somewhere, and set the table as I seldom saw it set out there. She propped Jim up with pillows, and laughed and played with him like a great girl. She described Sydney and Sydney life as I'd never heard it described before; and she knew as much about the bush and old digging days as I did. She kept old Brighten and me listening and laughing till nearly midnight. And she seemed quick to understand everything when I talked. If she wanted to explain anything that we hadn't seen, she wouldn't say that it was 'like a – like a' – and hesitate (you know what I mean); she'd hit the right thing on the head at once. A squatter with a very round, flaming red face and a white cork hat had gone by in the afternoon; she said it was 'like a mushroom on the rising moon.' She gave me a lot of good hints about children.

But she was quiet again next morning. I harnessed up, and she dressed Jim and gave him his breakfast, and made a comfortable place for him on the load with a possum rug and a spare pillow. She got up on the wheel to do it herself. Then was the awkward time. I'd half start to speak to her, and then turn away to go fixing up round the horses, and then make another false start to say good-bye. At last she took Jim up in her arms and kissed him, and lifted him on the wheel; but he put his arms tight round her neck, and kissed her – a thing Jim seldom did with anybody, except his mother, for he wasn't what you'd call an affectionate child – he'd never more than offer his cheek to me, in his old-fashioned way. I'd got up the other side of the load to take him from her.

'Here, take him,' she said.

I saw his mouth twitching as I lifted him. Jim seldom cried nowadays – no matter how much he was hurt. I gained some time fixing Jim comfortable.

'You'd better make a start,' she said. 'You want to get home early with that boy.'

I got down and went round to where she stood. I held out my hand and tried to speak, but my voice went like an ungreased wagon-wheel, and I gave it up, and only squeezed her hand.

'That's all right,' she said; then tears came into her eyes, and she suddenly put her hand on my shoulder and kissed me on the cheek. 'You be off – you're only a boy yourself. Take care of that boy; be kind to your wife, and take care of yourself.'

'Will you come to see us?'

'Some day,' she said.

I started the horses, and looked round once more. She was looking up at Jim, who was waving his hand to her from the top of the load. And I saw that haggard, hungry, hopeless look come into her eyes in spite of the tears.

I smoothed over that story and shortened it a lot when I told it to Mary – I didn't want to upset her. But, some time after I brought Jim home from Gulgong, and while I was at home with the team for a few days, nothing would suit Mary but she must go over to Brighten's shanty and see Brighten's sister-in-law. So James drove her over one morning in the spring-cart: it was a long way, and they stayed at Brighten's overnight and didn't get back till late the next afternoon. I'd got the place in a pig-muck, as Mary said, 'doing for' myself, and I was having a snooze on the sofa when they got back. The first thing I remember was someone stroking my head and kissing me, and I heard Mary saying 'My poor boy! My poor old boy!'

I sat up with a jerk. I thought that Jim had gone off again. But it seems that Mary was only referring to me. Then she started to pull grey hairs out of my head and put 'em in an empty match-box – to see how many she'd get. She used to do this when she felt a bit soft. I don't know what she said to Brighten's sister-in-law or what Brighten's sister-in-law said to her, but Mary was extra gentle for the next few days.

'WATER THEM GERANIUMS'

I

A LONELY TRACK

THE TIME Mary and I shifted out into the bush from Gulgong to 'settle on the land' at Lahey's Creek.

I'd sold the two tip-drays that I used for tank-sinking and dam-making, and I took the traps out in the wagon on top of a small load of rations and horse-feed that I was taking to a sheep station out that way. Mary drove out in the spring-cart. You remember we left little Jim with his aunt in Gulgong till we got settled down. I'd sent James (Mary's brother) out the day before, on horseback, with two or three cows and some heifers and steers and calves we had, and I'd told him to clean up a bit, and make the hut as bright and cheerful as possible before Mary came.

We hadn't much in the way of furniture. There was the four-poster cedar bedstead that I bought before we were married, and Mary was rather proud of it: it had 'turned' posts and joints that bolted together. There was a plain hardwood table, that Mary called her 'ironing-table,' upside down on top of the load, with the bedding and blankets between the legs; there were four of those common black kitchen-chairs – with apples painted on the hard board backs – that we used for the parlour; there was a cheap batten sofa with arms at the ends and turned rails between the uprights of the arms (we were a little proud of the turned rails); and there was the camp-oven, and the three-legged pot, and pans and buckets, stuck about the load and hanging under the tail-board of the wagon.

There was the little Wilcox & Gibb's sewing-machine – my present to Mary when we were married (and what a present, looking back to it!). There was a cheap little rocking-chair, and a looking-glass and some pictures that were presents from Mary's friends and sister. She had her mantelshelf ornaments and crockery and nick-nacks packed away, in the linen and old clothes, in a big tub made of half a cask and a box that had been Jim's cradle. The live stock was a cat in one box, and in another an old rooster, and three hens that formed cliques, two against one, turn about, as three of the same sex will do all over the world. I had my old cattle-dog, and of course a pup on the load – I always had a pup that I gave away, or sold and didn't get paid for, or had 'touched' (stolen) as soon as it was old enough. James had his three spidery, sneaking, thieving, cold-blooded kangaroo-dogs with him. I was taking out three months' provisions in the way of ration-sugar, tea, flour, and potatoes.

I started early, and Mary caught up to me at Ryan's Crossing on Sandy Creek, where we boiled the billy and had some dinner.

Mary bustled about the camp and admired the scenery and talked too much, for her, and was extra careful, and kept her face turned from me as much as possible. I soon saw what was the matter. She'd been crying to herself coming along the road. I thought it was all on account of leaving little Jim behind for the first time. She told me that she couldn't make up her mind till the last moment to leave him, and that, a mile or two along the road, she'd have turned back for him, only that she knew her sister would laugh at her. She was always terribly anxious about the children.

We cheered each other up, and Mary drove with me the rest of the way to the creek, along the lonely branch track, across native apple-tree flats. It was a dreary, hopeless track. There was no horizon, nothing but the rough ashen trunks of the gnarled and stunted trees in all directions, little or no undergrowth, and the ground, save for the coarse, brownish tufts of dead grass, as bare as the road, for it was a dry season: there had been no rain for months, and I wondered what I should do with the cattle if there wasn't more grass on the creek.

In this sort of country a stranger might travel for miles without seeming to have moved, for all the difference there is in the scenery. The new tracks were 'blazed' – that is, slices of bark cut off from both sides of trees, within sight of each other, in a line, to mark the track until the horses and wheel marks made it plain. A smart bushman, with a sharp tomahawk, can blaze a track as he rides. But a bushman a little used to the country soon picks out differences amongst the trees, half unconsciously as it were, and so finds his way about.

Mary and I didn't talk much along this track – we couldn't have heard each other very well, anyway, for the 'clock-clock' of the wagon and the rattle of the cart over the hard lumpy ground. And I suppose we both began to feel pretty dismal as the shadows lengthened. I'd noticed lately that Mary and I had got out of the habit of talking to each other – noticed it in a vague sort of way that irritated me (as vague things will irritate one) when I thought of it. But then I thought, 'It won't last long – I'll make life brighter for her by and by.'

As we went along – and the track seemed endless – I got brooding, of course, back into the past. And I feel now, when it's too late, that Mary must have been thinking that way too. I thought of my early boyhood, of the hard life of 'grubbin'' ' and 'milkin'' and 'fencin'' and 'ploughin'' and 'ring-barkin',' and all for nothing. The few months at the little bark school, with a teacher who couldn't spell. The cursed ambition or craving that tortured my soul as a boy – ambition or craving for – I didn't know what for! For something better and brighter, anyhow. And I made the life harder by reading at night.

It all passed before me as I followed on in the wagon, behind Mary in the spring-cart. I thought of these old things more than I thought of her. She had tried to help me to better things. And I tried too – I had the energy of half a dozen men when I saw a road clear before me, but shied at the first check. Then I brooded, or dreamed of making a home – that one might call a home – for Mary – some day. Ah, well!

And what was Mary thinking about, along the lonely, changeless miles? I never thought of that. Of her kind, careless, gentleman father, perhaps. Of her girlhood. Of her homes – not the huts and camps she lived in with me. Of our future? – she used to plan a lot, and talk a good deal of our future – but not lately. These things didn't strike me at the time – I was so deep in my own brooding. Did she think now – did she begin to feel now that she had made a great mistake and thrown away her life, but must make the best of it? This might have roused me, had I thought of it. But whenever I thought Mary was getting indifferent towards me, I'd think, 'I'll soon win her back. We'll be sweethearts again – when things brighten up a bit.'

It's an awful thing to me, now I look back to it, to think how far apart we had grown, what strangers we were to each other. It seems, now, as though we had been sweethearts long years before, and had parted, and had never really met since.

The sun was going down when Mary called out:

'There's our place, Joe!'

She hadn't seen it before, and somehow it came new and with a shock to me, who had been out here several times. Ahead, through the trees to the right, was a dark green clump of she-oaks standing out of the creek, darker for the dead grey grass and blue-grey bush on the barren ridge in the background. Across the creek (it was only a deep, narrow gutter – a watercourse with a chain of waterholes after the rain), across on the other bank, stood the hut, on a narrow flat between the spur and the creek, and a little higher than this side. The land was much better than on our old selection, and there was good soil along the creek on both sides: I expected a rush of selectors out here soon. A few acres round the hut were cleared and fenced in by a light two-rail fence of timber split from logs and saplings. The man who took up this selection left it because his wife died here.

It was a small oblong hut built of split slabs, and he had roofed it with shingles which he split in spare times. There was no veranda, but I built one later on. At the end of the house was a big slab-and-bark shed, bigger than the hut itself, with a kitchen, a skillion for tools, harness, and horse-feed, and a spare bedroom partitioned off with sheets of bark and old chaff-bags. The house itself was floored roughly, with cracks between the boards; there were cracks between the slabs all round – though he'd nailed strips of tin, from old kerosene-tins, over some of them; the partitioned-off bedroom was lined with old chaff-bags with newspapers pasted over them for wall-paper. There was no ceiling, calico or otherwise, and we could see the round pine rafters and battens, and the under ends of the shingles. But ceilings make a hut hot and harbour insects and reptiles – snakes sometimes. There was one small glass window in the 'dining-room' with three panes and a sheet of greased paper, and the rest were rough wooden shutters. There was a pretty good cow-yard and calf-pen, and – that was about all. There was no dam or tank (I made one later on); there was a water-cask, with the hoops falling off and the staves gaping, at the corner of the house, and spouting, made of lengths of bent tin, ran round the eaves. Water from a new shingle roof is wine-red for a year or two, and water from a stringy-bark roof is like tan-water for years. In dry weather the selector had got his house water from a cask sunk in the gravel at the bottom of the deepest waterhole in the creek, and the longer the drought lasted, the farther he had to go down the creek for his water, with a cask on a cart, and take his cows to drink, if he had any. Four, five, six, or seven miles – even ten miles to water is nothing in some places.

James hadn't found himself called upon to do more than milk old 'Spot' (the grandmother cow of our mob), pen the calf at night, make a fire in the kitchen, and sweep out the house with a bough. He helped me unharness and water and feed the horses, and then started to get the furniture off the wagon and into the house. James wasn't lazy, so long as one thing didn't last too long; but he was too uncomfortably practical and matter-of-fact for me. Mary and I had some tea in the kitchen. The kitchen was permanently furnished with a table of split slabs, adzed smooth on top, and supported by four stakes driven into the ground, a three-legged stool and a block of wood, and two long stools made of half-round slabs (sapling trunks split in halves) with auger-holes bored in the round side and sticks stuck into them for legs. The floor was of clay; the chimney of slabs and tin; the fire-place was about eight feet wide, lined with clay, and with a blackened pole across, with sooty chains and wire hooks on it for the pots.

Mary didn't seem able to eat. She sat on the three-legged stool near the fire, though it was warm weather, and kept her face turned from me. Mary was still pretty, but not the little dumpling she had been; she was thinner now. She had big dark hazel eyes that shone a little too much when she was pleased or excited. I thought at times that there was something very German about her expression; also something aristocratic about the turn of her nose, which nipped in at the nostrils when she spoke. There was nothing aristocratic about me. Mary was German in figure and walk. I used sometimes to call her 'Little Duchy' and 'Pigeon Toes.' She had a will of her own, as shown sometimes by the obstinate knit in her forehead between the eyes.

Mary sat still by the fire, and presently I saw her chin tremble.

'What is it, Mary?'

She turned her face farther from me. I felt tired, disappointed, and irritated – suffering from a reaction.

'Now, what is it, Mary?' I asked; 'I'm sick of this sort of thing. Haven't you got everything you wanted? You've had your own way. What's the matter with you now?'

'You know very well, Joe.'

'But I don't know,' I said. I knew too well.

She said nothing.

'Look here, Mary,' I said, putting my hand on her shoulder, 'don't go on like that; tell me what's the matter.'

'It's only this,' she said suddenly, 'I can't stand this life here; it will kill me!'

I had a pannikin of tea in my hand, and I banged it down on the table.

'This is more than a man can stand!' I shouted. 'You know very well that it was you that dragged me out here. You run me on to this. Why weren't you content to stay in Gulgong?'

'And what sort of a place was Gulgong, Joe?' asked Mary quietly.

(I thought even then in a flash what sort of a place Gulgong was. A wretched remnant of a town on an abandoned goldfield. One street, each side of the dusty main road three or four one-story square brick cottages with hip-roofs of galvanised-iron that glared in the heat – four rooms and a passage – the police station, bank-manager and schoolmaster's cottages. Half a dozen tumble-down weather-board shanties – the three pubs, the two stores, and the post office. The town tailing off into weather-board boxes with tin tops, and old bark huts – relics of the digging days – propped up by many rotting poles. The men, when at home, mostly asleep or droning over their pipes or hanging about the veranda-posts of the pubs, saying "Ullo, Bill!" or "Ullo, Jim!" – or sometimes drunk. The women, mostly hags, who blackened each other's and girls' characters with their tongues, and criticised the aristocracy's washing hung out on the line: 'And the colour of the clothes! Does that woman wash her clothes at all? or only soak 'em and hang 'em out?' – that was Gulgong.)

'Well, why didn't you come to Sydney, as I wanted you to?' I asked Mary.

'You know very well, Joe,' said Mary quietly.

(I knew very well, but the knowledge only maddened me. I had had an idea of getting a billet in one of the big wool-stores – I was a fair wool expert – but Mary was afraid of the drink. I could keep well away from it so long as I worked hard in the bush. I had gone to Sydney twice since I met Mary, once before we were married, and she forgave me when I came back; and once afterwards. I got a billet there then, and was going to send for her in a month. After eight weeks she raised the money somehow and came to Sydney and brought me home. I got pretty down that time.)

'But, Mary,' I said, 'it would have been different this time. You would have been with me. I can take a glass now or leave it alone.'

'As long as you take a glass there is danger,' she said.

'Well, what did you want to advise me to come out here for, if you can't stand it? Why didn't you stay where you were?' I asked.

'Well,' she said, 'why weren't you more decided?'

I'd sat down, but I jumped to my feet then.

'Good God!' I shouted, 'this is more than any man can stand. I'll chuck it all up! I'm damned well sick and tired of the whole thing.'

'So am I, Joe,' said Mary wearily.

We quarrelled badly then – that first hour in our new home. I know now whose fault it was.

I got my hat and went out and started to walk down the creek. I didn't feel bitter against Mary – I had spoken too cruelly to her to feel that way. Looking back, I could see plainly that if I had taken her advice all through instead of now and again, things would have been all right with me. I had come away and left her crying in the hut, and James telling her, in a brotherly way, that it was all her fault. The trouble was that I never liked to 'give in' or go half-way to make it up – not half-way – it was all the way or nothing with our natures.

'If I don't make a stand now,' I'd say, 'I'll never be master. I gave up the reins when I got married, and I'll have to get them back again.'

What women some men are! But the time came, and not many years after, when I stood by the bed where Mary lay, white and still; and, amongst other things, I kept saying, 'I'll give in, Mary – I'll give in,' and then I'd laugh. They thought I was raving mad, and took me from the room. But that time was to come.

As I walked down the creek track in the moonlight the question rang in my ears again, as it had done when I first caught sight of the house that evening:

'Why did I bring her here?'

I was not fit to 'go on the land.' The place was only fit for some stolid German, or Scotsman, or even Englishman and his wife, who had no ambition but to bullock and make a farm of the place. I had only drifted here through carelessness, brooding and discontent.

I walked on and on till I was more than half-way to the only neighbours – a wretched selector's family, about four miles down the creek – and I thought I'd go on to the house and see if they had any fresh meat.

A mile or two farther I saw the loom of the bark hut they lived in, on a patchy clearing in the scrub, and heard the voice of the selector's wife – I had seen her several times: she was a gaunt, haggard bushwoman, and I supposed the reason why she hadn't gone mad through hardship and loneliness was that she hadn't either the brains or memory to go farther than she could see through the trunks of the 'apple-trees.'

'You, An-nay!' (Annie.)

'Ye-es' (from somewhere in the gloom).

'Didn't I tell yer to water them geraniums!'

'Well, didn't I?'

'Don't tell lies or I'll break yer young back!'

'I did, I tell yer – the water won't soak inter the ashes.'

Geraniums were the only flowers I saw grow in the drought out there. I remembered this woman had a few dirty grey-green leaves behind some sticks against the bark wall near the door; and in spite of the sticks the fowls used to get in and scratch beds under the geraniums, and scratch dust over them, and ashes were thrown there – with an idea of helping the flowers, I suppose; and greasy dish-water, when fresh water was scarce – till you might as well try to water a dish of fat.

Then the woman's voice again:

'You, Tom-may!' (Tommy.)

Silence, save for an echo on the ridge.

'Y-o-u T-o-m-may!'

'Y-e-s!' shrill shriek from across the creek.

'Didn't I tell you to ride up to them new people and see if they want any meat or anything?' in one long screech.

'Well – I karn't find the horse.'

'Well-find-it-first-think-in-the-morning-and-don't-forgit-to-tell-Mrs-Wi'son-that-mother'll-be-up-as-soon-as-she-can.'

I didn't feel like going to the woman's house that night. I felt – and the thought came like a whipstroke on my heart – that this was what Mary would come to if I left her here.

I turned and started to walk home, fast. I'd made up my mind. I'd take Mary straight back to Gulgong in the morning – I forgot about the load I had to take to the sheep station. I'd say, 'Look here, Girlie' (that's what I used to call her), 'we'll leave this wretched life; we'll leave the bush for ever. We'll go to Sydney, and I'll be a man! and work my way up.' And I'd sell wagon, horses, and all, and go.

When I got to the hut it was lighted up. Mary had the only kerosene lamp, a slush-lamp, and two tallow candles going. She had got both rooms washed out – to James's disgust, for he had to move the furniture and boxes about. She had a lot of things unpacked on the table; she had laid clean newspapers on the mantelshelf – a slab on two pegs over the fire-place – and put the little wooden clock in the centre and some of the ornaments on each side, and was tacking a strip of vandyked American oilcloth round the rough edge of the slab.

'How does that look, Joe? We'll soon get things shipshape.'

I kissed her, but she had her mouth full of tacks. I went out in the kitchen, drank a pint of cold tea, and sat down.

Somehow I didn't feel satisfied with the way things had gone.

II

'PAST CARIN''

NEXT morning things looked a lot brighter. Things always look brighter in the morning – more so in the Australian bush, I should think, than in most other places. It is when the sun goes down on the dark bed of the lonely bush, and the sunset flashes like a sea of fire and then fades, and then glows out again, like a bank of coals, and then burns away to ashes – it is then that old things come home to one. And strange, new-old things too, that haunt and depress you terribly, and that you can't understand. I often think how, at sunset, the past must come home to new-chum black sheep, sent out to Australia and drifted into the bush. I used to think that they couldn't have much brains, or the loneliness would drive them mad.

I'd decided to let James take the team for a trip or two. He could drive all right; he was a better business man, and no doubt would manage better than me – as long as the novelty lasted; and I'd stay at home for a week or so, till Mary got used to the place, or I could get a girl from somewhere to come and stay with her. The first weeks or few months of loneliness are the worst, as a rule, I believe, as they say the first weeks in jail are – I was never there. I know it's so with tramping or hard graft: the first day or two are twice as hard as any of the rest. But, for my part, I could never get used to loneliness and dullness: the last days used to be the worst with me: then I'd have to make a move, or drink. When you've been too much and too long alone in a lonely place, you begin to do queer things, and think queer thoughts – provided you have any imagination at all. You'll sometimes sit of an evening and watch the lonely track, by the hour, for a horseman or a cart or someone that's never likely to come that way – someone, or a stranger, that you can't and don't really expect to see. I think that most men who have been alone in the bush for any length of time – and married couples too – are more or less mad. With married couples it is generally the husband who is painfully shy and awkward when strangers come. The woman seems to stand the loneliness better, and can hold her own with strangers, as a rule. It's only afterwards, and looking back, that you see how queer you got. Shepherds and boundary-riders, who are alone for months, must have their periodical spree, at the nearest shanty, else they'd go raving mad. Drink is the only break in the awful monotony, and the yearly or half-yearly spree is the only thing they've got to look forward to: it keeps their minds fixed on something definite ahead.

But Mary kept her head pretty well through the first months of loneliness. Weeks rather, I should say, for it wasn't as bad as it might have been farther up-country: there was generally someone came of a Sunday afternoon – a spring-cart with a couple of women, or maybe a family – or a lanky shy bush native or two on lanky shy horses. On a quiet Sunday, after I'd brought Jim home, Mary would dress him and herself – just the same as if we were in town – and make me get up on one end and put on a collar and take her and Jim for a walk along the creek. She said she wanted to keep me civilised. She tried to make a gentleman of me for years, but gave it up gradually.

Well. It was the first morning on the creek: I was greasing the wagon-wheels, and James out after the horse, and Mary hanging out clothes, in an old print dress and a big ugly white hood, when I heard her being hailed as 'Hi, missus!' from the front sliprails.

It was a boy on horseback. He was a light-haired, very much freckled boy of fourteen or fifteen, with a small head, but with limbs, especially his bare sun-blotched shanks, that might have belonged to a grown man. He had a good face and frank grey eyes. An old, nearly black cabbage-tree hat rested on the butts of his ears, turning them out at right angles from his head, and rather dirty sprouts they were. He wore a dirty torn Crimean shirt; and a pair of men's moleskin trousers rolled up above the knees, with a wide waistband gathered under a greenhide belt. I noticed, later on, that even when he wore trousers short enough for him, he always rolled 'em up above the knees when on horseback, for some reason of his own: to suggest leggings, perhaps, for he had them rolled up in all weathers, and he wouldn't have bothered to save them from the sweat of the horse, even if that horse ever sweated.

He was seated astride a three-bushel bag thrown across the ridge-pole of a big grey horse, with a coffin-shaped head, and built astern something after the style of a roughly put up hip-roofed box-bark humpy. His colour was like old box-bark, too, a dirty bluish-grey; and, one time, when I saw his rump looming out of the scrub, I really thought it was some old shepherd's hut that I hadn't noticed there before. When he cantered it was like the humpy starting off on its corner-posts.

'Are you Mrs Wilson?' asked the boy.

'Yes,' said Mary.

'Well, mother told me to ride acrost and see if you wanted anythink. We killed lars' night, and I fetched a piece er cow.'

'Piece of what?' asked Mary.

He grinned and handed a sugar-bag across the rail with something heavy in the bottom of it, that nearly jerked Mary's arm out when she took it. It was a piece of beef, that looked as if it had been cut off with a wood-axe, but it was fresh and clean.

'Oh, I'm so glad!' cried Mary. She was always impulsive, save to me sometimes. 'I was just wondering where we were going to get any fresh meat. How kind of your mother! Tell her I'm very much obliged to her indeed.' And she felt behind her for a poor little purse she had. 'And now – how much did you mother say it would be?'

The boy blinked at her, and scratched his head.

'How much will it be,' he repeated, puzzled. 'Oh – how much does it weigh I-s'pose-yer-mean. Well, it ain't been weighed at all – we ain't got no scales. A butcher does all that sort of thing. We just kills it, and cooks it, and eats it –and goes by guess. What won't keep we salts down in the cask. I reckon it weighs about a ton by the weight of it if yer wanter to know. Mother thought that if she sent any more it would go bad before you could scoff it. I can't see ——'

'Yes, yes,' said Mary, getting confused. 'But what I want to know is, how do you manage when you sell it?'

He glared at her, and scratched his head. 'Sell it? Why, we only goes halves in a steer with someone, or sells steers to the butcher – or maybe some meat to a party of fencers or surveyors, or tank-sinkers, or them sorter people ——'

'Yes, yes; but what I want to know is, how much am I to send your mother for this?'

'How much what?'

'Money, of course, you stupid boy,' said Mary. 'You seem a very stupid boy.'

Then he saw what she was driving at. He began to fling his heels convulsively against the sides of this horse, jerking his body backward and forward at the same time, as if to wind up and start some clockwork machinery inside the horse, that made it go, and seemed to need repairing or oiling.

'We ain't that sorter people, missus,' he said. 'We don't sell meat to new people that come to settle here.' Then, jerking his thumb contemptuously towards the ridges, 'Go over ter Wall's if yer wanter buy meat; they sell meat ter strangers.' (Wall was the big squatter over the ridges.)

'Oh!' said Mary, 'I'm so sorry. Thank your mother for me. She is kind.'

'Oh, that's nothink. She said to tell yer she'll be up as soon as she can. She'd have come up yesterday evening – she thought yer'd feel lonely comin' new to a place like this – but she couldn't git up.'

The machinery inside the old horse showed signs of starting. You almost heard the wooden joints creak as he lurched forward, like an old propped-up humpy when the rotting props give way; but at the sound of Mary's voice he settled back on his foundations again. It must have been a very poor selection that couldn't afford a better spare horse than that.

'Reach me that lump er wood, will yer, missus?' said the boy, and he pointed to one of my 'spreads' (for the team-chains) that lay inside the fence. 'I'll fling it back agin over the fence when I git this ole cow started.'

'But wait a minute – I've forgotten your mother's name,' said Mary.

He grabbed at his thatch impatiently. 'Me mother – oh! – the old woman's name's Mrs Spicer. (Git up, karn't yer!)' He twisted himself round, and brought the stretcher down on one of the horse's 'points' (and he had many) with a crack that must have jarred his wrist.

'Do you go to school?' asked Mary. There was a three-days-a-week school over the ridges at Wall's station.

'No!' he jerked out, keeping his legs going. 'Me – why I'm going on fur fifteen. The last teacher at Wall's finished me. I'm going to Queensland next month drovin'.' (Queensland border was over three hundred miles away.)

'Finished you? How?' asked Mary.

'Me edgercation, of course! How do yer expect me to start this horse when yer keep talkin'?'

He split the 'spread' over the horse's point, threw the pieces over the fence, and was off, his elbows and legs flying wildly, and the old saw-stool lumbering along the road like an old working bullock trying a canter. That horse wasn't a trotter.

And next month he did start for Queensland. He was a younger son and a surplus boy on a wretched, poverty-stricken selection; and as there was 'northin' doin'' in the district, his father (in a burst of fatherly kindness, I suppose) made him a present of the old horse and a new pair of blucher boots, and I gave him an old saddle and a coat, and he started for the Never-Never country.

And I'll bet he got there. But I'm doubtful if the old horse did.

Mary gave the boy five shillings, and I don't think he had anything more except a clean shirt and an extra pair of white cotton socks.

'Spicer's farm' was a big bark humpy on a patchy clearing in the native apple-tree scrub. The clearing was fenced in by a light 'dog-legged' fence (a fence of sapling poles resting on forks and X-shaped uprights), and the dusty ground round the house was almost entirely covered with cattle-dung. There was no attempt at cultivation when I came to live on the creek; but there were old furrow-marks amongst the stumps of another shapeless patch in the scrub near the hut. There was a wretched sapling cow-yard and calf-pen, and a cow-bail with one sheet of bark over it for shelter. There was no dairy to be seen, and I suppose the milk was set in one of the two skillion rooms, or lean-to's behind the hut – the other was 'the boys' bedroom.' The Spicers kept a few cows and steers and had thirty or forty sheep. Mrs Spicer used to drive down the creek once a week, in her rickety old spring-cart, to Cobborah, with butter and eggs. The hut was nearly as bare inside as it was out – just a frame of 'round-timber' (sapling poles) covered with bark. The furniture was permanent (unless you rooted it up), like in our kitchen: a rough slab table on stakes driven into the ground, and seats made the same way. Mary told me afterwards that the beds in the bag-and-bark partitioned-off room ('mother's bedroom') were simply poles laid side by side on cross-pieces supported by stakes driven into the ground, with straw mattresses and some worn-out bed-clothes. Mrs Spicer had an old patchwork quilt, in rags, and the remains of a white one, and Mary said it was pitiful to see how these things would be spread over the beds – to hide them as much as possible – when she went down there. A packing-case, with something like an old print skirt draped round it, and a cracked looking-glass (without a frame) on top, was the dressing-table. There were a couple of gin-cases for a wardrobe. The boys' beds were three-bushel bags stretched between poles fastened to uprights. The floor was the original surface, tramped hard, worn uneven with much sweeping and with puddles in rainy weather where the roof leaked. Mrs Spicer used to stand old tins, dishes, and buckets under as many of the leaks as she could. The saucepans, kettles and boilers were old kerosene-tins and billies. They used kerosene-tins, too, cut longways in halves, for setting the milk in. The plates and cups were of tin; there were two or three cups without saucers, and a crockery plate or two – also two mugs, cracked, and without handles, one with 'For a Good Boy' and the other with 'For a Good Girl' on it; but all these were kept on the mantelshelf for ornament and for company. They were the only ornaments in the house, save a little wooden clock that hadn't gone for years. Mrs Spicer had a superstition that she had 'some things packed away from the children.'

The pictures were cut from old copies of the Illustrated Sydney News and pasted on to the bark. I remember this, because I remembered, long ago, the Spencers, who were our neighbours when I was a boy, had the walls of their bedroom covered with illustrations of the American Civil War, cut from illustrated London papers, and I used to 'sneak' into 'mother's bedroom' with Fred Spencer whenever we got a chance, and gloat over the prints. I gave him the blade of a pocket-knife once, for taking me in there.

I saw very little of Spicer. He was a big, dark, dark-haired and whiskered man. I had an idea that he wasn't a selector at all, only a 'dummy' for the squatter of the Cobborah run. You see, selectors were allowed to take up land on runs or pastoral leases. The squatters kept them off as much as possible, by all manner of dodges and paltry persecution. The squatter would get as much freehold as he could afford, 'select' as much land as the law allowed one man to take up, and then employ dummies (dummy selectors) to take up bits of land that he fancied about his run, and hold them for him.

Spicer seemed gloomy and unsociable. He was seldom at home. He was generally supposed to be away shearin', or fencin', or workin' on somebody's station. It turned out that the last six months he was away it was on the evidence of a cask of beef and a hide with the brand cut out, found in his camp on a fencing contract up-country, and which he and his mates couldn't account for satisfactorily, while the squatter could. Then the family lived mostly on bread and honey, or bread and treacle, or bread and dripping, and tea. Every ounce of butter and every egg was needed for the market, to keep them in flour, tea and sugar. Mary found that out, but couldn't help them much – except by 'stuffing' the children with bread and meat or bread and jam whenever they came to our place – for Mrs Spicer was proud with the pride that lies down in the end and turns its face to the wall and dies.

Once, when Mary asked Annie, the eldest girl at home, if she was hungry, she denied it – but she looked it. A ragged mite she had with her explained things. The little fellow said:

'Mother told Annie not to say we was hungry if yer asked; but if yer give us anythink to eat, we was to take it an' say thenk yer, Mrs Wilson.'

'I wouldn't 'a' told yer a lie; but I thought Jimmy would split on me, Mrs Wilson,' said Annie. 'Thenk yer, Mrs Wilson.'

She was not a big woman. She was gaunt and flat-chested, and her face was 'burnt to a brick,' as they say out there. She had brown eyes, nearly red, and a little wild-looking at times, and a sharp face – ground sharp by hardship – the cheeks drawn in. She had an expression like – well, like a woman who had been very curious and suspicious at one time, and wanted to know everybody's business and hear everything, and had lost all her curiosity, without losing the expression or the quick suspicious movements of the head. I don't suppose you understand. I can't explain it any other way. She was not more than forty.

I remember the first morning I saw her. I was going up the creek to look at the selection for the first time, and called at the hut to see if she had a bit of fresh mutton, as I had none and was sick of 'corned beef.'

'Yes – of – course,' she said, in a sharp nasty tone, as if to say, 'Is there anything more you want while the shop's open?' I'd met just the same sort of woman years before while I was carrying swag between the shearing-sheds in the awful scrubs out west of the Darling River, so I didn't turn on my heels and walk away. I waited for her to speak again.

'Come – inside,' she said, 'and sit down. I see you've got the wagon outside. I s'pose your name's Wilson, ain't it? You're thinking' about takin' on Harry

Marshfield's selection up the creek, so I heard. Wait till I fry you a chop, and boil the billy.'

Her voice sounded, more than anything else, like a voice coming out of a phonograph – I heard one in Sydney the other day – and not like a voice coming out of her. But sometimes when she got outside her everyday life on this selection she spoke in a sort of – in a sort of lost groping-in-the-dark kind of voice.

She didn't talk much this time – just spoke in a mechanical way of the drought, and the hard times, 'an' butter 'n' eggs bein' down an' her husban' an' eldest son bein' away, an' that makin' it so hard for her.'

I don't know how many children she had. I never got a chance to count them, for they were nearly all small, and shy as piccaninnies, and used to run and hide when anybody came. They were mostly nearly as black as piccaninnies too. She must have averaged a baby a year for years – and God only knows how she got over her confinements! Once, they said she only had a black gin with her. She had an elder boy and girl, but she seldom spoke of them. The girl, 'Lisa,' was 'in service in Sydney.' I'm afraid I knew what that meant. The elder son was 'away.' He had been a bit of a favourite round there, it seemed.

Someone might ask her, 'How's your son Jack, Mrs Spicer?' or, 'Heard of Jack lately? and where is he now?'

'Oh, he's somewhere's up-country,' she'd say in the 'groping' voice, or 'He's drovin' in Queenslan',' or 'Shearin' on the Darlin' last time I heerd from him. We ain't had a line from him since – le's see – since Chris'mas 'fore last.'

And she'd turn her haggard eyes in a helpless, hopeless sort of way towards the west – towards 'up-country' and 'out back.'

The eldest girl at home was nine or ten, with a little old face and lines across her forehead: she had an older expression than her mother. Tommy, went to Queensland, as I told you. The eldest son at home, Bill (older than Tommy), was 'a bit wild.'

I've passed the place in smothering hot mornings in December, when the droppings about the cow-yard had crumpled to dust that rose in the warm, sickly, sunrise wind, and seen that woman at work in the cow-yard, 'bailing up' and leg-roping cows, milking, or hauling at a rope round the neck of a half-grown calf that was too strong for her (and she was tough as fencing-wire), or humping great buckets of sour milk to the pigs or the 'poddies' (hand-fed calves) in the pen. I'd get off the horse and give her a hand sometimes with a young steer, or a cranky old cow that wouldn't 'bail-up' and threatened her with her horns. She'd say:

'Thank yer, Mr Wilson. Do yer think we're ever goin' to have any rain?'

I've ridden past the place on bitter black rainy mornings in June or July, and seen her trudging about the yard – that was ankle-deep in black liquid filth – with an old pair of blucher boots on, and an old coat of her husband's, or maybe a three-bushel bag over her shoulders. I've see her climbing on the roof by means of the water-cask at the corner, and trying to stop a leak by shoving a piece of tin in under the bark. And when I'd fixed the leak:

'Thenk yer, Mr Wilson. This drop of rain's a blessin'! Come in and have a dry at the fire and I'll make yer a cup of tea.' And, if I was in a hurry, 'Come in, man alive! Come in! and dry yerself a bit till the rain holds up. Yer can't go home like this! Yer'll git yer death o' cold.'

I've even seen her, in the terrible drought, climbing she-oaks and apple-trees by a makeshift ladder, and awkwardly lopping off boughs to feed the starving cattle.

'Jist tryin' ter keep the milkers alive till the rain comes.'

They said that when the pleuro-pneumonia was in the district and amongst her cattle she bled and physicked them herself, and fed those that were down with slices of half-ripe pumpkins (from a crop that had failed).

'An' one day,' she told Mary, 'there was a big barren heifer (that we called Queen Elizabeth) that was down with the ploorer. She'd been down for four days and hadn't moved, when one mornin' I dumped some wheaten chaff – we had a few bags that Spicer brought home – I dumped it in front of her nose, an' – would yer b'lieve me, Mrs Wilson? – she stumbled onter her feet an' chased me all the way to the house! I had to pick up me skirts an' run! Wasn't it redic'lus?'

They had a sense of the ridiculous, most of those poor sundried bushwomen. I fancy that that helped save them from madness.

'We lost nearly all our milkers,' she told Mary. 'I remember one day Tommy came running to the house and screamed: 'Marther! [mother] there's another milker down with the ploorer!' Jist as if it was great news. Well, Mrs Wilson, I was dead-beat, an' I giv' in. I jist sat down to have a good cry, and felt for my han'kerchief – it was a rag of a han'kerchief, full of holes (all me others was in the wash). Without seein' what I was doin' I put my finger through the hole in the han'kerchief an' me thumb through the other, and poked me fingers into me eyes, instead of wipin' them. Then I had to laugh.'

There's a story that once, when the bush, or rather grass, fires were out all along the creek on Spicer's side, Wall's station-hands were up above our place, trying to keep the fire back from the boundary, and towards the evening one of the men happened to think of the Spicers: they saw smoke down that way. Spicer was away from home, and they had a small crop of wheat, nearly ripe, on the selection.

'My God! that poor devil of a woman will be burnt out, if she ain't already!' shouted young Bill Wall. 'Come along, three or four of you chaps' – it was shearing-time, and there were plenty of men on the station.

They raced down the creek to Spicer's, and were just in time to save the wheat. She had her sleeves tucked up, and was beating out the burning grass with a bough. She'd been at it for an hour, and was as black as a gin, they said. She only said when they'd turned the fire: 'Thenk yer! Wait an' I'll make some tea.'

After tea the first Sunday she came to see us, Mary asked:

'Don't you feel lonely, Mrs Spicer, when your husband goes away?'

'Well – no, Mrs Wilson,' she said in the groping sort of voice. 'I uster, once. I remember, when we lived on the Cudgegong River – we lived in a brick house then – the first time Spicer had to go away from home I nearly fretted my eyes out. And he was only goin' shearin' for a month. I muster bin a fool; but then we were only jist married a little while. He's been away drovin' in Queenslan' as long as eighteen months at a time since then. But' (her voice seemed to grope in the dark more than ever) 'I don't mind – I somehow seem to have got past carin'. Besides – besides, Spicer was a very different man then to what he is now. He's got so moody and gloomy at home, he hardly ever speaks.'

Mary sat silent for a minute thinking. Then Mrs Spicer roused herself:

'Oh, I don't know what I'm talkin' about! You mustn't take any notice of me, Mrs Wilson – I don't often go on like this. I do believe I'm gittin' a bit ratty at times. It must be the heat and the dullness.'

But once or twice afterwards she referred to a time 'when Spicer was a different man to what he was now.'

I walked home with her a piece along the creek. She said nothing for a long time, and seemed to be thinking in a puzzled way. Then she said suddenly:

'What-did-you-bring-her-here-for? She's only a girl.'

'I beg pardon, Mrs Spicer.'

'Oh, I don't know what I'm talkin' about! I b'lieve I'm gettin' ratty. You mustn't take any notice of me, Mr Wilson.'

She wasn't much company for Mary; and often, when she had a child with her, she'd start taking notice of the baby while Mary was talking, which used to exasperate Mary. But poor Mrs Spicer couldn't help it, and she seemed to hear all the same.

Her great trouble was that she 'couldn't git no reg'lar schoolin' for the children.'

'I learns 'em at home as much as I can. But I don't git a minute to call me own; an' I'm ginerally that dead-beat at night that I'm fit for nothink.'

Mary had some of the children up now and then later on, and taught them a little. When she first offered to do so, Mrs Spicer laid hold of the handiest youngster and said:

'There – do you hear that? Mrs Wilson is goin' to teach yer, an' it's more than yer deserve!' (the youngster had been 'cryin'' over something). 'Now, go up an' say "Thenk yer, Mrs Wilson." And if yer ain't good, and don't do as she tells yer, I'll break every bone in yer young body!'

The poor little devil stammered something, and escaped.

The children were sent by turns over to Wall's to Sunday-school. When Tommy was at home he had a new pair of elastic-side boots, and there was no end of rows about them in the family – for the mother made him lend them to his sister Annie, to go to Sunday-school in her turn. There were only about three pairs of anyway decent boots in the family, and these were saved for great occasions. The children were always clean and tidy as possible when they came to our place.

And I think the saddest and most pathetic sight on the face of God's earth is the children of very poor people made to appear well; the broken worn-out boots polished or greased, the blackened (inked) pieces of string for laces; the clean patched pinafores over the wretched threadbare frocks. Behind the little row of children hand-in-hand – and no matter where they are – I always see the worn face of the mother.

Towards the end of the first year on the selection our little girl came. I'd sent Mary to Gulgong for four months that time, and when she came back with the baby Mrs Spicer used to come up pretty often. She came up several times when Mary was ill, to lend a hand. She wouldn't sit down and condole with Mary, or waste her time asking questions, or talking about the time when she was ill herself. She'd take off her hat – a shapeless little lump of black straw she wore for visiting – give her hair a quick brush back with the palms of her hands, roll up her sleeves, and set to work to 'tidy up.' She seemed to take most pleasure in sorting out our children's clothes, and dressing them. Perhaps she used to dress her own like that in the days when Spicer was a different man from what he was now. She seemed interested in the fashion-plates of some women's journals we had, and used to study them with an interest that puzzled me, for she was not likely to go in for fashion. She never talked of her early girlhood; but Mary, from some things she noticed, was inclined to think that Mrs Spicer had been fairly well brought up. For instance, Dr Balanfantie, from Cudgegong, came out to see Wall's wife, and drove up the creek to our place on his way back to see how Mary and the baby were getting on. Mary got out some crockery and some table-napkins that she had packed away for occasions like this; and she said that the way Mrs Spicer handled the things, and helped set the table (though she did it in a mechanical sort of way) convinced her that she had been used to table-nap-kins at one time in her life.

Sometimes, after a long pause in the conversation, Mrs Spicer would say suddenly:

'Oh, I don't think I'll come up next week, Mrs Wilson.'

'Why, Mrs Spicer?'

'Because the visits doesn't do me any good. I git the dismals afterwards.'

'Why, Mrs Spicer? What on earth do you mean?'

'Oh, I-don't-know-what-I'm-talkin'-about. You mustn't take any notice of me.' And she'd put on her hat, kiss the children – and Mary too, sometimes, as if she mistook her for a child – and go.

Mary thought her a little mad at times. But I seemed to understand.

Once, when Mrs Spicer was sick, Mary went down to her, and down again next day. As she was coming away the second time Mrs Spicer said:

'I wish you wouldn't come down any more till I'm on my feet, Mrs Wilson. The children can do for me.'

'Why, Mrs Spicer?'

'Well, the place is in such a muck, and it hurts me.'

We were the aristocrats of Lahey's Creek. Whenever we drove down on Sunday afternoon to see Mrs Spicer, and as soon as we got near enough for them to hear the rattle of the car, we'd see the children running to the house as fast as they could split, and hear them screaming:

'Oh, marther! Here comes Mr and Mrs Wilson in their spring-cart.'

And we'd see her bustle round, and two or three fowls fly out the front door, and she'd lay hold of a broom (made of a bound bunch of 'broom-stuff' – coarse reedy grass or bush from the ridges – with a stick stuck in it) and flick out the floor, with a flick or two round in front of the door perhaps. The floor nearly always needed at least one flick of the broom on account of the fowls. Or she'd catch a youngster and scrub his face with a wet end of a cloudy towel or twist the towel round her finger and dig out his ears – as if she was anxious to have him hear every word that was going to be said.

No matter what state the house would be in she'd always say, 'I was jist expectin' yer, Mrs Wilson.' And she was original in that, anyway.

She had an old patched and darned white table-cloth that she used to spread on the table when we were there, as a matter of course ('The others is in the wash, so you must excuse this, Mrs Wilson'), but I saw by the eyes of the children that the cloth was rather a wonderful thing for them. 'I must really git some more knives and forks next time I'm in Cobborah,' she'd say. 'The children will break an' lose 'em till I'm ashamed ter ask Christians ter sit down ter the table.'

She had many bush yarns, some of them very funny, some of them rather ghastly, but all interesting, and with a grim sort of humour about them. But the effect was often spoilt by her screaming at the children to 'Drive out them fowls, karn't yer,' or 'Take yer maulies [hands] outer the sugar,' or 'Don't touch Mrs Wilson's baby with them dirty maulies,' or 'Don't stand starin' at Mrs Wilson with yer mouth an' ears in that vulgar way.'

Poor woman! she seemed everlastingly nagging at the children. It was a habit, but they didn't seem to mind. Most bushwomen get the nagging habit. I remember one, who had the prettiest, dearest, sweetest, most willing, and affec- tionate little girl I think I ever saw, and she nagged that child from daylight till dark – and after it. Taking it all round, I think that the nagging habit in a mother is often worse on ordinary children, and more deadly on sensitive youngsters, than the drinking habit in a father.

One of the yarns Mrs Spicer told us was about a squatter she knew who used to go wrong in his head every now and again, and try to commit suicide. Once, when the station-hand, who was watching him, had his eye off him for a minute, he hanged himself to a beam in the stable. The men ran in and found him hanging and kicking. 'They let him hang for a while,' said Mrs Spicer, 'till he went black in the face and stopped kicking. Then they cut him down and threw a bucket of water over him.'

'Why! what on earth did they let the man hang for?' asked Mary.

'To give him a good bellyful of it: they thought it would cure him of tryin' to hang himself again.'

'Well, that's the coolest thing I ever heard of,' said Mary.

'That's jist what the magistrate said, Mrs Wilson,' said Mrs Spicer.

'One morning,' said Mrs Spicer, 'Spicer had gone off on his horse somewhere, and I was alone with the children, when a man came to the door and said:

'For God's sake, woman, give me a drink!'

'Lord only knows where he came from! He was dressed like a new chum, his clothes was good, but he looked as if he'd been sleepin' in them in the bush for a month. He was very shaky. I had some coffee that mornin' so I gave him some in a pint-pot; he drank it, and then he stood on his head till he tumbled over, and then he stood up on his feet and said, "Thenk yer, mum."

'I was so surprised that I didn't know what to say, so I jist said, "Would you like some more coffee?"

'"Yes, thenk yer," he said – "about two quarts."

'I nearly filled the pint-pot, and he drank it and stood on his head as long as he could, and when he got right end up he said, "Thenk yer, mum – it's a fine day," and then he walked off. He had two saddle-straps in his hands.'

'Why, what did he stand on his head for?' asked Mary.

'To wash it up and down, I suppose, to get twice as much taste of the coffee. He had no hat. I sent Tommy across to Wall's to tell them that there was a man wanderin' about the bush in the horrors of drink, and to get someone to ride for the police. But they were too late, for he hanged himself that night.'

'O Lord!' cried Mary.

'Yes, right close to here, jist down the creek where the track to Wall's branches off. Tommy found him while he was out after the cows. Hangin' to the branch of a tree with the two saddle-straps.'

Mary stared at her, speechless.

'Tommy came home yellin' with fright. I sent him over to Wall's at once. After breakfast, the minute my eyes was off them, the children slipped away and went down there. They came back screamin' at the tops of their voices. I did give it to them. I reckon they won't want ter see a dead body again in a hurry. Every time I'd mention it they'd huddle together, or ketch hold of me skirts and howl.

"'Yer'll go agen when I tell yer not to,'" I'd say.

"'Oh no, mother,'" they'd howl.

"'Yer wanted ter see a man hangin','," I said.

"'Oh, don't, mother! Don't talk about it.'"

"'Yer wouldn't be satisfied till yer see it,'" I'd say; "yer had to see it or burst. Yer satisfied now, ain't yer?'"

"'Oh, don't, mother!'"

"'Yer run all the way there, I s'pose?'"

"'Don't, mother!'"

"'But yer run faster back, didn't yer?'"

"'Oh, don't, mother.'"

'But,' said Mrs Spicer, in conclusion, 'I'd been down to see it myself before they was up.'

'And ain't you afraid to live alone here, after all these horrible things?' asked Mary.

'Well, no; I don't mind. I seem to have got past carin' for anythink now. I felt it a little when Tommy went away – the first time I felt anythink for years. But I'm over that now.'

'Haven't you got any friends in the district, Mrs Spicer?'

'Oh yes. There's me married sister near Cobborah, and a married brother near Dubbo; he's got a station. They wanted to take me an' the children between them, or take some of the younger children. But I couldn't bring my mind to break up the home. I want to keep the children together as much as possible. There's enough of them gone, God knows. But it's a comfort to know that there's someone to see to them if anythink happens me.'

One day – I was on my way home with the team that day – Annie Spicer came running up the creek in terrible trouble.

'Oh, Mrs Wilson! something terrible's happened at home. A trooper' (mounted policeman – they called them 'mounted troopers' out there), 'a trooper's come and took Billy!' Billy was the eldest son at home.

'What?'

'It's true, Mrs Wilson.'

'What for? What did the policeman say?'

'He – he – he said, "I – I'm very sorry, Mrs Spicer; but I – I want William."'

It turned out that William was wanted on account of a horse missed from Wall's station and sold down-country.

'An' mother took on awful,' sobbed Annie; 'an' now she'll only sit stock-still an' stare in front of her, and won't take no notice of any of us. Oh! it's awful, Mrs Wilson. The policeman said he'd tell Aunt Emma' (Mrs Spicer's sister at Cobborah), 'and send her out. But I had to come to you, an' I've run all the way.'

James put the horse to the cart and drove Mary down.

'I found her just as Annie said; but she broke down and cried in my arms. Oh, Joe! It was awful. She didn't cry like a woman. I heard a man at Haviland cry at his brother's funeral, and it was just like that. She came round a bit after a while. Her sister's with her now ... Oh, Joe! You must take me away from the bush.'

Later on Mary said:

'How the oaks are sighing to-night, Joe!'

Next morning I rode across to Wall's station and tackled the old man; but he was a hard man, and wouldn't listen to me – in fact, he ordered me off his station. I was a selector and that was enough for him. But young Billy Wall rode after me.

'Look here, Joe!' he said, 'it's a blanky shame. All for the sake of a horse! As if that poor devil of a woman hasn't got enough to put up with already! I wouldn't do it for twenty horses. I'll tackle the boss, and if he won't listen to me, I'll walk off the run for the last time, if I have to carry my swag.'

Billy Wall managed it. The charge was withdrawn, and we got young Billy Spicer off up-country.

But poor Mrs Spicer was never the same after that. She seldom came up to our place unless Mary dragged her, so to speak; and then she would talk of nothing but her last trouble, till her visits were painful to look forward to.

'If it only could have been kep' quiet – for the sake of the other children; they are all I think of now. I tried to bring 'em all up decent, but I s'pose it was my fault, somehow. It's the disgrace that's killin' me – I can't bear it.'

I was at home one Sunday with Mary, and a jolly bush-girl named Maggie Charlsworth, who rode over sometimes from Wall's station (I must tell you about her some other time; James was 'shook after her'), and we got talkin' about Mrs Spicer. Maggie was very warm about old Wall.

'I expected Mrs Spicer up to-day,' said Mary. 'She seems better lately.'

'Why!' cried Maggie Charlsworth, 'if that ain't Annie coming running up along the creek. Something's the matter!'

We all jumped up and ran out.

'What is it, Annie?' cried Mary.

'Oh, Mrs Wilson! Mother's asleep, and we can't wake her!'

'What?'

'It's – it's the truth, Mrs Wilson.'

'How long has she been asleep?'

'Since lars' night.'

'My God!' cried Mary, 'since last night?'

'No, Mrs Wilson, not all the time; she woke wonst, about daylight this mornin'. She called me and said she didn't feel well, and I'd have to manage the milkin'.'

'Was that all she said?'

'No. She said not to go for you; and she said to feed the pigs and calves; and she said to be sure and water them geraniums.'

Mary wanted to go, but I wouldn't let her. James and I saddled our horses and rode down the creek.

Mrs Spicer looked very little different from what she did when I last saw her alive. It was some time before we could believe that she was dead. But she was 'past carin'' right enough.

A Double Buggy at
Lahey's Creek

I

SPUDS, AND A WOMAN'S OBSTINACY

EVER SINCE we were married it had been Mary's great ambition to have a buggy. The house or furniture didn't matter so much – out there in the bush where we were – but, where there were no railways or coaches, and the roads were long and mostly hot and dusty, a buggy was the great thing. I had a few pounds when we were married, and was going to get one then; but new buggies went high, and another party got hold of a second-hand one that I'd had my eye on, so Mary thought it over and at last she said, 'Never mind the buggy, Joe; get a sewing-machine and I'll be satisfied. I'll want the machine more than the buggy, for a while. Wait till we're better off.'

After that, whenever I took a contract – to put up a fence or wool-shed, or sink a dam or something – Mary would say, 'You ought to knock a buggy out of this job, Joe;' but something always turned up – bad weather or sickness. Once I cut my foot with the adze and was laid up; and, another time, a dam I was making was washed away by a flood before I finished it. Then Mary would say, 'Ah, well – never mind, Joe. Wait till we are better off.' But she felt it hard the time I built a woolshed and didn't get paid for it, for we'd as good as settled about another second-hand buggy then.

I always had a fancy for carpentering, and was handy with tools. I made a spring-cart – body and wheels – in spare time, out of colonial hardwood, and got Little the blacksmith to do the ironwork: I painted the cart myself. It wasn't much lighter than one of the tip-drays I had, but it was a spring-cart, and Mary pretended to be satisfied with it: anyway, I didn't hear any more of the buggy for a while.

I sold that cart for fourteen pounds, to a Chinese gardener who wanted a strong cart to carry his vegetables round through the bush. It was just before our first youngster came: I told Mary that I wanted the money in case of extra expense – and she didn't fret much at losing the cart. But the fact was that I was going to make another try for a buggy, as a present for Mary when the child was born. I thought of getting the turn-out while she was laid up, keeping it dark from her till she was on her feet again, and then showing her the buggy standing in the shed. But she had a bad time, and I had to have the doctor regularly, and get a proper nurse, and a lot of things extra; so the buggy idea was knocked on the head. I was set on it, too; I'd thought of how, when Mary was up and getting strong; I'd say one morning, 'Go round and have a look in the shed, Mary; I've got a few fowls for you,' or something like that – and follow her round to watch her eyes when she saw the buggy. I never told Mary about that – it wouldn't have done any good.

Later on I got some good timber – mostly scraps that were given to me – and made a light body for a spring-cart. Galletly, the coach-builder at Cudgegong, had got a dozen pairs of American hickory wheels up from Sydney, for light spring-carts, and he let me have a pair for cost price and carriage. I got him to iron the cart, and he put it through the paint-shop for nothing. He sent it out, too, at the tail of Tom Tarrant's big van – to increase the surprise. We were swells then for a while; I heard no more of a buggy until after we'd settled at Lahey's Creek for a couple of years.

I told you how I went into the carrying line, and took up a selection at Lahey's Creek – for a run for the horses and to grow a bit of feed – and shifted Mary and little Jim out there from Gulgong, with Mary's young scamp of a brother James to keep them company while I was on the road. The first year I did well enough carrying, but I never cared for it – it was too slow; and, besides, I was always anxious when I was away from home. The game was right enough for a single man – or a married one whose wife had got the nagging habit (as many bushwomen have – God help 'em), and who wanted peace and quietness sometimes. Besides, other small carriers started (seeing me getting on); Tom Tarrant, the coach-builder at Cudgegong, had another heavy spring-van built, and put it on the road, and he took a lot of the light stuff.

The second year I made a rise – out of 'spuds,' of all the things in the world. It was Mary's idea. Down at the lower end of our selection – Mary called it 'the run' – was a shallow watercourse called Snake's Creek, dry most of the year, except for a muddy waterhole or two; and, just above the junction, where it ran into Lahey's Creek, was a low piece of good black-soil flat, on our side – about three acres. The flat was fairly clear when I came to the selection – save for a few logs that had been washed up there in some big 'old man' flood, way back in blackfellows' times: and one day when I had a spell at home, I got the horses and trace-chains and dragged the logs together – those that wouldn't split for fencing timber – and burnt them off. I had a notion to get the flat ploughed and make a lucerne-paddock of it. There was a good waterhole, under a clump of she-oak in the bend, and Mary used to take her stools and tubs and boiler down there in the spring-cart in hot weather, and wash the clothes under the shade of the trees – it was cooler, and saved carrying water to the house. And one evening after she'd done the washing she said to me:

'Look here, Joe; the farmers out here never seem to get a new idea: they don't seem to me ever to try and find out beforehand what the market is going to be like – they just go on farming the same old way, and putting in the same old crops year after year. They sow wheat, and if it comes on anything like the thing, they reap and thresh it; if it doesn't they mow it for hay – and some of 'em don't have the brains to do that in time. Now I was looking at that bit of flat you cleared, and it struck me that it wouldn't be a half-bad idea to get a bag of seed potatoes, and have the land ploughed – old Corny George would do it cheap – and get them put in at once. Potatoes have been dear all round for the last couple of years.'

I told her she was talking nonsense, that the ground was no good for potatoes, and the whole district was too dry. 'Everybody I know has tried it one time or another, and made nothing of it,' I said.

'All the more reason why you should try it, Joe,' said Mary. 'Just try one crop. It might rain for weeks, and then you'll be sorry you didn't take my advice.'

'But I tell you the ground is not potato-ground,' I said.

'How do you know? You haven't sown any there yet.'

'But I've turned up the surface and looked at it. It's not rich enough, and too dry, I tell you. You need swampy, boggy ground for potatoes. Do you think I don't know land when I see it?'

'But you haven't tried to grow potatoes there yet, Joe. How do you know —?'

I didn't listen to any more. Mary was obstinate when she got an idea into her head. It was no use arguing with her. All the time I'd be talking she'd just knit her forehead and go on thinking straight ahead, on the track she'd started – just as if I wasn't there – and it used to make me mad. She'd keep driving at me till I took her advice or lost my temper – I did both at the same time, mostly.

I took my pipe and went out to smoke and cool down.

A couple of days after the potato breeze, I started with the team down to Cudgegong for a load of fencing-wire I had to bring out; and after I'd kissed Mary good-bye, she said:

'Look here, Joe, if you bring out a bag of seed potatoes, James and I will slice them, and old Corny George down the creek would bring his plough up in the dray, and plough the ground for very little. We could put the potatoes in ourselves if the ground were only ploughed.'

I thought she'd forgotten all about it. There was no time to argue – I'd be sure to lose my temper, and then I'd either have to waste an hour comforting Mary, or go off in a 'huff,' as the women call it, and be miserable for the trip. So I said I'd see about it. She gave me another hug and kiss. 'Don't forget, Joe,' she said as I started. 'Think it over on the road.' I reckon she had the best of it that time.

About five miles along, just as I turned into the main road, I heard someone galloping after me, and I saw young James on his hack. I got a start, for I thought that something had gone wrong at home. I remember the first day I left Mary on the creek, for the first five or six miles I was half a dozen times on the point of turning back – only I thought she'd laugh at me.

'What is it, James?' I shouted, before he came up – but I saw he was grinning.

'Mary says to tell you not to forget to bring a hoe out with you.'

'You clear off home!' I said, 'or I'll lay the whip about your young hide; and don't come riding after me again as if the run was on fire.'

'Well, you needn't get shirty with me!' he said. 'I don't want to have anything to do with a hoe.' And he rode off.

I did get thinking about those potatoes, though I hadn't meant to. I knew of an independent man in that district who'd made his money out of a crop of potatoes; but that was away back in the roaring fifties – fifty-four – when spuds went up to twenty-eight shillings a hundredweight (in Sydney), on account of the gold rush. We might get good rain now, and, anyway, it wouldn't cost much to put the potatoes in. If they came on well, it would be a few pounds in my pocket; if the crop was a failure, I'd have a better show with Mary next time she was struck by an idea outside housekeeping, and have something to grumble about when I felt grumpy.

I got a couple of bags of potatoes – we could use those that were left over; and I got a small iron plough and harrow that Little the blacksmith had lying in his yard and let me have cheap – only about a pound more than I told Mary I gave for them. When I took advice I generally made the mistake of taking more than was offered, or adding notions of my own. It was vanity, I suppose. If the crop came on well I could claim the plough-and-harrow part of the idea, anyway. (It didn't strike me that if the crop failed Mary would have the plough and harrow against me, for old Corny would plough the ground for ten or fifteen shillings.) Anyway, I'd want a plough and harrow later on, and I might as well get it now; it would give James something to do.

I came out by the western road, by Guntawang, and up the creek home; and the first thing I saw was old Corny George ploughing the flat. And Mary was down on the bank superintending. She'd got James with the trace-chains and the spare horses, and had made him clear off every stick and bush where another furrow might be squeezed in. Old Corny looked pretty grumpy on it – he'd broken all his ploughshares but one, in the roots; and James didn't look much brighter. Mary had an old felt hat and a new pair of 'lastic-side boots of mine on, and the boots were covered with clay, for she'd been down hustling James to get a rotten old stump out of the way by the time old Corny came round with his next furrow.

'I thought I'd make the boots easy for you, Joe,' said Mary.

'It's all right, Mary,' I said, 'I'm not going to growl.' Those boots were a bone of contention between us; but she generally got them off before I got home.

Her face fell when she saw the plough and harrow in the wagon, but I said that would be all right – we'd want a plough anyway.

'I thought you wanted old Corny to plough the ground,' she said.

'I never said so.'

'But when I sent Jim after you about the hoe to put the spuds in, you didn't say you wouldn't bring it,' she said.

I had a few days at home, and entered into the spirit of the thing. When Corny was done, James and I cross-ploughed the land, and got a stump or two, a big log, and some scrub out of the way at the upper end and added nearly an acre, and ploughed that. James was all right at most bushwork: he'd bullock so long as the novelty lasted; he liked ploughing or fencing, or any graft he could make a show at. He didn't care for grubbing out stumps, or splitting posts and rails. We sliced the potatoes of an evening – and there was trouble between Mary and James over cutting through the 'eyes.' There was no time for the hoe – and besides it wasn't a novelty to James – so I just ran furrows and they dropped the spuds in behind me, and I turned another furrow over them, and ran the harrow over the ground. I think I hilled those spuds, too, with furrows – or a crop of Indian corn I put in later on.

It rained heavens-hard for over a week: we had regular showers all through, and it was the finest crop of potatoes ever seen in the district. I believe at first Mary used to slip down at daybreak to see if the potatoes were up; and she'd write to me about them, on the road. I forget how many bags I got but the few who had grown potatoes in the district sent theirs to Sydney, and spuds went up to twelve and fifteen shillings a hundredweight in that district. I made a few quid out of mine – and saved carriage too, for I could take them out on the wagon. Then Mary began to hear (through James) of a buggy that someone had for sale cheap, or a dogcart that somebody else wanted to get rid of – and let me know about it, in an off-hand way.

II

JOE WILSON'S LUCK

THERE was good grass on the selection all the year. I'd picked up a small lot – about twenty head – of half-starved steers for next to nothing, and turned them on the run; they came on wonderfully, and my brother-in-law (Mary's sister's husband), who was running a butchery at Gulgong, gave me a good price for them. His carts ran out twenty or thirty miles, to little bits of gold rushes that were going on at th' Home Rule, Happy Valley, Guntawang, Tallawang, and Cooyal, and those places round there, and he was doing well.

Mary had heard of a light American wagonette, when the steers went – a tray-body arrangement, and she thought she'd do with that. 'It would be better than the buggy, Joe,' she said. 'There'd be more room for the children, and, besides, I could take butter and eggs to Gulgong, or Cobborah, when we get a few more cows.' Then James heard of a small flock of sheep that a selector – who was about starved off his selection out Talbragar way – wanted to get rid of. We'd had a heavy shower of rain, that came over the ranges and didn't seem to go beyond our boundaries. Mary said, 'It's a pity to see all that grass going to waste, Joe. Better get those sheep and try your luck with them. Never mind about the buggy – we'll get that when we're on our feet.'

So James rode across to Talbragar and drove a hard bargain with that unfortunate selector, and brought the sheep home. There were about two hundred, wethers and ewes, and they were young and looked a good breed too, but so poor they could scarcely travel; they soon picked up, though. The drought was blazing all round and out back, and I think that my corner of the ridges was the only place where there was any grass to speak of. We had another shower or two, and the grass held out. Chaps began to talk of 'Joe Wilson's luck.'

I would have liked to shear those sheep; but I hadn't time to get a shed or anything ready – along towards Christmas there was a bit of a boom in the carrying line. Wethers in wool were going as high as thirteen to fifteen shillings at the Homebush yards at Sydney, so I arranged to truck the sheep down from the river by rail, with another small lot that was going, and I started James off with them. He took the west road, and down Guntawang way a big farmer who saw James with the sheep (and who was speculating, or adding to his stock, or took a fancy to the wool) offered James as much for them as he reckoned I'd get in Sydney, after paying the carriage and the agents and the auctioneer. James put the sheep in a paddock and rode back to me. He was all there where riding was concerned. I told him to let the sheep go. James made a Greener shot-gun, and got his saddle done up, out of that job.

I took up a couple more forty-acre blocks – one in James's name, to encourage him with the fencing. There was a good slice of land in an angle between the range and the creek, farther down, which everybody thought belonged to Wall, the squatter, but Mary got an idea, and went to the local land office, and found out that it was unoccupied Crown land, and so I took it up on pastoral lease, and got a few more sheep – I'd saved some of the best-looking ewes from the last lot.

One evening – I was going down next day for a load of fencing-wire for myself – Mary said:

'Joe! Do you know that the Matthews have got a new double buggy?'

The Matthews were a big family of cockatoos, along up the main road, and I didn't think much of them. The sons were all 'bad-eggs,' though the old woman and girls were right enough.

'Well, what of that?' I said. 'They're up to their neck in debt, and camping like blackfellows in a big bark humpy. They do well to go flashing round in a double buggy.'

'But that isn't what I was going to say,' said Mary. 'They want to sell their old single buggy, James says. I'm sure you could get it for six or seven pounds; and you could have it done up.'

'I wish James to the devil!' I said. 'Can't he find anything better to do than ride round after cock-and-bull yarns about buggies?'

'Well,' said Mary, 'it was James who got the steers and the sheep.'

Well, one word led to another, and we said things we didn't mean – but couldn't forget in a hurry. I remember I said something about Mary always dragging me back just when I was getting my head above water and struggling to make a home for her and the children; and that hurt her, and she spoke of the 'homes' she'd had since she was married. And that cut me deep.

It was about the worst quarrel we had. When she began to cry I got my hat and went out and walked up and down by the creek. I hated anything that looked like injustice – I was so sensitive about it that it made me unjust sometimes. I tried to think I was right, but I couldn't – it wouldn't have made me feel any better if I could have thought so. I got thinking of Mary's first year on the selection and the life she'd had since we were married.

When I went in she'd cried herself to sleep. I bent over and, 'Mary,' I whispered.

She seemed to wake up.

'Joe – Joe!' she said.

'What is it, Mary?' I said.

'I'm pretty sure that old Spot's calf isn't in the pen. Make James go at once!'

Old Spot's last calf was two years old now; so Mary was talking in her sleep, and dreaming she was back in her first year.

We both laughed when I told her about it afterwards; but I didn't feel like laughing just then.

Later on in the night she called out in her sleep:

'Joe – Joe! Put that buggy in the shed, or the sun will blister the varnish!'

I wish I could say that that was the last time I ever spoke unkindly to Mary.

Next morning I got up early and fried the bacon and made the tea, and took Mary's breakfast in to her – like I used to do sometimes, when we were first married. She didn't say anything – just pulled my head down and kissed me.

When I was ready to start, Mary said:

'You'd better take the spring-cart in behind the dray, and get the tyres cut and set. They're ready to drop off, and James has been wedging them up till he's tired of it. The last time I was out with the children I had to knock one of them back with a stone: there'll be an accident yet.'

So I lashed the shafts of the cart under the tail of the wagon and mean and ridiculous enough the cart looked, going along that way. It suggested a man stooping along handcuffed, with his arms held out and down in front of him.

It was dull weather, and the scrubs looked extra dreary and endless – and I got thinking of old things. Everything was going all right with me, but that didn't keep me from brooding sometimes – trying to hatch out stones, like an old hen we had at home. I think, taking it all round, I used to be happier when I was mostly hard up – and more generous. When I had ten pounds I was more likely to listen to a chap who said, 'Lend me a pound note, Joe,' than when I had fifty; then I fought shy of careless chaps – and lost mates that I wanted afterwards – and got the name of being mean. When I got a good cheque I'd be as miserable as a miser over the first ten pounds I spent; but when I got down to the last I'd buy things for the house. And now that I was getting on, I hated to spend a pound on anything. But then, the farther I got away from poverty the greater the fear I had of it – and, besides, there was always before us all the thought of the terrible drought, with blazing runs as bare and dusty as the road, and dead stock rotting every yard, all along the barren creeks.

I had a long yarn with Mary's sister and her husband that night in Gulgong, and it brightened me up. I had a fancy that that sort of a brother-in-law made a better mate than a nearer one; Tom Tarrant had one, and he said it was sympathy. But while we were yarning I couldn't help thinking of Mary, out there in the hut on the creek, with no one to talk to but the children, or James, who was sulky at home, or Black Mary or Black Jimmy (our black boy's father and mother), who weren't over-sentimental. Or, maybe, a selector's wife (the nearest was five miles away) who could talk only of two or three things – 'lambin'' and 'shearin'' and 'cookin' for the men,' and what she said to her old man, and what he said to her – and her own ailments over and over again.

It's a wonder it didn't drive Mary mad! – I know I could never listen to that woman more than an hour. Mary's sister said:

'Now if Mary had a comfortable buggy, she could drive in with the children oftener. Then she wouldn't feel the loneliness so much.'

I said 'Good night' then and turned in. There was no getting away from that buggy. Whenever Mary's sister started hinting about a buggy, I reckoned it was a put-up job between them.

III

THE GHOST OF MARY'S SACRIFICE

WHEN I got to Cudgegong I stopped at Galletly's coach-shop to leave the cart. The Galletlys were good fellows: there were two brothers – one was a saddler and harness-maker. Big brown-bearded men – the biggest men in the district, 'twas said.

Their old man had died lately and left them some money; they had men, and only worked in their shops when they felt inclined, or there was a special work to do; they were both first-class tradesmen. I went into the painter's shop to have a look at a double buggy that Galletly had built for a man who couldn't pay cash for it when it was finished – and Galletly wouldn't trust him.

There it stood, behind a calico screen that the coach-painters used to keep out the dust when they were varnishing. It was a first-class piece of work – pole, shafts, cushions, whip, lamps, and all complete. If you only wanted to drive one horse you could take out the pole and put in the shafts, and there you were. There was a tilt over the front seat; if you only wanted the buggy to carry two, you could fold down the back seat, and there you had a handsome, roomy, single buggy. It would go near fifty pounds.

While I was looking at it, Bill Galletly came in and slapped me on the back.

'Now, there's a chance for you, Joe!' he said. 'I saw you rubbing your head round that buggy the last time you were in. You wouldn't get a better one in the colonies, and you won't see another like it in the district again in a hurry – for it doesn't pay to build 'em. Now you're a full-blown squatter, and it's time you took little Mary for a fly round in her own buggy now and then, instead of having her stuck out there in the scrub, or jolting through the dust in a cart like some old Mother Flourbag.'

He called her 'Little Mary' because the Galletly family had known her when she was girl.

I rubbed my head and looked at the buggy again. It was a great temptation.

'Look here, Joe,' said Bill Galletly in a quieter tone. 'I'll tell you what I'll do. I'll let you have the buggy. You can take it out and send along a bit of a cheque when you feel you can manage it, and the rest later on – a year will do, or even two years. You've had a hard pull, and I'm not likely to be hard up for money in a hurry.'

They were good fellows the Galletlys, but they knew their men. I happened to know that Bill Galletly wouldn't let the man he built the buggy for take it out of the shop without cash down, though he was a big-bug round there. But that didn't make it easier for me.

Just then Robert Galletly came into the shop. He was rather quieter than his brother, but the two were very much alike.

'Look here, Bob,' said Bill; 'here's a chance for you to get rid of your harness. Joe Wilson's going to take that buggy off my hands.'

Bob Galletly put his foot up on a saw-stool, took one hand out of his pocket, rested his elbow on his knee and his chin on the palm of his hand, and bunched up his big beard with his fingers, as he always did when he was thinking. Presently he took his foot down, put his hand back in his pocket, and said to me, 'Well, Joe, I've got a double set of harness made for the man who ordered that damned buggy, and if you like I'll let you have it. I suppose when Bill there has squeezed all he can out of you I'll stand a show of getting something. He's a regular Shylock, he is.'

I pushed my hat forward and rubbed the back of my head and stared at the buggy.

'Come across to the Royal, Joe,' said Bob.

But I knew that a beer would settle the business, so I said I'd get the wool up to the station first and think it over, and have a drink when I came back.

I thought it over on the way to the station, but it didn't seem good enough. I wanted to get some more sheep, and there was the new run to be fenced in, and the instalments on the selections. I wanted lots of things that I couldn't well do without. Then, again, the farther I got away from debt and hard-upedness the greater the horror I had of it. I had two horses that would do; but I'd have to get another later on, and altogether the buggy would run me nearer a hundred than fifty pounds. Supposing a dry season threw me back with that buggy on my hands. Besides, I wanted a spell. If I got the buggy it would only mean an extra turn of hard graft for me. No, I'd take Mary for a trip to Sydney, and she'd have to be satisfied with that.

I'd got it settled, and was just turning in through the big white gates to the goods-shed when young Black, the squatter, dashed past to the station in his big new wagonette, with his wife and a driver and a lot of portmanteaux and rugs and things. They were going to do the grand in Sydney over Christmas. Now it was young Black who was so shook after Mary when she was in service with the Blacks before the old man died, and if I hadn't come along – and if girls never cared for vagabonds – Mary would have been mistress of Haviland homestead, with servants to wait on her; and she was far better fitted for it than the one that was there. She would have been going to Sydney every holiday and putting up at the old Royal, with every comfort that a woman could ask for, and seeing a play every night. And I'd have been knocking around amongst the big stations out back, or maybe drinking myself to death at the shanties.

The Blacks didn't see me as I went by, ragged and dusty, and with an old, nearly black cabbage-tree hat drawn over my eyes. I didn't care a damn for them, or any one else, at most times, but I had moods when I felt things.

One of Black's big wool-teams was just coming away from the shed, and the driver, a big, dark, rough fellow, with some foreign blood in him, didn't seem inclined to wheel his team an inch out of the middle of the road. I stopped my horses and waited. He looked at me and I looked at him – hard. Then he wheeled off, scowling, and swearing at his horses. I'd given him a hiding, six or seven years before, and he hadn't forgotten it. And I felt then as if I wouldn't mind trying to give someone a hiding.

The goods clerk must have thought that Joe Wilson was pretty grumpy that day. I was thinking of Mary, out there in the lonely hut on a barren creek in the bush – for it was little better – with no one to speak to except a haggard, worn-out bushwoman or two that came to see her on Sunday. I thought of the hardships she went through in the first year – that I haven't told you about yet; of the time she was ill, and I away, and no one to understand; of the time she was alone with James and Jim sick; and of the loneliness she fought through out there. I thought of Mary, outside in the blazing heat, with an old print dress and a felt hat, and a pair of 'lastic-siders of mine on, doing the work of a station manager as well as that of a housewife and mother. And her cheeks were getting thin, and the colour was going: I thought of the gaunt, brick-brown saw-file voiced, hopeless and spiritless bushwomen I knew – and some of them not much older than Mary.

When I went back into the town, I had a drink with Bill Galletly at the Royal, and that settled the buggy; then Bob shouted, and I took the harness. Then I shouted, to wet the bargain. When I was going, Bob said, 'Send in that young scamp of a brother of Mary's with the horses: if the collars don't fit I'll fix up a pair of make-shifts, and alter the others.' I thought they both gripped my hand harder than usual, but that might have been the beer.

IV

THE BUGGY COMES HOME

I 'WHIPPED the cat' a bit, the first twenty miles or so, but then, I thought, what did it matter? What was the use of grinding to save money until we were too old to enjoy it. If we had to go down in the world again, we might as well fall out of a buggy as out of a dray – there'd be some talk about it, any-way, and perhaps a little sympathy. When Mary had the buggy she wouldn't be tied down so much to that wretched hole in the bush; and the Sydney trips need-n't be off either. I could drive down to Wallerawang on the main line, where Mary had some people, and leave the buggy and horses there, and take the train to Sydney, or go right on, by the old coach road, over the Blue Mountains: it would be a grand drive. I thought best to tell Mary's sister at Gulgong about the buggy; I told her I'd keep it dark from Mary till the buggy came home. She entered into the spirit of the thing, and said she'd give the world to be able to go out with the buggy, if only to see Mary open her eyes when she saw it; but she couldn't go, on account of a new baby she had. I was rather glad she couldn't, for it would spoil the surprise a little, I thought. I wanted that all to myself.

I got home about sunset next day, and, after tea, when I'd finished telling Mary all the news, and a few lies as to why I didn't bring the cart back, and one or two other things, I sat with James, out on a log of the wood-heap, where we general-ly had our smokes and interviews, and told him all about the buggy. He whis-tled, then he said:

'But what do you want to make it such a bushranging business for? Why can't you tell Mary now? It will cheer her up. She's been pretty miserable since you've been away this trip.'

'I want it to be a surprise,' I said.

'Well, I've got nothing to say against a surprise, out in a hole like this; but it 'ud take a lot to surprise me. What am I to say to Mary about taking the two horses in? I'll only want one to bring the cart out, and she's sure to ask.'

'Tell her you're going to get yours shod.'

'But he had a set of slippers only the other day. She knows as much about hors-es as we do. I don't mind telling a lie so long as a chap had only got to tell a straight lie and be done with it. But Mary asks so many questions.'

'Well, drive the other horse up the creek early, and pick him up as you go.'

'Yes. And she'll want to know what I want with two bridles. But I'll fix her – you needn't worry.'

'And, James,' I said, 'get a chamois leather and sponge – we'll want 'em anyway – and you might give the buggy a wash down in the creek, coming home. It's sure to be covered with dust.'

'Oh! – orlright.'

'And if you can, time yourself to get here in the cool of the evening, or just about sunset.'

'What for?'

I'd thought it would be better to have the buggy there in the cool of the evening, when Mary would have time to get excited and get over it – better than in the blazing hot morning, when the sun rose as hot as at noon, and we'd have the long broiling day before us.

'What do you want me to come at sunset for?' asked James. 'Do you want me to camp out in the scrub and turn up like a blooming sundowner?'

'Oh well,' I said, 'get here at midnight if you like.'

We didn't say anything for a while – just sat and puffed at our pipes. Then I said:

'Well, what are you thinking about?'

'I'm thinking it's time you got a new hat, the sun seems to get in through your old one too much,' and he got out of my reach and went to see about penning the calves. Before we turned in he said:

'Well, what am I to get out of the job, Joe?'

He had his eye on a double-barrel gun that Franca the gunsmith in Cudgegong had – one barrel shot, and the other rifle; so I said:

'How much does Franca want for that gun?'

'Five-ten; but I think he'd take my single barrel off it. Anyway, I can squeeze a couple of quid out of Phil Lambert for the single barrel.' (Phil was his bosom chum.)

'All right,' I said. 'Make the best bargain you can.'

He got his own breakfast and made an early start next morning, to get clear of any instructions or messages that Mary might have forgotten to give him overnight. He took his gun with him.

I'd always thought that a man was a fool who couldn't keep a secret from his wife – that there was something womanish about him. I found out. Those three days waiting for the buggy were about the longest I ever spent in my life. It made me scotty with every one and everything; and poor Mary had to suffer for it. I put in the time patching up the harness and mending the stockyard and the roof, and, the third morning, I rode up the ridges to look for trees for fencing timber. I remember I hurried home that afternoon because I thought the buggy might get there before me.

At tea-time I got Mary on to the buggy business.

'What's the good of a single buggy to you, Mary?' I asked. 'There's only room for two, and what are you going to do with the children when we go out together?'

'We can put them on the floor at our feet, like other people do. I can always fold up a blanket or possum rug for them to sit on.'

But she didn't take half so much interest in buggy talk as she would have taken at any other time, when I didn't want her to. Women are aggravating that way. But the poor girl was tired and not very well, and both the children were cross. She did look knocked up.

'We'll give the buggy a rest, Joe,' she said. (I thought I heard it coming then.) 'It seems as far off as ever. I don't know why you want to harp on it to-day. Now, don't look so cross, Joe – I didn't mean to hurt you. We'll wait until we can get a double buggy, since you're so set on it. There'll be plenty of time when we're better off.'

After tea, when the youngsters were in bed, and she'd washed up, we sat on the edge of the veranda floor, Mary sewing, and I smoking and watching the track up the creek.

'Why don't you talk, Joe?' asked Mary. 'You scarcely ever speak to me now: it's like drawing blood out of a stone to get a word from you. What makes you so cross, Joe?'

'Well, I've got nothing to say.'

'But you should find something. Think of me – it's very miserable for me. Have you anything on your mind? Is there any new trouble? Better tell me, no matter what it is, and not go worrying and brooding and making both our lives miserable. If you never tell one anything, how can you expect me to understand?'

I said there was nothing the matter.

'But there must be, to make you so unbearable. Have you been drinking, Joe – or gambling?'

I asked her what she'd accuse me of next.

'And another thing I was to speak to you about,' she went on. 'Now, don't knit up your forehead like that, Joe, and get impatient —'

'Well, what is it?'

'I wish you wouldn't swear in the hearing of the children. Now, little Jim to-day, he was trying to fix his little go-cart, and it wouldn't run right, and – and —'

'Well, what did he say?'

'He – he' (she seemed a little hysterical, trying not to laugh) – 'he said, "Damn it!"'

I had to laugh. Mary tried to keep serious but it was no use.

'Never mind, old woman,' I said, putting an arm round her, for her mouth was trembling, and she was crying more than laughing. 'It won't be always like this. Just wait till we're a bit better off.'

Just then a black boy we had (I must tell you about him some other time) came sidling along by the wall, as if he were afraid somebody was going to hit him – poor little devil! I never did.

'What is it, Harry?' said Mary.

'Buggy comin', I bin thinkit.'

'Where?'

He pointed up the creek.

'Sure it's a buggy?'

'Yes, missus.'

'How many horses?'

'One – two.'

We knew that he could hear and see things long before we could. Mary went and perched on the wood-heap, and shaded her eyes – though the sun had gone – and peered through between the eternal grey trunks of the stunted trees on the flat across the creek. Presently she jumped down and came running in.

'There's someone coming in a buggy, Joe!' she cried, excitedly. 'And both my white table-cloths are rough dry. Harry! put two flat-irons down to the fire, quick, and put on some more wood. It's lucky I kept those new sheets packed away. Get up out of that, Joe? What are you sitting grinning like that for? Go and get on another shirt. Harry – Why, it's only James – by himself.'

She stared at me, and I sat there, grinning like a fool.

'Joe!' she said. 'Whose buggy is that?'

'Well, I suppose it's yours,' I said.

She caught her breath, and stared at the buggy, and then at me again. James drove down out of sight into the crossing, and came up close to the house.

'Oh, Joe! what have you done?' cried Mary. 'Why, it's a new double buggy.' Then she rushed at me and hugged my head. 'Why didn't you tell me, Joe? You poor old boy! – and I've been nagging at you all day!' And she hugged me again.

James got down and started taking the horses out – as if it was an everyday occurrence. I saw the double-barrel gun sticking out from under the seat. He'd stopped to wash the buggy, and I suppose that's what made him grumpy. Mary stood on the veranda, with her eyes twice as big as usual, and breathing hard – taking the buggy in.

James skimmed the harness off, and the horses shook themselves and went down to the dam for a drink. 'You'd better look under the seats,' growled James, as he took his gun out with great care.

Mary dived for the buggy. There was a dozen of lemonade and ginger-beer in the candle-box from Galletly – James said that Galletly's men had a gallon of beer, and they cheered him, James (I suppose he meant they cheered the buggy), as he drove off; there was a 'little bit of a ham' from Pat Murphy, the storekeeper at Home Rule, that he'd 'cured himself' – it was the biggest I ever saw; there were three loaves of baker's bread, a cake, and a dozen yards of something 'to make up for the children,' from Aunt Gertrude at Gulgong; there was a fresh-water cod, that long Dave Regan had caught the night before in the Macquarie River, and sent out packed in salt in a box; there was a Holland suit for the black boy, with red braid to trim it; and there was a jar of preserved ginger, and some lollies (sweets) ('for the lil' boy') and a rum-looking Chinese doll and a rattle ('for lil' girl') from Sun Tong Lee, our storekeeper at Gulgong – James was chummy with Sun Tong Lee and got his powder and shot and caps there on tick when he was short of money. And James said that the people would have loaded the buggy with 'rubbish' if he'd waited. They all seemed glad to see Joe Wilson getting on – and these things did me good.

We got the things inside, and I don't think either of us knew what we were saying or doing for the next half hour. Then James put his head in and said, in a very injured tone:

'What about my tea? I ain't had anything to speak of since I left Cudgegong. I want some grub.'

Then Mary pulled herself together.

'You'll have your tea directly,' she said. 'Pick up that harness at once, and hang it on the pegs in the skillion; and you, Joe, back that buggy under the end of the veranda, the dew will be on it presently – and we'll put wet bags up in front of it to-morrow, to keep the sun off. And James will have to go back to Cudgegong for the cart – we can't have that buggy to knock about in.'

'All right,' said James – 'anything! Only get me some grub.'

Mary fried the fish, in case it wouldn't keep till the morning, and rubbed over the table-cloths, now the irons were hot – James growling all the time – and got out some crockery she had packed away that had belonged to her mother, and set the table in a style that made James uncomfortable.

'I want some grub – not a blooming banquet!' he said. And he growled a lot because Mary wanted him to eat his fish without a knife, 'and that sort of tommy-rot.' When he'd finished he took his gun, and the black boy, and the dogs, and went out possum-shooting.

When we were alone Mary climbed into the buggy to try the seat, and made me get up alongside her. We hadn't had such a comfortable seat for years; but we soon got down, in case any one came by, for we began to feel like a pair of fools up there.

Then we sat, side by side, on the edge of the veranda, and talked more than we'd done for years – and there was a good deal of 'Do you remember?' in it – and I think we got to understand each other better that night.

And at last Mary said, 'Do you know, Joe, why, I feel to-night just – just like I did the day we were married.'

And somehow I had that strange, shy sort of feeling too.

JOE WILSON'S MATES

THE CHINAMAN'S GHOST

'SIMPLE AS STRIKING matches,' said Dave Regan, bushman; 'but it gave me the biggest scare I ever had – except, perhaps, the time I stumbled in the dark into a six-foot digger's hole, which might have been eighty feet deep for all I knew when I was falling. (There was an eighty-foot shaft left open close by.)

'It was the night of the day after the Queen's birthday. I was sinking a shaft with Jim Bently and Andy Page on the old Redclay goldfield, and we camped in a tent on the creek. Jim and me went to some races that was held at Peter Anderson's pub, about four miles across the ridges, on Queen's birthday. Andy was a quiet sort of chap, a teetotaller, and we'd disgusted him the last time he was out for a holiday with us, so he stayed at home and washed and mended his clothes, and read an arithmetic book. (He used to keep the accounts, and it took him most of his spare time.)

'Jim and me had a pretty high time. We all got pretty tight after the races, and I wanted to fight Jim, or Jim wanted to fight me – I don't remember which. We were old chums, and we nearly always wanted to fight each other when we got a bit on, and we'd fight if we weren't stopped. I remember once Jim got maudlin drunk and begged and prayed of me to fight him, as if he was praying for his life. Tom Tarrant, the coach-driver, used to say that Jim and me must be related, else we wouldn't hate each other so much when we were tight and truthful.

'Anyway, this day, Jim got the sulks, and caught his horse and went home early in the evening. My dog went home with him, too; I must have been carrying on pretty bad to disgust the dog.

'Next evening I got disgusted with myself, and started to walk home. I'd lost my hat, so Peter Anderson lent me an old one of his, that he'd worn on Ballarat he said: it was a hard, straw, flat, broad-brimmed affair, and fitted my headache pretty tight. Peter gave me a small flask of whisky to help me home. I had to go across some flats and up a long dark gully called Murderer's Gully, and over a gap called Dead Man's Gap, and down the ridge and gullies of Redclay Creek. The lonely flats were covered with blue-grey gum-bush, and looked ghostly enough in the moonlight, and I was pretty shaky, but I had a pull at the flask and a mouthful of water at a creek and felt right enough. I began to whistle and then sing: I never used to sing unless I thought I was a couple of miles out of earshot of any one.

'Murderer's Gully was deep and pretty dark most times, and of course it was haunted. Women and children wouldn't go through it after dark; and even me, when I'd grown up, I'd hold my back pretty holler, and whistle, and walk quick going along there at night-time. We're all afraid of ghosts, but we won't let on.

'Someone had skinned a dead calf during the day and left it on the track, and it gave me a jump, I promise you. It looked like two corpses laid out naked. I finished the whisky and started up over the gap. All of a sudden a great 'old man' kangaroo went across the track with a thud-thud, and up the sidling, and that startled me. Then the naked, white, glistening trunk of a stringy-bark tree, where someone had stripped off a sheet of bark, started out from a bend in the track in a shaft of moonlight, and that gave me a jerk. I was pretty shaky before I started. There was a Chinaman's grave close by the track on the top of the gap. An old Chow had lived in a hut there for many years, and fossicked on the old diggings, and one day he was found dead in the hut, and the Government gave someone a pound to bury him. When I was a nipper we reckoned that his ghost haunted the gap, and cursed in Chinese because the bones hadn't been sent home to China. It was a lonely, ghostly place enough.

'It had been a smotheringly hot day and very close coming across the flats and up the gully – not a breath of air; but now as I got higher I saw signs of the thunderstorm we'd expected all day, and felt the breath of a warm breeze on my face. When I got into the top of the gap the first thing I saw was something white amongst the dark bushes over the spot where the Chinaman's grave was, and I stood staring at it with both eyes. It moved out of the shadow presently, and I saw that it was a white bullock, and I felt relieved. I'd hardly felt relieved when, all at once, there came a 'pat-pat-pat' of running feet close behind me! I jumped round quick, but there was nothing there, and while I stood staring all ways for Sunday, there came a 'pat-pat,' then a pause, and then 'pat-pat-pat-pat' behind me again: it was like someone dodging and running off that time. I started to walk down the track pretty fast, but hadn't gone a dozen yards when 'pat-pat-pat,' it was close behind me again. I jerked my eyes over my shoulder but kept my legs going. There was nothing behind, but I fancied I saw something slip into the bush to the right. It must have been the moonlight on the moving boughs; there was a good breeze blowing now. I got down to a more level track, and was making across a spur to the main road, when 'pat-pat, pat-pat-pat, pat-pat-pat!' it was after me again. Then I began to run – and it began to run too! 'pat-pat-pat' after me all the time. I hadn't time to look round. Over the spur and down the sidling and across the flat to the road I went as fast as I could split my legs apart. I had a scared idea that I was getting a touch of the 'jim-jams,' and that frightened me more than any outside ghost could have done. I stumbled a few times, and saved myself, but, just before I reached the road, I fell slithering on to my hands on the grass and gravel. I thought I'd broken both my wrists. I stayed for a moment on my hands and knees, quaking and listening, squinting round like a great goanna; I couldn't hear nor see anything. I picked myself up, and had hardly got on one end, when 'pat-pat!' it was after me again. I must have run a mile and a half altogether that night. It was still about three-quarters of a mile to the camp, and I ran till my heart beat in my head and my lungs choked up in my throat. I saw our tent-fire and took off my hat to run faster. The footsteps stopped, then something about the hat touched my fingers, and I stared at it – and the thing dawned on me. I hadn't noticed at Peter Anderson's – my head was too swimmy to notice anything. It was an old hat of the style that the first diggers used to wear, with a couple of loose ribbon ends, three or four inches long, from the band behind. As long as I walked quietly through the gully, and there was no wind, the tails didn't flap, but when I got up into the breeze, they flapped or were still according to how the wind lifted them or pressed them down flat on the brim. And when I ran they tapped all the time; and the hat being tight on my head, the tapping of the ribbon ends against the straw sounded loud, of course.

'I sat down on a log for a while to get some of my wind back and cool down, and then I went to the camp as quietly as I could, and had a long drink of water.

'"You seem to be a bit winded, Dave," said Jim Bently, "and mighty thirsty. Did the Chinaman's ghost chase you?"

'I told him not to talk rot, and went into the tent, and lay down on my bunk, and had a good rest.'

THE LOADED DOG

DAVE REGAN, Jim Bently, and Andy Page were sinking a shaft at Stony Creek in search of a rich gold quartz reef which was supposed to exist in the vicinity. There is always a rich reef supposed to exist in the vicinity; the only questions are whether it is ten feet or hundreds beneath the surface, and in which direction. They had struck some pretty solid rock, also water which kept them baling. They used the old-fashioned blasting-powder and time-fuse. They'd make a sausage or cartridge of blasting-powder in a skin of strong calico or canvas, the mouth sewn and bound round the end of the fuse; they'd dip the cartridge in melted tallow to make it watertight, get the drill-hole as dry as possible, drop in the cartridge with some dry dust, and wad and ram with stiff clay and broken brick. Then they'd light the fuse and get out of the hole and wait. The result was usually an ugly pot-hole in the bottom of the shaft and half a barrow-load of broken rock.

There was plenty of fish in the creek, fresh-water bream, cod, cat-fish, and tailers. The party were fond of fish, and Andy and Dave of fishing. Andy would fish for three hours at a stretch if encouraged by a 'nibble' or a 'bite' now and then – say once in twenty minutes. The butcher was always willing to give meat in exchange for fish when they caught more than they could eat; but now it was winter, and these fish wouldn't bite. However, the creek was low, just a chain of muddy waterholes, from the hole with a few bucketfuls in it to the sizable pool with an average depth of six or seven feet, and they could get fish by baling out the smaller holes or muddying up the water in the larger ones till the fish rose to the surface. There was the cat-fish, with spikes growing out of the sides of its head, and if you got pricked you'd know it, as Dave said. Andy took off his boots, tucked up his trousers, and went into a hole one day to stir up the mud with his feet, and he knew it. Dave scooped one out with his hand and got pricked, and he knew it too; his arm swelled, and the paid throbbed up into his shoulder, and down into his stomach, too, he said, like a toothache he had once, and kept him awake for two nights – only the toothache pain had a 'burred edge,' Dave said.

Dave got an idea.

'Why not blow the fish up in the big waterhole with a cartridge?' he said. 'I'll try it.'

He thought the thing out and Andy Page worked it out. Andy usually put Dave's theories into practice if they were practicable, or bore the blame for the failure and the chaffing of his mates if they weren't.

He made a cartridge about three times the size of those they used in the rock. Jim Bently said it was big enough to blow the bottom out of the river. The inner skin was of stout calico; Andy stuck the end of a six-foot piece of fuse well down in the powder and bound the mouth of the bag firmly to it with whipcord. The idea was to sink the cartridge in the water with the open end of the fuse attached to a float on the surface, ready for lighting. Andy dipped the cartridge in melted bees-wax to make it watertight. 'We'll have to leave it some time before we light it,' said Dave, 'to give the fish time to get over their scare when we put it in, and come nosing round again; so we'll want it well watertight.'

Round the cartridge Andy, at Dave's suggestion, bound a strip of sail canvas – that they used for making water-bags – to increase the force of the explosion, and round that he pasted layers of stiff brown paper – on the plan of the sort of fireworks we called 'gun-crackers.' He let the paper dry in the sun, then he sewed a covering of two thicknesses of canvas over it, and bound the thing from end to end with stout fishing-line. Dave's schemes were elaborate, and he often worked his inventions out to nothing. The cartridge was rigid and solid enough now – a formidable bomb; but Andy and Dave wanted to be sure. Andy sewed on another layer of canvas, dipped the cartridge in melted tallow, twisted a length of fencing-wire round it as an afterthought, dipped it in tallow again, and stood it carefully against a tent-peg, where he'd know where to find it, and wound the fuse loosely round it. Then he went to the camp-fire to try some potatoes which were boiling in their jackets in a billy and to see about frying some chops for dinner. Dave and Jim were at work in the claim that morning.

They had a big black young retriever dog – or rather an overgrown pup, a big, foolish, four-footed mate, who was always slobbering round them and lashing their legs with his heavy tail that swung round like a stock-whip. Most of his head was usually a red, idiotic slobbering grin of appreciation of his own silliness. He seemed to take life, the world, his two-legged mates, and his own instinct as a huge joke. He'd retrieve anything; he carted back most of the camp rubbish that Andy threw away. They had a cat that died in hot weather, and Andy threw it a good distance away in the scrub; and early one morning the dog found the cat, after it had been dead a week or so, and carried it back to camp, and laid it just inside the tent-flaps, where it could best make its presence known when the mates should rise and begin to sniff suspiciously in the sickly smothering atmosphere of the summer sunrise. He used to retrieve them when they went in swimming; he'd jump in after them, and take their hands in his mouth, and try to swim out with them, and scratch their naked bodies with his paws. They loved him for his good-heartedness and his foolishness, but when they wished to enjoy a swim they had to tie him up in camp.

He watched Andy with great interest all the morning making the cartridge, and hindered him considerably, trying to help; but about noon he went off to the claim to see how Dave and Jim were getting on, and to come home to dinner with them. Andy saw them coming, and put a pan full of mutton-chops on the fire. Andy was cook to-day; Dave and Jim stood with their backs to the fire, as bushmen do in all weathers, waiting till dinner should be ready. The retriever went nosing round after something he seemed to have missed.

Andy's brain still worked on the cartridge; his eye was caught by the glare of an empty kerosene-tin lying in the bushes, and it struck him that it wouldn't be a bad idea to sink the cartridge packed with clay, sand, or stones in the tin, to increase the force of the explosion. He may have been all out, from a scientific point of view, but the notion looked all right to him. Jim Bently, by the way, was-n't interested in their 'damned silliness.' Andy noticed an empty treacle-tin – the sort with the little tin neck or spout soldered on to the top for the convenience of pouring out the treacle – and it struck him that this would have made the best kind of cartridge-case: he would only have had to pour in the powder, stick the fuse in through the neck, and cork and seal it with bees-wax. He was turning to suggest this to Dave, when Dave glanced over his shoulder to see how the chops were doing – and bolted. He explained afterwards that he thought he heard the pan spluttering extra, and looked to see if the chops were burning. Jim Bently looked behind and bolted after Dave. Andy stood stock-still, staring after them.

'Run, Andy! Run!' they shouted back at him. 'Run! Look behind you, you fool!' Andy turned slowly and looked, and there, close behind him, was the retriever with the cartridge in his mouth – wedged into his broadest and silliest grin. And that wasn't all. The dog had come round the fire to Andy, and the loose end of the fuse had trailed and waggled over the burning sticks into the blaze; Andy had slit and nicked the firing end of the fuse well, and now it was hissing and spitting properly.

Andy's legs started with a jolt; his legs started before his brain did, and he made after Dave and Jim. And the dog followed Andy.

Dave and Jim were good runners – Jim the best – for a short distance; Andy was slow and heavy, but he had the strength and the wind and could last. The dog capered round him, delighted as a dog could be to find his mates, as he thought, on for a frolic. Dave and Jim kept shouting back, 'Don't foller us! Don't foller us, you coloured fool!' But Andy kept on, no matter how they dodged. They could never explain, any more than the dog, why they followed each other, but so they ran, Dave keeping in Jim's track in all its turnings, Andy after Dave, and the dog circling round Andy – the live fuse swishing in all directions and hissing and spluttering and stinking. Jim yelling to Dave not to follow him, Dave shouting to Andy to go in another direction – to 'spread out,' and Andy roaring at the dog to go home. Then Andy's brain began to work, stimulated by the crisis: he tried to get a running kick at the dog, but the dog dodged; he snatched up sticks and stones and threw them at the dog and ran on again. The retriever saw that he'd made a mistake about Andy, and left him and bounded after Dave. Dave, who had the presence of mind to think that the fuse's time wasn't up yet, made a dive and a grab for the dog, caught him by the tail, and as he swung round snatched the cartridge out of his mouth and flung it as far as he could; the dog immediately bounded after it, and retrieved it. Dave roared and cursed at the dog, who, seeing that Dave was offended, left him and went after Jim, who was well ahead. Jim swung to a sapling and went up it like a native bear; it was a young sapling, and Jim couldn't safely get more than ten or twelve feet from the ground. The dog laid the cartridge, as carefully as if it were a kitten, at the foot of the sapling, and capered and leaped and whooped joyously round under Jim. The big pup reckoned that this was part of the lark – he was all right now – it was Jim who was out for a spree. The fuse sounded as if it were going a mile a minute. Jim tried to climb higher and the sapling bent and cracked. Jim fell on his feet and ran. The dog swooped on the cartridge and followed. It all took but a very few moments. Jim ran to a digger's hole, about ten feet deep, and dropped down into it – landing on soft mud – and was safe. The dog grinned sardonically down on him, over the edge, for a moment, as if he thought it would be a good lark to drop the cartridge down on Jim.

'Go away, Tommy,' said Jim feebly, 'go away.'

The dog bounded off after Dave, who was the only one in sight now; Andy had dropped behind a log, where he lay flat on his face, having suddenly remembered a picture of the Russo-Turkish war with a circle of Turks lying flat on their faces (as if they were ashamed) round a newly-arrived shell.

There was a small hotel or shanty on the creek, on the main road, not far from the claim. Dave was desperate, the time flew much faster in his stimulated imagination than it did in reality, so he made for the shanty. There were several casual bushmen on the veranda and in the bar; Dave rushed into the bar, banging the door to behind him. 'My dog!' he gasped, in reply to the astonished stare of the publican, 'the blanky retriever – he's got a live cartridge in his mouth —'

The retriever, finding the front door shut against him, had bounded round and in by the back way, and now stood smiling in the doorway leading from the passage, the cartridge still in his mouth and the fuse spluttering. They burst out of that bar, Tommy bounded first after one and then after another, for, being a young dog, he tried to make friends with everybody.

The bushmen ran round corners, and some shut themselves in the stable. There was a new weather-board and corrugated-iron kitchen and wash-house on piles in the backyard, with some women washing clothes inside. Dave and the publican bundled in there and shut the door – the publican cursing Dave and calling him a crimson fool, in hurried tones, and wanting to know what the hell he came here for.

The retriever went in under the kitchen, amongst the piles, but, luckily for those inside, there was a vicious yellow mongrel cattle-dog sulking and nursing his nastiness under there – a sneaking, fighting, thieving canine, whom neighbours had tried for years to shoot or poison. Tommy saw his danger – he'd had experience from this dog – and started out and across the yard, still sticking to the cartridge. Half-way across the yard the yellow dog caught him and nipped him. Tommy dropped the cartridge, gave one terrified yell, and took to the bush. The yellow dog followed him to the fence and then ran back to see what he had dropped. Nearly a dozen other dogs came from round all the corners and under the buildings – spidery, thievish, cold-blooded kangaroo dogs, mongrel sheep- and cattle-dogs, vicious black and yellow dogs – that slip after you in the dark, nip your heels, and vanish without explaining – and yapping, yelping small fry. They kept at a respectable distance round the nasty yellow dog, for it was dangerous to go near him when he thought he had found something which might be good for a dog or cat. He sniffed at the cartridge twice, and was just taking a third cautious sniff when —

It was very good blasting-powder – a new brand that Dave had recently got up from Sydney; and the cartridge had been excellently well made. Andy was very patient and painstaking in all he did, and nearly as handy as the average sailor with needles, twine, canvas and rope.

Bushmen say that that kitchen jumped off its piles and on again. When the smoke and dust cleared away, the remains of the nasty yellow dog were lying against the paling fence of the yard looking as if he had been kicked into a fire by a horse and afterwards rolled in the dust under a barrow, and finally thrown against the fence from a distance. Several saddle-horses, which had been 'hanging-up' round the veranda, were galloping wildly down the road in clouds of dust, with broken bridle-reins flying; and from a circle round the outskirts, from every point of the compass in the scrub, came the yelping of dogs. Two of them went home, to the place where they were born, thirty miles away, and reached it the same night and stayed there; it was not till towards evening that the rest came back cautiously to make inquiries. One was trying to walk on two legs, and most of 'em looked more or less singed; and a little, singed, stumpy-tailed dog, who had been in the habit of hopping the back half of him along on one leg, had reason to be glad that he'd saved up the other leg all those years, for he needed it now. There was one old one-eyed cattle-dog round that shanty for years afterwards, who couldn't stand the smell of a gun being cleaned. He it was who had taken an interest, only second to that of the yellow dog, in the cartridge.

Bushmen said that it was amusing to slip up on his blind side and stick a dirty ramrod under his nose: he wouldn't wait to bring his solitary eye to bear – he'd take to the bush and stay out all night.

For half an hour or so after the explosion there were several bushmen round behind the stable who crouched, doubled up, against the wall, or rolled gently on the dust, trying to laugh without shrieking. There were two white women in hysterics at the house, and a half-caste rushing aimlessly round with a dipper of cold water. The publican was holding his wife tight and begging her between her squawks, to 'hold up for my sake, Mary, or I'll lam the life out of ye.'

Dave decided to apologise later on, 'when things had settled a bit,' and went back to camp. And the dog that had done it all, Tommy, the great, idiotic mongrel retriever, came slobbering round Dave and lashing his legs with his tail, and trotted home after him, smiling his broadest, longest, and reddest smile of amiability, and apparently satisfied for one afternoon with the fun he'd had.

Andy chained the dog up securely, and cooked some more chops, while Dave went to help Jim out of the hole.

And most of this is why, for years afterwards, lanky, easygoing bushmen, riding lazily past Dave's camp, would cry, in a lazy drawl and with just a hint of the nasal twang:

''Ello, Da-a-ve! How's the fishin' getting on, Da-a-ve?'

THE BUCK-JUMPER

 SATURDAY afternoon.

There were about a dozen bush natives, from anywhere, most of them lanky and easygoing, hanging about the little slab-and-bark hotel on the edge of the scrub at Capertee Camp (a teamster's camp) when Cobb & Co's mail-coach and six came dashing down the sidling from round Crown Ridge, in all its glory, to the end of the twelve-mile stage. Some dusty, wiry, ill-used hacks were hanging to the fence and to saplings about the place. The fresh coach-horses stood ready in a stockyard close to the shanty. As the coach climbed the nearer bank of the creek at the foot of the ridge, six of the bushmen detached themselves from veranda-posts, from their heels, from the clay floor of the veranda and the rough slab wall against which they'd been resting, and joined a group of four or five who stood round one. He stood with his back to the corner post of the stockyard, his feet well braced out in front of him, and contemplated the toes of his tight new 'lastic-side boots and whistled softly. He was a clean-limbed, handsome fellow, with riding-cords, leggings, and a blue sash; he was Graeco-Roman-nosed, blue-eyed, and his glossy, curly black hair bunched up in front of the brim of a new cabbage-tree hat, set well back on his head.

'Do it for a quid, Jack?' asked one.

'Damned if I will, Jim!' said the young man at the post. 'I'll do it for a fiver – not a blanky sprat less.'

Jim took off his hat and 'shoved' it round and 'bobs' were 'chucked' into it. The result was about thirty shillings.

Jack glanced contemptuously into the crown of the hat.

'Not me!' he said, showing some emotion for the first time. 'D'yer think I'm going to risk me blanky neck for your blanky amusement for thirty blanky bob? I'll ride the blanky horse for a fiver, and I'll feel the blanky quids in my pocket before I get on.'

Meanwhile the coach had dashed up to the door of the shanty. There were about twenty passengers aboard – inside, on the box-seat, on the tail-board, and hanging on to the roof – most of them Sydney men going up to the Mudgee races. They got down and went inside with the driver for a drink, while the stablemen changed horses. The bushmen raised their voices a little and argued.

One of the passengers was a big, stout, hearty man – a good-hearted, sporting man and a racehorse-owner, according to his brands. He had a round red face and a white cork hat. 'What's those chaps got on outside?' he asked the publican.

'Oh, it's a bet they've got on about riding a horse,' replied the publican. 'The flash-looking chap with the sash is Flash Jack, the horse-breaker; and they reckon they've got the champion outlaw in the district out there – that chestnut horse in the yard.'

The sporting man was interested at once, and went out and joined the bushmen.

'Well, chaps! What have you got on here?' he asked cheerily.

'Oh,' said Jim carelessly, 'it's only a bit of a bet about ridin' that blanky chestnut in the corner of the yard there.' He indicated an ungroomed chestnut horse, fenced off by a couple of long sapling poles in a corner of the stockyard. 'Flash Jack there – he reckons he's the champion horse-breaker round here – Flash Jack reckons he can take it out of that horse first try.'

'What's up with the horse?' inquired the big, red-faced man. 'It looks quiet enough. Why, I'd ride it myself.'

'Would yer?' said Jim, who had hair that stood straight up, and an innocent, inquiring expression. 'Looks quiet, does he? You ought to know more about horses than to go by the looks of 'em. He's quiet enough just now, when there's no one near him; but you should have been here an hour ago. That horse has killed two men and put another chap's shoulder out – besides breaking a cove's leg. It took six of us all the morning to run him in and get the saddle on him; and now Flash Jack wants to back out of it.'

'Euraliar!' remarked Flash Jack cheerfully. 'I said I'd ride that blanky horse out of the yard for a fiver. I ain't goin' to risk my blanky neck for nothing and only to amuse you blanks.'

'He said he'd ride the horse inside the yard for a quid,' said Jim.

'And get smashed against the rails!' said Flash Jack. 'I would be a fool. I'd rather take my chance outside in the scrub – and it's rough country round here.'

'Well, how much do you want?' asked the man in the mushroom hat.

'A fiver, I said,' replied Jack indifferently. 'And the blanky stuff in my pocket before I get on the blanky horse.'

'Are you frightened of us running away without paying you?' inquired one of the passengers who had gathered round.

'I'm frightened of the horse bolting with me without me being paid,' said Flash Jack. 'I know that horse; he's got a mouth like iron. I might be at the bottom of the cliff on Crown Ridge road in twenty minutes with my head caved in, and then what chance for the quids?'

'You wouldn't want 'em then,' suggested a passenger. 'Or, say! – we'd leave the fiver with the publican to bury you.'

Flash Jack ignored that passenger. He eyed his boots and softly whistled a tune.

'All right!' said the man in the cork hat, putting his hand in his pocket, 'I'll start with a quid; stump up, you chaps.'

The five pounds were got together.

'I'll lay a quid to half a quid he don't stick on ten minutes!' shouted Jim to his mates as soon as he saw that the event was to come off. The passengers also betted amongst themselves. Flash Jack, after putting the money in his breeches-pocket, let down the rails and led the horse into the middle of the yard.

'Quiet as an old cow!' snorted a passenger in disgust. 'I believe it's a sell!'

They waited and saw.

Flash Jack leisurely mounted the horse, rode slowly out of the yard, and trotted briskly round the corner of the shanty and into the scrub, which swallowed him more completely than the sea might have done.

Most of the other bushmen mounted their horses and followed Flash Jack to a clearing in the scrub, at a safe distance from the shanty; then they dismounted and hung on to saplings, or leaned against their horses, while they laughed.

At the hotel there was just time for another drink. The driver climbed to his seat and shouted, 'All aboard!' in his usual tone. The passengers climbed to their places, thinking hard. A mile or so along the road the man with the cork hat remarked, with much truth:

'Those blanky bushmen have got too much time to think.' The bushmen returned to the shanty as soon as the coach was out of sight, and proceeded to 'knock down' the fiver.

JIMMY GRIMSHAW'S WOOING

THE HALF-WAY House at Tinned Dog (out back in Australia) kept Daniel Myers – licensed to retail spirituous and fermented liquors – in drink and the horrors for upward of five years, at the end of which time he lay hidden for weeks in a back skillion, an object which no decent man would care to see – or hear when it gave forth sound. 'Good accommodation for man and beast'; but few shanties save his own might, for a consideration, have accommodated that sort of beast which the man Myers had become towards the end of his career. But at last the eccentric bush doctor, 'Doc. Wild' (who perhaps could drink as much as Myers without its having any further effect upon his temperament than to keep him awake and cynical), pronounced the publican dead enough to be buried legally; so the widow buried him, had the skillion cleaned out, and the sign altered to read, 'Margaret Myers, licensed, etc.' and continued to conduct the pub just as she had run it for over five years, with the joyful and blessed exception that there was no longer a human pig and pigsty attached, and that the atmosphere was calm. Most of the regular patrons of the Half-way House could have their horrors decently, and, comparatively, quietly – or otherwise have them privately – in the Big Scrub adjacent; but Myers had not been one of that sort.

Mrs Myers settled herself to enjoy life comfortably and happily, at the fixed age of thirty-nine, for the next seven years or so. She was a pleasant faced-dumpling, who had been baked solid in the droughts of Out Back without losing her good looks, and had put up with a hard life, and Myers, all those years without losing her good humour and nature. Probably, had her husband been the opposite kind of man, she would have been different – haggard, bad-tempered, and altogether impossible – for of such is woman. But then it might be taken into consideration that she had been practically a widow during at least the last five years of her husband's alleged life.

Mrs Myers was reckoned a good catch in the district, but it soon seemed that she was not to be caught.

'It would be a grand thing,' one of the periodical boozers of Tinned Dog would say to his mates, 'for one of us to have his name up on a pub; it would save a lot of money.'

'It wouldn't save you anything, Bill, if I got it,' was the retort. 'You needn't come round chewing my lug then. I'd give you one drink and no more.'

The publican at Dead Camel, station managers, professional shearers, even one or two solvent squatters and promising cockatoos, tried their luck in vain. In answer to the suggestion that she ought to have a man to knock round and look after things, she retorted that she had had one, and was perfectly satisfied. Few travellers on those tracks but tried 'a bit of bear-up' in that direction, but all to no purpose. Chequemen knocked down their cheques manfully at the Half-way House – to get courage and good will and 'put it off' till, at the last moment, they offered themselves abjectly to the landlady; which was worse than bad judgment on their part – it was very silly, and she told them so.

One or two swore off, and swore to keep straight; but she had no faith in them, and when they found that out, it hurt their feelings so much that they 'broke out' and went on record-breaking sprees.

About the end of each shearing the sign was touched up, with an extra coat of paint on the 'Margaret,' whereat suitors looked hopeless.

One or two of the rejected died of love in the horrors in the Big Scrub – anyway, the verdict was that they died of love aggravated by the horrors. But the climax was reached when a Queensland shearer, seizing the opportunity when the mate, whose turn it was to watch him, fell asleep, went down to the yard and hanged himself on the butcher's gallows – having first removed his clothes, with some drink-lurid idea of leaving the world as naked as he came into it. He climbed the pole, sat astride on top, fixed the rope to neck and bar, but gave a yell – a yell of drunken triumph – before he dropped, and woke his mates.

They cut him down and brought him to. Next day he apologised to Mrs Myers, said, 'Ah, well! So-long!' to the rest and departed – cured of drink and love apparently. The verdict was that the blanky fool should have dropped before he yelled; but she was upset and annoyed, and it began to look as though, if she wished to continue to live on happily and comfortably for a few years longer at the fixed age of thirty-nine, she would either have to give up the pub or get married.

Her fame was carried far and wide, and she became a woman whose name was mentioned with respect in rough shearing-sheds and huts, and round the camp-fire.

About thirty miles south of Tinned Dog one James Grimshaw, widower – otherwise known as 'Old Jimmy,' though he was little past middle age – had a small selection which he had worked, let, given up, and tackled afresh (with sinews of war drawn from fencing contracts) ever since the death of his young wife some fifteen years agone. He was a practical, square-faced, clean-shaven, clean and tidy man, with a certain 'cleanness' about the shape of his limbs which suggested the old jockey or hostler. There were two strong theories in connection with Jimmy – one was that he had had a university education, and the other that he couldn't write his own name. Not nearly such a ridiculous nor simple case out back as it might seem.

Jimmy smoked and listened without comment to the 'heard tells' in connection with Mrs Myers, till at last one night, at the end of his contract and over a last pipe, he said quietly, 'I'll go up to Tinned Dog next week and try my luck.'

His mates and the casual Jims and Bills were taken too suddenly to laugh, and the laugh having been lost, as Bland Holt, the Australian actor would put it in a professional sense, the audience had time to think, with the result that the joker swung his hand down through an imaginary table and exclaimed:

'By God! Jimmy'll do it.' (Applause.)

So one drowsy afternoon at the time of the year when the breathless day runs on past 7 p.m., Mrs Myers sat sewing in the bar-parlour, when a clean-shaved, clean-shirted, clean-neckerchiefed, clean-moleskinned, greased-bluchered – altogether a model or stage swagman came up, was served in the bar by the half-caste female cook, and took his way to the river-bank, where he rigged a small tent and made a model camp.

A couple of hours later he sat on a stool on the veranda, smoking a clean clay pipe. Just before the sunset meal Mrs Myers asked, 'Is that trav'ler there yet, Mary?'

'Yes, missus. Clean pfellar that.'

The landlady knitted her forehead over her sewing, as women do when limited for 'stuff' or wondering whether a section has been cut wrong – or perhaps she thought of that other who hadn't been a 'clean pfellar.' She put her work aside, and stood in the doorway, looking out across the clearing.

'Good day, mister,' she said, seeming to become aware of him for the first time.

'Good day, missus!'

Pause.

'Hot!'

'Hot!'

'Trav'lin'?'

'No, not particular!'

She waited for him to explain. Myers was always explaining when he wasn't raving. But the swagman smoked on.

'Have a drink?' she suggested, to keep her end up.

'No, thank you, missus. I had one an hour or so ago. I never take more than two a day – one before breakfast, if I can get it, and a night-cap.'

What a contrast to Myers! she thought.

'Come and have some tea; it's ready.'

'Thank you. I don't mind if I do.'

They got on very slowly, but comfortably. She got little out of him except the facts that he had a selection, had finished a contract, and was 'just having a look at the country.' He politely declined a 'shake-down,' saying he had a comfortable camp, and preferred being out this weather. She got his name with a 'by the way' as he rose to leave, and he went back to camp.

He caught a cod, and they had it for breakfast next morning, and got along so comfortably over breakfast that he put in the forenoon pottering about the gates and stable with a hammer, a saw, and a box of nails.

And, well – to make it short – when the big Tinned Dog Shed had cut out, and the shearers struck the Half-way House, they were greatly impressed by a brand-new sign whereon glistened the words:

HALF-WAY HOUSE HOTEL
By
JAMES GRIMSHAW
GOOD STABLING

The last time I saw Mrs Grimshaw she looked about thirty-five.

AT DEAD DINGO

IT WAS BLAZING hot outside and smothering hot inside the weather-board and iron shanty at Dead Dingo, a place on the Cleared Road, where there was a pub and a police station, and which was sometimes called 'Roasted,' and other times 'Potted Dingo' – nicknames suggested by the everlasting drought and the vicinity of the one-pub township of Tinned Dog.

From the front veranda the scene was straight-cleared road, running right and left to Out Back, and to Bourke (and ankle-deep in the red sand dust for perhaps a hundred miles); the rest blue-grey bush, dust, and the heat-wave blazing across every object.

There were only four in the bar-room, though it was New Year's Day. There weren't many more in the country. The girl sat behind the bar – the coolest place in the shanty – reading 'Deadwood Dick.' On a worn and torn and battered horse-hair sofa, which had seen cooler places and better days, lay an awful and healthy example, a bearded swagman, with his arms twisted over his head and his face to the wall, sleeping off the death of the dead drunk. Bill and Jim – shearer and rouseabout – sat at a table playing cards. It was about three o'clock in the afternoon, and they had been gambling since nine – and the greater part of the night before – so they were, probably, in a worse condition morally (and perhaps physically) than the drunken swagman on the sofa.

Close under the bar, in a dangerous place for his legs and tail, lay a sheep-dog with a chain attached to his collar and wound round his neck.

Presently a thump on the table, and Bill, unlucky gambler, rose with an oath that would have been savage if it hadn't been drawled.

'Stumped?' inquired Jim.

'Not a blanky, lurid deener!' drawled Bill.

Jim drew his reluctant hands from the cards, his eyes went slowly and hopelessly round the room and out the door. There was something in the eyes of both, except when on the card-table, of the look of a man waking in a strange place.

'Got anything?' asked Jim, fingering the cards again.

Bill sucked in his cheeks, collecting the saliva with difficulty, and spat out on to the veranda floor.

'That's all I got,' he drawled. 'It's gone now.'

Jim leaned back in his chair, twisted, yawned, and caught sight of the dog. 'That there dog yours?' he asked, brightening.

They had evidently been strangers the day before, or as strange to each other as bushmen can be.

Bill scratched behind his ear, and blinked at the dog. The dog woke suddenly to a flea fact.

'Yes,' drawled Bill, 'he's mine.'

'Well, I'm going out back, and I want a dog,' said Jim, gathering the cards briskly. 'Half a quid agin the dog?'

'Half a quid be —!' drawled Bill. 'Call it a quid?'

'Half a blanky quid!'

'A gory, lurid quid!' drawled Bill desperately, and he stooped over his swag. But Jim's hands were itching in a ghastly way over the cards.

'All right. Call it a — quid.'

The drunkard on the sofa stirred, showed signs of waking, but died again. Remember this, it might come in useful.

Bill sat down to the table once more.

Jim rose first, winner of the dog. He stretched, yawned 'Ah, well!' and shouted drinks. Then he shouldered his swag, stirred the dog up with his foot, unwound the chain, said 'Ah, well – so-long!' and drifted out and along the road toward Out Back, the dog following with head and tail down.

Bill scored another drink on account of girl-pity for bad luck, shouldered his swag, said 'So-long, Mary!' and drifted out and along the road towards Tinned Dog, on the Bourke side. A long, drowsy, half-hour passed – the sort of half-hour that is as long as an hour in the places where days are as long as years, and years hold about as much as days do in other places.

The man on the sofa woke with a start, and looked scared and wild for a moment; then he brought his dusty broken boots to the floor, rested his elbows on his knees, took his unfortunate head between his hands, and came back to life gradually.

He lifted his head, looked at the girl across the top of the bar, and formed with his lips, rather than spoke, the words:

'Put up a drink?'*

She shook her head tightly and went on reading.

He staggered up, and, leaning on the bar, made desperate distress signals with hand, eyes, and mouth.

'No!' she snapped. 'I means no when I says no! You've had too many last drinks already, and the boss says you ain't to have another. If you swear again, or bother me, I'll call him.'

He hung sullenly on the counter for a while, then lurched to his swag, and

*'Put up a drink' – i.e. 'Give me a drink on credit,' or 'Chalk it up.'

shouldered it hopelessly and wearily. Then he blinked round, whistled, waited a moment, went on to the front veranda, peered round through the heat with bloodshot eyes and whistled again. He turned and started through to the back door.

'What the devil do you want now?' demanded the girl, interrupted in her reading for the third time by him. 'Stampin'' all over the house. You can't go through there! It's privit! I do wish to goodness you'd git!'

'Where the blazes is that there dog o' mine got to?' he muttered. 'Did you see a dog?'

'No! What do I want with your dog?'

He whistled out in front again, and round each corner. Then he came back with a decided step and tone.

'Look here! that there dog was lyin' there agin the wall when I went to sleep. He wouldn't stir from me, or my swag, in a year, if he wasn't dragged. He's been blanky well touched [stolen], and I wouldn'ter lost him for a fiver. Are you sure you ain't seen a dog?' Then suddenly, as the thought struck him: 'Where's them two chaps that was playin'' cards when I wenter sleep?'

'Why!' exclaimed the girl, without thinking, 'there was a dog, now I come to think of it, but I thought it belonged to one of them chaps. Anyway, they played for it, and the other chap won it and took it away.'

He stared at her blankly, with thunder gathering in the blankness.

'What sort of dog was it?'

Dog described; the chain round the neck settled it.

He scowled at her darkly.

'Now, look here,' he said, 'you've allowed gamblin' in this bar – your boss has. You've got no right to let spielers gamble away a man's dog. Is a customer to lose his dog every time he has a doze to suit your boss? I'll go straight across to the police camp and put you away, and I don't care if you lose your licence. I ain't goin' to lose my dog. I wouldn'ter taken a ten-pound note for the blanky dog! I —'

She was filling a pewter hastily.

'Here! for God's sake have a drink an' stop yer row.'

He drank with satisfaction. Then he hung on the bar with one elbow and scowled out the door.

'Which blanky way did them chaps go?' he growled.

'The one that took the dog went towards Tinned Dog.'

'And I'll haveter go all the blanky way back after him, and most likely lose me shed! Here!' jerking the empty pewter across the bar, 'fill that up again; I'm narked properly, I am, and I'll take twenty-four blanky hours to cool down now. I wouldn'ter lost that dog for twenty quid.'

He drank again with deeper satisfaction, then he shuffled out, muttering, swearing, and threatening louder every step, and took the track to Tinned Dog.

Now the man, girl or woman, who told me this yarn has never quite settled it in his or her mind as to who really owned the dog. I leave it to you.

THE ROMANCE OF THE SWAG

THE ROMANCE OF THE SWAG

THE AUSTRALIAN SWAG fashion is the easiest way in the world of carrying a load. I ought to know something about carrying loads: I've carried babies, which are the heaviest and most awkward and heart-breaking loads in this world for a boy or man to carry, I fancy. God remember mothers who slave about the housework (and do sometimes a man's work in addition in the bush) with a heavy, squalling kid on one arm! I've humped logs on the selection, 'burning-off,' with loads of fencing-posts and rails and palings out of steep, rugged gullies (and was happier then, perhaps); I've carried a shovel, crowbar, heavy 'rammer,' a dozen insulators on an average (strung round my shoulders with raw flax) – to say nothing of soldiering kit, tucker-bag, billy and climbing spurs – all day on a telegraph line in rough country in New Zealand, and in places where a man had to manage his load with one hand and help himself climb with the other; and I've helped hump and drag telegraph-poles up cliffs and sidlings where the horses couldn't go. I've carried a portmanteau on the hot dusty roads in green old jackeroo days. Ask any actor who's been stranded and had to count railway sleepers from one town to another! he'll tell you what sort of an awkward load a portmanteau is, especially if there's a broken-hearted man underneath it. I've tried knapsack fashion – one of the least healthy and most likely to give a man sores; I've carried my belongings in a three-bushel sack slung over my shoulder – blankets, tucker, spare boots and poetry all lumped together. I tried carrying a load on my head, and got a crick in my neck and spine for days. I've carried a load on my mind that should have been shared by editors and publishers. I've helped hump luggage and furniture up to, and down from, a top flat in London. And I've carried swag for months out back in Australia – and it was life, in spite of its 'squalidness' and meanness and wretchedness and hardship, and in spite of the fact that the world would have regarded us as 'tramps' – and a free life amongst men from all the world!

The Australian swag was born of Australia and no other land – of the Great Lone Land of magnificent distances and bright heat; the land of self-reliance, and never-give-in, and help-your-mate. The grave of many of the world's tragedies and comedies – royal and otherwise. The land where a man out of employment might shoulder his swag in Adelaide and take the track, and years later walk into a hut on the Gulf, or never be heard of any more, or a body be found in the bush and buried by the mounted police, or never found and never buried – what does it matter?

The land I love above all others – not because it was kind to me, but because I was born on Australian soil, and because of the foreign father who died at his work in the ranks of Australian pioneers, and because of many things. Australia! My country! Her very name is music to me. God bless Australia! for the sake of the great hearts of the heart of her! God keep her clear of the old-world shams and social lies and mockery, and callous commercialism, and sordid shame! And heaven send that, if ever in my time her sons are called upon to fight for her young life and honour, I die with the first rank of them to be buried in Australian ground.

But this will probably be called false, forced or 'maudlin sentiment' here in England, where the mawkish sentiment of the music-halls, and the popular applause it receives, is enough to make a healthy man sick, and is only equalled by music-hall vulgarity. So I'll get on.

In the old digging days the knapsack, or straps-across-the-chest fashion, was tried, but the load pressed on a man's chest and impeded his breathing, and a man needs to have his bellows free on long tracks in hot, stirless weather. Then the 'horse-collar,' or rolled military overcoat style – swag over one shoulder and under the other arm – was tried, but it was found to be too hot for the Australian climate, and was discarded along with Wellington boots and leggings. Until recently, Australian city artists and editors – who knew as much about the bush as Downing Street knows about the British colonies in general – seemed to think the horse-collar swag was still in existence; and some artists gave the swagman a stick, as if he were a tramp of civilisation with an eye on the backyard and a fear of the dog. English artists, by the way, seem firmly convinced that the Australian bushman is born in Wellington boots with a polish on 'em you could shave yourself by.

The swag is usually composed of a tent 'fly' or strip of calico (a cover for the swag and a shelter in bad weather – in New Zealand it is oilcloth or waterproof twill), a couple of blankets, blue by custom and preference, as that colour shows the dirt less than any other (hence the name 'bluey' for swag), and the core is composed of spare clothing and small personal effects. To make or 'roll up' your swag: lay the fly or strip of calico on the ground, blueys on top of it; across one end, with eighteen inches or so to spare, lay your spare trousers and shirt, folded, light boots tied together by the laces toe to heel, books, bundle of old letters, portraits, or whatever little knick-knacks you have or care to carry, bag of needles, thread, pen and ink, spare patches for your pants, and bootlaces. Lay or arrange the pile so that it will roll evenly with the swag (some pack the lot in an old pillowslip or canvas bag), take a fold over of blanket and calico the whole length on each side, so as to reduce the width of the swag to, say, three feet, throw the spare end, with an inward fold, over the little pile of belongings, and then roll the whole to the other end, using your knees and judgment to make the swag tight, compact and artistic; when within eighteen inches of the loose end take an inward fold in that, and bring it up against the body of the swag. There is a strong suggestion of a roley-poley in a rag about the business, only the ends of the swag are folded in, in rings, and not tied. Fasten the swag with three or four straps, according to judgment and the supply of straps. To the top strap, for the swag is carried (and eased down in shanty bars and against walls or veranda-posts when not on the track) in a more or less vertical position – to the top strap, and lowest, or lowest but one, fasten the ends of the shoulder strap (usually a towel is preferred as being softer to the shoulder), your coat being carried outside the swag at the back, under the straps. To the top strap fasten the string of the nose-bag, a calico bag about the size of a pillowslip, containing the tea, sugar and flour bags, bread, meat, baking-powder and salt, and brought, when the swag is carried from the left shoulder, over the right on to the chest, and so balancing the swag behind. But a swagman can throw a heavy swag in a nearly vertical position against his spine, slung from one shoulder only and without any balance, and carry it as easily as you might wear your overcoat. Some bushmen arrange their belongings so neatly and conveniently, with swag straps in a sort of harness, that they can roll up the swag in about a minute, and unbuckle it and throw it out as easily as a roll of wall-paper, and there's the bed ready on the ground with the wardrobe for a pillow. The swag is always used for a seat on the track; it is a soft seat, so trousers last a long time. And, the dust being mostly soft and silky on the long tracks out back, boots last marvellously. Fifteen miles a day is the average with the swag, but you must travel according to the water: if the next bore or tank is five miles on, and the next twenty beyond, you camp at the five-mile water tonight and do the twenty next day. But if it's thirty miles you have to do it. Travelling with the swag in Australia is variously and picturesquely described as 'humping bluey,' 'waltzing Matilda,' 'humping Matilda,' 'humping your drum,' 'being on the wallaby,' 'jabbing trotters,' and 'tea and sugar burglaring,' but most travelling shearers now call themselves trav'lers, and say simply 'on the track,' or 'carrying swag.'

And there you have the Australian swag. Men from all the world have carried it – lords and low-class Chinamen, saints and world martyrs, and felons, thieves, and murderers, educated gentlemen and boors who couldn't sign their mark, gentlemen who fought for Poland and convicts who fought the world, women, and more than one woman disguised as a man. The Australian swag has held in its core letters and papers in all languages, the honour of great houses, and more than one national secret, papers that would send well-known and highly-respected men to jail, and proofs of the innocence of men going mad in prisons, life tragedies and comedies, fortunes and papers that secured titles and fortunes, and the last pence of lost fortunes, life secrets, portraits of mothers and dead loves, pictures of fair women, heart-breaking old letters written long ago by vanished hands, and the pencilled manuscript of more than one book which will be famous yet.

The weight of the swag varies from the light rouseabout's swag, containing one blanket and a clean shirt, to the 'royal Alfred,' with tent and all complete, and weighing part of a ton. Some old sundowners have a mania for gathering, from selectors' and shearers' huts, and dust-heaps, heart-breaking loads of rubbish which can never be of any possible use to them or any one else. Here is an inventory of the contents of the swag of an old tramp who was found dead on the track, lying on his face on the sand, with his swag on top of him, and his arms stretched straight out as if he were embracing the mother earth, or had made, with his last movement, the sign of the cross to the blazing heavens:

Rotten old tent in rags. Filthy blue blanket, patched with squares of red and calico. Half of 'white blanket' nearly black now, patched with pieces of various material and sewn to half of red blanket. Three-bushel sack slit open. Pieces of sacking. Part of a woman's skirt. Two rotten old pairs of moleskin trousers. One leg of a pair of trousers. Back of a shirt. Half a waistcoat. Two tweed coats, green, old and rotting, and patched with calico. Blanket, etc. Large bundle of assorted rags for patches, all rotten. Leaky billy-can, containing fishing-line, papers, suet, needles and cotton, etc. Jam-tin, medicine bottles, corks on strings, to hang to his hat to keep the flies off (a sign of madness in the bush, for the corks would |madden a sane man sooner than the flies could). Three boots of different sizes, all belonging to the right foot, and a left slipper. Coffee-pot, without handle or spout, and quart-pot full of rubbish – broken knives and forks, with the handles burnt off, spoons, etc., picked up on rubbish-heaps; and many rusty nails, to be used as buttons, I suppose.

Broken saw blade, hammer, broken crockery, old pannikins, small rusty frying-pan without a handle, children's old shoes, many bits of old bootleather and greenhide, part of yellow-back novel, mutilated English dictionary, grammar and arithmetic book, a ready reckoner, a cookery book, a bulgy anglo-foreign dictionary, part of a Shakespeare, book in French and book in German, and a book on etiquette and courtship. A heavy pair of blucher boots, with uppers parched and cracked, and soles so patched (patch over patch) with leather, boot protectors, hoop-iron and hobnails that they were about two inches thick, and weighed over five pounds. (If you don't believe me go into the Melbourne Museum, where, in a glass case in a place of honour, you will see a similar, perhaps the same, pair of bluchers labelled 'an example of colonial industry.') And in the core of the swag was a sugar-bag tied tightly with a whip-lash, and containing another old skirt, rolled very tight and fastened with many turns of a length of clothes-line, which last, I suppose, he carried to hang himself with if he felt that way. The skirt was rolled round a small packet of old portraits and almost indecipherable letters – one from a woman who had evidently been a sensible woman and a widow, and who stated in the letter that she did not intend to get married again as she had enough to do already, slavin' her finger-nails off to keep a family, without having a second husband to keep. And her answer was 'final for good and all,' and it wasn't no use comin' 'bungfoodlin'' round her again. If he did she'd set Satan on to him. 'Satan' was a dog, I suppose.

The letter was addressed to 'Dear Bill,' as were others. There were no envelopes. The letters were addressed from no place in particular, so there weren't any means of identifying the dead man. The police buried him under a gum, and a young trooper cut on the tree the words:

SACRED TO THE MEMORY OF
BILL
WHO DIED

THE BUSH-FIRE

I

SQUATTER AND SELECTOR

WALL WAS A squatter and a hard man. There had been long years of drought and loss, and then came the rabbit pest – the rabbits swarmed like flies over his run, and cropped the ground bare where even the poor grass might have saved thousands of sheep – and the rabbits cost the squatter hundreds of pounds in 'rabbit-proof' fences, trappers' wages, etc., just to keep them down. Then came arrangements with the bank. And then Wall's wife died. Wall started to brood over other days, and the days that had gone between, and developed a temper which drove his children from home one by one, till only Mary was left. She managed the lonely home with the help of a half-caste. Then in good seasons came the selectors.

Men remembered Wall as a grand boss and a good fellow, but that was in the days before rabbits and banks, and syndicates and 'pastoralists,' or pastoral companies instead of good squatters.

Runs were mostly pastoral leases for which the squatter paid the Government so much per square mile (almost a nominal rent). Selections were small holdings taken up by farmers under residential and other conditions and paid for by instalments. If you were not ruined by the drought, and paid up long enough, the land became freehold. The writer is heir to a dusty patch of three hundred acres or so in the scrub which was taken up thirty years ago and isn't freehold yet.

Selectors were allowed to take up land on runs or pastoral leases as well as on unoccupied Crown lands, and as they secured the best bits of land, and on water frontages if they could, and as, of course, selections reduced the area of the run, the squatters loved selectors like elder brothers. One man is allowed to select only a certain amount of land, and required by law to live on it, so the squatters bought as much freehold about the homestead as they could afford, selected as much as they are allowed to by law, and sometimes employed 'dummy' selectors to take up choice bits about the runs and hold them for them. They fought selectors in many various ways, and, in some cases, annoyed and persecuted them with devilish ingenuity.

Ross was a selector, and a very hard man physically. He was a short nuggety man with black hair and frill beard (a little dusty), bushy black eyebrows, piercing black eyes, horny knotted hands, and the obstinacy or pluck of a dozen men to fight drought and the squatter. Ross selected on Wall's run, in a bend of Sandy Creek, a nice bit of land with a black soil, flat and red soil sidings from the ridges, which no one had noticed before, and with the help of his boys he got the land cleared and fenced in a year or two – taking bush contracts about the district between whiles to make 'tucker' for the family until he got his first crop off.

Wall was never accused of employing dummies, or underhanded methods in dealings with selectors, but he had been through so much and had brooded so long that he had grown very hard and bitter and suspicious, and the reverse of generous – as many men do who start out in life too soft and good-hearted and with too much faith in human nature. He was a tall, dark man. He ordered Ross's boys off the run, impounded Ross's stock – before Ross had got his fencing finished, summoned Ross for trespass, and Ross retaliated as well as he could, until at last it mightn't have been safe for one of those men to have met the other with a gun. The impounding of the selector's cattle led to the last bad quarrel between Wall and his son Billy, who was a tall, good-natured Cornstalk, and who reckoned that Australia was big enough for all of us. One day in the drought, and in an extra bitter mood, Wall heard that some of his sheep had been dogged in the vicinity of Ross's selection, and he ordered Billy to take a station-hand and watch Ross's place all night, and, if Ross's cattle put their noses over the boundary, to drive them to the pound, fifteen miles away; also to lay poisoned baits for the dogs all round the selection. And Billy flatly refused.

'I know Ross and the boys,' he said, 'and I don't believe they dogged the sheep. Why, they've only got a Newfoundland pup and an old lame, one-eyed sheep-dog that couldn't hurt a flea. Now, father, this sort of thing has been going on long enough. What difference does a few paltry acres make to us? The country is big enough, God knows! Ross is a straight man and – for God's sake, give the man a chance to get his ground fenced in; he's doing it as fast as he can, and he can't watch his cattle day and night.'

'Are you going to do as I tell you, or are you not?' shouted Wall.

'Well, if it comes to that, I'm not,' said Billy. 'I'm not going to sneak round a place all night and watch for a chance to pound a poor man's cows.'

It was an awful row, down behind the wool-shed, and things looked so bad that old Peter, the station-hand, who was a witness, took off his coat and rolled up his sleeves, ready, as he said afterwards, ' to roll into' either the father or the son if one raised a hand against the other.

'Father!' said Billy, though rather sobered by the sight of his father's trembling, choking passion, 'do you call yourself an Englishman?'

'Yes!' yelled Wall, furiously. 'What the hell do you call yourself?'

'If it comes to that I'm an Australian,' said Billy, and he turned away and went to catch his horse. He went up-country and knocked about in the north-west for a year or two.

II

ROMEO AND JULIET

Mary Wall was twenty-five. She was an Australian bush girl every inch of her five-foot-nine; she had a pink-and-white complexion, dark blue eyes, blue-black hair, and 'the finest figure in the district,' on horseback or afoot. She was the best girl-rider too (saddle or bare-back), and they say that when she was a tomboy she used to tuck her petticoats under her and gallop man-fashion through the scrub after horses or cattle. She said she was going to be an old maid.

There came a jackeroo on a visit to the station. He was related to the bank with which Wall had relations. He was a dude, with an expensive education and no brains. He was very vain of his education and prospects. He regarded Mary with undisguised admiration, and her father had secret hopes. One evening the jackeroo was down by the homestead-gate when Mary came cantering home on her tall chestnut. The gate was six feet or more, and the jackeroo raised his hat and hastened to open it, but Mary reined her horse back a few yards and the 'dood' had barely time to jump aside when there was a scuffle of hoofs on the road, a 'Ha-ha-ha!' in mid-air, a landing thud, and the girl was away up the home-track in a cloud of dust.

A few days later the jackeroo happened to be at Kelly's, a wayside shanty, watching a fight between two bushmen, when Mary rode up. She knew the men. She whipped her horse in between them and struck at first one and then the other with her riding-whip.

'You ought to be ashamed of yourselves!' she said; 'and both married men, too!'

It evidently struck them that way, for after a bit they shook hands and went home.

'And I wouldn't have married that girl for a thousand pounds,' said the jackeroo, relating the incidents to some friends in Sydney.

Mary said she wanted a man, if she could get one.

There was no life at home nowadays, so Mary went to all the bush dances in the district. She thought nothing of riding twenty or thirty miles to a dance, dancing all night, and riding home again next morning. At one of these dances she met young Robert Ross, a clean-limbed, good-looking young fellow about her own age. She danced with him and liked him, and danced with him again, and he rode part of the way home with her. The subject of the quarrel between the two homes came up gradually.

'The boss,' said Robert, meaning his father, 'the boss is always ready to let bygones be bygones. It's a pity it couldn't be fixed up.'

'Yes,' said Mary, looking at him (Bob looked very well on horseback), 'it is a pity.'

They met several times, and next Prince of Wales's birthday they rode home from the races together. Both had good horses, and they happened to be far ahead of the others on the wide, straight clear road that ran between the walls of the scrub. Along, about dusk, they became very confidential indeed – Mary had remarked what a sad and beautiful sunset it was. The horses got confidential, too, and shouldered together, and touched noses, and, after a long interval in the conversation, during which Robert, for one, began to breathe quickly, he suddenly leaned over, put his arm round her waist and made to kiss her. She jerked her body away, threw up her whip-hand, and Robert ducked instinctively; but she brought her whip down on her horse's flank instead, and raced ahead. Robert followed – or, rather, his horse did: he thought it was a race, and took the bit in his teeth. Robert kept calling, appealing:

'Wait a while, Mary! I want to explain! I want to apologise! For God's sake listen to me, Mary!'

But Mary didn't hear him. Perhaps she misunderstood the reason of the chase and gave him credit for a spice of the devil in his nature. But Robert grew really desperate; he felt that the thing must be fixed up now or never, and gave his horse a free rein. Her horse was the fastest, and Robert galloped in the dust from his heels for about a mile and a half; then at the foot of a rise Mary's horse stumbled and nearly threw her over his head, and then he stopped like the good horse he was.

Robert got down feeling instinctively that he might best make his peace on foot, and approached Mary with a face of misery – she had dropped her whip.

'Oh, Bob!' she said, 'I'm knocked out;' and she slipped down into his arms and stayed there a while.

They sat on a log and rested, while their horses made inquiries of each other's noses, and compared notes.

And after a good while Mary said:

'No, Bob, it's no use talking of marrying just yet. I like you, Bob, but I could never marry you while things are as they are between your father and mine. Now, that'll do. Let me get on my horse, Bob. I'll be safer there.'

'Why?' asked Bob.

'Come on, Bob, and don't be stupid.'

She met him often and 'liked' him.

III

A TRAMP'S MATCH AND WHAT IT DID

It was Christmas Eve at Wall's, but there was no score or so of buggies and horses and dozens of strange dogs round the place as of old. The glasses and decanters were dusty on the heavy old-fashioned sideboard in the dining-room; and there was only a sullen, brooding man leaning over the hurdles and looking at his rams in the yard, and a sullen, brooding half-caste at work in the kitchen. Mary had ridden away that morning to visit a girl chum.

It was towards the end of a long drought, and the country was like tinder for hundreds of miles round – the ground for miles and miles in the broiling scrubs 'as bare as your hand,' or covered with coarse, dry tufts. There was feed grass in places, but you had to look close to see it.

Shearing had finished the day before, but there was a black boy and a station-hand or two about the yards and six or eight shearers and rouseabouts, and a teamster camped in the men's huts – they were staying over the holidays to shear stragglers and clean up generally. Old Peter and a jackeroo were out on the run watching a bush-fire across Sandy Creek.

A swagman had happened to call at the station that morning; he asked for work and then for tucker. He irritated Wall, who told him to clear out. It was the first time that a swagman had been turned away from the station without tucker.

Swaggy went along the track some miles, brooding over his wrongs, and crossed Sandy Creek. He struck a match and dropped it into a convenient tuft of grass in a likely patch of tufts, with dead grass running from it up into the scrubby ridges – then he hurried on.

Did you ever see a bush-fire? Not sheets of flame sweeping and roaring from tree-top to tree-top, but the snaky, hissing grass-fire of hardwood country.

The whole country covered with thin blue smoke so that you never know in what direction the fire is travelling. At night you see it like the lighted streets of cities, in the distant ranges. It roars up the hollows of dead trees and gives them the appearance of factory chimneys in the dusk. It climbs, by shreds of bark, the trunks of old dead white-box and blue-gums – solid and hard as cast-iron – and cuts off the limbs. And where there's a piece of recently ringbarked country, with the dead leaves still on the trees, the fire will roar from bough to bough – a fair imitation of a softwood forest fire. The bush-fire travels through the scrubs for hundreds of miles, taking the grass to the roots, scorching the living bush but leaving it alive – for gum-bush is hardest of any to kill. Where there is no undergrowth, and the country seems bare as a road for miles, the fire will cross, licking up invisible straws of grass, dusty leaves, twigs and shreds of bark on the hard ground already baking in the drought. You hear of a fire miles away, and next day, riding across the head of a gully, you hear a hissing and crackling and there is the fire running over the ground in lines and curves of thin blue smoke, snakelike, with old logs blazing on the blackened ground behind. Did you ever hear a fire where a fire should not be? There is something hellish in the sound of it. When the breeze is, say, from the east the fire runs round western spurs, up sheltered gullies – helped by an 'eddy' in the wind perhaps – and appears along the top of the ridge, ready, with a change in the wind, to come down on farms and fields of ripe wheat, with a 'front' miles long.

A selector might be protected by a wide sandy creek in front and wide cleared roads behind, and, any hour in the day or night, a shout from the farther end of the wheat paddock, and – 'Oh, my God! the wheat!'

Wall didn't mind this fire much; most of his sheep were on their way out back, to a back run where there was young grass; and the dry ridges along the creek would be better for a burning-off – only he had to watch his fences.

But, about dusk, Mary came galloping home in her usual breakneck fashion.

'Father,' she cried, 'turn out the men and send them at once. The fire is all down by Ross's farm, and he had ten acres of wheat standing, and no one at home but him and Bob.'

'How do you know?' growled Wall. Then suddenly and suspiciously, 'Have you been there?'

'I came home that way.'

'Well – let Ross look after his own,' snarled the father.

'But he can't, father. They're fighting the fire now, and they'll be burnt out before the morning if they don't get help – for God's sake, father, act like a Christian and send the men. Remember it is Christmas-time, father. You're surely not going to see a neighbour burnt out.'

'Yes, I am,' shouted Wall. 'I'd like to see every selector in the country burnt out, hut and all! Get off that horse and go inside. If a man leaves the station to-night he needn't come back.' (This last for the benefit of the men's hut.)

'But, father —'

'Get off that horse and go inside,' roared Wall.

'I–I won't.'

'What!' He darted forward as though to drag her from the saddle, but she swung her horse away.

'Stop! Where are you going?'

'To help Ross,' said Mary. 'He had no one to send for help.'

'Then go the same way as your brother!' roared her father; 'and if you show your nose back again I'll horse-whip you off the run!'

'I'll go, father,' said Mary, and she was away.

IV

THE FIRE AT ROSS'S FARM

Ross's farm was in a corner between the ridges and the creek. The fire had come down from the creek, but the siding on that side was fairly clear, and they had stopped the fire there. It went behind the ridge and ran up and over. The ridge was covered thickly with scrub and dead grass; the wheat-field went well up the siding, and along the top was a bush fence with only a narrow bridle-track between it and the long dead grass. Everything depended on the wind. Mary saw Ross and Mrs Ross and the daughter Jenny, well up the siding above the fence, working desperately, running to and fro, and beating out the fire with green boughs. Mary left her horse, ran into the hut, and looked hurriedly round for something to wear in place of her riding-skirt. She only saw a couple of light print dresses. She stepped into a skillion room, which happened to be Bob's room, and there caught sight of a pair of trousers and a coat hanging on the wall.

Bob Ross, beating desperately along a line of fire that curved down-hill to his right, and half-choked and blinded with the smoke, almost stumbled against a figure which was too tall to be his father.

'Why! Who's that?' he gasped.

'It's only me, Bob,' said Mary, and she lifted her bough again.

Bob stared. He was so astonished that he almost forgot the fire and the wheat. Bob was not thin – but –

'Don't look at me, Bob!' said Mary, hurriedly. 'We're going to be married, so it doesn't matter. Let us save the wheat.'

There was no time to waste; there was a breeze now from over the ridges, light, but enough to bear the fire down on them. Once, when they had breathing space, Mary ran to the creek for a billy of water. They beat out the fire all along the siding to where a rib of granite came down over the ridge to the fence, and then they thought the wheat was safe. They came together here, and Ross had time to look and see who the strange man was; then he stared at Mary from under his black, bushy eyebrows. Mary, choking and getting her breath after her exertions, suddenly became aware, said 'Oh!' and fled round the track beyond the point of granite. She felt a gust of wind and looked up the ridge. The bush fence ended here in a corner, where it was met by a new wire fence running up from the creek. It was a blind gully full of tall dead grass, and glancing up, Mary saw the flames coming down fast. She ran back.

'Come on!' she cried, 'come on! The fire's the other side of the rocks!'

Back at the station, Wall walked up and down till he cooled. He went inside and sat down, but it was no use. He lifted his head and saw his dead wife's portrait on the wall. Perhaps his whole life ran before him in detail – but this is not a psychological study.

There were only two tracks open to him now: either to give in, or go on as he was going – to shut himself out from human nature and become known as 'Mean Wall,' 'Hungry Wall,' or 'Mad Wall, the Squatter.' He was a tall, dark man of strong imagination and more than ordinary intelligence. And it was the great crisis of his ruined life. He walked to the top of a knoll near the homestead and saw the fire on the ridges above Ross's farm. As he turned back he saw a horseman ride up and dismount by the yard.

'It that you, Peter?'

'Yes, boss. The fences is all right.'

'Been near Ross's?'

'No. He's burnt out by this time.'

Wall walked to and fro for a minute longer. Then he suddenly stopped and called, 'Peter!'

'Ay, ay!' from the direction of the huts.

'Turn out the men!' and Wall went into a shed and came out with his saddle on his arm.

The fire rushed down the blind gully. Showers of sparks fell on the bush fence, it caught twice, and they put it out, but the third time it blazed and roared and a fire-engine could not have stopped it.

'The wheat must go,' said Ross. 'We've done our best,' and he threw down the blackened bough and leaned against a tree, and covered his eyes with a grimy hand.

The wheat was patchy in that corner – there were many old stumps of trees, and there were bare strips where the plough had gone on each side of them. Mary saw a chance, and climbed the fence.

'Come on, Bob,' she cried, 'we might save it yet. Mr Ross, pull out the fence along there,' and she indicated a point beyond the fire. They tramped down and tore up the wheat where it ran between the stumps – the fire was hissing and crackling round and through it, and just as it ran past them in one place there was a shout, a clatter of horses' hoofs on the stones, and Mary saw her father riding up the track with a dozen men behind him. She gave a shriek and ran straight down, through the middle of the wheat, towards the hut.

Wall and his men jumped to the ground, wrenched green boughs from the saplings, and, after twenty minutes' hard fighting, the crop was saved – save for a patchy acre or so.

When it was all over Ross sat down on a log and rested his head on his hands, and his shoulders shook.

Presently he felt a hand on his shoulder, looked up, and saw Wall.

'Shake hands, Ross,' he said.

And it was Christmas Day.

But in after years they used to nearly chaff the life out of Mary. 'You were in a great hurry to put on the breeches, weren't you, Mary?' 'Bob's best Sunday-go-meetin's too, wasn't they, Mary?' 'Rather tight fit, wasn't they, Mary?' 'Couldn't get 'em on now, could you, Mary?'

'But,' reflected old Peter apart to some cronies, 'it ain't every young chap as gits an idea of the shape of his wife afore he marries her – is it? An' that's sayin' somethin'.'

And old Peter was set down as being an innercent sort of ole cove.

A Droving Yarn

ANDY MACULLOCH had heard that old Bill Barker, the well-known overland drover, had died over on the Westralian side, and Dave Regan told a yarn about Bill.

'Bill Barker,' said Dave, talking round his pipe stem, 'was the quintessence of a drover —'

'The whatter, Dave?' came the voice of Jim Bentley, in startled tones, from the gloom on the far end of the veranda.

'The quintessence,' said Dave, taking his pipe out of his mouth. 'You shut up, Jim. As I said, Bill Barker was the quintessence of a drover. He'd been at the game ever since he was a nipper. He run away from home when he was fourteen and went up into Queensland. He's been all over Queensland and New South Wales and most of South Australia, and a good deal of the Western, too: over the great stock routes from one end to the other, Lord knows how many times. No man could keep up with him riding out, and no one could bring a mob of cattle or a flock of sheep through like him. He knew every trick of the game; if there was grass to be had Bill'd get it, no matter whose run it was on. One of his games in a dry season was to let his mob get boxed with the station stock on a run where there was grass, and before Bill's men and the station-hands could cut 'em out, the travelling stock would have a good bellyful to carry them on the track. Billy was the daddy of the drovers. Some said that he could ride in his sleep, and that he had one old horse that could jog along in his sleep, too, and that – travelling out from home to take charge of a mob of bullocks or a flock of sheep – Bill and his horse would often wake up at daylight and blink round to see where they were and how far they'd got. Then Bill would make a fire and boil his quart-pot, and roast a bit of mutton, while his horse had a mouthful of grass and a spell.

'You remember Bill, Andy? Big dark man, and a joker of the loud sort. Never slept with a blanket over him – always folded under him on the sand or grass. Seldom wore a coat on the route – though he always carried one with him, in case he came across a bush ball or a funeral. Moleskins, flannel waistcoat, cabbage-tree hat and 'lastic-side boots. When it was roasting hot on the plains and the men swore at the heat, Jim would yell, "Call this hot? Why, you blanks, I'm freezin'! Where's me overcoat?" When it was raining and hailing and freezing on Bell's Line in the Blue Mountains in winter, and someone shivered and asked, "Is it cold enough for yer now, Bill?" "Cold!" Bill would bellow, "I'm sweatin'!"

'I remember it well. I was little more than a youngster then – Bill Barker came past our place with about a thousand fat sheep for the Homebush sale-yards at

Sydney, and he gave me a job to help him down with them on Bell's Line over the mountains, and mighty proud I was to go with him, I can tell you. One night we camped on the Cudgegong River. The country was dry and pretty close cropped and we'd been "sweating" the paddocks all along there for our horses. You see, where there weren't sliprails handy we'd just take a tomahawk and nick the top of a straight-grained fence-post, just above the mortise, knock out the wood there, lift the top rail out and down, and jump the horses in over the lower one – it was all two-rail fences around there with sheep wires under the lower rail. And about daylight we'd have the horses out, lift back the rail, and fit in the chock that we'd knocked out. Simple as striking matches, wasn't it?

'Well, the horses were getting a good bellyful in the police horse paddock at night, and Bill took the first watch with the sheep. It was very cold and frosty on the flat and he thought the sheep might make back for the ridges, it's always warmer up in the ridges in winter out of the frost. Bill roused me out about midnight. "There's the sheep," he says, pointing to a white blur. "They've settled down. I think they'll be quiet till daylight. Don't go round them; there's no occasion to go near 'em. You can stop by the fire and keep an eye on 'em."

'The night seemed very long. I watched and smoked and toasted my shins, and warmed the billy now and then, and thought up pretty much the same sort of old things that fellers on night watch think over all over the world. Bill lay on his blanket, with his back to the fire and his arm under his head – freezing on one side and roasting on the other. He never moved. I itched once or twice to turn him over and bake the front of him – I reckoned he was about done behind.

'At last daylight showed. I took the billy and started down to the river to get some water to make coffee; but half-way down, near the sheep camp, I stopped and stared, I was never so surprised in my life. The white blur of sheep had developed into a couple of acres of long dead silver grass!

'I woke Bill, and he swore as I never heard a man swear before – nor since. He swore at the sheep, and the grass, and at me; but it would have wasted time, and besides I was too sleepy and tired to fight. But we found those sheep scattered over a scrubby ridge about seven miles back, so they must have slipped away back of the grass and started early in Bill's watch, and Bill must have watched that blessed grass for the first half of the night and then set me to watch it. He couldn't get away from that.

'I wondered what the chaps would say if it got round that Bill Barker, the boss overland drover, had lost a thousand sheep in clear country with fences all round; and I suppose he thought that way too, for he kept me with him right down to Homebush, and when he paid me off he threw in an extra quid, and he said:

"'Now, listen here, Dave! If I ever hear a word from any one about watching that gory grass, I'll find you, Dave, and murder you, if you're in wide Australia. I'll screw your neck, so look out."

'But he's dead now, so it doesn't matter.'

There was silence for some time after Dave had finished. The chaps made no comment on the yarn, either one way or the other, but sat smoking thoughtfully, and in a vague atmosphere as of sadness – as if they'd just heard of their mother's death and had not been listening to an allegedly humorous yarn.

Then the voice of old Peter, the station-hand, was heard to growl from the darkness at the end of the hut, where he sat on a three-bushel bag on the ground with his back to the slabs.

'What's old Peter growlin' about?' someone asked.

'He wants to know where Dave got that word,' someone else replied.

'What word?'

'Quint-essents.'

There was a chuckle.

'He got it out back, Peter,' said Mitchell, the shearer. 'He got it from a new chum.'

'How much did yer give for it, Dave?' growled Peter.

'Five shillings, Peter,' said Dave, round his pipe stem. 'And stick of tobacco thrown in.'

Peter seemed satisfied, for he was heard no more that evening.

'Shall We Gather at
the River?'

God's preacher, of churches unheeded,
God's vineyard, though barren the sod,
Plain spokesman where spokesman is needed,
Rough link 'twixt the Bushman and God.
—The Christ of the Never.

TOLD BY JOE WILSON

I NEVER told you about Peter M'Laughlan. He was a sort of bush missionary up-country and out back in Australia, and before he died he was known from Riverina down south in New South Wales to away up through the Never-Never country in western Queensland.

His past was a mystery, so, of course, there were all sorts of yarns about him. He was supposed to be a Scotchman from London, and some said that he had got into trouble in his young days and had had to clear out of the old country; or, at least, that he had been a ne'er-do-well and had been sent out to Australia on the remittance system. Some said he'd studied for the law, some said he'd studied for a doctor, while others believed that he was, or had been, an ordained minister. I remember one man who swore (when he was drinking) that he had known Peter M'Laughlan as a medical student in a big London hospital, and that he had started in practice for himself somewhere near Gray's Inn Road in London. Anyway, as I got to know him he struck me as being a man who had looked into the eyes of so much misery in his life that some of it had got into his own.

He was a tall man, straight and well built, and about forty or forty-five, when I first saw him. He had wavy dark hair, and a close, curly beard. I once heard a woman say that he had a beard like you see in some Bible pictures of Christ. Peter M'Laughlan seldom smiled; there was something in his big dark brown eyes that was scarcely misery, nor yet sadness – a sort of haunted sympathy.

He must have had money, or else he got remittances from home, for he paid his way and helped many a poor devil. They said that he gave away most of his money. Sometimes he worked for a while himself as bookkeeper at a shearing-shed, wool-sorter, shearer, even rouseabout; he'd work at anything a bushman could get to do. Then he'd go out back to God-forgotten districts and preach to bushmen in one place, and get a few children together in another and teach them to read. He could take his drink, and swear a little when he thought it necessary. On one occasion, at a rough shearing-shed, he called his beloved brethren 'damned fools' for drinking their cheques.

Towards the end of his life if he went into a 'rough' shed or shanty west of the Darling River – and some of them were rough – there would be a rest in the language and drinking, even a fight would be interrupted, and there would be more than one who would lift their hats to Peter M'Laughlan. A bushman very rarely lifts his hat to a man, yet the worst characters of the West have listened bareheaded to Peter when he preached.

It was said in our district that Peter only needed to hint to the squatter that he wanted fifty or a hundred pounds to help someone or something, and the squatter would give it to him without question or hesitation.

He'd nurse sick boundary-riders, shearers, and station-hands, often sitting in the desolate hut by the bedside of a sick man night after night. And, if he had time, he'd look up the local blacks and see how they were getting on. Once, on a far out back sheep station, he sat for three nights running, by the bedside of a young Englishman, a B.A. they said he was, who'd been employed as tutor at the homestead and who died a wreck, the result of five years of life in London and Paris. The poor fellow was only thirty. And the last few hours of his life he talked to Peter in French, nothing but French. Peter understood French and one or two other languages, besides English and Australian; but whether the young wreck was raving or telling the story of a love, or his life, none of us ever knew, for Peter never spoke of it. But they said that at the funeral Peter's eyes seemed haunted more than usual.

There's the yarn about Peter and the dying cattle at Piora Station one terrible drought, when the surface was as bare as your hand for hundreds of miles, and the heat like the breath of a furnace, and the sheep and cattle were perishing by thousands. Peter M'Laughlan was out on the run helping the station-hands to pull out cattle that had got bogged in the muddy waterholes and were too weak to drag themselves out, when, about dusk, a gentlemanly 'piano-fingered' parson, who had come to the station from the next town, drove out in his buggy to see the men. He spoke to Peter M'Laughlan.

'Brother,' he said, 'do you not think we should offer up a prayer?'

'What for?' asked Peter, standing in his shirt sleeves, a rope in his hands and mud from head to foot.

'For? Why, the rain, brother,' replied the parson, a bit surprised.

Peter held up his finger and said 'Listen!'

Now, with a big mob of travelling stock camped on the plain at night, there is always a lowing, soughing or moaning sound, a sound like that of the sea on the shore at a little distance; and, altogether, it might be called the sigh or yawn of a big mob in camp. But the long, low moaning of cattle dying of hunger and thirst on the hot barren plain in a drought is altogether different, and, at night, there is something awful about it – you couldn't describe it. This is what Peter M'Laughlan heard.

'Do you hear that?' he asked the other preacher.

The little parson said he did. Perhaps he only heard the weak lowing of cattle.

'Do you think that God will hear us when He does not hear that?' asked Peter.

The parson stared at him for a moment and then got into his buggy and drove away, greatly shocked and deeply offended. But, later on, over tea at the homestead, he said that he felt sure that the 'unfortunate man,' Peter M'Laughlan, was not in his right mind; that his wandering, irregular life, or the heat, must have affected him.

I well remember the day when I first heard Peter M'Laughlan preach. I was about seventeen then. We used sometimes to attend service held on Sunday afternoon, about once a month, in a little slab-and-bark school-house in the scrub off the main road, three miles or so from our selection, in a barren hole amongst the western ridges of the Great Dividing Range. School was held in this hut for a few weeks or a few months now and again, when a teacher could be got to stay there and teach, and cook for himself, for a pound a week, more or less contributed by the parents. A parson from the farming town to the east, or the pastoral town over the ridges to the west, used to come in his buggy when it didn't rain and wasn't too hot to hold the service.

I remember this Sunday. It was a blazing hot day towards the end of a long and fearful drought which ruined many round there. The parson was expect-ed, and a good few had come to 'chapel' in spring-carts, on horseback, and on foot; farmers and their wives and sons and daughters. The children had been brought here to Sunday-school, taught by some of the girls, in the morning. I can see it all now quite plain. The one-roomed hut, for it was no more, with the stunted blue-grey gum scrub all round. The white, dusty road, so hot that you could cook eggs in the dust. The horses tied up, across the road, in the supposed shade under clumps of scraggy saplings along by the fence of a cattle-run. The little crowd outside the hut: selectors in washed and mended tweeds, some with paper collars, some wearing starched and ironed white coats, and in blucher boots, greased or blackened, or the young men wearing 'larstins' (elastic-side boots). The women and girls in prints and cottons (or cheap 'alpaca,' etc.), and a bright bit of ribbon here and there amongst the girls. The white heat blazed everywhere, and 'dazzled' across light-coloured surfaces – dead white trees, fence-posts, and sand-heaps, like an endless swarm of bees passing in the sun's glare. And over above the dry box-scrub-covered ridges, the great Granite Peak, glaring like a molten mass.

The people didn't like to go inside out of the heat and sit down before the minister came. The wretched hut was a rough school, sometimes with a clay fire-place where the teacher cooked, and a corner seemed off with sacking where he had his bunk; it was a camp for tramps at other times, or lizards and possums, but today it was a house of God, and as such the people respected it.

The town parson didn't turn up. Perhaps he was unwell, or maybe the hot, dusty ten-mile drive was too much for him to face. One of the farmers, who had tried to conduct service on a previous occasion on which the ordained minister had failed us, had broken down in the middle of it, so he was out of the question. We waited for about an hour, and then who should happen to ride along but Peter M'Laughlan, and one or two of the elder men asked him to hold service. He was on his way to see a sick friend at a sheep station over the ridges, but he said that he could spare an hour or two. (Nearly every man who was sick, either in stomach or pocket, was a friend of Peter M'Laughlan.) Peter tied up his horse under a bush shed at the back of the hut, and we followed him in.

The 'school' had been furnished with a rough deal table and a wooden chair for 'the teacher,' and with a few rickety desks and stools cadged from an old 'provisional' school in town when the new public school was built; and the desks and stools had been fastened to the floor to strengthen them; they had been made for 'infant' classes, and youth out our way ran to length. But when grown men over six feet high squeezed in behind the desks and sat down on the stools the effect struck me as being ridiculous. In fact, I am afraid that on the first occasion it rather took my attention from the sermon, and I remember being made very uncomfortable by a school chum, Jack Barnes, who took a delight in catching my eye and winking or grinning. He could wink without changing a solemn line in his face and grin without exploding, and I couldn't. The boys usually sat on seats, slabs on blocks of wood, along the wall at the far end of the room, which was comfortable, for they had a rest for their backs. One or two of the boys were nearing six feet high, so they could almost rest their chins on their knees as they sat. But I squatted with some of my tribe on a stool along the wall by the teacher's table, and so could see most of the congregation.

Above us bare tie-beams and the round sapling rafters (with the bark still on), and the inner sides of the sheets of stringy-bark that formed the roof. The slabs had been lined with sacking at one time, but most of it had fallen or dry-rotted away; there were wide cracks between the slabs and we could see the white glare of sunlight outside, with a strip of dark shade, like a deep trench in the white ground, by the back wall. Someone had brought a canvas water-bag and hung it to the beam on the other side of the minister's table, with a pint-pot over the tap, and the drip, drip from the bag made the whole place seem cooler.

I studied Peter M'Laughlan first. He was dressed in washed and mended tweed vest and trousers, and had on a long, light-coloured coat of a material which we called 'Chinese silk.' He wore a 'soft' cotton shirt with collar attached, and blucher boots.

He gave out a hymn in his quiet, natural way, said a prayer, gave out another hymn, read a chapter from the Bible, and then gave out another hymn. They liked to sing, out in those places. The Southwicks used to bring a cranky little harmonium in the back of their old dog-cart, and Clara Southwick used to accompany the hymns. She was a very pretty girl, fair, and could play and sing well. I used to think she had the sweetest voice I ever heard. But – ah, well.

Peter didn't sing himself, at first. I got an idea that he couldn't. While they were singing he stood loosely, with one hand in his trouser-pocket, scratching his beard with his hymn-book, and looking as if he were thinking things over, and only rousing himself to give another verse. He forgot to give it once or twice, but we got through all right. I noticed the wife of one of the men who had asked Peter to preach looking rather black at her husband, and I reckoned that he'd get it hotter than the weather on the way home.

Then Peter stood up and commenced to preach. He stood with both hands in his pockets, at first, his coat ruffled back, and there was the stem of a clay pipe sticking out of his waistcoat-pocket. The pipe fascinated me for a while, but after that I forgot the pipe and was fascinated by the man. Peter's face was one that didn't strike you at first with its full strength, it grew on you; it grew on me, and before he had done preaching I thought it was the noblest face I had ever seen.

He didn't preach much of hope in this world. How could he? The drought had been blazing over these districts for nearly a year, with only a shower now and again, which was a mockery – scarcely darkening the baked ground. Wheat crops came up a few inches and were parched by the sun or mown for hay, or the cattle turned on them; and last year there had been rust and smut in the wheat. And, on top of it all, the dreadful cattle plague, pleuro-pneumonia, had somehow been introduced into the district. One big farmer had lost fifty milkers in a week.

Peter M'Laughlan didn't preach much of hope in this world; how could he? There were men there who had slaved for twenty, thirty, forty years; worked as farmers have to work in few other lands – first to clear the stubborn bush from the barren soil, then to fence the ground, and manure it, and force crops from it – and for what? There was Cox, the farmer, starved off his selection after thirty years and going out back with his drays to work at tank-sinking for a squatter. There was his eldest son going shearing or droving – anything he could get to do – a stoop-shouldered, young-old man of thirty. And behind them, in the end, would be a dusty patch in the scrub, a fence-post here and there, and a pile of chimney-stones and a hardwood slab or two where the hut was – for thirty hard years of the father's life and twenty of the son's.

I forget Peter's text, if he had a text; but the gist of his sermon was that there was a God – there was a heaven! And there were men there listening who needed to believe these things. There was old Ross from across the creek, old, but not sixty, a hard man. Only last week he had broken down and fallen on his knees on the baked sods in the middle of his ploughed ground and prayed for rain. His frightened boys had taken him home, and later on, the same afternoon, when they brought news of four more cows down with 'the pleuro' in an outer paddock, he had stood up outside his own door and shaken his fist at the brassy sky and cursed high heaven to the terror of his family, till his brave, sun-browned wife dragged him inside and soothed him. And Peter M'Laughlan knew all about this.

Ross's family had the doctor out to him, and persuaded him to come to church this Sunday. The old man sat on the front seat, stooping forward, with his elbow resting on the desk and his chin on his hand, bunching up his beard over his mouth with his fingers and staring gloomily at Peter with dark, piercing eyes from under bushy eyebrows, just as I've since seen a Scotchman stare at Max O'Rell all through a humorous lecture called 'A nicht wi' Sandy.'

Ross's right hand resting on the desk was very eloquent: horny, scarred and knotted at every joint, with broken, twisted nails, and nearly closed, as though fitted to the handle of an axe or a spade. Ross was an educated man (he had a regular library of books at home), and perhaps that's why he suffered so much.

Peter preached as if he were speaking quietly to one person only, but every word was plain and every sentence went straight to someone. I believe he looked every soul in the eyes before he had done. Once he said something and caught my eye, and I felt a sudden lump in my throat. There was a boy there, a pale, thin, sensitive boy who was eating his heart out because of things he didn't understand. He was ambitious and longed for something different from this life; he'd written a story or two and some rhymes for the local paper; his companions considered him a 'bit ratty' and the grown-up people thought him a 'bit wrong in his head,' idiotic, or at least 'queer.' And during his sermon Peter spoke of 'unsatisfied longings,' of the hope of something better, and said that one had to suffer much and for long years before he could preach or write;

and then he looked at that boy. I knew the boy very well; he has risen in the world since then.

Peter spoke of the life we lived, of the things we knew, and used names and terms that we used. 'I don't know whether it was a blanky sermon or a blanky lecture,' said long swanky Jim Bullock afterwards, 'but it was straight and hit some of us hard. It hit me once or twice, I can tell yer.' Peter spoke of our lives: 'And there is beauty – even in this life and in this place,' he said. 'Nothing is wasted – nothing is without reason. There is beauty even in this place —'

I noticed something like a hint of a hard smile on Ross's face; he moved the hand on the desk and tightened it.

'Yes,' said Peter, as if in answer to Ross's expression and the movement of his hand, 'there is beauty in this life here. After a good season, and when the bush is tall and dry, when the bush-fires threaten a man's crop of ripened wheat, there are tired men who run and ride from miles round to help that man, and who fight the fire all night to save his wheat – and some of them may have been wrangling with him for years. And in the morning, when the wheat is saved and the danger is past, when the fire is beaten out or turned, there are blackened, grimy hands that come together and grip – hands that have not joined for many a long day.'

Old Palmer, Ross's neighbour, moved uneasily. He had once helped Ross to put a fire out, but they had quarrelled again since. Ross still sat in the same position, looking the hard man he was. Peter glanced at Ross, looked down and thought a while, and then went on again:

'There is beauty even in this life and in this place. When a man loses his farm, or his stock, or his crop, through no fault of his own, there are poor men who put their hands into their pockets to help him.'

Old Kurtz, over the ridge, had had his stacked crop of wheat in sheaf burned – some scoundrel had put a match to it at night – and the farmers round had collected nearly fifty pounds for him.

'There is beauty even in this life and in this place. In the blazing drought, when the cattle lie down and cannot rise from weakness, neighbours help neighbours to lift them. When one man has hay or chaff and no stock, he gives it or sells it cheaply to the poor man who has starving cattle and no fodder.'

I only knew one or two instances of this kind; but Peter was preaching of what man should do as well as what they did.

'When a man meets with an accident, or dies, there are young men who go with their ploughs and horses and plough the ground for him or his widow and put in the crop.'

Jim Bullock and one or two other young men squirmed. They had ploughed old Leonard's land for him when he met with an accident in the shape of a broken leg got by a kick from a horse. They had also ploughed the ground for Mrs Phipps when her husband died, working, by the way, all Saturday afternoon and Sunday, for they were very busy at home at that time.

'There is beauty even in this life and in this place. There are women who were friends in girlhood and who quarrelled bitterly over a careless word, an idle tale, or some paltry thing, who live within a mile of each other and have not spoken for years; yet let one fall ill, or lose husband or child, and the other will hurry across to her place and take off her bonnet and tuck up her sleeves, and set to work to help straighten things, and they will kiss, and cry in each other's arms, and be sisters again.'

I saw tears in the eyes of two hard and hard-faced women I knew; but they were smiling to each other through their tears.

'And now,' said Peter, 'I want to talk to you about some other things. I am not preaching as a man who has been taught to preach comfortably, but as a man who has learned in the world's school. I know what trouble is. Men,' he said, still speaking quietly, 'and women too! I have been through trouble as deep as any of yours – perhaps deeper. I know how you toil and suffer, I know what battles you fight, I know. I too fought a battle, perhaps as hard as any you fight. I carry a load and am fighting a battle still.' His eyes were very haggard just then. 'But this is not what I wanted to talk to you about. I have nothing to say against a young man going away from this place to better himself, but there are young men who go out back shearing or droving, young men who are good-hearted but careless, who make cheques, and spend their money gambling or drinking and never think of the old folk at home until it is too late. They never think of the old people, alone perhaps, in a desolate hut on a worked-out farm in the scrub.'

Jim Bullock squirmed again. He had gone out back last season and made a cheque, and lost most of it on horse-racing and cards.

'They never think – they cannot think how, perhaps, long years agone in the old days, the old father, as a young man, and his brave young wife, came out here and buried themselves in the lonely bush and toiled for many years, trying – it does not matter whether they failed or not – trying to make homes for their children; toiled till the young man was bowed and grey, and the young wife brown and wrinkled and worn out. Exiles they were in the early days – boy-husbands and girl-wives some of them, who left their native lands, who left all that was dear, that seemed beautiful, that seemed to make life worth living, and sacrificed their young lives in drought and utter loneliness to make homes for their children. I want you young men to think of this. Some of them came from England, Ireland, Bonnie Scotland.' Ross straightened up and let his hands fall loosely on his knees. 'Some from Europe – your foreign fathers

– some from across the Rhine in Germany.' We looked at old Kurtz. He seemed affected.

Then Peter paused for a moment and blinked thoughtfully at Ross, then he took a drink of water. I can see now that the whole thing was a battle between Peter M'Laughlan and Robert Ross – Scot met Scot. 'It seemed to me,' Jim Bullock said afterwards, 'that Peter was only tryin' to make some of us blanky well blubber.'

'And there are men,' Peter went on, 'who have struggled and suffered and failed, and who have fought and failed again till their tempers are spoiled, until they grow bitter. They go in for self-pity, and self-pity leads to moping and brooding and madness; self-pity is the most selfish and useless thing on the face of God's earth. It is cruel, it is deadly, both to the man and to those who love him, and whom he ought to love. His load grows heavier daily in his imagination, and he sinks down until it is in him to curse God and die. He ceases to care for or to think of his children who are working to help him.' (Ross's sons were good, steady, hard-working boys.) 'Or the brave wife who has been so true to him for many hard years, who left home and friends and country for his sake. Who bears up in the blackest of times, and persists in looking at the bright side of things for his sake; who has suffered more than he if he only knew it, and suffers now, through him and because of him, but who is patient and bright and cheerful while her heart is breaking. He thinks she does not suffer, that she cannot suffer as a man does. My God! he doesn't know. He has forgotten in her the bright, fresh-faced, loving lassie he loved and won long years agone – long years agone —'

There was a sob, like the sob of an over-ridden horse as it sinks down broken-hearted, and Ross's arms went out on the desk in front of him, and his head went down on them. He was beaten.

He was steered out gently with his wife on one side of him and his eldest son on the other.

'Don't be alarmed, my friends,' said Peter, standing by the water-bags with one hand on the tap and the pannikin in the other. 'Mr Ross has not been well lately, and the heat has been too much for him.' And he went out after Ross. They took him round under the bush shed behind the hut, where it was cooler.

When Peter came back to his place he seemed to have changed his whole manner and tone. 'Our friend, Mr Ross, is much better,' he said. 'We will now sing –' he glanced at Clara Southwick at the harmonium – 'we will now sing "Shall We Gather at the River?"' We all knew that hymn; it was an old favourite round there, and Clara Southwick played it well in spite of the harmonium.

And Peter sang – the first and last time I ever heard him sing. I never had an ear for music; but I never before nor since heard a man's voice that stirred me as Peter M'Laughlan's. We stood like emus, listening to him all through one verse, then we pulled ourselves together.

> *Shall we gather at the River,*
> *Where bright angels' feet have trod*

The only rivers round there were barren creeks, the best of them only strings of muddy waterholes, and across the ridge, on the sheep-runs, the creeks were dry gutters, with baked banks and beds, and perhaps a mudhole every mile or so, and dead beasts rotting and stinking every few yards.

> *Gather with the saints at the River,*
> *That flows by the throne of God.*

Peter's voice trembled and broke. He caught hisbreath, and his eyes filled. But he smiled then – he stood smiling at us through his tears. The beautiful, the beautiful

> *The beautiful, the beautiful River,*
> *That flows by the throne of God.*

Outside I saw women kiss each other who had been at daggers drawn ever since I could remember, and men shake hands silently who had hated each other for years. Every family wanted Peter to come home to tea, but he went across to Ross's, and afterwards down to Kurtz's place, and bled and inoculated six cows or so in a new way, and after tea he rode off over the gap to see his friend.

ABOUT THE AUTHOR

THE WRITER Henry Lawson was born on 17 June 1867 on the goldfields near Grenfell, New South Wales. Today an obelisk nearly two kilometres from the township marks his place of birth. His father was Niels Larsen, a former Norwegian mariner who had arrived in Australia during the gold rushes in 1855 and had married Lawson's mother, Louisa Albury, at Mudgee in 1866. Niels anglicised his name to Peter Lawson and named his first son Henry Lawson, though there is no record of his baptism.

The family lived briefly at Gulgong, where gold had been discovered, and later on a selection at New Pipeclay (now Eurunderee) near Mudgee. Four more children were born to Peter and Louisa Lawson before they separated in 1883. After working with his father as a builder, Henry left to join his mother to Sydney, where he was to spend most of his life. Yet his memories of his early years in the bush became the inspiration and the raw material for much of his writing. From boyhood Henry Lawson was afflicted by a sense of loneliness. When he was nine he became partly deaf and, by fourteen, he had completely lost his hearing. 'It was to cloud my whole life,' he later wrote, 'to drive me into myself, and to be, perhaps, in a great measure responsible for my writing.' Like his brother Charlie, he also suffered periods of deep depression which increased in severity in later life and would eventually drive him into alcoholism.

In Sydney Louisa Lawson, now celebrated as a pioneer feminist, founded the progressive journal the *Republican* to which Henry, who shared her radical and reformist beliefs, contributed articles. His first verse, 'Song of the Republic' and the first of his short stories, 'His Father's Mate', were published in the *Bulletin* (the latter in December 1888, just after his father's death) and he thereafter became a regular contributor to the journal. The onset of the economic depression in the early 1890s resulted in some of Lawson's most popular and powerful verse but the *Bulletin's* editor J.F. Archibald encouraged him to write more short stories, sending him out in 1892 to western New South Wales to gather material and observe conditions there. In 1894 his mother, who both encouraged and infuriated her son, published his first collection of writings in book form, *Short Stories in Prose and Verse*.

Lawson's first collection of short stories, *In the Days When the World Was Wide*, was published by Angus & Robertson early in 1896 and a second collection, *While the Billy Boils*, later in the year. In the same year Lawson married Bertha Bredt (whose sister later married the future Labor premier Jack Lang). After working as a teacher in New Zealand, Lawson returned to Sydney in 1898 and put together two more books of short stories, *On the Track* and *Over the Sliprails* and one of poems, *Verses Popular and Humorous*. He left for London in their year of publication, 1900, with his wife and two children, Joseph and Gertrude. English critics such as Edward Garnett had acclaimed Lawson's stories as equal to Anton Chekhov's in their simplicity and power, and two of his books were published in London. But neither the climate nor the prospects appealed to Lawson, and he and his family returned to Australia in 1902. Lawson's strained marriage now broke up and he turned to drink.

Thereafter his life was one of decline. Constantly impoverished and forced to cadge money for drink from his publishers and acquaintances, often jailed for failure to pay alimony, Lawson survived thanks to the loyalty of a few devoted friends who were convinced of his genius. He continued to write, but much of his verse emerged from the stimulus of alcohol and is now forgotten.

Henry Lawson died of a stroke in a cottage at Abbotsford, a Sydney suburb, on 2 September 1922. He was accorded the honour of a State Funeral at St Andrew's Cathedral, attended by Prime Minister William Morris Hughes. 'They buried Harry like a Lord,' his brother-in-law J.T. Lang commented. 'A week before they would have dodged by on the other side of the road to avoid him. Now they wanted to bask in his reflected glory.'

Henry Lawson stands with 'Banjo' Paterson as a founding father of Australian literature. Since his death, his writings have never been out of print. Despite his hardships and the afflictions over which he could never triumph, Lawson regarded his fellow man with humorous and often sardonic affection; this is what gives the best of his writings a humanity and a dignity that has made him beloved.